of the

CRESCENT MOON˙

JEROME J. FOODY

First published in the United States of America in 2010
by Buckhead Publishing House, LLC.
25 Buckhead Court
Aiken, South Carolina

Cover design by Dana Cooke

JEROME J. FOODY

* * * * * * *

RISE OF THE CRESCENT MOON

Printed in the United States of America

Other "*Flynn Series*" books by Jerome J. Foody:

A Capitol Conspiracy

Flynn's Revenge

Black Mamba

RISE OF THE CRESCENT MOON

ABOVE THE ARCTIC CIRCLE, ALASKA

The Buccaneer's prop strained through the driving September wind blowing down from the Arctic Circle along the Cascade Mountains. His location was about eighty miles northeast of Circle, Alaska, having taken off from Wainwright Field at Fairbanks, two hours earlier. A storm was building quickly as the temperature dropped and the first snowfall of a long Alaskan winter was imminent.

Jeremiah Flynn had flown in many different storms since assigned by the Agency to Air America, the CIA's "private" airline which had origins in Southeast Asia during the Viet Nam War era. Flynn, however, was the most experienced South American, 'Air America' pilot having just survived his latest mission in Colombia, along the border with Venezuela. His Beechcraft King Air B200, was unceremoniously shot down by a Russian made surface to air missile fired by an old enemy, Lorenzo Milazzo, the head of the *Brigate Rosse,* during a drug-sting operation that went bad. Flynn, wounded in the ambush, narrowly escaped capture from Milazzo's Brigade after bailing out over the rain forest. It took an injured Flynn weeks to force his way through the rain forest ultimately making his way across the Llanos. After following the Meta River, he was fortunately discovered by friendly Colombians who kept him safe while he recovered from his gunshot wound.

He was one of the Agency's best "Black Ops" specializing in the most clandestine missions. Flynn always drew the toughest and most difficult assignments, but now this was vacation. He had chosen to venture deep into the Alaskan wilderness to hunt wildlife with a camera. Flynn, although no stranger to killing, believed that there was no need to kill animals merely for sport. Instead, it was more challenging for him to hunt them in their natural environment with a camera. He wasn't foolish nor naïve, though. Flynn packed his Remington, 30.06, survival knife, and .44 magnum Smith & Wesson —just in case. Anything could happen in the wilderness and it was prudent to be prepared.

Flynn was looking forward to this vacation, his first in a long time. He needed to spend time alone after his Washington, D.C. 'experience' during the past year. While having been ostensibly assigned back to the Company's "home office" in Langley, for a refresher seminar on the International Economics of Energy, Flynn found himself in a complicated and conflicted year-long love affair with Patricia Bunnell, the Vice President of the United States.

Flynn met the Vice President at a diplomatic party hosted by the Crown Prince of Saudi Arabia. Flynn generally avoided these functions whenever possible. However, the Deputy Director of Special Operations, George Dimmler, insisted that Flynn attend because Flynn was an authority on the international oil cartel. Flynn had never before met Patricia Bunnell only knowing about her from the television news.

The Vice President was more strikingly beautiful in person than any television camera could portray. When Flynn first saw Patricia Bunnell in person he understood why President Harper chose this Congresswoman to be his running mate. She had charisma, charm, intelligence, and beauty. And how, as Flynn discovered, it became easier for the media to identify her as every American man's heartthrob--being widowed the prior year when her husband was killed in an automobile accident on the Beltway.

"She's quite a beauty, eh, Flynn," Deputy Director Dimmler remarked noticing Flynn's stare.

"Once again, General, you have understated the obvious," Flynn replied sarcastically. Then he asked, "Who's the sailor with her?"

"That sailor, my boy, is Admiral Michael Allen Moorehouse, White House Chief of Staff." Dimmler placed his hand on Flynn's shoulder and added, "Looks like you've been in the field too long, Flynn. There's talk around town that she and the Admiral are an 'item', if you know what I mean. But," Dimmler concluded, "it's strictly on the 'Q.T.', mind you. He's still married."

Flynn's interest peaked. "Really?"

"Come on over with me and I'll introduce you." Dimmler started toward the Vice President and Admiral Moorehouse. Flynn eagerly joined his boss.

Flynn could not take his eyes off the Vice President. She was radiant in a black sleeveless dress cut fashionably above the knee. Her flaming red hair was shoulder length and totally natural in color. She looked ten years younger than her thirty-nine years. Flynn's focus became obvious to the Vice President who was accustomed to, and whom appeared to enjoy, the attention. Vice President Bunnell returned Flynn's fixed gaze as he and Dimmler approached.

"Why, good evening, George," Patricia Bunnell greeted the Deputy Director before he could. "It's so nice to see you." The Vice President offered her hand to

Dimmler who took it with grace. Her eye contact then focused on Flynn. "I'm Patricia Bunnell," she said extending her hand to Flynn.

"Flynn. Jeremiah Flynn, Madam Vice President," Flynn introduced himself in return. Flynn held on to her hand for an extra second while he looked deeply into her ocean blue eyes. The Vice President smiled warmly at Flynn allowing him to hold on to her hand while an unusual electricity flowed over her body. There was a very brief pause between them which seemed like an eternity.

Composing himself, Flynn looked over at Admiral Moorehouse shook his hand and introduced himself. The Admiral had not missed the non-verbal exchange between Flynn and the Vice President, but quickly dismissed it as what generally occurs when men meet the lovely woman to his right.

"Mister Flynn," the Admiral said coolly, "nice to meet you." He turned and shook hands with Dimmler, "George, how are you this evening?"

"Very well, Admiral. Thank you," the Deputy Director replied.

Instinctively, Flynn sensed he was compromising himself. "If you'll excuse me, Madam Vice President...Admiral. It's been a pleasure to meet you both." Flynn began to turn and walk away.

"It's Pat, Mister Flynn." The Vice President wanted him to stay. "What brings you here tonight?"

"Well, Ma'am," Flynn knew his cover story perfectly, "I do a good deal of legal consulting work in the international oil community for American oil companies and I find I spend a great deal of time in Saudi Arabia and the Middle East. I've known Sheik Ahmad

Arcazi for many years and never miss an opportunity to attend one of his lavish receptions." Then looking deep into her eyes Flynn added, "And I sometimes meet new and interesting people. Some of whom become close friends."

The Vice President was aware of Flynn's lack of subtlety and laughed out loud, "Oh, Mister Flynn, I can just imagine that you have, indeed." She quickly glanced at Dimmler then back to Flynn asking, "So, what's your connection to the Deputy Director?"

"The General was a law school professor of mine at Cornell. We've been friends ever since."

"Oh, I see," Patricia Bunnell coyly responded while turning to the Deputy Director. "George, you shouldn't keep friends like Mister Flynn as secretive as you do the affairs of your Agency."

Dimmler smiled, "It would be impossible to keep too many secrets from you, Patricia, for very long."

"Yes, and I hope you keep that in mind, George."

Admiral Moorehouse was tugging at her arm which did not escape the watchful eyes of the two Agency men. Flynn bade off first, "I hope to see you again, Madam Vice President. Admiral, it's been a pleasure." The four then parted.

"Yes, perhaps..." Patricia coyly replied, "I'll look forward to it."

Admiral Moorehouse forced a slight smile but did not respond while he led the Vice President away.

During the remainder of the evening Vice President Bunnell kept herself in a position to watch Flynn and study his every movement. She found Flynn fascinating in a dangerously exciting way. She also didn't believe one word of his cover story. She made a mental note to question Deputy Director Dimmler about his mysterious friend, Jeremiah Flynn, while she saw him approach Sheik Ahmad Arcazi.

"Sheik Ahmad," Flynn greeted the Saudi Oil Minister. "Thank you for inviting me. It's so good to see you again, my friend."

"Ah, Mister Flynn," Sheik Ahmad delighted to see him replied. "Welcome. Welcome. You are always welcome here and in my country." Then steering Flynn aside for privacy he asked softly, "What do you make of the Iranian situation, my friend?"

Flynn looked around respecting the Sheik's desire for privacy before he answered. "Well contrary to what most believe, Ahmad, I think I understand what President Jahmir and the Ayatollah are doing. Although the consequences of their actions are dangerous and far-reaching, I believe they have a hidden international agenda under the guise of Arab unity. It's basically the destruction of Israel and the West."

"Do you sincerely believe that, Flynn?" Sheik Ahmad asked.

"Yes, I do. And, I wouldn't be surprised that they are closer to obtaining a nuclear weapon than most governments would believe."

"Oh, Flynn," Sheik Ahmad laughed in disbelief. "You have too vivid an imagination."

"You may be right, Ahmad, but in my judgment Iran has formed an unholy alliance with Syria's al-Anzarisad, Kim Moon-Jung of North Korea and Victor Escobar of Venezuela--three of most dangerous men in the world. The four of them would make the Axis Powers of World War Two look like kindergärteners."

"This is all too much for me to believe, my friend.

The United Nations would never let that happen."

"Ahmad, I hope that I am wrong. The world's balance of power could very well hang in the outcome. And, as you know, Jahmir believes that Allah has destined him to strike down all infidels and unify the world under Islam."

"But the enrichment of uranium in order to make a bomb would never be tolerated by the world. Your own government would never stand still for that to happen, nor would the Israeli's."

"Perhaps so, Ahmad, but the alternative scenario doesn't sound promising either..." Flynn was interrupted by the Vice President making her way toward them. She had overheard the last words of Flynn's comment to Ahmad.

"And what does sound promising to you, Flynn?" Patricia Bunnell seductively asked.

"Frankly, Madam Vice President, not much."

"Mister Flynn, I told you to call me Pat."

"I'm sorry Madam Vice President, but I don't know you well enough to take the liberty of calling you by anything other than your title--out of respect for your position."

"I see," Patricia smiled. "Well perhaps then we should start to get to know one another a whole lot better. Would you be kind enough to escort me home?"

Flynn was taken aback by her directness. "I was under the impression, Madam, that you came with Admiral Moorehouse?"

"Oh, I did come with the Admiral," she said distinctly, "but I'm leaving with you. Shall we go?"

For the better part of that next entire year, Vice President Patricia Bunnell and Jeremiah Flynn got to know each other very, very well, indeed.

ABOVE THE ARCTIC CIRCLE, ALASKA

The snowfall became more intense as Flynn banked the plane to the left. He checked his gauges and nosed the Buccaneer down to land on the pond below him. Flynn engaged full flaps to make his final approach. He couldn't wait to get this plane on the water and begin his vacation. He wanted Washington and Patricia Bunnell to be far away and long ago.

Flynn made a final check of his compass and altimeter. The plane was in a total white-out and instrument flight rules were in effect. He was confident in his many thousands of hours of flying experience and his intimate knowledge of this turbo-charged pusher aircraft. He knew just how far he could push her and when to allow a gentle touch to get what he needed from her. "The way it once was with Patricia." Flynn forced that thought from his mind while he pushed the nose of the Lake down in one banking thrust. At fifty feet above the pond he flared out and pulled back on the power. He brushed the underside of his plane on the tree tops surrounding this isolated pond

"Someday she's not going to like you doing that, Sport," Flynn said feeling the plane gently caress the water. He pulled back all power and slowly moved toward shore.

The snow hammered the plane's skin so hard it could be heard inside the cabin. His world was a total blizzard. Flynn was at last alone. No one would find him now. But then, no one was looking for him either.

P'YONGYANG, NORTH KOREA

Kim Moon Jung was lost in deep thought while he studied the international market exchange reports spread out before him on his desk. The timing was almost perfect. The price of benchmark crude was steadily rising. And, while the price of oil continued to rise, the economies of many of the world's countries were being pushed to the breaking point. The United States' dollar continued to plummet on the world's currency markets. It was time for something to be done. Drastic action was not out of the question.

Kim Moon Jung picked up his cell phone and found the private number he was looking for in the phone's memory. The call was placed to Houston, Texas.

"This is the 'Tiger' we are ready to initiate 'Operation Lifeblood'. We must meet with all parties in two days time. You are responsible to arrange it." Kim Moon Jung disconnected the call. He stared out of his office window at the bleak city of P'yongyang. He was a powerful man in North Korea. The 'Divine One' looked to him to propel the county's economy. Oil was a major necessity for the government to become strong and stable. 'Operation Lifeblood' was necessary not only for his survival as a power broker, but also for North Korea to emerge as the world power he envisioned. North Korea had the atomic bomb which made them a nuclear threat and now with 'Operation Lifeblood', nuclear North Korea would control the world's supply of oil!

WASHINGTON, D. C.

Another cell phone rang on a private, secured line

in Washington, D.C.

"Yes?" The receiver answered the call.

"Tiger has called for us to meet in Houston, in two days."

"You know you should never call me here. What if someone was with me in my office?"

"I had no other choice. Time is of the essence."

"Two days! That does not give me, er, us, much time, does it?"

"Some things cannot be helped. The Tiger has called for the meeting."

"I understand. I'll be there. Same place--what time?"

"Nine o'clock sharp in my office." The call was disconnected.

AMSTERDAM, HOLLAND

Kristen Shults was at her office at British Petroleum Limited until six. She was the Senior Marketing Vice President in the Netherlands Office owing in part because Kristen had dual citizenship with Great Britain and the Netherlands. This was a result of her mother's marriage to Hans Shults after World War II. Her mother, the former Phyllis Saunders, was a British foreign correspondent in Holland during World War II. And Kristen's mother loved her husband so much that she readily stayed in the Netherlands after the War rather than return to Mother England and the BBC.

Kristen was educated at Oxford where she received her Doctorate in International Marketing. She became a frequent companion of Jeremiah Flynn soon after meeting him a few years ago at an International Oil

Industry Symposium in Amsterdam. Kristen found that she had a good deal in common with Flynn. Both enjoyed each others company and frequently dated when he was in town. Kristen suspected that Flynn might be more than the Special Analyst for the Holland-American Oil Company. However, she was a rare woman who never asked personal questions to which she might not like the answer. This was a character trait passed down to her-- making her more like her father than her mother, in that regard.

It was early autumn and Kristen was preparing for a two week holiday in London to visit relatives and friends. "It would be good to get away from the office for a while," Kristen thought while preparing to leave work. She took one last look on her computer at the oil futures being traded on the commodities market. "What's going on? I don't understand what is causing all of the sudden volatility these past weeks."

Kristen was alone in her wonderment. "The price of oil has been rising sharply without any real explanation. OPEC members have not cut production, yet speculators are driving up the world's price for crude oil for some inexplicable reason. It appears that market driven forces are largely coming from these speculators in the United States, Venezuela and Asia. It's times like these when I need a vacation."

Although her favorite date, Jeremiah Flynn, had not been in the Netherlands for several months they talked weekly by cell phone and chatted on the Internet nearly daily. He had mentioned that he was due back in Amsterdam in three weeks after his Alaskan camera--hunt vacation. "It would be good to see him again," Kristen reflected while leaving her office. "Maybe he would have some insight on the oil market developments--he often did."

LONDON, ENGLAND

There was a business card imprinted with a picture of a tiger's head placed under the windshield wiper of a car at the garage at the British Foreign Ministry. This was a predetermined signal that a message was to be picked up at the usual drop. The importance of the message would be understood by the recipient at once. Extreme caution would have to be exercised by this British government official when he drove to the rendezvous destination later that evening.

WASHINGTON, D.C.

"Madam Vice President," Patricia Bunnell's male secretary, Scot, announced into the intercom. "It's Deputy Director George Dimmler on line two."

"George, thank you for returning my call."

"My pleasure, Madam Vice President," Dimmler said, "How can I help you?"

"George, could you come over to the Executive Office this afternoon?"

"Certainly, Ma'am. What's going on?"

"I'd like you to bring Flynn's file with you." Patricia Bunnell demanded.

"Pat," Dimmler appealed, "I don't understand. Flynn has been re-assigned at his own request after he gets back from vacation in Alaska. He's going back to Amsterdam in three weeks."

The Vice President responded to the Deputy

Director sharply. "Jeezus, George, I know that! But I want to know why?"

The Deputy Director of Clandestine and Black Operations for the Central Intelligence Agency understood the Vice President's apparent frustration with Flynn's sudden exit from her and Washington. Flynn was an enigma. "Look," Dimmler tried to explain, "let me say this to you as a friend. It's best for both of you right now and Flynn knows it."

"I don't give a shit, Deputy Director," Patricia was livid. "Bring his file over with you this afternoon!"

Dimmler acquiesced. "Of course, Madam Vice President. But you understand that regulations on field men are highly classified, strictly confidential, and of the utmost secret."

"George, don't give me that shit, please. I don't think I have to remind you how many years I supported your Agency when I was in Congress."

"No, ma'am, I know what a loyal supporter of the Agency you have been."

"Beside," Patricia softened, "no one will have to know anything about this except you and me. Consider it a favor which I won't forget."

"But Madam Vice President," Dimmler protested, "your request is highly irregular!"

"George, it's Pat. We've been friends too long. Don't make me order you," the Vice President warned. "Neither you nor the Agency will be compromised, I promise."

"Very well," Dimmler reluctantly agreed. "What time should I come over?"

"Two thirty," the Vice President said triumphantly while hanging up her phone. Patricia Bunnell turned in her chair as she gazed out over toward the White House. "What is it about you, Flynn, that interests me so much? Even though we've been together almost a year I feel as if I don't really know you at all."

DAMASCUS, SYRIA

Sheik Mohammad el Zelawi was driving his red BMW, Z-8 out of Damascus at his usual high rate of speed on his way to Deir-ez Zoi, for an important meeting with his Oil Ministry advisors when his cell phone ringtone alerted him to a call.

el Zelawi switched on his hands free device on the steering wheel. "Yes?"

"Sheik el Zelawi," a woman's voice began, "there is a mandatory meeting of the 'Elite' scheduled in two days in Houston, Texas. The meeting will take place at the Executive offices, President's private suite, at United Petroleum. All of the usual arrangements have been made. Tiger expects you to be there."

"In two days? Allah be praised. I will be there." Sheik Mohammad el Zelawi disconnected the call while his foot tromped down on the accelerator. He needed to make up some time. Once again, he activated his hands free cell phone and placed a call to his office back in Damascus.

"Abdul, have my personal jet meet me tonight in Deir-ez Zoi. Tell the pilot to prepare a flight plan for Houston, Texas, U.S.A. I must be there the day after tomorrow." The Sheik continued to dictate orders into his phone while he raced on. "Also, contact the Oil Ministry's office and have all OPEC's production reports prepared along with the estimates of current reserves and distribution schedules. Fax them to me on my car-fax. You have the number. There can be no delays, do you understand?"

"Consider it done, Excellency. May Allah go with you."

WASHINGTON, D. C.

Deputy Director of Operations George Dimmler was perplexed and more than slightly annoyed with his phone call from the Vice President. Her request to personally review Flynn's status file was highly irregular and was contrary to standard operating practices. Although Patricia Bunnell was a close friend and strong supporter of the Agency's clandestine operations, Dimmler was not pleased that confidential files on field operatives, like Flynn, should be read by other than "Need-to-Know" personnel. After all, men like Flynn were the shadows of the government. While others knew that they existed they never really knew the 'who' or 'where' or the 'what' about them. The less known about these people the better for everyone. Their very safety depended on the fact that they were invisible. Dimmler looked over Flynn's file in thought.

"Why Flynn? And why all of a sudden? Sure, I know that they were lovers," Dimmler continued, "but I thought that the 'Affair' between them was over. Why won't she let him go? Too many field men get themselves killed over so-called love."

Dimmler reached over to his computer keyboard and began to type in his access codes for the top secret and confidential files. It took the Deputy Director a few minutes to access the fourth level of files.

The Deputy Director of Operations continued through all twenty-one pages in Flynn's file which consisted of in depth physical, psychological, and service profiles. While Dimmler reviewed Flynn's file, he knew that he had recruited the perfect operative. He was highly intelligent, well-educated, creative, imaginative, a Gulf War hero--awarded the Silver Star--single with no known relatives, and only one close friend, Nicholas Cokely, of Boothbay Harbor, Maine, a former Sergeant in Flynn's command.

This information was not new to Dimmler. Flynn was like a son to him in many ways. He first met Flynn when he was a professor at Cornell Law School and Flynn was one of his brightest students. He had recruited Flynn for the Agency. And for many weeks, when the news of Flynn being shot down over the Colombia-Venezuela border was reported, Dimmler felt a personal loss. No one was more joyed than he when Flynn walked out of the rain forest across the Llanos and was rescued by friendly, Colombian forces. Of course Flynn went through a troublesome and dark period of 'adjustment' after learning that his high school girlfriend, Kathleen Murphy, married Michael O'Toole, a restaurant owner in Cleveland, Ohio while he was on that protracted 'shadow' assignment in Colombia.

The Deputy Director also knew of the Dutch girl, Kristen Shults. He knew of Flynn and Kristen's on-again-off-again affair. It was not love though, Dimmler believed, but a different relationship. "Or could I be wrong?" Dimmler knew that the Shults woman, extremely beautiful and sensual, gave Flynn an intellectual challenge. Naturally, there was also a strong physical attraction to each other. The Agency did a thorough background investigation on her and she was cleared as a non-security threat. She was exactly whom she appeared to be.

Vice President Bunnell was another matter, entirely. Flynn was different, almost overly protective around her. She, like Kristen Shults, was very beautiful. Interestingly, both had red hair, were about the same age, and physical appearance and strikingly similar to Kathleen Murphy. And, Dimmler noted, both Kristen Shults and Patricia Bunnell had Dutch heritage. However, as the Vice President, Patricia Bunnell was only a heart beat away from being the most powerful woman in the world.

Deputy Director Dimmler ordered the 'print' mode to activate while he closed the file and pondered. "Why is Patricia fixated on a man like Flynn? Flynn is a trained, cold blooded killer, if necessary, with little emotion. He disregards his personal feelings and he has proven his worth to his country many times." Dimmler could not understand what the Vice President wanted to know about Flynn that she already didn't know.

"Well," George Dimmler said as an idea came to him, "if you want a file on Flynn, I think I'll run one on you, Madam Vice President, too." The Deputy Director of Operations picked up his office phone and dialed the Assistant Deputy Director of Operations, Daniel Kent.

"Dan, George. I need a complete breakout on Patricia Bunnell, ASAP."

Daniel Kent was alarmed by the request. "Jesus Christ, George, she's the sitting Vice President. What's up?"

"I know fucking well who she is," Dimmler barked into the phone. "Just get it to me before lunch."

"Okay, you're the boss."

Dimmler concluded, "And Dan, I don't think I have to tell you that this is most sensitive in nature. Your complete discretion is required. Understood?"

"Yes, sir. I understand completely," Dan Kent assured him. "I'll have it brought up to you before noon."

"No, Dan," Dimmler admonished his assistant, "I want you to personally bring it to me. No copies, no tracers." He discontinued the call.

Daniel Kent couldn't believe what he was just ordered to do. In all the years he was in Operations, no one ever ordered a "DOGS" --a Document of Operational Government Security--on a sitting Vice President. "Christ," Kent mumbled, "Hoover, when he was the Director of the Bureau, before Stanton, almost got himself shit-canned over this kind of internal 'spying' back in the 1960's." Daniel Kent made a handwritten memo to himself noting the date, time, and request from Deputy Director Dimmler. He was going to cover his own bureaucratic ass, just in case. He sealed the memo in an envelope and locked it in his safe.

"Lois," Kent pushed his secretary's intercom button.

"Yes, sir, Mister Kent?"

"Lois, I have an urgent request from the Deputy Director which I must complete by noon. Please hold all calls. And no visitors."

"Yes, sir."

Daniel Kent spun his chair around to a bank of computer screens and immediately began to access the security files. He had set up this computer program and knew it better than anyone else at the Agency. On more than one occasion, Kent would surreptitiously access files on his own but, in this case, he didn't want any possible trace back to him, nor the Deputy Director. In setting up this program, Kent had installed a back-door access to the files which would not trigger the automatic logging system. In effect, he had a secret way in and out of any file which could never be traced nor discovered. No other person knew of his back-door access and it had served him well in the past. He impishly smiled at his own brilliance while logging on.

Kent was into the file within a minute. He called up all information accumulated on Patricia Bunnell and ordered it printed--two copies. Within seconds the laser printers spewed out the fifty-six pages of intelligence gathered on the Vice President--twice. Everything anyone ever knew about the Vice President all the way from Kindergarten to the present was copied.

"This one is for the Deputy Director," Kent mused. "Now, let's have some fun."

Once again he began typing on his keyboard. This file would require a lot more time. "I need to access the FBI's and NSA's secret files, but I don't want them to detect my entry."

It took Kent nearly two hours to break into the Bureau's and NSA's data banks. His high speed computers were sent on a clandestine mission talking in encoded language to other high speed computers throughout Washington, D.C. This 'global' search for all information on Patricia Bunnell was secretly copied into Kent's computer memory while simultaneously erasing any trace that he was there.

It was eight minutes to noon when the task was completed by Daniel Kent. He took one of the two copies and placed it in a security envelope which could not be re-sealed, once opened. The other he put in a folder and again locked it in his safe.

"Lois," Kent called his secretary. "I'm going up to Dimmler's office." Kent went out his private door which opened onto a back stairway and marched himself up the two flights to Dimmler's office. Kent buzzed the Deputy Director's private door. Dimmler checked his security monitor and seeing that it was Daniel Kent, pressed the lock release under his desk allowing Kent to enter.

"Here is the information that you requested, sir," Kent said handing Dimmler the sealed security envelope. "Is there anything else, boss?"

"No, that's all. Thank you, Dan." Dimmler opened the envelope and added, "Is this file complete?"

"Up to the minute, General."

"No traces like I asked?"

"None, General. There can be no trace, either." Kent answered proud of himself and his ability.

"Good," Dimmler said. "That will be all for now. Good job. Leave by the same door, understood?"

"Yes, sir." Kent left by the rear, private door and descended the two floors to his own office.

Meanwhile, George Dimmler began to read the report very carefully. There would be no lunch today. Dimmler checked his watch. He had less than two hours before his meeting with the Vice President.

ABOVE THE ARCTIC CIRCLE, ALASKA

Flynn secured the Buccaneer's nose with the bow line to the nearest scrub pine on the shore. The wind-whipped snow obscured his vision to not more than a few feet in front of him. It was going to be quite a storm for several more hours. Flynn made the trips back and forth to his plane and to the shore without incident unloading all of his gear. The pounding blizzard was actually comforting to Flynn. He needed to be alone in his thoughts. Altogether, too much had happened to Flynn in the past year which made him lose sight of his career. He needed to get his focus back and regain his edge. That edge had been what had kept Flynn alive in the field as a Special Ops agent over the years.

Patricia Bunnell had been a major distraction. There was no room in Flynn's life for such a distraction. She was different than the other women that Flynn had known, except perhaps his old girl friend, Kathleen. Even Kristen Shults, beautiful and intelligent as she was, was never a distraction--she was a good friend. Flynn paused for a moment while thinking of Kristen. "It would be nice to see her again," he smiled. "Maybe she would take my mind off of the Vice President."

All of his gear unloaded, Flynn sought cover between a pine thicket which would offer some shelter from the raging storm. He pitched his tent and settled in waiting out the storm that howled around him. The Alaskan twilight at this time of year soon became total darkness for the next fifteen hours. Flynn checked his BlackBerry for any text-messages or missed calls. "I wish I was never forced to bring this damn cell phone with me," Flynn griped to himself. "Agency regulations, you know," Flynn mocked his old friend the Deputy Director of Operations, George Dimmler. There were no messages which was a relief to Flynn. If there were it meant that he would have to return to work. And, right now, that was the last thing Flynn wanted to do.

Flynn reached into his back-pack and retrieved a

bottle of Jack Daniel's. "Time to relax, Sport," he said downing a long hit on the bottle. The Tennessee sour mash instantly warmed him from the inside. While the storm continued outside Flynn's tent another storm was bubbling inside his head. "Fuck you, Jeremiah," a drunken Flynn screamed. "You know you couldn't fall in love with her. You don't belong in that shitty circle of political phony mother-fuckers! And besides, she doesn't love you. She's in fucking love with that sonofabitch Admiral, fucking Allen, fucking Moorehouse! She's no different than Kathleen, either. Kathleen's the one that shouldn't have gotten away."

Two days later the storm stopped and Flynn awoke from his stupor.

CARACAS, VENEZUELA

Don Carols Escobar, brother of Venezuelan Vice-President, Victor Escobar, was addressing a meeting of the regional drug-lords of Venezuela and Colombia at his six thousand acre estate. It was more like a fortress than an estate, however. Security systems, with the latest technology, encompassed the entire grounds. The main compound consisted of several small buildings, workers' quarters, a warehouse, laboratory, and a main living mansion with in-ground, Olympic sized pool. The interior compound was surrounded by a fifteen foot high stone wall complete with surveillance cameras and a computerized system of fifty caliber machine guns--activated by motion detection devices when armed at night--which would cover every foot of the grounds. A turbo helicopter sat on its pad directly behind the mansion adjacent to the pool.

Don Carlos Escobar employed nearly one hundred--highly trained and combat ready--men who lived in the compound and provided twenty-four hour security. In the basement of the mansion, Don Carlos also had a high-tech information center. This information center kept Don Carlos Escobar fully informed of world events and in touch with the major distribution centers world-wide. His computer networks rivaled many of the largest corporations in the world and even some governments.

It was Don Carlos's job to run the multi-billion dollar drug business and he never left anything to chance. At this moment he was taking care of business. Don Carlos Escobar opened his meeting to outline his operational plan to increase production and distribution of his drug empire.

"Gentlemen, it gives me a great deal of pleasure to tell you that within the next few days, I will be attending a very important meeting which will have world-wide impact. And it will mean more gold for all of you, *amigos*."

HOUSTON, TEXAS

The top two floors of the United Petroleum Building were occupied by David R. Laird, Chief Executive Officer of the world's largest petroleum corporation. There was an ostentatious display of wealth in his executive suite which was both home and office to Laird. Most of Laird's work was done at a teak desk adjacent to his private swimming pool. He surrounded himself with beautiful women and handsome young men whose primary purpose was to serve Laird's every pleasure. He indulged himself with these 'pleasures' several times each day.

"Marge," Laird said to his private executive assistant and Laird's primary 'pleasure unit', "have all the arrangements been made for the meeting with the Tiger and the other members of the 'Elite'?

"Yes, Dave, they have. All members have been contacted...." There was a sudden and unexpected blow to her face. The force of his backhanded slap knocked her off balance and to the floor. She was in obvious pain and trembling in fear.

"You filthy SLUT!" Laird screamed at her. "Don't you EVER call me by my first name. Who the fuck gave you that right, you bitch?"

Choking on her tears Marge cried, "I'm sorry, Mister Laird."

Just as sudden as had been his uncontrollable rage, Laird, as if a switch had been thrown, bent over and helped her to her feet. Laird embraced the stricken woman while she sobbed deeply.

"There, there, my little Margie, you're all better now. I've got you. You'll do better from now on won't you, my dear?"

"Yes, sir. I'm so sorry, sir. It won't ever happen again."

With a sinister grin he replied, "No, Marge, that's for sure. It won't ever happen...again." The executive assistant immediately understood what Laird meant by his remark. "Now, let me ask you again, is everything taken care of for the meeting with Tiger?"

"Yes sir, Mister Laird." Marge fought back her tears. She had taken care of everything to the last detail. Her life depended on making certain that a problem was never reported to Laird which she could correct. She had seen first hand how David Laird eliminated hundreds of others who tried to give him, one of the most powerful men in the world, a problem. He took pleasure in crushing those who got in his way or tried to usurp his control. Laird derived pleasure from the most bizarre things.

WASHINGTON, D.C.

The Deputy Director of Operations, George Dimmler, arrived at the Office of the Vice President on schedule and with Flynn's file in his metal attache case.

"Good afternoon, Mister Dimmler. The Vice President is expecting you. Please go right in."

"Thank you, Scot," Dimmler said wondering why Patricia Bunnell would have a male secretary for all these years. After all, Scot wasn't really very handsome. "Oh well," Dimmler thought, "this is the era of political correctness and all that shit, maybe he fetches her Starbucks."

The Deputy Director was greeted by the Vice President. "Hello, George. Right on time as usual."

"Madam Vice President," Dimmler returned the greeting shaking her out-stretched hand. "God!," he thought looking at her, "She is so strikingly beautiful. If I were only twenty years younger..."

Patricia Bunnell gestured for the Deputy Director to be seated. "George, I assume you brought Flynn's file. May I see it, please?"

Dimmler opened his brief case and presented her the file. "Madam Vice President," Dimmler protested, "I must express my official position that your request is highly irregular and places me and my section in an uncomfortable situation. The precedent for such a request is..."

Patricia Bunnell interrupted him. "George, let's cut through the bureaucratic and political bullshit for a moment, please. I've known you long enough to appreciate your position. Let me assure you again that this file will remain confidential. No one will ever know anything from me or from this office about Flynn, or that he even exists in your Agency."

"Goddamnit, Madam Vice President," Dimmler exploded, "Flynn is one of, no he is the best field operative the Agency has. And now I feel that I have placed him in personal jeopardy. What possible explanation can you give me for wanting his file?"

"Relax," she replied. "Let me assure you that my only interest is for Flynn's professional career."

"Professional career!" Dimmler exclaimed, "What in heaven's name would possess you to be solely interested in Flynn's professional career? He's a Special Operations ghost! Why Flynn and why now? I thought you two had parted company?"

"Look, George, my reasons are my reasons. And they will stay my reasons. I needn't tell you..."

It was Dimmler's turn to interrupt. "No, Madam, you don't need to tell me who you are. I realize you are the Vice President."

"Fuck you, George," Patricia fired back at his pedantry. "You have no right to pull this shit on me. I've been the best friend your department has ever had. I've supported every request you ever made while I was in Congress. I don't think I have to remind you that your ass would be fried over that mess up in Central America a few years ago if I hadn't covered for you." Patricia Bunnell was a tough politician for all her beauty. And she knew how and when to play a trump card.

Dimmler was instantly angry at her for reminding him about the Company's fuck-up in Central America. "That's a low blow, Patricia, and you know it."

The Vice President knew that she had won this round. "Come on, George," she charmed, "we're on the same team, you know that." She came out from behind her desk and walked over near where Dimmler was sitting. She sat on the corner of her desk and crossed her legs teasing, just a little, as her skirt pulled back to the top of her thigh exposing a pair of legs a model would kill for. The move wasn't lost on the Deputy Director, who smiled.

"Now, George," Patricia said coyly, "tell me what Mister Flynn's been up to these days."

AMSTERDAM, HOLLAND

Kristen Shults left her apartment around seven. She had packed only one suitcase and threw the rest of her personal belongings in her matching overnight bag which she carried slung over her shoulder. The drive to the airport only took about twenty minutes and Kristen would have plenty of time to catch her nine o'clock flight to London's Heathrow airport.

Kristen parked her Audi in the long term lot and took the shuttle to the KLM counter to check in. She checked her suitcase and picked up her boarding pass. She passed through security and stopped for a cup of tea at one of the terminal's shops. While sipping her tea, she made a call on her cell phone to her uncle in London. He was going to meet her at the airport. Kristen set her shoulder bag down next to her while she waited for her uncle to answer.

"Hello, Uncle James. This is Kris. I just wanted to let you know that I'll be in London around midnight. Is there any problem with meeting me? I could catch a taxi... Are you certain? Very well. I'm on KLM flight 214. See you later, Uncle James. Bye, bye."

Kristen finished her tea and picked up an identical bag that had been switched on her by an oriental man who was sitting in the next booth. The Korean watched while Kristen walked to the boarding gate with the bag slung over her shoulder.

WASHINGTON, D.C.

White House Chief of Staff Admiral Moorehouse was in his office when a call came in on his private line.

"Admiral, this is Dan."

Moorehouse was surprised to hear from Daniel Kent on his office phone. "Dan, I hope this is a secure line."

"Of course, Admiral," Kent said smugly.

"Okay, then cut the shit. What's up?" Admiral Moorehouse had no respect for this twit, but he was an inside informant on things going on at the CIA. And, as such, he was useful to Moorehouse.

"Well, Admiral...Dimmler just had me run a complete 'DOGS' on your girlfriend."

Admiral Moorehouse was curious and shocked by Kent's message. "What the fuck for?"

"I don't know. But if I were you I'd be a little more discreet with your love life. It's all over the report from

NSA." Kent thought he had the upper hand for once.

"Listen to me, you shithead," Moorehouse was livid.

"Whoa, easy, Admiral," Kent interrupted. "Don't sweat it. I only gave the Deputy Director what we have. He doesn't know that I ran the search through the Bureau and NSA. Your ass is covered, again."

The Chief of Staff didn't like being blackmailed or even the threat of a blackmail by this man. He recovered his composure enough to disguise his rage. "Dan, I need you to get me that complete file, TODAY!"

"I suspected that you would. That's why I called you. Why don't we meet later for a drink at the *Dubliner*? I'll bring the file with me."

"All right. About eight o'clock. Back booth as usual." Moorehouse hung up.

The Chief of Staff was concerned. He couldn't understand why the Deputy Director of Operations at the CIA would have a 'DOGS' run on the Vice President. "What's that sly old General up to now?" he thought. Then he had an idea. He placed a call to the Vice President on her private line.

"Hello," Patricia Bunnell answered.

"Pat, it's Michael."

"I was just thinking about you. Are we still on for dinner?"

"No, something's come up. I won't be able to make it. But how about I drop by your place around eleven, Babe?"

"All right," Patricia said. "I'll be still up. I'll see you then, I guess."

As soon as Admiral Moorehouse hung up he pushed his intercom button. "Susan?"

"Yes, sir?"

"I have plans for this evening. Don't schedule me for anything after seven tonight. Is everything set for the President's flight to Houston tomorrow? You know that we'll be leaving at dawn and returning tomorrow night."

"All arrangements have been made at our end, sir. Air Force One will be ready."

"Thank you, Susan," Moorehouse concluded. This promised to be an informative evening for the Chief of Staff.

LONDON, ENGLAND

It was rainy and foggy in London when KLM flight 214, touched down just before midnight. Kristen Shults had spent the time on the flight drifting away in her thoughts. She tried to push thoughts of work from her mind. She was going on holiday, and work could wait. Besides, she hadn't been able to understand why the oil futures market was so volatile. Market conditions didn't make any sense anymore. The economic factors of supply and demand were in equilibrium, but the prices were rising anyway. She kept thinking, "There is some influencing factor in the price equation that I'm missing. And, I don't know what it is."

This thought then led to Jeremiah Flynn. She smiled when her thoughts turned to him. "I think I'm in love with him, but he doesn't know it. Maybe it's that certain mystery about him that I find attractive. I always enjoy being with him. Flynn makes me feel comfortable and secure." While she watched the plane taxi to the terminal she whispered, "I do miss you, Flynn."

The 747 taxied to the gate and came to a stop.

Kristen deplaned and proceeded to customs with her carry on bag. Because she was a frequent visitor to England, Kristen was completely familiar to all of the customs agents who also knew that she was the niece of Foreign Minister James Saunders. It was not out of the ordinary for the customs agents to merely wave her on through without checking her luggage. They did so again on this trip.

Nearby, a Korean man watched the entire proceeding with great interest. As soon as Kristen Shults had cleared customs, he made a call on his cell phone.

"Uncle James," Kristen called out seeing her uncle.

"Kristen, my dear," the Foreign Minister greeted his niece. "How are you, dear? My, you look more like your mother every time I see you....but more beautiful, of course."

"Oh, Uncle. You always say that. Maybe it's time for you to see the eye doctor for new spectacles," she laughed.

"Come along, my dear," Foreign Minister Saunders said taking Kristen's arm. "William will see to your bags." When they got in the government car her Uncle James asked, "What plans have you made for your holiday?"

Nothing definite, Uncle. A few days shopping and some time in the country. I need a little time to clear my head. Nothing at work seems to make sense right now. Nor does anything else for that matter."

"Ah," Saunders replied, "And what of that Yank friend of yours? What's his name?"

"Flynn, Uncle. Jeremiah Flynn."

"Yes, of course. Has he asked you to marry him,

yet?"

Kristen blushed. "No, he hasn't. And I don't think he will."

"What's the matter with that man? Is is he daft? Why he should be begging you to marry him."

"You're sweet, Uncle James," Kristen added.

William, the Foreign minister's personal driver, returned with her suitcase. Kristen handed William her carry on bag which he took to the back of the Bentley. He opened the trunk and placed it inside along with Kristen's suitcase and her original carry on shoulder bag. His personal stash of cocaine was delivered along with a million dollars in blood diamonds.

ABOVE THE ARCTIC CIRCLE, ALASKA

The sun came out after the storm had passed. It turned warmer and the snow began to melt. Flynn crawled out from his tent and was blinded by the brightness of the sun reflecting off the snow. His head ached and his eyes hurt right into the back of his brain. Flynn's mouth was as dry as cotton. He attempted to shield his eyes from the glare by putting on his dark flying glasses. He walked the few yards to the pond with his tin drinking cup and dipped it into the ice-cold, clear water. When he raised his cup to drink, however, Flynn became aware that he was not alone at the pond.

A bull moose was wading in the pond and feeding only fifty yards away. Flynn instinctively froze any movement. The wind was in his face and the moose had not picked up Flynn's human scent. Slowly, and with as little movement as possible, Flynn inched his way back to his tent for his digital camera with telephoto lens.

Flynn began stalking the enormous animal with all the skill of a professional hunter trained in the art of silent killing. This was indeed a trophy moose. The giant's pans were at least fifty inches across and full. His large 'bell' below the moose's jaw and his height told Flynn that the animal was between twelve and fifteen years of age. He probably weighed close to fifteen hundred pounds. Flynn crawled closer to the moose taking numerous pictures as he went.

The clicking action of the shutter opening and closing suddenly alerted the moose of potential danger. Alarmed, the moose quickly lifted his huge head and turned toward the noise while testing the air for any scent of danger. Flynn tensed. He stopped taking pictures when the giant moose snorted. It was rutting season and this animal was dangerous.

Flynn quickly assessed his situation preparing for the charge that he was certain would follow at any moment. Over to Flynn's left was the ice cold pond. To his right a thick copse of small evergreen scrub pines. To Flynn's rear, more scrub pines and eventually the Buccaneer. Now directly in front of Flynn, no more than thirty feet, was a curious and dangerous bull moose who was in a very bad disposition.

"What a strategic position you put yourself in, Sport," Flynn thought knowing that his only real avenue of escape was the ice-cold pond. At that very moment the wind shifted and the moose had caught Flynn's scent. The moose charged! Flynn dropped his camera and launched himself into the frigid water just as the moose trampled his former position and trashed his campsite. The moose raged on bellowing and trumpeting--then disappeared into the dense forest.

Flynn surfaced gasping for breath from the icy water. "Well that was fucking special, you dumb sonofabitch!" Flynn cursed. Then while surveying what used to be his campsite he shouted out loud, "You never stop fucking over me do you, Patricia!"

After a few minutes he began the task of re-assembling his camp. Fortunately, the moose's charge only knocked over his tent. There was no damage to his weapons nor his BlackBerry. Flynn went back to the plane for a change of clothing and a towel. "What the hell," Flynn mumbled, "I might as well take a bath. I'm already soaked." Flynn stripped and jumped back into the cold pond. Within a few minutes in the ice-cold water Flynn's hangover was gone. He climbed out of the water now sober and in better spirits. The sun was warm and felt good on his naked body. "Yes, this is vacation," he laughed.

Flynn hung his wet clothes over several tree branches and got himself dressed in dry and warm clothes. "Time to go exploring," Flynn thought packing his back-pack for a trek into the vast Alaskan wilderness. He slung his 30.06 over his shoulder, checked his side-arm, and made a quick GPS location and bearing on his BlackBerry. Then he set off on his march away from his base camp.

Flynn brought along an extra battery pack for his cell phone just in case he needed it. The snow was dry and powdery, deeper in places where it had been blown into drifts by the wind. The walk was not too difficult, however. After hiking for several hours, Flynn calculated that he was only a few hours away from the Porcupine River and about twelve miles from his base camp. Once he got to the Porcupine he would fish for salmon and camp for the night. He hoped he could get some pictures of a grizzly bear fishing for salmon, too.

Flynn walked on about another mile before he suddenly stopped in his tracks. The quiet of the forest was deafening. All of Flynn's senses came to full alert. The hunter was being watched. A movement to his right caught Flynn's attention but the image disappeared as he turned to locate what it was. Another shadow to his left. A muffled noise behind him. Flynn un-shouldered his 30.06 and prepared it to fire. He unbuckled his holster to ready the .44 magnum side-arm for a quick draw if necessary. Flynn scanned the trees around him while flashbacks of the rain forest jungle came to mind when he was shot down near the Venezuelan-Colombian border.

Less than twenty yards away Flynn saw his 'enemy'. It was a gray wolf. He realized that he was surrounded by a small pack of Alaskan timberwolves. Flynn slowly relaxed, setting his rifle down against a tree. He took out his camera from his pack and started to take pictures. Two of nature's ultimate killing machines were face to face with guarded curiosity. Flynn snapped a picture which caused the wolf's ears to perk straight up at full attention. The wolf studied the unfamiliar figure before him. His nose twitched inhaling the scent. Then, when Flynn snapped another picture, the wolves disappeared as quickly as they had appeared. Flynn reviewed his pictures in the digital camera and smiled. "This is great!"

Flynn replaced his camera back into the backpack and picked up his rifle. He slung the weapon over his shoulder and walked on with a renewed vigor in his step. A short time later, Flynn was at the banks of the Porcupine River. He found a level spot and made his camp. Then Flynn took the fishing line from his pack. He rolled over a nearby rock and found a grub which he used for bait. It wasn't long after the hook went into the water that he had a strike. It was a native cut-throat trout about fifteen inches in length. He landed the fish and threw out his line again. Within seconds he had another trout on the hook. It was nearly identical to the first one. Pulling it to shore, Flynn was satisfied that he had enough for dinner and breakfast. Flynn marveled at their beautiful, deep coloring. He was about to take his catch back to camp when he noticed a huge grizzly upstream on the opposite bank of the river.

The giant bear paid no attention to Flynn who once again started snapping pictures of the beautiful beast doing a little fishing of his own. After the bear had caught and eaten his fill he climbed back up the bank and vanished silently into the woods. Flynn was amazed that such a large animal could be so quiet going through the forest.

While darkness came over the small valley on the banks of the Porcupine River, Flynn took his catch--which he now cleaned--back to his temporary campsite. Flynn filleted the trout and cooked them over a small fire. The taste of the trout was sweet and juicy. After he ate, Flynn looked up into the clear Alaskan sky. The stars were brighter in the clean air. Flynn looked to the north, and was treated to a fabulous light-show flashing across the sky. Flynn enjoyed the Aurora Borealis, remembering only a few other times in his life that he had ever seen this phenomena. Tonight was an exceedingly brilliant display. Flynn lay back in his sleeping bag and while he started to fall asleep remembered other flashes of light in the night sky. Those flashes, however, were man made--

caused by weapons of war--all from another time and another place.

WASHINTON, D. C.

Admiral Moorehouse waited in his private car outside the *Dubliner*. He had arrived at seven forty-five, fifteen minutes before his scheduled meeting with Daniel Kent. He was positioned so that he could easily see the restaurant's front entrance. At eight-ten Daniel Kent arrived by cab. Admiral Moorehouse could see that Kent had his attache case with him and, he suspected, the full file on the Vice President. Moorehouse waited a few extra minutes as a precautionary measure making certain that Kent was not being followed. The Admiral was not a novice in the art of shady meetings and clandestine affairs. He had thought, however, that he had been more clever in cheating on his wife with the beautiful Vice President. Kent's earlier phone comment's now gave him cause for concern. When he was confident that Kent was not being followed, Admiral Moorehouse got out of his car and walked across the street to the *Dubliner* then went inside.

Moorehouse walked through the cocktail crowd at the bar area. He made his way to the last booth in the back where he saw the back of Kent's head. Kent was alone.

"Okay, Dan," Admiral Moorehouse said placing his hand on the shoulder of Daniel Kent, "let me see what you've got."

The White House Chief of Staff stopped in immediate shock as the force of his hand on Kent's shoulder caused the man's body to slump forward--his

41

lifeless body falling on top of the table, spilling his drink.

"Jeezus!" Moorehouse exclaimed in shock. Kent was dead and the attache case was gone! Intuitively, Moorehouse lifted Kent's body back upright. The horrified look of death on Kent's face glared back at a frightened Moorehouse. Beads of sweat formed on the Chief of Staff's face while a chill shot through his body. Quickly, the Admiral looked around the restaurant to see if anyone had witnessed the scene. Panic overcame the Admiral. He quickly turned and hastened back through the crowd toward the front door. He clutched at his necktie trying to loosen it in an attempt to get some air. By the time Admiral Moorehouse hit the street his stomach wrenched and he vomited. He staggered to his car hoping to get away from the restaurant as quickly as possible.

"Fucking drunk," a passerby said in disgust seeing Moorehouse vomit and stagger.

The Chief of Staff fumbled with his keys trying to get them into the ignition. Finally successful, the engine raced. Moorehouse composed himself just enough to pull out into traffic and speed off into the Washington night. He drove around for quite some time unsure of exactly where he was or where he was going. As if by instinct, he found himself on a familiar street. It was the street where Patricia Bunnell, Vice President of the United States, lived. Michael Allen Moorehouse parked his car down the block from the Vice President's residence. He was still trembling while fumbling with his cell phone to retrieve her private number.

The Vice President's caller ID told her it was Michael calling. "Hello, Michael."

"Patricia, thank God you're home! I need to see

you right away."

The Vice President could sense there was something wrong by the tone of his voice. "Michael, what's the problem?"

"I'll be right up. I'm just down the block. Don't move."

"Use the back door," Patricia advised sensing that there was a problem with Michael.

"Yes, of course," Moorehouse stammered.

The Chief of Staff to President I.W. Harper walked down the street and turned up an alley to the back door of the Vice President's home. She was waiting at the door.

"Michael, what's wrong?"

"Pat, Daniel Kent was murdered tonight at the *Dubliner.* I was going to meet him for a drink. But, when I got there, he was in the back booth and already dead!"

"Why?"

"How the fuck do I know why?" Moorehouse snapped. "He was just dead!"

"Calm down, Michael," Patricia began slowly. "What were you meeting Kent for? And who do you think might have killed him?"

Admiral Moorehouse looked at her in an obvious confused state of mind. "I haven't a clue. Pour me a drink will you?"

The Vice President walked over to her cabinet and took out a bottle of Napoleon Brandy. She poured it in a snifter glass and handed it to Moorehouse. "Michael, you've got to pull yourself together," Patricia was taking charge of his dilemma. "Can anyone put you and Kent together tonight?"

"I'm not sure," Michael tried to think. "I don't

believe so. Unless someone saw us at the *Dubliner*. I can't be sure of anything, right now."

"Well," Patricia said thinking out loud. "then you were here with me all evening."

"Yes, that's possible I suppose. But what about the person who killed Kent? He knows differently?"

"Michael, whomever killed Kent did it for another reason. Why would anyone want him dead? Do you know?"

"Goddamn it, Pat, Kent told me he had a complete file on you. That's why I was going to meet him to look at the file and see just what the fuck was in there."

A surprised and concerned Patricia exclaimed, "A complete file on me? Why would he want a complete file on me?"

Moorehouse took a drink of the brandy regaining some of his composure. "I don't know. But it's obvious that someone has a keen interest in you and your association with me." The Chief of Staff thought for a moment and then asked, "What about that fuck, Flynn? You two had some torrid affair for the past year. Maybe he killed Kent"

"Be serious, Michael," Patricia Bunnell dismissed his reasoning. "Flynn is up in Alaska somewhere. Besides we're both single. What motive would he have?"

"Who knows about that sonofabitch. He's a fucking killer isn't he? Shit, he could have had one of his assassin buddies at the Agency do it for him. If you could have seen Kent, you'd believe it was a professional job. There was no blood, no wounds, no weapon. He was just dead! It had the earmarks of the Company all over it."

"I can't believe that Jeremiah Flynn had anything to do with it. I won't ever believe that, Michael."

A flash of jealousy emerged in the White House Chief of Staff. "You're in love with that cold-blooded bastard, aren't you?"

"Cut the bullshit, Michael. Whatever is or was between us is over," Patricia replied in anger. "Flynn is not in love with me and I don't think he is capable of being in love with anyone, except maybe his cheerleader girlfriend, Kathleen Murphy." Then the Vice President switched the subject away from Flynn. "Look, Michael, you'd better try to figure out a way to remove yourself from this situation and forget about Flynn."

"I'll think of something so don't worry about me. The real puzzle is why and who wants to know so much about you? It still comes back to the CIA. Kent worked there under another one of your other pals, Dimmler, right?" Moorehouse didn't wait for her to answer the question. "Look, Pat," he said as he held her in his arms, "I'm worried about you. You know how I feel about you."

She pushed him away and responded, "Go home to your wife, Michael."

Moorehouse left by the back door and didn't see that Patricia Bunnell had tears in her eyes. She was alone and she ached inside. She realized that she could never love Admiral Moorehouse. He could never be the man that Flynn was. Nobody could.

The next morning's *Washington Post,* made no mention of Daniel Kent's murder. In fact, there was no report of any trouble at the Dubliner last night whatsoever.

HOUSTON, TEXAS

United Petroleum President and CEO, David

Laird's private line rang. It was a secured and scrambled line but the caller ID indicated it was a call from a known source in Washington, D.C.

Laird answered. "What have you to report?"

The scrambled voice on the other end began, "Daniel Kent, Assistant Deputy Director of Operations at the CIA, has been terminated. A certain file he had copied has been stolen."

"What does this mean?" Laird asked.

"It means that there is now a potential for a remote contingency that could complicate things," the mysterious voice answered.

"What exactly do you mean by a 'remote contingency'?" Laird questioned.

"We anticipated that the file Kent had copied contained information that would have been useful to us. The only information we do know, is that it had something to do with Vice President Patricia Bunnell. What that information is, is unknown. The remote contingency is that which we are not certain."

Laird, not used to political or clandestine double-talk, was angry. "Jeezus, can't you fucking 'Spooks' ever speak in plain English? Why is there all of this bullshit?"

"Listen, Laird," the caller admonished, "Don't use that tone with me! Remember who you're dealing with."

Laird backed off, "Okay, okay. I'm sorry. What am I supposed to tell Tiger and the other members of the 'Elite'? That all is well...but?"

"My advice to you is to say nothing about this at all. I told you that he was a remote contingency, and only a potential problem. If anything comes of it, I think he can be handled without too much difficulty at this end."

"He?" Laird shouted. "Who the fuck is the 'HE'?"

"That he, is Jeremiah Flynn. He is very protective of the Vice President. He is a Special Operations specialist who is a very capable operative. He is fearless, stealthy and efficient. He eliminates problems for the Agency."

Laird couldn't help but laugh. "You're telling me that we need to be worried about one man? You can't be serious. We will crush him like a bug, if necessary."

"I'm warning you not to take him lightly. I know that he and the Vice President were lovers for some time and that they have a strong relationship. If she is threatened, he will stop at nothing to protect her."

"Well, then maybe you have just solved the problem, don't you see."

"What do you mean, Laird?"

"If Vice President Bunnell becomes a liability, we use her as bait and draw him out. Then we can can deal with this Flynn. If he is in love with her, it will be his Achilles heel. So, I don't give a rat's ass if they are lovers or not."

"Well, I do." The voice from Washington concluded and hung up.

LONDON, ENGLAND

The next morning Kristen Shults awoke at her Uncle James Saunders's estate. She was surprised at breakfast.

"Good morning, Uncle," Kristen greeted him at the breakfast table.

The Foreign Minister was already dressed. He had packed a small overnight bag which was waiting by the front entrance. "Good morning, my dear," returning her greeting. Then turning to her he explained, "Kristen, I have been called away for a few days on urgent business in the U.S., for a meeting on the oil problem of late, in Houston. I'm so sorry to have to rush off like this so soon after you got here."

"Oh, Uncle, I did so want to visit with you..."

"Don't worry, my dear," Saunders said getting up from the table. "We'll have plenty of time to talk when I return. It shouldn't be more than a few days, I suspect. William will see to you if you need anything."

"Very well." Kristen resigned herself that her uncle was a very important man in the British government and if he had business, he needed to attend to it. "Have a safe trip, Uncle James." Kristen kissed her uncle on the cheek.

The Foreign Minister smiled and went to the waiting car. William carried his bag and placed it in the trunk of the Bentley. Right beside James Saunders suitcase was the shoulder bag containing the diamonds that Kristen had unknowingly brought through Customs. The British government plane that would take Foreign Minister Saunders to Houston would not have to worry about customs. He had Diplomatic immunity, in any case.

WASHINGTON, D. C.

Air Force One lifted off the runway at Andrews Air Force Base at dawn. On board was President Irwin W. Harper, Secretary of State James Makoweic, Chief of Staff Moorehouse, and National Security Advisor William Pfohl.

President Harper and Secretary of State Makoweic were engaged in a private discussion over developments with OPEC, and the apparent stranglehold that the oil cartel was putting on the consumer nations with the continuous increase in the price for oil. "Jim," President Harper asked, "what do you make of the oil situation?"

"Frankly, Mister President," Makoweic began opening his brief case and removing a file, "I don't understand what is happening. When I met with the Oil Ministers just last month, I was under the impression that we had an agreement that they would hold the production levels at the present rate, stabilizing the price per barrel for at least six months. As a trade-off, we would continue our military contracts through next year. Unfortunately, with the Iranian government in a turmoil and the Israelis nervous about them getting weapons grade enriched uranium, not everyone was on board. Syria's al-Anzarisad has been stirring up the Iranians and that's worrying the Saudis, too."

President Harper asked, "Well, Mister Secretary, that doesn't seem to explain why the price hasn't stopped going up, does it?"

"No, Mister President, I don't believe so. But that's not the only place that the pressure to raise prices is coming from. North Korea's and Venezuela's latest saber rattling-anti U.S. policy is causing the speculators, like your friend Gerry Pearson, who seem to be hedging on the oil futures market. In essence, this is directly influencing the price per barrel. There are, in summary, Mister President, several external forces involved driving the price."

The President looked out the window of Air Force One in thought. Finally, President Harper asked his Secretary of State, "What do our friends thinks, Jim?"

The Secretary of State was perplexed by this

question. "What does he mean? What friends?", Makoweic thought. "Our allies, the press, the American public? Who knows what this Texan means." Makoweic was unsure what to say so he asked for clarification. "I'm sorry, Mister President, I don't understand the question."

"Our friends for Christ's sake!" Harper bellowed. "What do our friends think of the oil situation?"

"Well, sir, our allies..." Makoweic was instantly cut off.

"Our fuckin' allies? Who's talking' about our allies?" President Harper leaned over the table at the Secretary of State. "I'm talkin' about our own oil people. Our friends. I swear, are all you egg-heads that dense?"

James Makoweic was riled over the obvious insult. "That's not my bailiwick, Mister President. I don't meet with our own oil people. As the Secretary of State, I meet with foreign governments. And only confer with them."

"I don't need a fucking civics lesson, Mister Secretary. I know who the fuck you are and who the fuck put you in that job. If you ever climbed down from that Ivy League tower you live in, you might learn that the oil companies—the American Oil Corporations, like United Petroleum, run themselves like another fucking goddamn country. And, only maybe, pay homage to the United States of America by paying a few dollars in fucking taxes!"

"Sir," the Secretary of State said in a higher pitch, "you are the Texas oil man, Mister President. You should know more about what are 'friends' think."

President Harper sat back in the plush chair and let out a hearty laugh. "You're fuckin'-A-right on that, pardner. That's why we're taking this little two day trip to

Houston. You tell the rest of those diplomatic assholes what our position is."

"And, what is the official U.S. position, Mister President?"

"It's real simple, Mister Secretary of State," the sarcasm ringing in his voice. "Fuck 'em all and the horse they rode in on." He slapped Makoweic on the knee and smiled, "Send Pfohl in here, will you."

The Secretary of State got up from his seat very quickly then shoved the file back into the brief case and slammed it shut. He was still angry when he reached the National Security Advisor.

"Bill," Makoweic sneered, "Cowboy Harper wants to 'palaver' with you, Pard."

The National Security Advisor understood Makoweic's frustration. The President was not an easy man to deal with. He was an opinionated bully, bullheaded, and a rough and a gruff sonofabitch who thought he was John Wayne.

President Harper remained in his plush chair when Pfohl joined him. President Harper motioned for Pfohl to have a seat. "Bill, what's the latest analysis on the oil situation? OPEC and any other outside factors driving the price of crude up?"

"Our latest analysis at NSA, Mister President, confirms that there is a movement in the Middle East to de-stabilize the current production and distribution supply lines. These include Iran and Syria, primarily. Outside the Middle East, there is a strong influence down in Venezuela and, strangely enough, North Korea. There seems to be some triangle of interest going on among these players. Oil and drugs for nuclear materials, as far as we can tell. However, we have not been able to identify all of the players. Especially here in this country."

"People here in this country?" The President appeared shocked.

"Yes, sir," William Pfohl continued. "There are powerful people in this country who are operating within this cabal, I'm positive of it, sir. I just can't prove it. Many may be even members of Congress, or people in this administration."

"You've got to be shitting me, Pfohl!" President Harper bellowed. "You're telling me that elected members of Congress are cashing in on the plight of the American people?"

"Yes, I am saying that, Mister President. And, perhaps, some in this administration."

"Well, the American people are getting pretty damn fed up with the spiraling cost of gasoline and heating oil." President Harper said emphatically. "And it appears to me that your analysis is way off base. Do we or do we not have a threat to our National Security? Goddamn it, Pfohl, if our supplies are cut off we're damn well not going to sit around while some camel jockey jerks us off."

"Sir, President Jahmir of Iran is becoming a serious threat with that country's enrichment of uranium. If they develop a nuclear bomb, with the missile capabilities that they already have, Israel is a prime target."

President Harper became concerned, "What the fuck are you telling me, Pfohl, that that asshole is going to start World War Three?"

"Mister President," William Pfohl tried to explain, "Jahmir and the Ayatollah believe that they are destined to unite all of the Arab world. And that Allah has ordained them to wipe out all infidels and make one world under Muslim rule."

"Bullshit! Bull-fucking-shit!" President Harper was irate. "Are you trying to set me up for another fiasco like Kennedy's Bay of Pigs?"

"On the contrary, Mister President," Pfohl tried again. "I'm merely trying to point out what our intelligence reports from telephone traffic tell us. I have not suggested that we take any military action at this time. Secretary of State Makoweic has a good handle on the situation of the politics in the Middle East. And we believe, as he does, that we can apply enough pressure from the United Nations, including additional economic sanctions, to make Jahmir ineffective for some time. They do not have enough oil refining capacity to sustain their demand for gasoline..."

"What about our friends, Bill?" Harper queried. "What do they think?"

"Most of our allies are with us on this...."

President Harper cut him off, "What allies are you talking about? You sound like that other asshole, Makoweic, William. I'm talking about our friends for Chrissake. The American Oil Companies!"

The National Security Agency Chief looked at President Harper with confusion all over his face and in his mind. Pfohl, a career NSA employee who had risen through the ranks of that Agency, was not unaware of the national political picture. He knew that President Irwin W. Harper was a Texas oilman and that his political clout came from oil money and power. Harper was a better politician than he was an intellectual. "The President is very much a one-dimensional person," Pfohl thought. "He has a great deal of difficulty understanding the global picture and what is the role of the United States in that global picture."

Pfohl finally said, "I don't know what they think, Mister President."

"Jeezus H. Christ," Harper bellowed, "can't anyone give me the answer?" Then turning his ire on Pfohl he said, "You'd better find out what they do think, William. I want to know before we leave Houston tomorrow, Buckaroo, or somebody's ass is going to be grass and I'm the power mower!" Harper swiveled in his plush chair and poured himself a tall glass of bourbon. Then turning back to William Pfohl, he concluded, "Do I make myself clear?"

There was no need to comment Pfohl thought. He rose from his chair and left the Presidential compartment.

President Harper put his feet up on the chair across from him. He took a long drink from his glass then switched on the cabin CD player. The entire plane was filled with the music of Hank Williams, Jr.

Chief of Staff Moorehouse picked up the intercom phone and rang up the pilot. "How much longer to Houston, Colonel?"

Colonel Bob Paxson, command pilot of Air Force One replied, "We should be touching down at seven forty-eight, Admiral."

"Thanks, Colonel." Moorehouse hung up the intercom and walked back to talk with President Harper.

Upon seeing his Chief of Staff Harper smiled, "Michael, my old friend, what's up?"

"Colonel Paxson told me that we should be in Houston in about an hour. Are there any last minute details that need to be taken care of, sir?"

President I. W. Harper smiled broadly while

motioning for Moorehouse to sit down. "Michael, tell me something will you?"

Admiral Moorehouse returned the President's smile and while he sat down said, "Of course, Mister President. What is it?"

"Michael," Harper asked, "what's it like to fuck the Vice President? Is she any good in bed?"

Moorehouse turned red with embarrassment and anger but managed to control himself. However, before he could formulate an appropriate response to such an outrageous question, Harper continued. "Shit, Pardner, don't get your ass too tight in the saddle. I've known all along you were banging her. Can't say that I blame you, either. Wouldn't mind slammin' the pork to her myself." Harper then got personal. "Does your wife know that you're fuckin' Bunnell?"

"Sir, my personal life is not..."

The President cut him off cold. "Your personal life is relevant to me, ol boy, especially if it might fuck me up." Harper was enjoying watching Moorehouse suffer from his verbal abuse. "I know more than you think I do, Michael. Especially about last night!"

Admiral Moorehouse was in shock. He began to feel himself getting dizzy. "Last night?"

"Yeah, last night," President Harper's tone was sinister and cutting. "Who do you think cleaned up your mess at the *Dubliner*? What the fuck were you meeting Kent for any way? And don't lie to me, Mikey, I already know."

The Chief of Staff was pale, sweat soaking his back and underarms. "He had a file..."

"I know all about the file," Harper reached in his desk drawer and pulled out the 'DOGS' file on Vice

President Patricia Bunnell. He tossed it on top of the desk. "Do you know who killed Kent?"

"No, sir, I'm still in shock about it. I have no idea in the world why he was murdered," Moorehouse offered.

"Well, I've got a couple of hunches who the bad guys might be," Harper interjected. "But I'm going to play my cards a little closer to the vest for now." The President took another drink from his glass before he added. "Michael, let me tell you something for your own good and for the good of my administration."

"What's that, Mister President?" Moorehouse asked meekly.

"Keep your pecker in your pants from now on and watch out for those two bushwhackers up front."

Astonished at the inference and the admonishment, Admiral Moorehouse exclaimed, "Who? You can't mean the Secretary of State and..."

Harper cut him off again, "Yessiree, Admiral. Makoweic and Pfohl! Those two ride with a peculiar posse. Keep your eyes on them for both of us. I'm not sure I can trust either of those two sidewinders."

"You can't be serious, Mister President. They are your closest advisors," Moorehouse was stunned.

"And lately, their advice sucks!" Harper said flipping through a few pages of the file on Vice President Bunnell. After reading over a few pages the President looked up at Moorehouse and continued, "It appears that your little heifer had you sucking hind tit for about a year. Who's this Flynn fellow she was doing?"

"He's a Special Black Ops guy that works in Dimmler's unit at CIA" Moorehouse sneered glad for an opportunity to turn on Flynn. "A cold blooded killer, Mister President."

"Do you think he killed Kent?"

"I wouldn't put it past him or one of his pals. Pat, er, I mean, the Vice President, said that Flynn was in Alaska on vacation. But who knows? Those ghosts are never where they say they're going to be..."

"Are you telling me that the Vice President knows about Kent's murder?" Harper was shocked at this revelation.

"Yes, sir. You see, last night I was all confused and in shock after I saw Kent being dead and all. I guess I wasn't thinking too clearly and next thing I know I'm at the Vice President's door...."

President Harper was angry and disgusted. He leaned over and blasted his Chief of Staff. "You dumb fucking sonofabitch! What the fuck is wrong with you? Is she that good of a piece of ass?"

"Sir, I..."

"Let me tell you one more thing, you sorry excuse for a man," Harper snarled. "Don't be like the coyote who lost his head over a little tail. Put some distance between you and that Bitch right now, Admiral. That's an order. Do you understand me, Mikey?"

The Chief of Staff hated to be called Mikey and he bristled inside but manged to hide his resentment. "Yes, sir, I understand. Perfectly!" Admiral Moorehouse got up to leave.

President Harper called after him, "Don't forget what I told you about those two bushwhackers, Admiral. And remember to keep your powder dry, Pard."

"Go fuck yourself, Cowboy," Moorehouse thought, leaving the compartment.

LONDON, ENGLAND

Kristen Shults awoke at her usual time of six o'clock in the morning. She started to get herself out of bed when she realized that she was in her Uncle James' house and she was on holiday. A smile came over her lips while she pulled the covers over her naked body and was soon back to sleep.

Kristen found herself in a dream--walking hand in hand with Jeremiah Flynn. They had just made love and were in a field of bright colored tulips. Suddenly, there was a loud crash which sounded like thunder. Kristen was confused because in her dream the sun had been shining. She felt a force pulling her away from Flynn. Then feeling fear--jolted awake.

Two masked men were carrying her out of the bedroom. Kristen began to fight her abductors. When she began to scream she felt the needle jam into her. She was unconscious again but this was not a dream. When Kristen awoke her arms were handcuffed to a brass headboard. She was lying naked on an old mattress without any blanket. She was in an unfamiliar room. An ugly man with bad teeth was sitting on the end of the bed and grinning at her when she began to realize what had happened.

"Well, princess, you are awake at last," the ugly man greeted Kristen with a heavy Cockney accent.

Kristen was terrified, "Who are you? Where am I?" She began to cry uncontrollably.

"Don't you worry your pretty little head about a thing. You'll be ours for a little while, now." The ugly little man tossed her a large sweatshirt. "Here put this on, love." He got up from the bed and stood. "Now, you be a good lass and I'll unhook you so you can cover yourself."

When he unlocked the handcuffs, Kristen realized she was still naked. Her thighs hurt and were bruised. She screamed through her tears of fright, "What do you want with me? Who are you? Don't you know who I am?"

The ugly little man looked at her and snarled, "Of course we know who you are, princess. Both of us know you really well by know, don't you think?" He laughed grabbing his crotch in an insulting and sexually suggestive manner. "And we're going to know you some more, too."

Kristen tried to kick at him but he slapped her legs aside and pounced on her with his hands on her throat. "Don't ever try that again or I kill you!"

"Go ahead," Kristen coughed out as he squeezed her neck tighter, "I'd rather be dead now anyway."

ABOVE THE ARCTIC CIRCLE, ALASKA

It was still dark when Flynn awoke. A cold chill ran through his body. He lay motionless listening. He could only hear the wind whispering through the Alaskan pines and the water as it lapped against the river's rocks. Everything seemed quiet and peaceful, yet Flynn was uneasy and tense. He felt danger but was unable to identify the source of his discomfort. Flynn remained motionless for over an hour trying to focus his mind on the cause of his concern. His instincts told him all was not well somewhere in his world.

WASHINGTON, D. C.

Vice President Patricia Bunnell arrived at her office before eight. She had spent an unsettled night after

Michael Moorehouse had left. Patricia scoured the morning papers for any news on Daniel Kent's death last night at the *Dubliner*. There was none. She tried to comprehend why Daniel Kent had been killed and why did he have a complete 'DOGS' file prepared on her. Moreover, Patrica wondered who was behind the cover up of Kent's murder.

"Must be CIA," she thought. "Who else would cover up Kent's killing so fast and so thoroughly?" Patricia put down the papers and decided to call Deputy Director Dimmler to see if she could get some answers.

"Scot," Patricia called into the intercom to her male secretary. "Would you get me Dimmler at CIA-- Langley, please."

"Yes, Ma'am."

While she waited for George Dimmler to come on the line, Patrica Bunnell went over what Michael had told her about last night. She kept stopping on the part that he said it looked like an Agency job. And, that Flynn was somehow behind it all. "That's just not possible," she thought, "Flynn's in Alaska. He has no knowledge nor any motive for either ordering such a file or for killing Kent."

Her thoughts were interrupted by Scot on the intercom. "Deputy Director of Operations Dimmler is on, Madam Vice President."

"Good morning, George,"

"Good morning, Madam Vice President. To what do I owe the privilege of your call first thing this morning?"

"Daniel Kent, George."

"I'm as sorry as you are to hear of his untimely death," Dimmler answered her statement.

"Don't fuck with me, George," Patricia growled.

"We both know that Daniel Kent was murdered last night at the Dubliner. And I want some answers."

Dimmler appeared to be confused, "I'm sorry, Madam Vice President, I don't know what you're talking about. Daniel Kent died last night but he had a heart attack at home."

"Bullshit, George!" the Vice President exclaimed, "He was murdered at the Dubliner and you know it. And who the fuck authorized a 'DOGS' on me, Deputy Director?"

"Leave it alone, Patricia," Dimmler warned his friend. "Leave it alone for your own good."

Don't you dare threaten me, George. I want to know what the fuck is going on. And I want to know right now!"

"I am not threatening you, Pat," Dimmler tried to be calm and persuasive. "I am your friend. And I'm trying to give you some friendly advice, that's all. I am looking into the matter. I will let you know something as soon as I know something."

"Damn it, General, did Flynn have anything to do with this?"

Dimmler was shocked at her suddenly bring Flynn's name up in connection with this. "What's wrong with you, Patricia? Flynn? Flynn is in Alaska. You know that."

"Are you certain, George?"

"Yes. His GPS chip in his BlackBerry indicates that he's up over the Arctic Circle as we speak." Dimmler thought for a moment before he continued. "Why would you think Flynn would have anything..."

The Vice President cut him off, "I don't give a shit about Flynn. And he doesn't give a shit about me either. I was just asking if you knew whether or not he really was in Alaska, that's all." Patricia realized she was ranting off base, "George, call me when you know something." She hung up.

HOUSTON, TEXAS

Four separate private jests arrived within an hour of each other shortly after midnight at George Bush Intercontinental Airport at Houston, Texas. Each private jet landed and taxied to the United Petroleum Company hanger under the utmost security. Each member of the 'Elite' was met with a limousine and a car with four armed guards supplied by United Petroleum's CEO, David R. Laird, the 'host' of the meeting.

The British Foreign Minister James Saunders' arrival at Houston occurred just prior to dawn. Laird had Saunders met at the diplomatic gate by four men dressed in business suits. They escorted the Foreign Minister to United Petroleum's Corporate headquarters where he and the other three 'Elite' members had their individual suites in the corporate building.

The seventh and final member of the 'Elite' would be arriving by Air Force One at seven forty-eight that very morning.

ABOVE THE ARCTIC CIRCLE, ALASKA

Flynn remained on edge, still uncertain why he felt the way he did. He went about his normal duties cleaning up camp and packing his gear in haste. He had decided to head back to his base camp and fly further northwest. An inexplicable urgency filled Flynn while he checked his smart phone's GPS and began his forced march. Flynn's pace would have left any other man, not so well, conditioned exhausted within a few hours. He was walking like a man on a mission but Flynn didn't know why. He was relying on his instincts which he had done many times before. They were usually right.

Flynn made fast time over the uneven terrain and arrived at his base camp before dawn. The sky was clear and a full moon illuminated the snow covered ground. Flynn loaded the Buccaneer with all of his gear then untied the plane from the scrub pine. Using the paddle he had brought along, he shoved himself out onto the pond's icy water. While the plane moved back and forth with each paddle stroke, Flynn could hear the thin ice shattering like glass under the fuselage and around the pontoons. When he felt he was clear of the shoreline, Flynn buckled his seat belt and ran through his pre-flight checklist.

The Buccaneer's engine cranked over a few times until it finally ignited. The plane shook and rattled while Flynn tested the controls and adjusted the prop's pitch. Within a few minutes the oil pressure gauge indicated normal temperature and pressure. Flynn was prepared for take-off. Flynn closed the the front hatch and gave the rudder peddle a hard left. He pushed the throttle forward accelerating the aircraft through the water breaking the ice underneath it. There was no noticeable wind and and the water was very calm. Flynn was going to have to create a circular, short take off. He taxied to the approximate center of the pond, the nose of the plane crunching through the ice and water. Flynn made his last instrument check and scanned the moonlit shoreline for the best lift-off point over the lowest trees.

Flynn engaged full forty degrees of flaps and eased the throttle forward until he achieved full power. Flynn kept the Buccaneer in a tight left turn gaining both ground speed and lift from the wake he created in the water. The pusher prop was well to the task while the experienced pilot held the plane's nose down. Soon Flynn had the plane hydroplaning. The airspeed indicator increased. When he felt it was just right, Flynn pulled back on the yoke. The plane jumped into the air. He engaged the turbo charger which thrust the plane forward with additional power and speed. Flynn continued to pull back on the yoke gaining altitude as the Lake cleared the shoreline trees by inches. He was airborne and flying. He raised his flaps and disengaged the turbo charger while adjusting the prop's pitch and trimming the aircraft. Flynn checked his instruments and marked his compass heading. He was heading northwest and along the great Alaskan pipeline below him.

Flynn turned on his CD player which was loaded with Patsy Cline's greatest hits. The words to *"Walkin' After Midnight"* played which brought back memories of Patricia Bunnell. He sensed that she was in some sort of danger and something was not right in her world. He felt compelled to help her but for some reason he was flying in the opposite direction. It was as if the Buccaneer had the answer for him and it was taking him to it.

The moonlight reflected off the snow covered tundra below casting eerie shadows over the mysterious Alaskan terrain. Flynn looked down on the rugged land and thought how much it reminded him of his own life— cold, lonely, unforgiving and empty. Flynn flew on for about an hour then looked for a place to land. Ahead of him he could see what appeared to be a flat narrow strip tucked in a valley among four hills. He calculated that he was less than a hundred miles from Prudhoe Bay on the Beaufort Sea. Flynn prepared to set his plane down. He made a straight-in final approach and landed smoothly on a frozen lake. The snow made a whispering sound on the hull while Flynn taxied to a spot facing outward for a quick and unencumbered takeoff. Before Flynn cut the engine, he made a note of his position using his GPS and his relative position to Fairbanks. He quickly estimated his distance, fuel and flight time to Wainwright Field. Confident that he had enough fuel to get him back, Flynn unlatched his seat belt and crawled over the seat to stretch out in the fuselage to sleep. Flynn felt secure in her body and within minutes he was asleep. Flynn had a disturbing dream about Kristen Shults.

LONDON, ENGLAND

When Kristen came to, she was disoriented. There were muffled sounds of voices shouting angrily on the floor above her. Her body ached and her face was swollen and sore. She was still handcuffed to the headboard. While continuing to focus her eyes, Kristen saw a figure of a man standing at the foot of her bed. Not the ugly little man, but some other man--much larger--with a shaved head and muscular build. His face exposed a long scar down one side of his cheek. This man was holding a tray with a can of sardines, a few crackers and a cup of tea.

Upon seeing Kristen awake the man sneered, "Well, Love, you're with us again. Here's your supper."

Kristen summoned all of her strength and kicked up at the man knocking the tray from his hands and sending it crashing across the room.

"Why you little bitch," he screamed. "I'll teach you a lesson!" He reached down and grabbed Kristen by the hair in one of his giant hands. With his other hand he slapped her across the face opening a cut on the side of Kristen's mouth. The crashing noise of the tray was heard upstairs which alarmed the two additional captors. They rushed down the stairs with guns drawn. When they reached the bottom of the stairs they witnessed the large man slapping Kristen across the face.

"Stop it, Arthur, you dumb, retarded bastard!" One of the men shouted at the larger man.

Arthur immediately stopped slapping Kristen and spun around in anger at the man shouting. In his anger and, as an explanation for his actions, Arthur shouted back, "She needs a lesson in manners and so do you!"

Arthur started to come at the smaller man but halted in his tracks when the third man leveled his .45 caliber pistol at him and warned, "That's enough from both of you assholes! Remember we have a job to do and the boss will be pissed if we blow it. Now, cut the shit. Arthur, leave the bitch alone."

"All right, Falso. This time." Arthur replied staring at the weapon. "But that little rat is going to get it good if he ever calls me names again."

"Hey, Arthur," the little man said attempting to appease the giant. "I didn't mean nothing by it. I just didn't want you to damage the goods, that's all. You don't know your own strength, especially when you get mad."

Arthur's expression immediately went from anger to smiles hearing the little man apologize. "Yeah, you're right, Willie. But you know that I don't like to be yelled at or called names. I'm not retarded."

Falso looked at the two of them and thought, "These two fucking idiots are as stupid as a box of rocks. How did I ever get mixed up with two morons like this?" Falso glanced over at Arthur who was grinning like an imbecile. He was dim-witted but as strong as a bull and potentially as dangerous. Willie, on the other hand, was a weasel. Willie would just as soon knife you in the back as say, 'hello.' He could not be trusted. Falso noticed that Kristen was unconscious and bleeding from the mouth. He knew that she would be no use to them if she were dead.

"Get a wet cloth and clean her up, Willie," Falso ordered. "Arthur, you go up stairs and wait by the telly. The boss should be calling soon." Turning back to Willie, Falso concluded, "And, Willie, don't fondle the merchandise no more." He and Arthur went back up the stairs.

Willie went over to the laundry tub and wet a rag. He walked to the bed and sat down next to Kristen and started to wipe her face. "There, there, my beauty," Willie said softly. "You'll be as good as new now. Then we can play some more."

Kristen started to come around. When she opened her eyes she saw Willie right over her dabbing her mouth with the wet cloth. Kristen immediately withdrew in fright trying in vain to get away from him. She was still handcuffed to the brass headboard and couldn't move far enough away from Willie's groping hands. Willie rubbed his hand over her breasts slowly pinching her nipples. Then he moved his hand down between Kristen's legs. She kicked and squirmed trying to get away from him. Willie forced his fingers inside her. Kristen started to let out a scream but Willie stuffed the rag in her mouth muffling her cries. Kristen was filled with hate, fear, and pain as Willie had his way with her--again. Kristen soon passed out from shock.

HOUSTON, TEXAS

Air Force One landed at Bush Intercontinental on schedule and was met with the usual dignitaries and a medium sized crowd of on-lookers trying to catch a glimpse of their native son, the President of the United States. Security was extremely tight and no one would get very close to the President. The Secret Service motorcade into downtown Houston was scheduled to be routine. Only a few insiders knew that President Harper was not going to be part of that motorcade since he was taking a private helicopter directly to the top of the United Petroleum Company building. Secretary of State Makoweic, National Security Administration Director William Pfohl, and Chief of Staff Moorehouse were the only members of the government who were riding in the motorcade along with the mayor of the city.

The six members of the 'Elite' were already gathered in the conference room of United Petroleum's CEO, David Laird. The members were watching the arrival of President Harper on the large flat-screen television.

At the head of the table was Kim Moon Jung-- 'Tiger'--as he was known. Tiger spoke to Laird. "How long will it take for Harper to get here?"

"Laird looked at his watch and replied, "It'll be about eight minutes from the airport to the top of this building."

"Very well," Tiger said. "Gentlemen, we will begin in fifteen minutes. I would suggest that you use that time to review the packet in front of you. We have much to cover in the next few hours. I need not remind you that we must move quickly with our plan. And there can be no mistakes. In a few weeks Operation Lifeblood will be a reality and we will have a strangle hold on the world's economy."

The President landed and was immediately ushered down the stairs to the conference room. The entire 'Elite' was now assembled. Secret Service agents were posted outside the conference room under President Harper's orders. This made Agent-in-Charge, Pete Eisenmann, very apprehensive. He did get the President to agree to carry a pocket signaling device in the event of an emergency. Eisenmann had posted agents on the roof, the floor below and at the two doors which lead into the closed conference room.

After the usual greetings, handshakes and small talk were over, Kim Moon Jung took his seat at the head of the table. "Gentlemen, we have a good deal of work to accomplish in order for our plan, Operation Lifeblood, to become fully implemented. It will take each of you to make certain that every phase of this plan is carefully and perfectly executed.

"As you may know, I have ordered Don Carlos to increase our cocaine supply through Alaska for distribution in the U.S. It is my projection that within two months we will control enough money to buy out the major oil refineries. Once that is accomplished, we will have achieved a monopoly on oil production thus controlling the world's supply of petroleum products at whatever price we demand."

"Hold on a minute, Tiger," President Harper interrupted. "How the fuck are we going to do all of this without starting World War Three?"

"That, Mister President," Kim Moon Jung answered without hesitation, "is a distinct possibility. It is your part of the plan to make sure that before it does begin, the United States moves quickly into the Middle East with the assistance of Sheik Mohammed al-Anzarisad and Iranian President Jahmir...."

Harper interrupted again. "You're fucking nuts. If the United States suddenly backed Syria and Iran, the Israelis and the rest of the A-rab camel jockeys in the Mid East would be screaming bloody hell! Why, for shit sake, we've been slapping sanctions on Iran for years trying to stop them from getting the fucking bomb!"

The obvious rudeness to Syria's 'Elite' representative Sheik Mohammed al-Anzarisad and Iran's representative to this meeting President Jahmir caused everyone to turn on President Harper. It took several minutes for Tiger to calm everyone down.

"Why are you so short-sighted, Harper?" Tiger began. "When we finish here today, I will show you how this can all be done. And you, and the U.S., will be the guardians of the world's economy and nuclear weapons. Of course, certain concessions must be made and certain sacrifices must take place."

"Hey, Don Carlos," Harper leaned over toward Escobar of Venezuela, "I think the Tiger has been sucking on too much of your shit. He's out of his fucking mind."

"Please, Mister President," Sheik Mohammad el-Anzarisad spoke up. Let us hear all of what Tiger has to say and listen to his entire plan before we make any comments."

"Bullshit!" Harper was feeling defensive and lashed out. "If you think this half pint Gook is going to tell me that I'm going to start World War Three so his fucking shit hole of a country can become a world power, you're all fucking loco."

James Saunders had been sitting and listening to the bickering going around. "Mister President, let's keep this on a professional and business level if you would, please, sir. We formed this group in order to unify the world's economy and nuclear weapons with a goal of one world government where we, as members of the 'Elite', are in control. I, for one, am enthusiastic about about this concept and I would ask you, sir, to refrain from making any further comments until the entire proposal has been put out before us."

"Fuck you too, you Limy bastard!" Harper was indignant. "Have you all lost your senses? We are supposed to be sensible, intelligent men. Look, if you want to make a few hundred million here or there, I'm all for it. And, I'll do what I can to help, as I always have. But you start talking about controlling the world by seven men, or starting World War Three, then Jumpin' Jezeeus, I can't let you do it. It's that fucking simple."

There was a sudden silence in the room while each of the seven members looked at each other. David Laird took his cue from the Tiger and assumed his role as host of the meeting.

"Gentlemen, Gentlemen," Laird began trying to ease the obvious tension caused by President Harper. "Let's all relax here a minute. We haven't gotten where we are because we're stupid or irrational. When we formed this group we did so for all of our mutual economic benefit and because we control the power base in this world. We have not always agreed on every idea proposed by any one of us. But, we have all been willing to listen to every proposal that any member has put forth with the respect that each of us owes it to the proposer. I can understand President Harper's geo-political position with respect to the United States. On the other hand, I think we owe Tiger the courtesy to listen to his entire plan before we make any judgments on its merit. Remember, it was Tiger's idea to smuggle the cocaine from Venezuela into Alaska for distribution throughout the western world in tankers of our oil. I needn't tell you how successful that this has been for the past few years—for all of us." Laird saw that he was making some headway and that calm was being restored, so he continued. "Now, might I suggest that we all give Tiger our undivided attention and hold all comments and questions until he has completed his presentation. Is this agreeable to all of you?" There were no objections. "Very well. Tiger, you have the floor."

WASHINGTON, D. C.

Vice President Patricia Bunnell was not a woman who took being told to 'leave it alone' very well. When she wanted an answer she was determined to get it. She fumed over Dimmler's comment for nearly an hour. She decided to take matters into her own hands and find out for herself.

"Scot, get me Senator Conness, please."

A few moments later her secretary announced, "Madam Vice President, Senator Conness is on the line."

"Hello, Senator."

"Hello, Madam Vice President," Senator Conness was curious about her call. "How may I help you?"

"Senator," Patricia Bunnell began, "As Chairman of the Joint Intelligence Oversight Committee, do you have access to personnel files of the CIA, NSA and the Bureau?"

"If I understand your question, Madam Vice

President, if you're asking whether or not we know the names of each and every employee then the answer is no. As you are aware, we don't get into those day-to-day operations. We are mainly concerned with policy issues. National Security considerations would naturally override our desire to discover, for example, the names of every field operative, or undercover agent. In fact, we are prevented by law from asking for such information. You'd have to talk with the Agencies directly. However, I don't think they'll volunteer any information. They're pretty sensitive about anyone poking into their operations on this level."

"I was aware of that Senator, but I thought that perhaps you had access to their files."

"No, Madam Vice President, we do not." Senator Conness then asked, "May I inquire what your interest is?"

"Not at this time, Senator Conness, thank you." The Vice President hung up her phone.

Patricia Bunnell spun around in her chair and began to think how she could get the answer she was looking for. "Who would have a record of Daniel Kent's murder?" No sooner had she formulated the question when Patricia had an idea.

"Scot, get me the D.C. Chief of Police."

"Is there a problem, Ma'am?"

"No, but there will be if you don't get me the Chief of Police."

Within a few moments the Vice President's intercom announced, "Chief Williams is on for you, Ma'am."

"Chief Williams, this is Vice President Bunnell."

"Yes, Ma'am. How may I help you?"

"Chief, it's my understanding that there was a man found dead at the *Dubliner* last night. Could you tell me what you have in your report on the identity of this man?"

"Madam Vice President, I don't have any report on anyone being found dead at the *Dubliner* last night or any night. We did not respond to any calls to that location at all, Ma'am," Chief Williams said sincerely.

"Are you absolutely certain, Chief Williams?" Patricia asked.

"Positive, Madam Vice President. We don't have anything."

"All right, Chief. Thank you." Patricia Bunnell hung up. She was getting nowhere. "Who is covering up Daniel Kent's murder?" She mumbled, frustration showing on her face.

Her thoughts were interrupted by Scot's voice over the intercom. "Madam, your driver is here to take you to the airport."

"What?" Patricia was momentarily puzzled.

"Madam, you are scheduled to address the National Education Association luncheon in Chicago at noon today."

"Oh, shit, I forgot that was today! Is the information file available?"

"It's in your briefcase. Agent Wilkins has it out here in the front office."

"Okay, Scot, give me a minute and we'll be off." The Vice President went into her private bathroom to check her make-up. She looked into the mirror and moved closer to the reflection then said, "I certainly could use you right now, Flynn. Something is definitely wrong here and I don't know who or what is behind it. Where are you?"

The Vice President didn't hear an answer so she turned off the bathroom light and left her office. Air Force Two left Andrews Air Force Base at ten thirty Eastern time. She would be in Chicago in time for her address before the NEA. "Call me mushroom, assholes," she thought to herself. "Feed me shit and keep me in the dark!"

NORTH OF THE ARCTIC CIRCLE, ALASKA

Flynn snapped awake thinking he heard someone call his name. He checked his Rolex and it was a little before five in the morning. "Time to get moving, Sport," Flynn said packing his gear. "Maybe I can get some shots of the Caribou migration today." Flynn packed his digital camera and lenses, binoculars, two extra clips for his .44 Magnum, a box of 30.06, 180 grain bullets for the rifle, his razor-sharp hunting knife, his cell phone, compass, and canteen. He also packed some dry food packs, enough for a couple of days, if he ate light.

Flynn left the Buccaneer and shouldered his rifle. He strapped on snowshoes then started off to the northwest towards the coastal area. The moon was still bright and nearly full and the stars shined like Christmas tree lights in the festive looking sky. Flynn figured he could make eight to ten miles before it became light. Of course, at this time of year, the sun was so low in the sky that it never really got too light, more like dusk for the few hours it was visible this far north.

The Arctic air was cold. Flynn started out walking towards the hill before him. Flynn marched on for a few hours reaching the top of the hill. He found the walking more difficult than he expected because of the uneven ground and the lack of deep snow. On the summit of the hill, Flynn stopped for the first time to have a small drink from his canteen. His body was warm and he was careful not to overheat himself which would cause him to sweat. That would be a dangerous thing as he would then become wet and cold. Flynn noticed a slight wind picking up and clouds rolling in. The sky was turning an ashen gray and it looked like snow within the hour.

Flynn put down his pack and took out his binoculars. He could see for several miles from atop of this ridge. Off in the distance Flynn saw a migrating herd of caribou. The line of animals appeared to extend for miles. He watched them move gracefully over the snow. "There must be thousands of them," he whispered. Then he saw the wolves. Nature doing its thing in the Alaskan wilderness. The wolf pack was scouting the perimeter of the migrating herd. Flynn watched the wolves shadow the caribou until they were out of sight. Then he turned back towards the northwest. Surprisingly, Flynn caught sight of a plume of rising smoke.

"Probably Eskimos on a hunting party," Flynn mumbled. "This might be interesting." Flynn made a mental note of the location of the smoke, checked his compass and GPS on his cell then started in that direction.

Flynn hiked for about an hour and climbed up another ridge. The scrub pines were thick and provided him with adequate cover. He didn't want to spook any game or otherwise interfere with what he believed to be a native hunting party. When Flynn scanned the terrain below him he was surprised at what he saw. It wasn't a hunting party at all. Only a few hundred yards below him,

Flynn watched while several men in white snowsuits were loading boxes on sleds behind powerful snow machines. Three tents were set up to the left of a small log hut. The smoke that Flynn had seen was coming from a fire inside the hut.

Instinctively, Flynn dove into the snow and rolled himself under a copse of trees. He quickly undid his pack and retrieved his binoculars. Then Flynn swung his 30.06 around and cradled it under his arms. Flynn knew that this was not a hunting party but he wasn't sure just what these men were doing. He focused his gaze on the hut. Two men stepped from the hut carrying automatic weapons.

"What the fuck is this?" Flynn thought training his binoculars on the man's face. Flynn could see that the man was Oriental, either Chinese or Korean. Flynn continued to study the entire camp for every detail while his curiosity heightened. Two of the sleds were fully loaded. Flynn watched while one of the men appeared to be giving orders or directions to the other. The man made a slight bow and climbed on the snow machine and drove off down the valley to Flynn's left. The same scenario occurred with the second sled which closely followed the first.

Flynn spent the next hour looking over the entire area and observing the operation below him. He had memorized every detail of the camp. Flynn estimated the distances between the tents and the hut and the tents to the tents. This information would be necessary for his reconnaissance after it became totally dark. There were many unanswered questions racing through his mind while he watched and waited for darkness to fall.

A great deal of activity had been going on right up

until it became dark. Now, Flynn could see that things were quieting down. Six men went--two each--into the three tents. Another three were in the hut. Flynn prepared to go down to the camp and find out what he could. He took his .44 Magnum Smith & Wesson and two quick-loads along with his digital camera, infrared lens, and night vision lens. Flynn reached his objective behind the hut within a few minutes totally undetected. He listened at the back wall while two men were talking. It took Flynn only a moment to recognize that they were speaking Korean. "What the fuck are the Koreans doing here in Alaska?" Flynn wondered.

Flynn worked his way around the side of the hut away from the tents. While doing so he bumped into a box. He froze listening to whether anyone heard the noise. He waited, hand on his .44 Magnum for a minute. No one came. There wasn't enough light for him to make out the lettering on the box. He attached the night vision lens on his camera and took a picture of the top and three exposed sides, hoping that the camera would pick up the lettering. He felt the box. It was sealed shut. Flynn took out his knife and inserted the blade between the wooden boards of the box near the bottom. There was something soft inside the box. Flynn withdrew the blade and wet it, inserting the knife blade back into the box. He withdrew the blade again. This time, with his dry fingers, he wiped the knife blade. Flynn tasted the substance. It was pure cocaine!

A high pitched whine in the distance alerted Flynn that another snow machine was in-coming. He made his way to the back of the hut and waited while the machine drew closer. A light leaked through a crack in the hut's wall. Flynn squinted inside. He could make out a portable radio receiver and transmitter in one corner. Three men were sitting around a stove keeping themselves warm. One man, another Korean, was facing in Flynn's direction and was speaking to another in Korean. The third man, with his back to Flynn didn't appear to be involved in the conversation. This man stood up when he heard the snow machine approaching. Flynn could see that he was considerably taller than the others. When he turned for the door, Flynn noticed that he was not Korean. The non-Asian man blurted out something in Spanish. The other two Koreans joined him with their automatic weapons and went to meet the machine.

Flynn, keeping hidden in the shadows, moved to the side of the hut while the headlights of the in-coming snow machine lit up the camp area. The machine pulled near the hut and stopped. Two men got off greeting the other man from the camp in Spanish. Flynn listened as they spoke.

"Don Carlos sends his greetings, Juan. I am to relieve you here and you are wanted back on the ship. We are to prepare for additional shipments which are already on the way. We must step up our efforts here to move the goods."

"*Si,* I will prepare to leave at once, *Jaffe.* Juan went back into the hut to pack his meager belongings. The snow machine driver started to talk to the Koreans.

"I have a message from Tiger with me, *amigo.*" He reached inside of his parka and retrieved an envelope and handed it to the Korean. The two men went inside the hut in order to read the message by the light.

Flynn retraced his steps to the back of the hut and peeked through the crack in the hut wall again. The man called Juan was ready to leave. He bowed to the Korean and hugged his fellow Caucasian. He left the hut and within a minute the snow machine turned around and returned in the direction from which it had come.

Flynn watched while the Korean read the message. The man's face turned from somber to a broad smile as he read. He turned to the new man and said, "We have begun Operation Lifeblood, my friend. Soon we will control the destiny of the world. Join me in a drink to our success." The Korean took two tin cups and reached for a bottle of liquor. He poured each a drink and they toasted to their success.

Flynn left his position behind the hut and made his way back up the slope to his original position on the ridge. A light snow had begun to fall by the time he made his way back up the slope. Flynn wasn't exactly sure what was going on although it was definitely illegal. He needed to find out more of this plan called, 'Operation Lifeblood'.

LONDON, ENGLAND

When Kristen awoke, she was alone. The room was dark except for a dim light coming through the basement window. Her entire body ached. She was surprised to find that she was no longer handcuffed to the bed. She had been shackled around the ankle to a center support post. The length of chain allowed her to walk in a circle around the post, and to easily reach the bed, the wash tub and the portable toilet. She was cold, still only dressed in the sweatshirt. Kristen was confused and in a state of despair. She began to cry--fighting back her tears.

"I need to escape, or they will kill me. I've seen their faces, so I know they won't let me live," She thought trying to stay calm and think rationally.

Kristen walked around looking for anything that she might use to help her escape. The dim light prevented her from seeing very far. She moved to the wash basin and splashed some water on her face. Kristen winced in pain when the water hit her swollen and cut face. She ran her fingers through her hair trying to untangle it as best she could.

"I've got to think straight," she told herself. "I've got to stay alive. There must be a way, there must be a way."

HOUSTON, TEXAS

Kim Moon Jung outlined his plan for Operation Lifeblood for the next ninety minutes. The only interruptions came in the form of groans of disbelief from President I. W. Harper. The other members of the 'Elite' gave Tiger their undivided attention. When he concluded his presentation, Kim Moon Jung--Tiger, opened the floor for questions.

"Well, pardners," President Harper began sarcastically, "the way I see it is you're puttin' my ass in a tight spot with the rest of the world, especially the industrial countries. And, I gotta tell you, the United States Navy patrols the northern Pacific and any unusual shipping activity will certainly be detected. Not to mention that we have satellites that can tell the time on a man's watch anywhere in the world. So, what am I supposed to do about all of this activity in Alaska and on our coast?""

"I have to agree that President Harper makes some sense," Foreign Minister Saunders added. "My question,

Tiger, is how can the U.S. and Great Britain increase a military presence in the Middle East? We are already in Pakistan and Afghanistan."

There was an immediate outburst from the members as they all began talking at once to anyone who would listen. Kim Moon Jung rose calmly and slowly from his chair at the head of the table. When he stood, the murmuring came to a halt.

"Gentlemen," Tiger began, "the plan will work. Let me show you again. First of all, we have been using the Alaskan supply route for many years now and it is still undetected. Our increase in activity will also go unnoticed since we are basically increasing the size of each delivery and only slightly increasing the frequency of the deliveries. The vastness of the Alaskan wilderness provides us with the mathematical probability that any detection remains the same—near zero! We move our base camps every three days as we do the supply routes. Any random satellite detection will disappear by the time it comes around again by these moves. We know the times that the satellites pass overhead and activity halts until it passes.

"Now, to answer Foreign Minister Saunders question," Kim Moon Jung continued. "You must trust that I have calculated all possible contingencies to a mathematical certainty. With President Jahmir and the Ayatollah agreeing to assist Sheik Mohammad al-Anzarisad and his allies, the Hamas, and by increasing terrorist strikes in the Middle East, Great Britain and the U.S. will be welcome to show additional force. These terrorist strikes will allow us to pollute the oil fields of Iraq and Saudi Arabia with nuclear waste rendering the world's oil supply useless for hundreds of years. Only

Venezuela and our protected sources will have the oil that is non-contaminated."

Don Carlos Escobar stood up and was heard. "I endorse Tiger's plan with all of my resources!"

"You would you fucking banditio," Harper shouted. "You have nothing to lose. You can always find a market for that shit you peddle."

The Venezuelan was irate at the insult by President Harper. "Senior Harper," Escobar said with anger, "I have listened to your shit long enough. You have the balls of a monkey and the brain of a toad! You are the most arrogant asshole I have ever known. If you could see beyond the nose on your face you could see that Tiger has worked out this plan thoroughly!"

There was immediate tension in the room and Laird sensed it. He quickly jumped up between the two men knowing fully well that both were emotionally overloaded. "Senior Escobar, President Harper, please!" Laird pleaded. "Gentlemen, please sit down and remain calm. Let us all stop the name calling. Perhaps we need to take a break."

It was decided that in the best interest of all parties to this meeting, that a break was necessary. Kim Moon Jung announced, "That is a very good idea, Mister Laird. Let us meet here again tomorrow at nine"

"I second that, Tiger," James Saunders quickly added.

President Harper stormed out ahead of the rest. He refused to speak to any of the others. It was evident that he was still outraged at Escobar and Kim Moon Jung. The other six members waited until Harper had cleared the room.

Don Carlos was still fuming. "Harper is too

pigheaded. He has become a liability to our organization. We must do something to neutralize his stubbornness."

No one else spoke out loud but there was a general consensus that Escobar was right.

ABOVE THE ARCTIC CIRCLE, ALASKA

Flynn did not sleep the entire night keeping a vigil on the camp below his location. He tried to understand and rationalize what was going on. "The only answer I can come up with, that makes any sense to me, is there is illegal drug traffic coming into the United States via Alaska by some joint operation with Korea and some South American country.--either Colombia or Venezuela."

Flynn spent most of the time trying to devise a plan of action. He considered several options including charging in with guns blazing or just watching and noting the activity level and supply routes. He dismissed the first —guns blazing option as foolish. The second, sitting and waiting, was not an action plan at all.

The light snowfall continued for the next few hours well past daylight. As first light approached, Flynn heard the whine of an incoming snow machine which was pulling another trailer-sled behind. The load looked similar to the one he had seen the day before. Flynn watched through his binoculars while the sled came to a stop near the hut. A tarp that was covering the trailer-sled had come loose enough that Flynn could see some lettering on one of the boxes. The words 'United Petroleum' were clearly visible. Flynn thought, "United Petroleum is one of the world's largest oil companies." His interest was peaked continuing his thought. "Kiss my ass. Somebody is running illegal drugs through the cover of an American Oil Company!"

Flynn considered the magnitude of the operation. "It looks like I've stumbled upon a major drug cartel of international proportions. The Koreans, the South Americans, and a world-wide major oil company. I wonder how long this has been going on and who else is involved?"

Flynn knew that he had to report this find to the proper officials. Flynn would have to make a call on his cell phone. "If I can get Langley they can connect me to the FBI or the DEA," Flynn mumbled activating his cell to CIA Headquarters.

The call was answered on the first ring. "Boswick Library. May I help you?" the woman's voice answered.

Flynn new the drill, "Reference department please." The call was immediately switched to a scrambled line that was constantly recorded in Operations.

"May I have your Library Card number, please."

Flynn thought, "This is Mickey Mouse", but he played by the rules set up and texted the code: 3-11-15-144.

"Yes, Mister Flynn. What's your report?"

Flynn recognized the female's voice. "Mollie, where's the Old Man?"

"He's up on the Hill. What's up, Flynn?"

"I've uncovered an international drug smuggling operation involving the Koreans, some South Americans and maybe United Petroleum, or it could just be their cover."

"What's the GPS location?" Mollie asked.

"West 137 degrees, 22 minutes; North 14 degrees 16 minutes. Visual contact of Niner. Positive for cocaine.

Using snow machines from coast to another, as yet unknown, location. Overheard discussion of an 'Operation Lifeblood'. Unknown meaning. Visual of 'United Petroleum' on one of the crates. Suggest satellite surveillance with infrared pass at night."

"Anything else, Jeremiah?"

"Can you connect me to the Bureau or DEA? It's more in their line of work, I think, and I am up here on vacation as you know. So, I really don't want to get too involved. You understand."

"Look, I'll take care of notification. I think that NSA should be involved, too. You lay low and keep your eyes on them for now. I'll get back to you in a little while," Mollie explained.

Flynn sat back and waited for Mollie Farnham, Special Assistant to the Deputy Director, George Dimmler, to call back with any further instructions from DEA, the FBI or NSA. Meanwhile, he continued to watch the camp below from his cover in the scub pines.

At two minutes past seven Alaskan time, Flynn's BlackBerry vibrated. He took it off ring tone so that he would remain silent as long as possible. Flynn noticed it was a Seven Series Activator Code which meant that the call was on a secured line in the Deputy Director's Office at Langley.

"Mollie, what's the good word?"

Mollie was all business, "Listen to your instructions carefully. You are to remain secluded for the next twenty-four hours. Make observations on traffic flow in and out of camp and approximate number of loads and number of personnel involved. Satellites will do recon. You are not to attempt any personal adventures..."

"Personal adventures?" Flynn interrupted in

disbelief. "What are you talking about? I never...." Flynn was cut short by an all-business Mollie Farnham.

"NSA wants you to stay hidden and watch. Do not, I repeat, do not attempt anything that will disclose your presence. Do you copy?"

"Aye, Aye, my cap-ee-tan," Flynn replied in a mocking manner. "What does the Old Man want me to do?"

"I told you he was up on the Hill. He suggested NSA. NSA relayed the message I just gave you." Mollie had worked with Flynn for many years and knew that he didn't like taking orders that just called for 'wait and see.' She added, "Flynn, you're the only eyes we have and it is important that you follow these orders. You take care and call back in twenty four hours with a report."

"I copy," Flynn said resigned to stay put. The call ended and Flynn thought, "Christ, don't they ever think that we can think? Personal adventure...my ass."

LONDON, ENGLAND

"When we move her tonight," Falso advised his two fellow kidnappers, "you both know what to do, right?"

"Yeah, Falso," Arthur responded, "but I don't know why we have to move her. This place seems safe enough."

"Because the boss wants it that way. It's part of his plan and we're getting paid to do it his way. And, if he says move her, we move her." Then Falso turned to Willie and asked, "Is the van all set and loaded properly?"

"All set," Willie answered. "What time do we go, Falso?"

"We'll leave at eleven forty-five. We have to be set up by one A.M. Then tomorrow morning it's showtime!" All three laughed.

HOUSTON, TEXAS

The Tiger, Kim Moon Jung, was on the balcony of his suite looking over the Houston skyline when his cell phone rang. The call interrupted his thoughts while he was going over the day's meeting. He identified the caller and answered annoyed. "Yes?"

"Did the meeting go as you planned?"

"Everything went as I expected," Tiger said. "Are you prepared for tomorrow?"

"Yes, but there is a slight problem up in Alaska?" The mysterious voice advised.

Tiger expressed concern. "What is the problem?"

"The CIA has an operative named Flynn on vacation, so I understand, in Alaska who has seen the operation and has reported it back to Langley."

"How much does this man Flynn know?"

"Apparently he stumbled upon the operation. He has been ordered to sit and watch for the next twenty four hours. From what I have learned from the interception of the call he has identified Koreans and some Latin American personnel. He also overheard the code name 'Operation Lifeblood', but does not know what it is."

"I will notify our people and have them take care of this man Flynn. It should not be very difficult. After all, he is only one man." Tiger then changed the subject by advising the caller, "Now be prepared. For tomorrow the United States will have a new President who will be putty in our hands."

ABOVE THE ARCTIC CIRCLE, ALASKA

Flynn spent the rest of the day as ordered. He watched a number of shipments come in and re-fuel then leave. There didn't appear to be any set pattern he could identify except that four sleds arrived within an hour of each other--then nothing for three hours--and then four sleds again. Late in the afternoon, while Flynn was eating a packet of dehydrated food he had taken from his backpack, he heard a louder more powerful--sounding machine coming over the horizon from the northwest. Flynn put down his 'lunch' and picked up his binoculars. What he saw gave him concern. Before him, advancing toward the camp, were four snow-track machines similar to half-tracks. These machines carried additional men, supplies of gasoline, food and water to replenish the camp. Flynn watched and counted twenty men with automatic assault rifles and enough ammunition to start a small war. Instinctively, Flynn knew that something was out of the ordinary.

When it was nearly dark Flynn was altered to a flurry of activity at the base camp. Men were moving quickly and snow machines were dispersing in several directions. A squad started up the hill directly at Flynn's location.

"They're looking for something or someone," he whispered. "They can't know that I'm here. It's gotta be a routine recon for base security. Either way, I got to get the hell out of here or they'll run right over me."

Flynn retreated down the back side of the slope circling to his left in an attempt to flank the search party while drawing them away from where he had his aircraft. Flynn didn't have enough time to eradicate his footprints while he quicken his pace. "If they're good they'll find them and then the hunt will be on." By the time he reached the bottom of the hill a loud whine off in the distance grew louder. A quick look around for cover told Flynn his only hope was to climb up another slope to a denser thicket of scrub pines. It was his only option.

Flynn moved quickly up the hill carefully dodging in and out of the small overgrowth in an attempt to hide himself as much as possible knowing that the human eye, like every predator, watches for movement. Crouching behind a scub pine, Flynn glanced back over his shoulder across the valley of his former position. He spotted two men who had discovered his tracks and were on the move. One of the men was speaking into a walkie-talkie. Flynn knew that this was a call for the pack of hunters to close in.

Suddenly, Flynn was in the jungle on the Colombian-Venezuelan border. He was being hunted again. Flynn's only thought was survival at all cost. And that meant he could not be captured. A bullet ricocheted off a rock in front of him spraying snow into the air. He had been spotted! Flynn sprang from his crouch and took off on the run as fast as he could through the knee high snow struggling to get to the top of the rise—his objective and cover.

Another bullet whistled inches over his head. Flynn lunged for the top of the rise and cover behind two trees. The limb in front of his face was ripped away by another round of automatic fire. Flynn threw himself down into the snow and rolled for protection behind a fallen tree. The original two that had picked up his tracks were now joined by two more on a snow machine. Flynn un-slung his 30.06, and readied it to fire. The man with the walkie-talkie was centered in his scope's cross-hairs. Flynn squeezed the trigger. The Korean was lifted off his feet--dead before he hit the snow. His radio went flying backwards and was lost under the snow. The other Korean who was on foot leaped for cover while the two on the snow machine raced up the hill at Flynn as fast as it would go.

The nature of the terrain made it impossible for Flynn to get off another shot before the two on the snow machine were on top of him. It was going to be close quarters combat. Flynn would be able to make the first strike since they didn't know precisely where he was located and Flynn had the element of surprise on his side while the machine closed in.

Flynn quickly slipped off his pack and parka and positioned his rifle between the two trees he had been using as cover. The make-shift dummy might fool the two rushing attackers just long enough for Flynn to catch them by surprise. He unsheathed his knife and readied himself for his counter-attack. The snow machine came rushing up over the hilltop. The rider opened fire on the dummy. In an instant, as the driver slowed to make a turn to avoid crashing into one of the trees, Flynn launched himself at the pair on the sled. The two Koreans were knocked off the machine by the force of Flynn's lunge. The machine wedged itself between the trees and stalled. Flynn had the driver around the neck and without hesitation drove his knife up into the Korean's throat while slashing his jugular. Flynn twisted the blade and drove it deeper up into the man's brain--killing him instantly. The other Korean tried to get to his feet but Flynn was on top of him before he could get up. The Korean's eyes were wide open with the grimace of fear and death on his face when Flynn's knife was hammered into the man's chest. Flynn felt the would-be attacker stiffen and then his body completely relaxed.

Flynn rushed to recover his parka and put it on. He slipped the pack over his back and grabbed his rifle. With a huge pull Flynn was able to free the snow machine from the trees. He started it up and drove off down the valley putting distance between himself and his enemies. Flynn drove on for nearly fifteen minutes until he came upon denser forest cover where he hid himself and the machine while darkness fell. Flynn knew that more men would be coming after him soon. But for the moment he was safe. He would have to get to the Buccaneer if he were to ever get out of Alaska alive.

A cold Arctic wind began to blow down from the northeast bringing storm clouds over the frozen land. Flynn gathered his thoughts. His first thought was to call Langley to report what had happened but something about that idea bothered him. "I don't know how they discovered me," Flynn's mind raced looking for an answer. "No, I'll wait til seven tomorrow as planned."

Flynn couldn't get past the idea that somehow those Koreans had known that he was there. "My only contact was on my cell phone talking to Mollie at Headquarters. So, how did they find me? It must be coincidental," he mumbled trying not to believe she had betrayed him or anybody else at the Agency. "But they sure as hell knew I was there." This though kept returning to Flynn while he tried to figure out how he was going to get back to his plane and escape.

LONDON, ENGLAND

"Arthur," Falso said looking at his watch. "It's time to get the van. Bring it around." Then turning to Willie, Falso continued to give orders, "Take these clothes down to the princess and have her put them on. Don't tell her anything else. And Willie," Falso added sternly, "don't touch her, understand?"

"Right Gov'," Willie acknowledged, "I wouldn't lay a hand on her, you know that." Willie picked up the clothing which consisted of a pair of slacks, a blouse, and shoes, and took them downstairs to where Kristen was still chained to the center post.

Kristen was sitting on the bed when Willie opened the door. He walked over to her and put the clothes on the bed. "Put these on my pretty and be quick about it." He leered at her and started to put his hand on her leg but Kristen twisted away. She thought he was going to rape her again so in an attempt to protect herself Kristen dug her fingernails deep into Willie's hand drawing blood as she raked him.

"You dirty little bitch of a whore! You'll pay for this when we get you to the farmhouse tonight. Now get dressed."

Willie went back up the stairs in pain from Kristen's clawing, mumbling under his breath. Kristen now realized that they were going to move her to some other location out in the country to a farmhouse. "I've got nothing to lose," she told herself. "I've got to make a run for it at the first opportunity."

Arthur pulled the van up to the front of the row house. The street was dark and there was no traffic. Falso was watching from the window and when he saw the van stop he yelled over to Willie. "Arthur's here. Come with me while we get the girl. Bring the rifle and the hood."

Willie was about to pick up the rifle but Falso snapped at him, "Goddamn it, Willie, you dumb bastard, put the rubber gloves on first. You want your prints all over it for Chrissake?"

"Sorry, Falso, I almost forgot," Willie apologized. His hand was still bleeding when he stretched the glove over his fingers. A few drops of blood dropped onto the barrel and trickled unnoticed between the barrel and the stock. The glove snapped over his hand and he picked up the Weatherby 301 rifle. Willie admired the craftsmanship of the weapon. He looked at Falso who had been watching. "Seems a bloody shame to waste such a beautiful and expensive rifle for only one shot, eh, Falso?"

"It won't be wasted if you make it a good shot."

"Don't you worry about that," Willie smiled, "I'll make it a good shot."

Falso picked up the hood from the chair while the two men went down to collect Kristen. As they approached the door Falso whispered to Willie, "Don't let her see the gun. Wait til I get the hood over her face then shove it into her."

"It's a rifle, Falso, not a fuckin' gun. Don't sweat it. I got the plan." Willie felt superior for a moment, correcting Falso.

Kristen was still sitting on the bed undressed when Falso enter the room. "Why aren't you dressed?"

"How am I supposed to get dressed with this chain around my leg like a dog?"

Falso immediately understood that Willie could not proceed to step two in a logical sequence nor did he remember to give Willie the key. Falso took the key from his pocket and bent down then unlocked the shackle around her ankle. Kristen rubbed her ankle and foot as she sat back down on the bed. Falso picked up the bundle of clothing and snarled, "Put 'em on."

"What's the rush?" Kristen asked.

"Shut up. Just put them on....Now."

Kristen looked at both men and thought about rushing the door. She dismissed that thought quickly realizing that she couldn't get past them both not knowing where the big galoot, Arthur, might be. "How about a little privacy?" Kristen asked stalling for time.

Both Falso and Willie laughed simultaneously. It was Willie who spoke first. "Ain't nothin' private about you and us, honey. Isn't that right Falso?"

"Yeah, that's right Willie," Falso laughed. Then he snapped back at Kristen, "Get dressed right now or I'll have Willie here dress you."

Seeing the perverted smile on Willie's face convinced Kristen to get dressed immediately. She slipped the sweatshirt on over the blouse to keep warm.

"Okay, let's get going," Falso directed. He grabbed Kristen by the arm and led her to the door. As she passed him he slipped the hood over her head. Kristen cried out in fright at the sudden move. "Don't worry, princess," Falso reassured her. Then he motioned to Willie. "Give it to her, NOW!"

Willie shoved the rifle stock first into Kristen's stomach. She instinctively recoiled and crabbed the wooden stock. She realized in a moment that it was a weapon and when she groped for the trigger Kristen pulled it hoping the gun was loaded. Only a click was heard as the firing pin hit an empty chamber. The damage had been done. Kristen's fingerprints were all over the weapon just as it had been planned.

"That ought to do it...just right," Falso said with a grin. He grabbed Kristen's arms and pushed her up the stairs. "Willie," Falso called back. "Get the gun!"

"It a rifle, mate. I told you before. It's not a gun," Willie retorted in disgust, carefully picking up the Weatherby with his gloved hands.

"I don't give a good fuck," Falso screamed. "Let's get moving!" He pushed Kristen into the stairway causing her to stumble as her shins crashed into the step. Falso then realized it would be easier for her to walk without the hood over her head so he ripped it from her head and dragged her to her feet. "Get moving!" Falso ordered Kristen pulling her arm up the staircase.

Kristen in obvious pain and fright began to cry, "Where are you taking me?" She sobbed, "What do you want with me?"

"You'll see soon enough," Willie sneered.

The two men led Kristen up the stairs and through the row house to the front door. Arthur had the van running when they came out. Falso had a tight grip on Kristen's arm. The street was dark and there was no traffic.

Falso took a studied look up and down the street and he warned Kristen, "Not a sound now, princess, or you're dead."

Kristen could feel a hard pointed object held tightly into her side. All thoughts of a dash for freedom quickly evaporated in her mind. Within a few seconds all of them were in the van. Kristen was blindfolded and she and Willie sat in the back out of sight. Falso joined Arthur up front. Falso then directed Arthur to move out. Kristen, blindfolded, sat motionless and silent trying to understand why her world was turned upside down. She had no clue as to why she was being held prisoner. Kristen Shults would not find out for several more hours.

HOUSTON, TEXAS

President Irwin W. Harper was still seething while pacing in his suite. Chief of Staff Michael Moorehouse was sitting by the desk watching the President pace back and forth and mumbling to himself.

"Michael," President Harper finally exclaimed, "I want a full briefing from the boys when they get here. What time are they supposed to be breaking up with those sand-niggers?"

"The plan was originally to work through lunch and work with the ministers until about two."

"Fine," Harper said. "Order us some bourbon and some lunch. Make sure they bring up plenty of ice. We've got to straighten out a few of these bastards real quick. And, by the way, we'll be staying until tomorrow afternoon."

"Sir?" Moorehouse was concerned about the sudden change in plans.

"There are some loose ends that I have to tie up with the people at United Petroleum. There are some bushwhackers over there that don't seem to remember who the fuck is President of these United States!"

Admiral Moorehouse knew better than to ask any more questions. He got up from his chair and walked into the other room to make the necessary phone calls concerning the change of plans. After he alerted Air Force One's crew and the White House, he ordered lunch.

Country music came blasting from the other room. "Still the Cowboy." Moorehouse thought.

The motorcade with Secretary of State Makoweic and National Security Director Pfohl arrived back at the hotel shortly after two o'clock that afternoon. Both men were informed by Secret Service agents that they were needed immediately to meet with the President in his suite. They were ushered to the elevator.

"Mister Secretary," NSA Director Pfohl said to Secretary of State Makoweic, "I need to stop by my room for just a minute. Will you please tell the President I'll be right along?"

"Sure, Bill," Makoweic replied, "but don't be too long. You know how Ol' Tex gets when he pulls the strings and the puppets don't jump fast enough."

"All too well, 'Pardner'," Pfohl laughed. "I gotta take a shit and I don't want to stink up his bathroom. Why he might string me up on the spot if I ever did."

Secretary of State Makoweic broke out with a wide grin. "Why don't we both take a five minute break. Then I'll meet you at the 'ranch'."

The elevator stopped on their floor and the two men walked in opposite directions to their respective suites.

"Goddamn it, Mikey," President Harper bellowed. "Where are those two sons'bitches, Pfohl, and Makoweic? It's almost two-fucking-thirty. Where are they? I don't like being kept waiting!"

Admiral Moorehouse bristled inside at being called 'Mikey'. He reined his emotions while he went to the phone to call their rooms. As he began pushing the numbers Pfohl arrived. Moorehouse looked over at the NSA Director and nodded toward the other room where

President Harper was sitting with his feet up on the desk. The sounds of Willie Nelson blared from the suite before Pfohl cracked open the door. Moorehouse rolled his eyes at the noise and Pfohl gave him a wink of understanding. Moorehouse then asked the NSA Director, "Where's Mak? The President's been waiting for both of you?"

William Pfohl appeared confused, "I thought Mak would be here by now. I'm sure he'll be right along. The Director leaned over to Moorehouse and joked, "How's things here at the ranch, buckaroo?"

"Oh, we're still ridin' and ropin' and punchin' dogies."

President Harper looked over his Gouchie cowboy boots and caught a glimpse of Pfohl talking to Chief of Staff Moorehouse. "Jeezus Christ, William, I've been waitin' for you guys for over an hour." Harper didn't see the Secretary of State. "Where's Makoweic? What do you think I am, cowshit? I'm still the fucking President and you assholes are working for me."

"Mister President," Pfohl began firmly, "we just arrived a few minutes ago. The Secretary and I just stopped by our suites to freshen up a bit."

The President let out a disgusting laugh. "Freshen up? What the fuck is 'freshen up'? You mean you had to piss? Faggots and Bitches 'freshen up'. Real men shit and piss! Now fix yourself a drink and let's get started."

Just as President Harper was finishing his rude remarks Secretary of State Makoweic entered the room beginning to anger over Harper's last remark. "Mister President, I'm a little sick of your ill manners and guttural references about me. I have always shown you the utmost respect for your Office even though you act like a country bumpkin on many occasions!"

"Why you educated nit-wit," Harper shot back. "My Administration wouldn't be in the shit it's in if you bastards had any common sense. The whole lot of you are nothing but a pack of bushwhackers scheming behind my back! You all think that you're smarter than me. But let me remind y'all that I am the President and y'all work for me! If you don't like the rules of the game get the fuck out!"

There was a momentary silence in the room while the men glared at each other. The tension was broken when Secretary of State Makoweic calmly spoke up. "Mister President I'll be submitting my resignation immediately."

"Fine!" President Harper screamed. Then he turned toward Pfohl and Admiral Moorehouse. "What about you two?"

National Security Director Pfohl attempted to lessen the tension and defuse the situation. "Look, gentlemen, Mister President. We are all under a lot of pressure these days. Might I suggest that we all think of the overall good of the country and leave our individual personalities out of our professional lives? Mister President, might I also suggest that no one wishes to quit the work we have undertaken for the country and the Administration. Moreover, I don't believe that Secretary Makoweic really wishes to resign. Today's talks with the oil ministers didn't go as well as we all hoped. It seems that instead of fighting amongst ourselves we should be pulling together to resolve our position with respect to the oil producers in a unified fashion."

The President's mood changed immediately. He was now more compassionate and in better spirits. "William, you are exactly right. We have to pull together.

Those camel drivers are going to be the ruin of us all if we let them get the upper hand." Then he turned to James Makoweic and extended his hand. "Jim, I apologize. There's not any other man I would rather have as my Secretary of State than you. I shouldn't have blown off like that." Secretary of State Makoweic smiled shaking the President's hand. There was a sigh of relief from Admiral Michael Allen Moorehouse when the tension broke.

Over the next three hours the men discussed the meetings which they had attended and fully briefed the President on the events of the morning. President Harper listened intently sorting through the information and reflecting on what was said at the meeting of the 'Elite', and what position he might take at tomorrow morning's resumption of talks.

The President, Chief of Staff, NSA Director and the Secretary of State concluded their meeting around six o'clock. It was decided that the President would have a statement to deliver to the press corps outlining the steps he intended to take on the volatile oil situation, the growing dependency on imported oil, and the vulnerability of America to the recent radical price increases.

When the men started to leave the Presidential suite, President Harper called the Secretary of State aside. "Jim, what do you think of the possibility of our troops having to invade Iran to stabilize that Mid-east region?"

"Mister President, I can't foresee that happening unless the Iranian government gets enough enriched uranium to make a bomb."

"Well, Mister Secretary, I think that that may have already occurred." Secretary of State Makoweic appeared shocked by this news and was at a loss for words. President Harper noticed that he had one-upped the intellectual and smiled while continuing. "Mak, I'd like you to meet with the Saudis—in private--and let them know what I just said. That our intelligence has confirmed that the Iranians have enough uranium to make the bomb. However, assure them that the U.S. will do whatever is necessary to deter any aggression against our Arab allies or the Israelis."

Secretary of State James Makoweic looked at the President and directly asked, "Is any of this true, Mister President?"

"Of course it's true. I wouldn't lie to you, Mister Secretary! But keep this between the two of us for now. I don't want to tip my hand--just yet. I told you boys that I wasn't as stupid as y'all thought."

"Mister President, I never said, nor ever implied, that you were stupid." Makoweic was embarrassed. "All I implied is that you come across a little too 'country' for us sometimes."

"That's down home common sense, buckaroo. Something you Ivy Leaguer's need more of. Now, can you get this message to the Saudis by tomorrow?"

"Yes, I can arrange it."

"Stop by here about six A.M. and I give you more details on this. That way you'll be able to answer most of their questions. We'll give them some of the answers, but not all. Trust me on this one, Pard."

The President ushered the Secretary of State to the door. Then he went to his desk and turned on his CD player bringing George Jones bursting into song. The President poured himself a tall bourbon. He sat back with his boots up on the desk and smiled to himself. "There's

going to be an ambush at Devil's Pass and you fuckers are
gonna pay!"

ABOVE THE ARCTIC CIRCLE, ALASKA

Flynn took his knife and cut two pine branches
from a tree an notched one end of each. He put the
notched ends into the handle bars of the snow machine
and jammed the opposite ends into the seat against the
back support. Flynn then removed one of the strings from
his pack and tightly wrapped it around the throttle control
to hold it firmly open. Aiming the snow machine down
the long open valley while holding the brake, Flynn
prepared to let it go. He released his hold on the brake
and the machine lurched forward and down the path that
Flynn hoped would lead his pursuers off in the wrong
direction while he cut across the hill and headed for his
aircraft on foot.

Flynn swept the snow behind him for about a
hundred yards covering his footprints. Then he discarded
the pine branch and picked up his pace to make time. He
hoped he would be able to get to his plane before the
snow machine ruse was discovered.

Flynn made excellent time and reached the top of
the ridge where his Buccaneer was waiting below covered
with snow. Although it was now pitch dark the stars
illuminated the snowscape sufficiently for Flynn to make
out the silhouette of the plane's outline. The Alaskan
night was cold and silent and the only sound Flynn could
hear was his own breathing and the crunch of the snow
under his feet as he approached the plane.

Suddenly, Flynn froze. In the distance the
unmistakable high pitch whine signaled that his trail had

been found. Flynn rushed to open the hatch then climbed into the left seat as the lights from the first snow machine hit the top of the ridge. Flynn pumped the throttle four times. He turned the key but the Buccaneer's cold engine protested. Bullets ripped into the skin of the plane while the machines raced down the slope toward him. The prop turned faster. Flynn pushed the throttle to full when the engine began to fire. Finally, the entire plane shook and vibrated when the engine came alive. Flynn relaxed the throttle easing the plane loose from the snow and ice. There wasn't a moment to spare while additional bullets tore into the plane and below him.

The Buccaneer picked up momentum and Flynn pulled on the stick freeing the ailerons while moving his feet to shake any ice from the rudder. The wake from the pusher's prop created a white-out behind him. The men on the snow machines were blinded by the blizzard. Many of their shots rang wild from their reckless firing. Flynn was totally focused on getting the plane airborne. When the plane picked up sufficient speed Flynn pulled back on the stick and the plane leaped into the air. The plane roared while he climbed out of danger into the safety of the night air. The oil temperature began to rise and the engine quieted. Flynn set the manifold and rpms to twenty-four square. By making a final adjustment for the propeller's pitch and trim with full carburetor heat on, the plane was practically flying itself. Flynn continued to climb to eight thousand feet and set his heading and VOR for Wainwright Field at Fairbanks.

Jeremiah Flynn took a deep breath to relax. He turned on his radio to call 'approach control' to get the proper frequency. Then he tuned it and the plane's transponder as directed. Flynn estimated his flight time to be about two hours. When he guided the plane southeast he turned on his CD. Patsy Cline was singing, *"I Fall to Pieces"*, and Flynn smiled.

The flight to Fairbanks went smoothly. During the flight Flynn re-assessed the events of the past few days. He couldn't shake the feeling that his location had been compromised and that the illegal drug dealers had known it. Flynn needed to know more about 'Operation Lifeblood', and why Koreans and Latinos were connected to United Petroleum--an American Oil conglomerate. Flynn was determined to find out more about all of this tomorrow when he returned to the lower forty-eight.

OUTSIDE LONDON, IN RURAL ENGLAND

Arthur pulled the van up the gravel drive to the old stone farmhouse and stopped by the side door. Falso stepped out and looked around making certain that no one was about. He removed a key from his jacket pocket and unlocked the farmhouse door. Falso went inside and turned on a light while Willie and Arthur remained in the van with a blindfolded Kristen Shults.

In a minute, Falso reappeared in the doorway and signaled for them to bring Kristen inside. Willie and Arthur escorted Kristen into the farmhouse. Once inside, Falso removed her blindfold. The light momentarily blinded Kristen and she squinted from the stabbing pain.

"Take her upstairs and lock her in the bedroom at the top of the stairs," Falso ordered Willie.

"Right," Willie replied. He grabbed Kristen's arm and led her to the stairs. Kristen's eyes, now accustomed to the light, saw what looked like a dining room table covered with a map. There were several coils of wire and sticks of explosives. She remained silent pretending that she couldn't see clearly while Willie dragged her to the stairway and shoved her up. As soon as Willie and Kristen reached the bedroom Willie unlocked the door and pushed her inside. He locked the door and hurried back down the steps joining his co-kidnappers.

Kristen was locked in a room with only a single bed. A small window gave her little light as she tried to make out her surroundings. The shadows didn't betray much of the landscape and now thoroughly exhausted, Kristen lay down and fell asleep.

Downstairs Falso was assembling the bomb while Arthur watched in amused amazement. Willie paced nervously in the kitchen waiting for the pot of water to boil for tea. The plank board in the floor creaked beneath his pacing steps. Finally Falso yelled out, "Willie, goddamnit, stop the fuckin' pacing. Just make the bloody tea and light somewhere. You're driving me bonkers."

Willie was startled by Falso's voice and came to an immediate halt. "Sorry, Gov', I'm a bit anxious about this morning I guess." Willie poured out three cups of tea and brought them into the next room for Falso and Arthur.

Arthur looked over at the small man and said, "You better not be too anxious, Willie. You can't afford to miss."

"Ah, don't worry about me," Willie came back, "I won't miss if I can get a clear shot."

Falso looked up from the bomb. "You'll have a clear shot." He patted the bomb lightly concluding, "This 'ere will guarantee it." Then he turned to Arthur and asked, "What time have you got?"

"Three-fifteen."

"Okay lads, let's drink our tea and get moving."

After they drank their tea, Falso picked up the bomb and wrapped it in a nice box. "Willie, check on the princess. And don't forget to leave her door unlocked this time. Hurry we got to make tracks."

Willie walked up the stairs as quietly as the old house would let him while Falso and Arthur got into the van. Willie unlocked the door and peeked inside. Kristen was sound asleep. He closed the door and went back down the stairs and joined the other two in the van. Arthur drove them off back toward London.

Kristen was awaken by the bright sunlight shining through the small bedroom window. She sat up in fright disoriented and momentarily confused by her new surroundings. In a few seconds the realization of her predicament set in. She jumped to the window but it was nailed shut. She looked out. Below was an open field which stretched out of her line of sight. A few scattered trees and gently rolling hills off in the distance was all she could see. Kristen went to the door and listened for any sound. It was quiet. She thought that they might be asleep, uncertain what time of day it was. She tried the door knob and was surprised to find that the door was unlocked. Slowly she opened the door. The creaking under each step echoed throughout the farmhouse when she walked across the hallway. Kristen tip-toed to the stairs all the while straining to hear any sounds.

By the time she reached the ground floor she realized that they were not around. "Run!" A voice inside of her screamed! Kristen burst out of the door and ran down the driveway and onto the road. She had no idea where she was nor in which direction she should go. Her only thoughts were to get away before they came back for her.

The autumn sun was already high in the sky but Kristen was unaware of it. She had run for about a mile before she was too tired to run again. She slowed her escape to a walk. Kristen kept looking back over her shoulder to see if they were following her. Finally, Kristen reached a cross roads. She looked up and down in all directions. She was full of indecision. At last the words of her father came to her.

"If you always go right, then you'll never go wrong."

Kristen chose the right road and walked nearly another mile approaching a slight rise in the road. Before her was a village. A wave of elation came over her for the first time since her capture.

"Thank God!" Kristen said out loud. A smile crossed her lips as she picked up her pace towards the village.

There was very little activity in the streets as Kristen, surprised by this, reached the village. Kristen walked on and reached a small shop. Looking in the store window, Kristen was shocked at the reflection she saw. She was a mess. Her hair was was uncombed, her face puffy and dirty and her clothes were wrinkled and dirty as well. She ran her fingers through her red hair trying to comb it some. She wiped her eyes and her face with the inside of her sleeve of the sweatshirt.

When she prepared to walk inside the shop, the newspaper rack holding the *London Times* caught her attention.

"Prime Minister Assassinated!" Kristen was shocked at what she read. She pulled out the paper and began reading the story. "Prime Minister Nigel Sommerset was assassinated early this morning outside the Foreign Ministry by a single shot from a high powered rifle. A bomb exploded in a nearby building at the moment the Prime Minister was gunned down. Authorities speculate that the attack was part of of a terrorist plot.

"Security agents from MI-6, and Scotland Yard have reportedly found the weapon used in the assassination in a building across from the Foreign Ministry. Prime Minister Sommerset was scheduled to meet with government leaders regarding the recent oil crisis and the threat by Iran to obtain nuclear materials to make an atomic bomb.

"No arrests have been made as yet, and officials are not discussing any leads they might have at this time. However, sources at the scene report that no group has yet, claimed responsibility...."

The paper was ripped from Kristen's hands. "Excuse me, Miss," the man's voice startled Kristen. "But this ain't no library. If you want to read the paper, you'll have to buy it."

Kristen was taken aback. Instinctively she reached in her pocket for some money. There was none, of course. She was penniless. Kristen was overcome with a new fear. How was she ever going to get anywhere without money?

The shopkeeper glared back at her and sneered, "We don't need your kind around her. Now, get along with ya before I call a copper."

Kristen turned and walked away. She was depressed, hungry, and every muscle in her body ached. "I need to think," she told herself. She continued along the street until she came to a small church. Kristen looked at the church for a moment before she tried the door. It was open and she went in. The empty church was quiet and dark with only a few devotional lights near the altar giving off any light. Kristen sat herself down in the very last pew and began to weep.

HOUSTON, TEXAS

Special Secret service Agent Samuel Adams picked up the Presidential hotline at 2:47 A.M. He put the Home Secretary on hold while he entered the President's bedroom to wake President Harper to take the call. The President was not a sound sleeper and he awoke immediately. Agent Adams handed the President the phone and waited for his directions from the President.

"This is President Harper. Good morning, Mister Secretary." There was a pause from the President while listening to the caller. President Irwin W. Harper's expression was somber when he heard of the assassination of British Prime Minister Sommerset.

"Please accept my deepest regrets," Harper replied to the Home Secretary, "and the sincerest condolences of the American people. I will be speaking with the Foreign Minister right away. Please keep me informed of any further developments. Let me assure you, sir, that America will stand ready to assist you in any way necessary. I considered Prime Minister Sommerset a personal friend and I am deeply shocked and outraged by this horrible and cowardly act. Secretary of State Makoweic will be contacting you later this morning. Thank you for calling me, Mister Secretary."

"Sonofabitch!" Harper exclaimed to Special Agent Adams. "They've shot and killed the British Prime Minister. Have the operator contact the Cabinet and the others--she's got a list. First, though, get me the Joint Chiefs. We'd better put our military on alert, just in case." Harper handed the phone to the Secret Service man and went back to sleep.

FAIRBANKS, ALASKA

Flynn touched down at Wainwright Field at twelve thirty in the morning. He was tired and hungry. He parked the Buccaneer by a remote hangar off to the far side taxiway. Flynn noticed a light on in the office room and thought maybe someone was still up to whom he could tell about his plane and that he would be back later in the morning for his gear. As Flynn approached the office door a military jeep came around the corner of the building with its red lights flashing. Flynn halted and the jeep came forward stopping right in front of him. Flynn couldn't see into the vehicle because the headlights were shining into his eyes. Two armed AP's jumped out when the jeep screeched to a halt.

One of the Air Patrolmen shouted, "Sir, you are in a restricted area. Raise your arms away from your sides and don't move."

Flynn did as he was ordered. The other AP came around to Flynn's right holding his automatic weapon on Flynn while he approached. "Sir, put your hands on the vehicle and spread your legs apart."

Flynn complied with the direction. "Cover him while I pat him down," the AP told his partner. The airman removed Flynn's .44 Magnum Smith & Wesson, knife and BlackBerry and placed them on the hood of the jeep. After the pat-down, no additional weapons were found on Flynn and the airman then addressed Flynn.

"What's your name and why are you in this restricted area?"

"My name is Flynn. Jeremiah Flynn. I just landed in the Lake aircraft behind me. I was on a vacation hunting trip in the north and just got back."

"I've never known anyone to hunt with a .44 Magnum," the Airman replied smugly.

"It's only a side arm," Flynn explained. "My rifle is in the plane with the rest of my gear. I planned on coming back for it later to get it all."

"Sir, this is a restricted area. You are going to have to come with us. Please get in the jeep."

Flynn pushed himself back from the vehicle and stood erect. He walked around the jeep and got in the front seat. The Airman picked up Flynn's pistol, cell phone and knife and returned to the rear seat in the jeep.

The jeep driver was on the radio, "We have apprehended a man in restricted area Bravo. We are bringing him to HQ." The driver swung the jeep around and drove back around the building down the taxiway to a concrete block building which had a sign, 'Base Security' over the doorway.

"Sir, come with us." The Airman ordered Flynn out of the jeep. Flynn gave the man a passive look while he walked to the door. There, two additional armed AP's met Flynn and escorted him to the Duty Officer's Office.

Flynn saw that the Duty Officer was a second lieutenant and his name plate identified him as Reed. Flynn noticed that second lieutenant Reed was a very young man probably in his early twenties. The DO looked Flynn over and asked the AP, "What do we have here, Airman?"

"Sir, this man was picked up in red sector Bravo.

He landed a private aircraft on the restricted runway. In his possession he had this weapon--a .44 caliber Smith & Wesson, a knife and a cellular phone. Airman Onacki and Jones are searching the aircraft at this moment, sir."

The second lieutenant looked at the cellular phone, the .44 Magnum, and the hunting knife. He picked up the knife and removed it from its sheath. The young officer was fascinated by the knife and there was a long pause before he he spoke to Flynn directly.

"Well, Rambo," the Duty officer began sarcastically, "what's your story?"

Flynn smiled while thinking, "What a cocky little shit this guy is." Flynn answered the officer. "Lieutenant, my name is Flynn. And, before we go any further, I'd suggest that you call your commanding officer, Colonel Alexander, and tell him that I am here."

"I'll make all of the decisions on who to call. I don't need you to tell me what to do. I'm the Duty Officer and in charge of this watch! I'd suggest, Rambo, that you answer my questions. You may not know it but your ass is mine right now."

"Look, Lieutenant," Flynn tried to rationalize with the young officer although he knew it was hopeless, "I'm tired. I'd like to get some sleep. I'm merely trying to save us all a lot of time."

The young officer flipped the knife in his hands catching the handle with the blade pointed at Flynn in a threatening manner. Flynn, although not intimidated by the young officer's gesture, warned, "Don't threaten me with that knife, Lieutenant. I'm liable to shove it up your ass."

The airman who was still guarding Flynn made a move to grab Flynn's arm. When he did so, Flynn's elbow caught him right under the jaw and sent him crashing unconscious into the wall. In the same motion Flynn's left hand grabbed the second lieutenant's wrist holding the knife. With one swift tug, Flynn pulled the young officer over the desk. The razor sharp blade just touching him under the chin. The Lieutenant's face was a picture of surprised terror.

In a very calm and cold voice Flynn said, "Now, Lieutenant, I told you that I was tired and wanted to get some sleep. Call Colonel Alexander and tell him that Jeremiah Flynn is here and we can both relax."

Flynn moved the phone over to the still sprawled out second lieutenant. The frightened officer pushed the speed dial button for the commanding officer's home phone. Colonel Alexander answered on the second ring.

"Colonel, this is Lieutenant Reed. We have a situation here, sir." Reed's voice was noticeably trembling. "There's a man here who identified himself as a Mister Flynn. He landed in red sector Bravo, a restricted area, and..."

The Lieutenant was interrupted by the Commanding Officer. "Put Flynn on, Lieutenant!"

Lieutenant Reed handed the phone to Flynn. "Mister Flynn, the Colonel would like to speak to you."

Flynn relaxed the man's wrist and took the knife in his own hand while taking the receiver in the other. "Hello, Frank," Flynn said into the phone. "No, there's no problem. The Lieutenant was just a little over-in-charge at first. Look, Colonel, I hate to impose but, is there a nearby cot I could crash on for a few hours. I ran into a little situation up north and I need to get back home tomorrow morning. But right now, as I told the Lieutenant, I'm tired and a bit irritable and need some sleep... Thanks Frank. It's good to talk to you again, too. Flynn handed the phone back to Lieutenant Reed.

"Yes, sir, Colonel. I'll take care of it. Anything Mister Flynn wants...I understand, sir."

There was a new man now addressing Flynn. "Mister Flynn, please let me show you to Colonel Alexander's Quarters. This way, sir. I hope you will be comfortable. If there is anything you need let me know, sir."

Flynn couldn't stand the puke coming from the Lieutenant's mouth but he let him go on as a lesson to him to be a bit more respectful. However, Flynn finally broke a grin and said, "Relax, Reed. Do your job but just don't overdo it until you know all the facts."

The young officer, still embarrassed, nodded that he understood what Flynn meant. Then he led Flynn to Colonel Alexander's quarters. Flynn found the cot and he was asleep before Lieutenant Reed closed the commanding officer's door.

Flynn snapped awake shortly after five. He got up and started out of Colonel Alexander's quarters. Outside the door an airman came to attention. Before Flynn could say anything the airman spoke.

"Good morning, Captain Flynn. Lieutenant Reed assigned me to see that you were not disturbed."

"Thank you, airman," Flynn responded, somewhat amused by the attention. "Could you get me a ride to my plane so I could get my gear so I can shower, shave and change?"

"Sir, Lieutenant Reed took the liberty of having all of your gear brought over here earlier to save you some time. It's right here, sir." The airman indicated a neat pile of Flynn's things, including rifle, next to his station by the door.

"Thank Lieutenant Reed for me, airman Onacki," Flynn said reading the name tag on the airman's uniform.

Flynn picked up his duffel and started back into the Colonel's room to shower. He stopped before opening the door and addressed the airman with a question. "Airman, I'd like to catch a ride, if possible, back to Washington, D.C., this morning." Flynn went inside smiling, thinking that he would clue airman Onacki in on the joke after he showered and changed.

Flynn was showered, shaved and dressed within twenty minutes. When he left Colonel Alexander's quarters, Flynn was surprised to see Lieutenant Reed dressed in full flight suit waiting for him.

"Captain Flynn, we're ready for takeoff as soon as you are," Lieutenant Reed said.

"Where are we going, Lieutenant?" Flynn asked in disbelief.

"Sir, Colonel Alexander has given me permission, er, an order, sir, to fly you to Fort Lewis, Tacoma, Washington. There he has had us arrange for you to hop on with an F-16, heading to Andrews later this morning. All connections have been cleared by Colonel Alexander himself, Captain."

Flynn was completely surprised by this fortunate turn of events but he never let on that he expected anything less. This was good fortune indeed. "Very well, Lieutenant. Let me grab a cup of coffee and a bit of chow. Give me fifteen minuets, can you?"

"Take your time, sir. Our Hornet will get us there in plenty of time. Your connect won't leave until you get there anyway, sir. I'll meet you at Hangar Bravo, at say 0600, Captain Flynn?"

"Roger, Lieutenant. 0600. Bravo!" The pun was lost on the young Lieutenant. Flynn couldn't believe all of this but it would get him back to Washington where he could get some answers a lot sooner than he expected. Flynn pondered the still unanswered questions in his mind concerning the events of the past few days. He still hadn't made his report to Langley but they weren't expecting his call till seven local Alaskan time which was about an hour from now. "I can text them from the air," he thought.

Flynn made his way to the mess hall and ate a light breakfast. By 0600, he was at the F-16 Fighting Falcon and met Lieutenant Reed.

The Lieutenant gave Flynn a flight suit. "Sir, I'll have your gear shipped to you stateside. What do you want us to do with the Buccaneer?"

"It's a rental from Anchorage," Flynn replied reaching for a card in his pocket and handing it to the young Lieutenant. They have my address and credit card so call them and tell them to pick it up here."

"That won't be necessary, sir. We'll drop it off for you. No problem."

"Thank you, again," Flynn was amazed at the change in this man's attitude.

The Falcon lifted off the runway at 0604 and shot skyward with full throttle and afterburners climbing almost straight up through the dense clouds in a dark sky. Flynn thought that this was as close to being in a rocket as he'd ever get. The young pilot was good, although Flynn thought he was showing off a bit with the hot-dog takeoff. They leveled off at eighteen thousand feet and headed southeast into the rising sun.

"Mister Flynn," Lieutenant Reed's voice came into

the the headset in Flynn's helmet. "We should be at Fort Lewis by nine local time. With your connection you should be in D.C. for supper."

"Roger that, Lieutenant," Flynn replied. "And you can drop the Mister, Lieutenant."

"Okay. And you can call me Bob." The young aviator curiously added, "You must know Colonel Alexander pretty well for him to arrange this ride for you, Flynn. If you don't mind me asking, what's up with you two?"

"Frank...Colonel Alexander was a flight instructor of mine. I was the only hot shot jet jock to ever beat him in a mock dog fight. More importantly, he taught me several tricks on how to stay alive in the air. It came in handy more than once and actually saved my life in Colombia." Flynn only told the young man half the story. There was no need to relate how he saved Frank Alexander after he was shot down in Iraq. Or how Flynn made an impossible landing in his Air America recon plane on a roadway which just happened to be in the right spot at the right time for then, Captain Alexander, while under heavy shelling by in-coming fire. Flynn was unorthodox even then. Captain Alexander was forever grateful that he was. "Oh, and I remember," Flynn added, "I gave him a ride once."

Lieutenant Reed sensed that there was more to the story than Flynn had told him but he decided to leave it alone.

About one hour into the flight Flynn's Rolex told him it was time to check in with Langley. He took out his BlackBerry and texted the message: "Safe. Unable to communicate by voice from present location. Be back soon."

The F-16 Fighting Falcon landed at Fort Lewis, Tacoma, Washington around nine that morning Pacific Time. Lieutenant Reed taxied the plane over to the end of the hangar where the other F-16 was waiting. Flynn and the young Lieutenant walked over to the jet together.

Flynn stopped and looked at the young man. He shook his hand and said, "Thanks for the ride, Bob. I hope we meet again. I owe you a couple of stiff drinks."

"Roger that, Flynn," Reed answered with a salute. "Thank you, sir. I learned something from you that I'll never forget. Have a safe flight and good luck."

The two men parted and Flynn climbed into the Falcon for his last leg of his trip back to Washington, D.C. Flynn smiled while he watched the young Lieutenant walk away back to his plane. "He'll be a good officer. He's a good man," Flynn thought.

"Welcome aboard, Mister Flynn. I'm Captain Johnson. We should be arriving at Andrews before dark."

"Nice to meet you, Captain. Thanks for the lift."

Within a few short minutes the Falcon was barreling down the runway and rocketing skyward. "So much for vacation," Flynn smirked while being pressed by the 'G-force' back into the seat.

HOUSTON, TEXAS

"Mister President, Foreign Minister Saunders is on the line for you, sir." Special Agent Adams announced.

President Harper picked up the phone. "Mister Foreign Minister, please accept my condolences over the loss of Prime Minister Sommerset. You know what a friend he was to me."

"Thank you, Mister President," Foreign Minister

Saunders replied,."Yes, we have all lost a true friend."
There was a rather long pause on both ends before
Saunders spoke again. "Mister President, I fear for my
life."

"Don't worry, Jim," Harper reassured the Foreign
Minister. "You'll be all right."

No, Mister President, you don't understand. I have
some close friends at the Yard who have told me they
have identified the fingerprints on the weapon used to kill
the Prime Minister as those belonging to my niece,
Kristen Shults!"

"Sonofabitch!" President Harper exclaimed in
shock. "Why would she do it?"

"I can't believe that Kristen could or would do
such a thing. I feel that this is some sort of conspiracy—a
frame up, if you will. To disgrace me and remove me
from office."

"Who's out to get, Jim?" Harper asked.

"I can't imagine. However, as you know, we make
a lot of enemies in political life. And, as Foreign Minister,
any number of foreign countries could use this
opportunity to pressure me out of the way. At any rate, I
must leave for London immediately."

"Of course," President Harper concurred. "Have
you told Tiger, yet?"

"No. I wanted to phone you first. I will call him
straight away. You know that I support a reasonable
position on this 'Operation Lifeblood' affair. But," James
Saunders added, "with this latest development at home,
Mister President, I am not certain what lies ahead."

"Well, don't you worry about that. As I said
before, I 'm not about to start World War Three for that
slant-eyed prick.. Now, let me know if there is anything I

can do to help you out."

"Be careful, Mister President," the Foreign Minister warned, "Tiger is an ambitious man."

The President smiled confidently to himself. "I know all about Tiger and his global dream of conquest. He hasn't seen me in a pissin' contest before. I'm not worried. What the fuck can he do to the President of the United States?"

WASHINGTON, D. C.

Vice President Patricia Bunnell was back from Chicago the same evening she addressed the NEA luncheon. She went straight to her Georgetown apartment upon arrival. She rarely went to the official Vice Presidential residence because there were too many empty rooms and she felt more comfortable in her apartment that she had ever since first coming to the Nation's Capital as a freshman Congressman.

Patricia was awaken around five o'clock by a phone call from the White House informing her of the assassination of Prime Minister Sommerset. She was advised to standby for directions from President Harper on whether he or she would be going to London to attend the State funeral as the official representative of the United States.

Across the Potomac River at Langley, Virginia, at CIA headquarters, analysts were sorting out the field data pouring in from London and all over the world pertaining to the the assassination of the British Prime Minister. This information was being cross-referenced by high speed computers which were spewing out volumes of paper for some analysts while other more classified information was being directed to other computers. This information was only accessible by specific codes to teams of economists, political scientists, military strategists, and social scientists for interpretation. The primary objective was the security of the United States' interests around the world.

Among the data that was received was information which identified the fingerprints of Kristen Shults, niece to Foreign Minister James Saunders, as the ones found on the weapon which was used in the assassination. All pertinent information regarding Kristen Shults was rated high priority—high security. This information was only accessible to those Agency personnel with the highest security clearance. One person who took special interest in reading this information was Mollie Farnham. She noted that Jeremiah Flynn's name was in the report as one of Kristen Shults' 'close friends, frequent companion, and probable lover.'

It was just about this time that Mollie received Flynn's text message which she believed was being sent from his location in Alaska. Mollie read, "Safe. Unable to communicate by voice from current location. Be back soon." She made the assumption that that Flynn had moved to another location and that he would be calling back soon.

Mollie thought it would be nice to hear Flynn's voice. She also couldn't wait to get his reaction to his little girlfriend being the subject of the most massive manhunt in recent British history. "You see, Flynn," Mollie thought, "you really don't know how to pick a real woman."

SOMEWHERE IN RURAL ENGLAND

"Can I help you, lass?" The man's Irish brogue startled Kristen while she wept in the pew. She looked up to see that the man was a priest. Kristen stared up at him choking back her tears.

"Father, where am I?"

"You're in God's house, child. What's troubling you now?" the priest asked sympathetically. "Would ye like to talk about it, child?"

"Oh, Father, I need to get to London. I don't know where I am. I have no money. I mean I have money, Father, but I don't have any on me. I'm supposed to be on holiday. No one knows where I am. My Uncle James will be worried sick." Kristen was rambling. "Don't let them get me, Father, please."

"Now, now, my child, calm yourself down. Nobody is going to get you. You're safe here in God's house. Tell me what it tis that's troubling ye." The priest sat in the pew next to Kristen who went on to relate her frightening story of the past few days.

When she had finished her tale of terror, the priest took Kristen by the hand and gently held it in his. He looked at her and offered to help. "I think I know a few people who can help you, lass." He stood up and led Kristen up toward the altar and through the sacristy into a hallway that led to the rectory. "Come along, child. Let's get you something to eat."

Kristen sat at the kitchen table while the priest made her a cup of tea and warmed up some oatmeal he had left over from his breakfast. Kristen ate it quickly.

While Kristen ate the remaining oatmeal, the priest began, "Listen now, my dear. I have to go out for a short while and talk to a few people I know who I think can help you. While I am gone you stay inside here. You'll be safe. I shall return very soon."

"Very well, Father. How long will you be gone?"

Not long. You sit still now and don't fret. I'll be back before you know it. Everything will be all right."

Kristen watched the priest leave the rectory by the side door until he was out of sight. She walked into the parlor and took a seat next to the radio that was on to the BBC. The news broadcast was all about the assassination of Prime Minister Sommerset. Kristen listened intently to the tragic news thinking how upset her Uncle James would be. Her thoughts drifted to what he would do, what the government would do, and who could be responsible for such a horrible crime. "A whole lot of horrible things have happened in the past few days," she mumbled. "What was the world coming to?"

Suddenly there was news which caused Kristen's heart to stop. "Police sources indicate that they believe the assailant has been identified as Kristen Shults, the niece of Foreign Minister James Saunders. Apparently, the Shults woman acted alone but details are still being sorted out. No motive has been given at this time although authorities from Scotland yard and MI-6 have issued an all points bulletin for the Shults woman who, thus far, has eluded capture. The alleged assassin, Kristen Shults, was identified from fingerprints taken from the Weatherby rifle found at the Whitehall location where the fatal shot was fired.

"Speculation continues on the motive. It is not clear whether or not Miss Shults has ties with the IRA. However, it is generally known that the Irish terrorist organization has been threatening an attempt on the Prime

Minister. What is particularly shocking is that Shults is the niece of Foreign Minister James Saunders. The Foreign Minister is returning from America where he has been engaged in talks with world leaders relative to the current oil crisis and the troubles in the Middle East and has been unavailable for comment...."

Kristen couldn't believe what she had just heard. She was in total shock. She was being sought as the murderer of the Prime Minister! "This can't be true!," she screamed. "I haven't been in London. I have been kidnapped, raped and beaten for the past two days!" Kristen stood paralyzed unable to walk from shock. "I couldn't ever kill anyone. Why would they think I did this horrible thing?"

Finally, reality set in. Kristen rethought what had happened to her. The three kidnappers: Willie, Falso, and the brute Arthur had set her up. They must have killed the Prime Minister. The weapon! "Oh my God! They shoved it in my stomach and when I tried to shoot them they got my fingerprints all over it. Oh, Lord, help me. What am I to do?"

At that moment the priest and another man entered the parlor. Kristen looked at them both, still standing in shock. Then she blurted out, "Father, they think I killed the Prime Minister!"

"We know, child. We know," the priest comforted her. "This good lad is Timothy Hartnett," the priest introduced the tall thin man. "He can help you get away safely."

"Get away?" Kristen cried, "Get away to where? I don't want to get away. I have to get to London...to my Uncle James and get this straightened out. I didn't kill anyone."

"I'm afraid, Kristen," Timothy Hartnett said calmly, "you would not be safe in London. Your only hope for safety is to come with us. We can get you out of England and into a safe house."

"I didn't kill him! Those three men who kidnapped me did it, don't you see?"

The priest put his arm around her shoulder to reassure her. He spoke in a very calm voice. "Listen, my child, we believe you. But the police have you as the prime suspect. And right now, the way things are, you'll be safer with Timothy and our friends out of England. Then when the real killer or killers are caught you can return. There's no way you can help yourself in jail, is there? And sure as the Pope is Catholic that's where ye'd be til hell froze over."

Kristen was frightened and confused. So much had happened to her in the past few days. She was having difficulty believing anyone or anything. Nothing was real. She was supposed to be on holiday. It was now a terrible nightmare. Finally, with no other recourse for help, she agreed in her mind, that maybe this priest was right. Maybe he really did want to help her. It made sense to stay free in the hope that the real assassins would be caught and Kristen could have her life back.

"All right, Father," Kristen resigned, "I guess you're right. There's no way I can help myself from prison."

"You'll come to see, my child," the priest reassured her, "that this is the for best."

"Father, could you do me a favor?"

"What is it, lass?"

"I need to contact a friend of mine. He's an American. I know that he can help me."

"I don't think it's wise to contact anyone right now, my child."

"I must, Father," Kristen protested, "Or I will turn myself in. So help me God."

The two men looked at each other for a moment. Timothy Hartnett broke the momentary silence. "Tell us his name and where he lives. We'll get a message to him in America through our Yank friends."

Kristen felt relieved. "His name is Flynn. Jeremiah Flynn. He has an office in Washington, D.C., but a residence in Amsterdam. He's a consultant, an international attorney, for a plastics company with offices in Holland. I think the company's name is American Plastics."

"We'll find him, Kristen," Hartnett lied. "Now, why don't you get yourself ready to travel."

The priest added, "Come. There's a guest room up stairs where ye can clean up and rest for a bit. I'll find ye some clean duds to put on. Then we'll have a hot supper to eat and you and Tim can be on your way as soon as it is dark. Don't worry about a thing. Everything will be just fine. You'll see."

Kristen went upstairs as directed. She found the bath and filled the tub with hot water. She climbed into the tub and felt the dirt and tension leave while she soaked. She dozed off in the tub and was awaken by a gentle rapping on the bathroom door.

"Kristen?" The priest announce softly. "Are ye all right?"

Startled for a moment, Kristen splashed when she moved too quickly. "I'm fine, Father. I guess I just dozed off for a moment."

The priest smiled behind the door and said, "I've

laid out some clean clothes for ye on the bed. They're not the latest in fashion, but they should fit ye." Then he added, "Supper is about ready and it'll be dark enough to travel soon."

"Thank you, Father. I'll be down in a minute."

Kristen emptied the tub and dried herself. She wrapped herself in the towel and went into the guest room. Just as the priest had said, there was a clean shirt, starched and pressed, a pair of trousers, socks, a wool sweater, and a cap. She put on the clothes and studied herself in the mirror. With her red hair tucked up under the cap, she could pass for a young lad. She turned and saw that there was a small desk by the window. Kristen opened a drawer and found some writing paper, a pen and envelopes. Kristen thought for a moment. Then she quickly decided to write Flynn. She sat down and wrote a short letter to Flynn at his Amsterdam address, which she remembered from more pleasant times where they made love on many happier occasions.

"Flynn," Kristen wrote, "I am frightened and need your help. I have been falsely accused of killing the Prime Minister. I have been kidnapped by three horrible men, who probably are the real assassins. It's a long, horrible story that I hope to forget.

"I'm being helped by an Irish priest and a man called Timothy Hartnett. I believe they are IRA or have connections to the IRA. They are taking me out of England tonight, probably to Ireland, although they haven't said. I don't know that you will ever find me or even if you will receive this letter. Or even if I will be alive when you do. I am very frightened and need your help desperately! You were the first person I thought of who would help me without asking any questions.

"Please let my Uncle James know that I love him,
Signed, "Kristen"

"P.S. I love you, too."

Kristen folded the paper and stuffed it into the envelope. She addressed it and sealed it. She went to put the pen back into the drawer and noticed that there were a number of postage stamps. She put two on the envelope and then shoved it into her pants' pocket. She grabbed two more stamps and put them in her pocket, also. She thought, "I'll find a way to mail this myself."

It was nearly dark when Kristen descended the stairs of the rectory. She found the priest and Hartnett drinking tea at the kitchen table. They were talking quietly but ceased when she entered the room. Both men stood up when she came in. Kristen looked much different than before, both thought. She exuded a kind of radiance and confidence they had not seen.

"These men can help me remain free," Kristen thought looking at the two men. "I don't trust them completely, but if I can stay free long enough Flynn will find me. I pray to God that he will find me."

The priest spoke first. "Good evening, Lass. Are ye feeling better?"

"I'll be fine, Father." Kristen hoped.

"Indeed, ye shall, child. Now, Tim here is prepared to take ye to some friends of ours who will assist ye." The priest reached in his pocket and took out some money and placed it in her hand. "Take this with ye, now. Tis only a few pounds but it might come in handy."

Kristen smiled gratefully and said, "Thank you, Father. For everything."

"Come now. Sit and have some supper. Then ye both can be on your way." The three sat down and the priest served out their bowls of stew from a large pot that sat in the middle of the table.

After they had eaten, Timothy looked at the kitchen clock and announced, "Tis time that we be a goin'"

"Go in Almighty God's peace," the priest blessed Kristen and Timothy as they left the rectory and slipped into the darkness.

The pair kept to the back of the church then turned down a dark alley which brought them out to a side street. They walked along for a block to a dimly lighted garage. Timothy glanced up and down the street before knocking on the door. A small man with a large nose opened the door slightly.

"Come in, come in," he said softly while opening the door wider to let them enter.

"Is the automobile ready?" Hartnett asked.

"It is. It's out back and full of petrol. You'd best be on your way."

"That we are," Timothy replied. "Thank you, Darby. You won't be forgotten."

"Aw, be off with ye now," Darby said "Tis for the cause."

Timothy Hartnett led Kristen out the back, "This way, Lass."

They found the auto and Timothy got behind the wheel. Kristen sat in the passenger side as they drove off into the darkness. They had driven for a long time in silence before Hartnett spoke.

"There is identification papers for you in the glove box."

Kristen realized that she was wanted by every police agency in the British Empire by now and, for the first time, she understood that she would need a new identity in order to travel safely. Kristen removed the papers from the glove box and looked them over.

"Maureen Hartnett?" She exclaimed. "Am I, 'Maureen Hartnett', your, er...wife?"

Timothy broke into a wide smile and laughed. "No, Lass, not my wife, my sister. And we're on our way to Belfast to visit our dying mother, Anna." Then he added, "If anyone asks that's the story. Have you got it?"

"Yes, I can remember it, dear brother." Kristen sighed. "So we're going to Belfast," she thought looking out the window into the night. A wave of despair overcame her. "Flynn will never find me in Belfast. What is happening to me? How will I ever clear my name? Oh Uncle James, what is to become of me?"

Her thoughts were interrupted when Timothy Hartnett spoke. "We'll be coming into Liverpool in a bit. I'm certain that the 'coppers' will have road blocks up. Let me do all the talkin', Lass. If they ask ye anything direct, you stick to the story, now. And, 'Maureen'," Timothy added as a caution, "both of our lives depend on what ye say and how ye behave."

Kristen turned toward him and asked directly, "You're the IRA, aren't you?"

Hartnett returned her gaze, but said nothing. His silence was as clear a statement as if he had spoken it. Kristen closed her eyes then put her head back against the seat. A final tear trickled from her eyes and down her cheek.

Flashing lights appeared up ahead in the road. "Tis the road block," Timothy announced. "Keep your wits about ye, now." He stopped the vehicle between two of the police cars where the officers were standing.

"Good evening, Constable." Timothy addressed the officer. "What's about this evening?"

"Good evening, sir," the policeman returned the greeting politely. "May I see your and the lady's identifications, please?" The policeman shined a flashlight into the car on Kristen's face.

Timothy handed the constable his and Kristen's papers which she had still been holding in her hands.

The constable leaned into the car while he reviewed the papers in his light. "Are you Maureen Hartnett?"

"Yes, she's my sister," Timothy spoke up answering for her.

"Where are you coming from?" the constable continued to study Kristen who sat motionless.

"Sheffield, sir," Timothy answered quickly noticing the policeman's interest in Kristen.

"Where are you bound?"

"We're on our way home to see our dying mother and we're trying to catch the midnight ferry," Hartnett offered as an explanation.

"Constable!" Kristen spoke out to the amazement of Hartnett who shot a tense look at her. "My brother and I are in a bit of a hurry. So if you don't mind we'd like to be getting along."

"Yes, very well. Right." The policeman responded, caught off guard. Then he quickly handed the identification papers back to Timothy and added, "Sorry for the delay. Off with you, now."

Hartnett started the car forward clearing the road block. When he rolled up his window he glanced back into the rear view mirror and snarled at Kristen. "I thought I told you not to say anything."

133

"I didn't want to diddle any longer. Didn't you notice how he was giving me the once over? It was getting creepy. We needed to get along so I did what I thought had to be done. And, it worked didn't it, 'Brother'," Kristen said confidently.

Hartnett looked over at her as he thought in silence, "She's different than I first assumed. She's unpredictable and will need to be watched more closely, I fear."

They drove through the city of Liverpool and at last made their way down to the port and to the docks. Timothy pulled the car over and set the hand brake. "Stay put, Lass," he ordered. "I have to check to make certain that all is set for us to board. I'll just be a moment." He left her in the car and Kristen watched while Timothy walked into one of the buildings along the wharf.

Kristen noticed that just up ahead was a mail box drop next to a telephone booth. She opened the car door and got out. Kristen looked about and didn't see anyone. She quickly made her way to the mail box. Then taking the letter to Flynn out of her pocket, she prayed he would get it soon. Kristen quickly slipped the letter into the slot just as Timothy Hartnett reappeared from the building's doorway.

Thinking that Kristen was about to make a phone call, Hartnett rushed up to her and took her by the arm. "Look it here, now!" he shouted, "We can't be makin' any calls to anyone. I told you to wait in the car. If you want me to get us out of here alive you'll have to do as I say."

Kristen pulled away from him, fire in her eyes as she lashed back, "Don't you ever touch me again! I wasn't about to make any call. I merely wanted to stretch my legs a little."

Timothy's mood changed while he studied her closely. "Sorry, Lass," he said softly. "But I'd ask ye to trust me on this, please. You're my responsibility until I can get us to Belfast. And I can't have you goin' off on your own. It isn't safe for either of us."

"I understand. But I'm not going to be treated like a prisoner either. You'll have to trust me a little, too."

"Very well," Timothy agreed. "Let's be goin' down the pier to the boat. We'll be leaving in a few minutes."

The two walked down the pier to where a small launch was moored. Hartnett helped Kristen aboard then he called below deck. "Andrew?"

"Hello, Tim," the man below answered coming topside. The two men shook hands.

The man called Andrew, the skipper, looked Kristen over. "This must be your sister, Maureen."

"It is," Timothy answered. "Maureen, this is Andrew Owens, our skipper."

Owens smiled obviously delighted at Kristen's beauty. "Nice to meet you, Maureen."

"Thank you, sir," Kristen answered coolly extending her hand. "It's a pleasure to make your acquaintance."

"She's a real pretty one, Tim, me boy," Andrew Owens remarked to Hartnett.

Timothy ignored the familiarity and responded, "Are we about ready to shove off, Andrew?"

Andrew got the message to stay away. "Indeed we are. Will ye cast off the bow line, Timo?" Then as he started the engines he looked back at Kristen. "Maureen? Can ye cast off the stern line for us?"

Kristen Shults cast off the stern line and the boat pulled away from the pier. In her thoughts she wondered if she had symbolically cast off her prior life as Kristen Shults and if she would ever return to England as a free woman. Kristen remained lost in her thoughts while the boat made its way out of the Mersey estuary and into the waters of the Irish Sea. Her thoughts merged into a prayer that Flynn would find her soon.

HOUSTON, TEXAS

President Irwin W. Harper was dressed and watching the television morning news channel. The news was all about the assassination of Prime Minister Sommerset. Harper was scheduled for a twenty minute briefing on this development from his staff. He was also scheduled to be meeting with the 'Elite' at nine o'clock. "I'll have a few surprises for that Korean bastard, Tiger," Harper mumbled while he adjusted his tie. Then his phone rang.

"Mister President, it's Deputy Director Dimmler from CIA, sir." Special Agent Eisenmann announced.

President Harper asked, "Where's Agent Adams, Pete?"

"He'll be right along, sir."

"Takin' a piss, eh, " Harper joked. "Okay, Pete, put the top spy through."

"Good morning, Mister President," Dimmler said. "I trust you have been informed about Prime Minister Sommerset?"

"I don't live in a vacuum, George. You're as bad as that guy Pfohl. Do any of my Security and Intelligence people know anything for Chrissake. Tell me something new, George. What's the Agency's take on this."

"We've learned that the alleged assailant is the

niece of Foreign Minister Saunders and we believe she's connected to the IRA," Dimmler reported.

President Harper didn't let on that he already knew this from Saunders directly, hours before. He thought, "I know more about things than either the NSA, or the CIA." Then he said to Dimmler, "How reliable is your information, George?"

"Quite reliable, sir. Although the IRA connection is still speculative at this time. She may have been newly recruited."

"What the fuck for?" Harper asked.

Deputy Director of Special Operations Dimmler caught himself before he answered. He had been down this road on previous occasions with the President, never knowing what the real question was. "Does the President mean, 'what was she recruited for?' or, 'what was the reason she killed the P.M. for?', or was there some other convoluted reason for the question?" Dimmler thought. He then took a chance and answered, "We don't know yet, Mister President."

"Okay," Harper retorted, "When you do you let me know."

"Yes, sir," Dimmler replied totally confused, since he didn't know what he was supposed to let the President know, if he found out.

President Harper hung up the phone and stood up looking out his window for a long moment. He shrugged his shoulders as if this action would clear his mind. "I'm surrounded by fucking idiots," he mumbled walking into the next room. Special Agent Adams had returned and was at his usual station by the door near the phone.

The President's private secretary Cynthia Miano was busy handling the affairs of State as only secretaries to powerful people know how to do.

Harper signaled to Agent Adams who walked over to the President. "Yes, sir?"

"Has the Vice President been informed that she is going to represent me at the Prime Minister's state funeral?"

"Sir," Agent Adams answered, "I believe Misses Miano has notified the Vice President that she might be going but wasn't sure whether or not you would rather attend."

"Well, it's sure as shit it ain't gonna be me. She's the Vice President. That's one of her two jobs. Go to State Funerals and babysit the fucking Senate. Vice President's aren't much good for anything else." The President chuckled to himself as if he were letting the Secret Service Agent in on a secret. Harper whispered, "'Cept with Vice President Bunnell being a good looking woman, she's probably a hell of a good ride in the saddle, don't you think?"

Secret Service Agent Adams did not respond. He had been assigned to other Presidents before and would probably be assigned to others in the future. In fact, it may even be the Vice President herself. So, being professional, Adams simply answered, "I'll notify Misses Miano of your decision, sir."

"Goddamnit, Adams, you boys don't have a sense of humor," Harper bellowed, upset that the Secret Service Agent did not get the joke. "Trouble with you boys is your underwear is too tight and your nuts get all twisted."

"Yes, sir," Adams responded with a straight face. "Will that be all?"

"We'll be leaving for United Petroleum at ten til nine. Notify your crew."

"We'll be ready, Mister President."

President Harper shook his head disgusted with everyone around him. "Not only am I surrounded by idiots but I'm being protected by robots," he mumbled walking back into the other room.

WASHINGTON, D. C.

The F-16 Fighting Falcon taxied to the Air Force hangar and cut its engine. Flynn gathered his gear and thanked the pilot for the ride. When he stepped down the ladder of the fighter jet, Flynn immediately thought of a shore dinner of Blue Crab fresh from the Chesapeake. Flynn made his way towards the hangar. While he walked over the tarmac to his left, Flynn saw there was a lot of activity around either Air Force One, meaning the President was going somewhere, or it was Air Force Two, which meant that the Vice President was about to leave. "Either way," Flynn thought, "someone is going somewhere." Flynn hoped it was the President because, for a brief moment, he thought he could call Patricia and ask her out for dinner. "That's not going to happen," Flynn muttered while he continued his walk towards the main building.

"No, we're long ago through," Flynn said. "She's got her own political life. And the Chief of Staff is on her like stink on shit. I'm not the kind of guy that can give up what I do to be the man-in-waiting. Besides, she's in love with Admiral Moorehouse and everybody in Washington knows it--except his wife."

Flynn decided that he would check into the Willard, dine alone--or find a companion to join him. After all, he was still on vacation. Jackie Armstrong, a close friend at Langley, would be a welcomed guest. She always seemed to have a 'thing' for Flynn every time he was in town or around at the Agency. Flynn never dated her but the thought was intriguing. She was about his age, bright as hell, and had a gorgeous body.

Flynn was enjoying this thought until he saw the headline of the *Washington Post* that was displayed on the table of the flight room. "PRIME MINISTER SOMMERSET ASSASSINATED!!!" Flynn grabbed the newspaper and began to read. He had only been out of touch with the world for a few days and no one called him with this information which he thought was odd. The Deputy Director of Operations for Special Ops certainly would have contacted him. "Why didn't the General call me?" Flynn thought, "What's the problem? Vacation or not, I thought he'd call me."

An airman greeted Flynn and asked, "Sir, Colonel Alexander has requested that I assist you in any way that I can."

Flynn was distracted by the news in the *Post* but looked up briefly and said, "Can you get me a taxi or a ride into D.C.?"

The airman picked up a phone and began talking while Flynn, engrossed in the news, didn't hear him.

"Captain Flynn," the young airman announced. "Your ride to the Capital is waiting, sir."

"What?" Flynn said momentarily distracted. "Oh, yes, thank you, airman."

Flynn picked up his duffel and walked out to the roadway behind the operations building where he had been. There was a car waiting for him.

"Where to, sir?" The airman asked.

"The Willard." Flynn said automatically. He was

still trying to comprehend what he had read in the newspaper and why he wasn't notified by either the Deputy Director or Mollie Farnham about Prime Minister Sommerset's murder. Both of them had his cell phone number. The rest of the trip into Washington was uneventful. Flynn was lost in thought. Before he realized it the car had stopped in front of the Willard hotel.

Flynn thanked the young airman and walked into the lobby. The night manager recognized Flynn immediately and rang for the bell captain.

"Good evening, Mister Flynn. It's always a pleasure to see you, sir."

Flynn put down his duffel bag and said, "Andre, I need my usual suite, if you please. I realize that I don't have a reser...."

"Not a problem, Mister Flynn, we always have your room available for you, sir." Andre knew that Flynn was a frequent and special guest who always tipped everyone in the hotel extremely well and he would make certain that Flynn would be accommodated.

"Andre," Flynn asked picking up the card key, "do you have today's *Post*?"

"Certainly, sir." Andre stepped back for a moment and retrieved a copy of the *Washington Post*. "Here you are, sir."

Flynn dropped a five dollar bill on the counter, never expecting any change. "Thank you, Andre." Flynn said following the bell captain to the elevator.

The elevator went up to the penthouse suite where Flynn had, on occasion, entertained a number of female guests including the former Congresswoman Patricia Bunnell, now the Vice President. As far as the Willard was concerned, Mister Flynn could do anything he wanted.

Flynn handed the bell captain a ten dollar bill just for opening the door. Flynn dismissed the man and turned on the room's television. Before he unpacked, Flynn took a glass and poured himself a tall Jack Daniels's from the bottle in his duffel which he had brought with him from Alaska.

The evening news was just coming on with the lead story concerning the assassination of British Prime Minister Nigel Sommerset.

"British Prime Minister Nigel Sommerset was shot and killed outside his government office this morning here in London.

"All of Great Britain and most of the Western world were shocked this morning as a lone shooter, tentatively identified as Kristen Shults...." Kristen's picture was flashed on the screen and Flynn dropped his glass of Tennessee sour mash to the floor.

"There's no fucking way Kristen could have done this!" Flynn shouted at the television. "This has to be one big mistake."

The reporter continued while Flynn watched in total disbelief. "Scotland yard officials and representatives of the British Secret Service were able to identify the Shults woman from her fingerprints found on the Weatherby 301, rifle used in the assassination and discovered at the scene directly across the Whitehall street where the Prime Minister was gunned down.

"The Irish Republican Army has not, as yet, claimed responsibility for Prime Minister Sommerset's death. But sources at the scene are convinced that Kristen Shults has IRA ties.

"In a bizarre note to this act of terrorism," the

reporter continued, "Kristen Shults is the niece of British Foreign Minister James Saunders. Saunders, as you know, Dan, had been in Houston, Texas at a meeting of foreign ministers and President Harper dealing with the recent oil crisis and the looming crisis in Iran.

"Kristen Shults," the reporter added while her picture flashed back up on the screen, "is the subject of of the most intensive manhunt in recent British history. Although she remains at large at this report, authorities to whom I have spoken feel that her capture is imminent."

The network anchorman came back on the screen as he read, "White House Press Secretary Jonathan Bradley said that President Harper expressed his outrage at the shooting of the British Prime minister. Bradley went on to tell Fox news that Vice President Patricia Bunnell would be representing the United States at the State funeral in London later this week.

"In other news today, Iranian President Jahmir announced that his country has made a break through in Iran's efforts at enriching uranium for peaceful nuclear power purposes. Jahmir also issued a warning to the West that it does not intend to allow any United Nations inspectors into Iran to, as he says, 'spy' on their program.

"Fox news will continue in a moment." A commercial announcement began while Flynn paced his hotel suite talking to himself.

"That poor girl. I wonder what has happened to her? I can't believe that Kris would do anything like that. There is no fucking way that she could have done it or be involved with the IRA for Chrissake! And if those Irish bastards have done anything to hurt her they'll have to deal with me."

As suddenly as Flynn had burst into his tirade, he

became totally silent. He stared out the penthouse window overlooking the Nation's Capital. He knew that he would have to go to Europe not only to find Kristen but also to clear her name. Flynn began making mental preparations for his departure.

After a long while gazing out into the darkness of Washington, Flynn's exhaustion from his day long journey finally overcame him. Flynn lay down on the king sized bed and fell asleep.

Waking up in a cold sweat, Flynn looked at the alarm clock. It was two-thirty. He was still tired but his senses were wide awake and he knew he would never be able to sleep again that night. Flynn got out of the bed and showered. He was going to go over to CIA headquarters at Langley to run through the computer files that he knew were pouring in information on the recent assassination of Prime Minister Sommerset from field agents and analysts in London. Flynn also wanted to get an update on Kristen to see if he could possibly find something that might tip him off where she might be—if she were still alive. In addition, he would write a brief 'in-house' report on what he had discovered in Alaska and turn that over to some other division who could contact the Bureau and NSA, or Homeland Security.

Flynn grabbed a cab outside the Willard. The ride to Langley, Virginia was uneventful while Flynn prioritized his early morning tasks. A light rain began to fall when the cab pulled into Agency Headquarters. Flynn paid the fare and entered the building. He showed the security guard his ID and clipped it on his shirt, as required. Flynn walked to the elevators. He pushed the sixth floor number for the Operations Section. The elevator automatically stopped on the fourth floor where two security guards re-checked his Identification badge. Satisfied that Flynn was a legitimate employee with proper clearance, they allowed the elevator to proceed to the sixth floor. Upon reaching the sixth floor, Flynn used his ID to swipe the computer lock on the door allowing him access to the office complex where most of the United States' Intelligence policy was made and directed to be carried out. Down the hallway, analysts were reviewing their computer screens and printing out reports from all over the world from other field operatives.

Flynn looked through the glass window and caught the attention of an old friend, Jackie Armstrong, the senior supervisor of this shift. Jackie saw Flynn and smiled. She rushed to the locked door and let Flynn enter.

"Well, look at you," Jackie Armstrong said still beaming at Flynn. "Is is you, Flynn. Jeremiah L. Flynn, is it not?"

"How are you darlin'?" Flynn smiled giving Jackie a big hug.

"Don't you darlin me, you scoundrel. I'm still waiting for your call."

"You know I meant to call you, Jackie, but..."

Flynn was interrupted before he could finish while Jackie joked, "But nothing you sonofabitch. You stood me up again."

"Duty dragged me away from you, my lovely. I would never stand you up, darlin, darlin', Jackie."

"Cut the Irish Bullshit and tell the truth. You fell in love with me and then got scared that I'd never let you out of my sight, so you ran."

"Ah, smart as a whip as always. I admit it. I could never fool you."

Jackie laughed, "It's good to see you, Jerry. But

what really brings you here at this hour?"

Flynn was now all business. "Jackie, I need to get on one of your terminals for a few hours."

"No problem. You can use the one in my office. No one will bother you. Is there anything I can help you get?"

"Maybe later," Flynn answered. "Right now I need to dig around and run some tracers." Jackie understood Flynn's guardedness about telling anybody anything. So she left it alone and took him to her office.

Flynn sat down at her desk. "Do you remember how to access one of these?" Jackie asked in jest when Flynn turned on her computer.

"That's why I love you so, Jackie, darlin'" Flynn smiled. "You're the only other person in this whole silly business with a sense of humor."

"I've been trying to tell you that for years, handsome. I know we have a lot in common. Why else would I be saving myself for only you all this time?" Then, as she was about to leave Flynn alone, she added seriously, "If I can help you, Jerry, let me know."

Flynn knew she was sincere in her offer. "Thanks, I will."

The woman closed the office door and walked back on the floor amidst the sea of computers while Flynn watched her through the glass. He always thought very fondly of Jackie Armstrong. She was the only person in the Agency that ever and always called him, 'Jerry'. Flynn thought, "Jackie is a good friend. She's very attractive and very bright. I wonder why I have never dated her?" Flynn dropped his thoughts of Jackie Armstrong and focused on the computer before him.

Flynn began inputting data and cross referencing it

with other data, searching for any leads that might connect United Petroleum, the Koreans, and some Spanish speaking drug country, probably in South America—either Colombia, or Venezuela. After nearly an hour, Flynn could not find any connection other than United Petroleum had offices all over the world. Finally, Flynn decided to print the information and transfer it to another section in the Company and let them run with it.

Next, Flynn turned his attention to Kristen Shults. He called up for any file which had her name in it to see if he could find any connection between her and the assassinated British Prime Minister. The menu file caught his attention. Right before him there was his own name! Flynn called for that file. The screen flashed back, "ACCESS DENIED"! Flynn tried several codes which he had memorized to override, but none of them worked.

Flynn looked at his watch. He needed to finish up in order to catch the early morning trans-Atlantic flight to London.

"Having a problem, Jerry?" Flynn was startled and a little embarrassed that Jackie Armstrong was standing in front of him and he hadn't seen her come into the room.

"Yeah, as a matter of fact," Flynn answered, "What do you make of this?"

Jackie came around her desk and looked at the screen. "Let me see what I can do," she said calmly. Flynn yielded the chair and Jackie sat down. Her fingers flashed across the keyboard while she tried several access codes of her own. None of the codes would allow access to the file. "This is very unusual," she said quietly but determined to continue.

Within a few minutes she stopped and looked up at Flynn. "There's a Director's stop on all access not only to this file but also to your own personal file, Jerry. Either the Director, or someone at his direction, has locked out any access to these files. I've tried to cross check any other files with your reference and have discovered that you are now a *persona non grata,* for some inexplicable reason. Do you have a clue?"

Flynn thought for a minute. "Only thing I can think of is that I am a friend of Kristen Shults."

"What? The woman who assassinated Sommerset?"

Flynn came to Kristen's defense. "She couldn't have done it. I know her too well..."

"Ah, ha! You've been two timing on me, again."

Flynn wasn't in the mood for any levity at this point. He gave Jackie a stern look which she saw meant, "Not Now!"

Jackie went back to the keyboard, "Let me try one more thing." Still nothing. "I'll bet it's the work of Mollie Farnham," Jackie announced.

"Mollie?" Flynn was puzzled, "Why?"

"Don't know. But maybe she's trying to protect you. She works directly under the Director, as you know. Does she know where you are?"

"I believe she might think I'm still on vacation in Alaska. I texted her yesterday..." Flynn thought of the message he sent. "I told her that I was okay, that I couldn't talk from my present location and that I'd be back..."

Jackie smiled, "I'll bet she thought that you were going to call her back, not be back in Washington."

"I think you're right," Flynn replied. "But what does this all mean--the computer locked out?"

"There's something serious going on here." Jackie worked the terminal keys until a new screen came up.

"From what I can tell, you've been placed on the report or 'burn list', and your classification has been revoked, starting at nine today." She looked up at Flynn with a worried looked on her face and continued. "Who did you piss off this time, Jerry?"

A confused and serious Flynn answered, "I haven't a clue."

"Well, handsome, you'd better go into hiding or whatever you special ops people do until you can figure this whole mess out. 'Cuz right now, you are wanted by our own people as a possible traitor and accomplice to Kristen Shults." She turned the flat screen monitor towards Flynn who read the same words she just spoke.

Flynn shook his head. He couldn't believe what he read. "How can I figure this out when I don't really know what it is all about?"

"Think about it. You'll figure it out, I know you will," Jackie assured him. "I'll do whatever I can here to help you. But, I don't want to read about you in the Obits, or me, for that matter waking up dead some morning."

Flynn looked her in the eyes and said, "Don't do anything that might jeopardize yourself or your career. I can take care of myself. I don't want you to get into any trouble on my account."

"Too late. All keystrokes are recorded and guess who gets to see them?"

Flynn had no idea. "I couldn't tell you."

"Mollie Farnham!" Jackie revealed. Then added, "She'll know that you were in the building by nine o'clock when she gets here. And, she'll know we were looking in her programs."

"What will she do to you?" Flynn asked concerned for his friend.

"Probably nothing. I'll tell her that I let you use my office, you know, for old times sake, blah, blah, blah, and that you did it all by yourself."

"Good idea. Blame it all on me," Flynn meant it. "Do you think Mollie will buy it?"

"Sure. Why not? The official notice about your status being revoked doesn't hit all the computers in our system until nine A.M. That's why you were allowed access this morning. No one knows 'til it becomes official, see? She probably didn't think she needed to make it active any sooner because you were, or so she thought, still up in Alaska."

"Jackie," Flynn was still puzzled, "I don't understand why, just because I know Kristen Shults, that the Agency would suspend my classification. It seems a little too extreme, doesn't it?"

"Yes, you're right. It is extreme. But the Company has to cover its political ass and appear squeaky clean. And, for the moment, you're tainted goods because of your 'relationship' with a suspected terrorist."

"Kristen is no more of a terrorist than I am," Flynn growled.

"That's neither here nor there at the moment." Jackie Armstrong started to write down some numbers on a piece of paper and handed it to Flynn. "Here, these are some codes that you can use to contact me directly from anywhere in the world. And, no one from our Agency will ever know, or be able to connect them to me. All you have to do is ask for 'Alice Long'."

"Alice Long?" Flynn asked. "Why Alice Long?"

"Oh, come on, Jerry," Jackie smiled. "Tommy Boyce and Bobby Hart.... 'You're still my favorite girlfriend, Alice Long'..."

Flynn smiled, "You're one wild woman. Christ, you should be in the field."

"I've learned a few little tricks from you guys in the field these past fifteen years. You'd best haul ass, lover."

"Oh, one other thing before I go," Flynn added. "I ran some info on United Petroleum but couldn't make any connections." He passed over his notes and the computer print out that he made. "Would you look this over and see if you can find any correlation between them and activity in South America—probably Venezuela or Colombia—North Korea, and Alaska? You might check satellite recon photos."

"No sweat. I'll run it over when things are clear. You take care of that body for me." Jackie gave Flynn a hug and concluded, "I really do love you, you know." Then she took her keys and handed them to Flynn.

"What's this, the key to your place?"

"Not exactly. Those are the keys to my car. You take it and park it at Dulles in the short term lot. Have a safe flight to Europe. And don't forget to call me on those codes I gave you."

"What kind of a car is it?" Flynn teased, "A Ford Grand Torino?"

Jackie gave him a wink as she smiled, "Not quite. It's the red Corvette over by the guard gate. Hey, one last thing."

"Yes, mother."

"I don't have to tell you to change your name, ID, etc, do I, smart ass?"

"No, I think I have that part covered." Flynn looked at the keys and leaned over and gave Jackie a long, deep kiss. "Thanks, darlin'."

Jackie was breathless, shocked by his kiss. She grinned while she watched Flynn leave her office and walk to the elevators. "Be careful, Jerry," Jackie whispered.

Flynn took the elevator down and signed out at the main guard desk before leaving the building. He went to the parking garage and found Jackie's red 'Vette just where she said it would be. "Hot car," Flynn commented, "Just like the woman. Makes sense." He unlocked the door, got in and hit the ignition. The Corvette's engine purred just like the cat she was. Flynn drove out of the CIA compound and headed for the Interstate and Dulles. He would have about an extra hour before he could catch his flight to Amsterdam, thanks to Jackie Armstrong and her red Corvette.

The drive to Dulles International Airport was lonely for Flynn. He was now on everyone's radar. He didn't know exactly why while he thought, "it must have something to do with Kris Shults. If I can find her, assuming that she's still alive, and prove her innocence, she would be cleared and so would I. But that's going to take some time and work and a few thousand miles. And who knows what else," Flynn wondered as he drove on. "Shit, can't anything about this job ever be easy?"

Flynn pulled into the short-term lot. "There's an ATM machine at the airport that would allow me to withdraw enough cash to hold me over until I can reach my safety deposit box in Amsterdam." Once in Amsterdam, Flynn knew he had stashed away nearly a quarter of a million in cash, along with new ID's, passports and credit cards. He was on a mission. Solo. Since he, for all intents and purposes, was a man without a country or at least was no longer an Agency operative.

Flynn would have to go this mission alone. "Alone is good," Flynn thought. "It lets me focus on what I have to do without distraction. I like being this way. Alone. That's where I need to be."

The rain continued to fall while Flynn parked the car in the short-term lot, as Jackie had requested. When he walked toward the terminal the loud blast of the planes taking off momentarily caused Flynn to have a flashback to the time he was just shot down over the jungle near the Llanos, on the border between Colombia and Venezuela. "I was set up then, and I think I'm being set up now."

Flynn tried to dismiss that thought but somewhere back in his brain he couldn't let it go. He went to the ticket counter of KLM and bought a first-class seat on the first flight to Amsterdam. Since there was at least an hour and a half before check in at the gate, Flynn, with no baggage, went through security and proceeded to the gates. "I can get a cup of coffee and maybe a doughnut or something to hold me over," Flynn thought walking down the concourse.

His ticket on the 5:50 A.M. flight was a non-stop to Amsterdam and indicated that his plane would board at gate 53. Flynn familiarized himself with where the gate was and walked back to the only open coffee kiosk to have a cup of coffee and something to eat.

Flynn was going 'home' to his apartment in Amsterdam. In a few more hours he would be on familiar ground. From there he hoped he would be able to trace Kristen's trip to England. He needed to start at the first square before he could go any further. He had some well paid for 'friends' who might know something that they would be willing to share with him, for a price. "I need to get the scent of the rabbit," Flynn thought, "before I can find the trail."

What Flynn would soon find out--that he too, was a prey being hunted by those who didn't want him to ever find the trail.

Flynn bought his coffee at the kiosk and walked over to the KLM boarding gate, Gate 53. Flynn stood off to the side behind a pillar and looked over the passengers who were to be traveling on this flight. When he scanned the crowd, Flynn caught sight of of a British MI-6, operative, David Greene. There was an unwritten code among the world's operatives--'recognize and report', but do nothing to blow each others cover. And, if you were doing business, neither would speak except as causal travelers in light conversation. The proper words, codes as they were called, would indicate whether or not a meeting or a further discussion was needed.

David Greene, pretending to be reading a newspaper, was doing what Flynn had been doing, scanning the crowd. He caught Flynn's abrupt about face movement and watched as Flynn went into the men's rest room. Casually, Greene put down the paper and slowly made his way into the restroom.

Flynn was at the sink when Greene came in. Flynn signaled that all was clear before he spoke. "Hello, David."

"Hello, Flynn. Look, Old Man, we need your help finding your bird. She's gone bad and is lost."

Flynn did not let on that he knew anything. "What are you talking about?"

"Let's be blunt, shall we. We know that your girl friend, Kristen Shults, murdered the Prime Minister and we'd appreciate your help in finding her."

"I don't know any such thing, David," Flynn

replied. "I don't believe Kris could kill anyone. And, if you ask me, the whole thing stinks of a set-up."

"You might be right, of course," Greene said realizing that Flynn was sincere in his belief. "Which is all the more reason to bring her in and find out what it is she knows of the matter so we can apprehend the rightful killer. Now, will you help us, Old Man?"

Flynn washed his hands and, still watching David Greene in the mirror, reached over for a paper towel. "You've known me for long time, David. We've worked together before. But this time I can't help you."

"Can't or won't?"

Flynn dropped the paper towel in the waste basket. "A little of both, I guess. I truly don't have any idea where Kristen might be. And I stick by what I said earlier. I can't believe she had anything to do with this business."

"You know, Flynn, we're not supposed to fall in love."

"I am not in love with her, David." There was a cold chill in his voice as Flynn continued. "If I find her, and she is the one you're looking for, I'll bring her in. If she's not, I'll find out who is and I'll let you know. But right now, I can't help you."

"Let me say this to you, Old Man," Green responded, "if we find her, and we will. Don't get in our way. We both know what will happen if you do—friends or not, Flynn."

"I hope it never comes to that, David," Flynn countered. Greene left him alone in the restroom. Flynn stared into the mirror for a long moment. "And you'd better not get in my way either, David. Friends or not."

The public address announcement came on calling

for boarding for KLM Flight 2143, non-stop to Amsterdam at Gate 53. Flynn walked out of the rest room to the boarding area. Most of the passengers were assembling in line and beginning to hand the Flight Attendant their tickets and began boarding. Flynn spotted David Greene sitting in a chair, slightly slumped over to one side. Flynn felt instant danger when he walked over to the MI-6 man. Greene was dead. Stuffed in his hand was a business card which Flynn took and looked at it. Printed on the card was the head of a tiger. Flynn placed the card into his pocket.

Flynn noticed a wheelchair over near the gate and he hurried to retrieve it. Flynn wheeled the chair over to Greene's seat and started to talk to the dead man as he assisted the body into the chair. While doing so, Flynn exchanged his passport and plane ticket for Greene's. Flynn took a pair of sunglasses out of Greene's coat pocket and put them on the dead man covering his opened eyes. Then Flynn wheeled him over to the front of the line where the flight attendant took his ticket and allowed Flynn to cut in--stopping the line.

"I'm Mister Flynn's aide," Flynn announced to the flight attendant while handing her the ticket. "He's dead tired, Miss. If I could put him in his seat, I'll be right back. There is another associate of Mister Flynn's who will meet him in Amsterdam."

The flight attendant answered, "Of course, go right in. Do you need any assistance, sir?"

"No, thank you. We'll be fine." Flynn wheeled Greene's body down the rampway and on to the plane. He picked up the dead man and placed him in what would have been Flynn's first class seat. Flynn buckled David Greene's seat belt and continued to talk as if the dead man were alive. "All set, Mister Flynn. Good. Mister Johannsen will meet you in Amsterdam, sir. Have a pleasant flight, sir." Flynn folded up the wheelchair and as he deplaned he whispered to another flight attendant. "Mister Flynn has been ill and needs his rest. Would you see to it that he is not disturbed at all until he arrives in Amsterdam?"

"Certainly, sir. As you wish."

Flynn took the wheelchair back down the rampway and returned it next to the gate. He looked around at the crowd studying them quickly before he disappeared in the main terminal. Without hesitation, Flynn walked out of the main terminal and went straight to where he had parked Jackie's Corvette.

"Forgive me Jackie, but I need to borrow your car for a little while longer. He turned the key and drove out to the parking gate, paid the attendant then headed for the Interstate. He planned on being in Shaker Heights, Ohio by sunset. He was going home all right, but not home to Amsterdam, Holland. It was his secret home he had bought under an assumed name. He was an attorney and closing on the house without the buyer being present was not a problem so long as all the proper papers were signed and in proper order. Flynn had made certain of that and that the purchase would never be traced back to him.

HOUSTON, TEXAS

The Secret Service agents were busy checking and re-checking preparations to escort President Irwin W. Harper from his suite to United Petroleum's corporate office wing. It was eight-fifty A.M. according to Special Agent Adams' watch.

"Have you directed the building management that we will be using elevator Number 3?" Adams barked into his radio.

The reply came back over his radio, "Yes, sir. I have the key for the manual override. They've assured me that no one has been allowed on that particular car from eight this morning. The car has been waiting on the President's floor for the last half hour."

Agent Adams made a note of this on his checklist in a metal binder. He turned to another agent and started the run-through of security measures in place for the President from the time he was to leave his suite until he returned after the scheduled meeting.

The intercom rang and Adams picked it up. "Special Agent Adams."

"Agent Adams, this is Pete Eisenmann."

Adams recognized the voice of his superior, the head of the White House detail. "Yes, sir, Agent Eisenmann."

"John, I am on my way back to Washington. I will be escorting the detail for Vice President Bunnell for her trip to London for the State funeral of Prime Minister Sommerset. You should have gotten my written directive this morning from Williams."

"Yes, sir, I have it. We are going over everything now."

"Good. I don't expect any problems but stay on your toes." Pete Eisenmann concluded.

"Roger that. Good bye, sir."

Secret Service Agent Adams went back to his checklist. This was his first assignment as Agent-in-Charge, and he was a little edgy. Adams ran through the entire checklist again with all his men. Then he went to see the President to find out if he had made any other changes in his itinerary.

"No plans for any side trips today, Adams," President Harper assured the Secret Serviceman. "It's all business today. And make a note, Pardner, today President Harper is gonna kick some Korean ass."

Adams thought to himself without showing any emotion, "No wonder they call you the 'Cowboy'." Then he said, "Thank you, Mister President. We are ready whenever you are, sir."

"I'll be ready in two minutes after I take a final piss before we go. Just give a knock and I'll be with you."

After two minutes, Adams knocked on the President's door. "Mister President, it's time to go, sir."

The door to the President's suite opened and President Harper stepped out. He was dressed in a dark blue pin-stripped suit with cowboy boots and a ten gallon Stetson. "Let's get on with this rodeo, Pardner," Harper bellowed at the Secret Serviceman. "This is gonna be a day to mark down in history, boys."

The President marched forward and Adams began talking into his radio, "He's on the move." Secret Service Agents scurried about opening doors, checking the hallways, and forming a protective barrier around the President while he strode into the waiting elevator car. Adams was joined by three other men. When the elevator doors closed President Harper turned to Agent Adams. "Loosen up, Pard. When is the Admiral going to join us?"

"Sir, Admiral Moorehouse, and Secretary of State Makoweic have already gone down. Only Director Pfohl is still in his suite. He will be the last to leave the floor, sir."

It only took less than two minutes for elevator car Number 3, to descend the thirty-three floors to the lobby. The elevator arrived exactly on time. However, when the doors to the car opened the President of the United States of America and four Secret Service Agents were all dead!

WASHINGTON, D. C.

A private cell phone call was answered. A scrambled voice spoke, "Yes. I have just learned that Flynn arrived in Washington. A 'burn notice' has been issued since nine this morning. We believe he will run to Europe. We have anticipated everything so far. But there was a minor incident. MI-6 intercepted him unexpectedly at Dulles. The fool we had watching him lost him and terminated the wrong man. We will see to it that Flynn gets blamed so that our 'cousins' will be hunting him as well....The roundup in Houston is over....Perfect.......No, no, he will never get to her. It is impossible....Of course we have someone with her...Yes, I will double check with them.....Yes, I will see to it personally....Very well.... Until then."

NEAR BELFAST, NORTHERN IRELAND

Kristen Shults stared into the early morning sky. Behind her the sun was just coming up over the water. In front of her were the dimming lights of a small Northern Irish town on the outskirts of Belfast. A safe harbor for transients. "Safe for whom?" Kristen thought to herself. She was in despair. She was now the most hunted person in recent British history. Only Jack the Ripper was more notorious. Kristen felt lonely and alone as she sank deeper into depression. "I was a respected International Analyst only a few days ago. Today, I'm an outlaw. A suspected murderer, now in the hands of the IRA." To them Kristen was a heroine. In reality she was a victim. She had been a victim of a kidnapping. A victim of rape. And now, an accused victim of murdering someone whom she had respected.

"Where is the Justice, Lord?" Kristen thought, "Where is Flynn, Lord?" While she stared into the water again she thought of times she and Flynn talked. "Didn't he warn me how circumstances could turn someone's life around for good or bad? Hadn't he said how the system manipulated many people and that an innocent person could be placed in jeopardy of his own life? How did Flynn know all of these things? Was he just more worldly or was there more to him than he ever told me as I often suspected?"

The power boat's engines slowed when they entered the hidden harbor. Captain Andrew Owens guided the craft expertly into the slip. Timothy Hartnett was at the bow on the starboard side and fastened the the bowline to the mooring cleat.

"Maureen," Owens called out to Kristen, "grab the

pier post and hold her fast."

Kristen responded to the order which snapped her back to the present moment. She was surprised to see Timothy on the pier ahead of her. Owens cut the engines and Timothy helped Kristen out of the launch and onto the dock. Owens followed them. They all walked in silence. Kristen's vision began to blur again as tears filled her eyes.

"Thank you, Andrew," Hartnett said to the seaman. "You'll be taken care of at the pub, as usual."

Owens looked over at Kristen and said, "You have done the cause proud, lass. May God bless you, Maureen."

Hartnett took Kristen by the arm and led her away from the pier and up a narrow street into town. The two had walked about three blocks when Kristen stopped suddenly. "Where are you taking me?"

"Someplace where you'll be safe. With friends who will look after ye." Hartnett regained his grip on her arm and led her another block and half where they turned down an alley between row houses. Timothy brought them to a halt. Then he knocked on a door. Within seconds the door was opened and an old man stood before them.

"Paddy," Timothy addressed the old gent. "We need to sit a spell."

"Timo!" The old man exclaimed happy to see young Hartnett. "Come in with ye lad and out of the damp air and have a cup of tea." The old Irishman looked at Kristen but didn't speak to her, knowing full well who she was, and why they were at his door. Instinctively, the old man looked up and down the alley before he shut the door and bolted it.

"Sit, sit, now," Paddy said ushering them to the wooden kitchen table. He took two mugs from an open cupboard and placed them before Timothy and Kristen. He added loose tea to the cups and poured hot water in each. Then he poured himself a little more hot water in his own mug and placed the pot back on the stove before he joined them at the table.

Timothy sipped his tea before he spoke to the old man. "Paddy, our Colleen here needs safe passage...."

He was interrupted by the wave of an old man's hand. A gesture which spoke volumes. "Hold your whist now, me boy," Paddy said. "You don't need to tell me a thing, lad." Then he switched into Gaelic and continued, "I know who this woman is and why she is wanted by the police, the army and the entire bloody British Empire. All arrangements have been made for us to take her to the convent of the Sisters of Charity at Noch Sheegan. She will be accepted as a novice into the Order without question. Mother Superior has her orders, too."

"But, Paddy," Hartnett answered in Gaelic, "won't the nuns suspect anything? Won't they talk?"

"Timo, me boy, if ye spent more time in the Church instead of the Pub, you'd be knowin' that the convent at Noch Sheegan is cloistered. They all have a taken a vow of silence!"

WASHINGTON, D. C.

The Vice President had already boarded Air Force Two while the crew were making their final preparations for takeoff from Andrews Air Force Base for the flight to London where Patricia Bunnell would be attending the State funeral of slain British Prime Minister, Nigel

Sommerset. The hotline call came in just as the big jet started to taxi towards the main, active runway.

Secret Service Special Agent Gordon Young looked at the phone and knew that it meant one of two things. Either the United States was at War, or something happened to the President.

He answered the call apprehensively, "Agent Young."

"Gordon, this is Agent Thompson in Houston. The President has been killed!"

"Say again. Repeat that, please,." Agent Young was in shock and disbelief.

"President Harper is dead. He was assassinated in the elevator along with four of our own agents. Take all precautions to guard the Vice President. She must be sworn in ASAP. Get her to the White House as quickly and as safely as possible."

There was a brief pause while Agent Young tried to comprehend what had been said.

Agent Thompson nearly shouted into the phone. "Agent Young do you copy?"

"Yes, I copy. What the fuck is going on?"

"We don't know. But get her ass to the White House. One of the Justices will be there to meet her and swear her in as President."

"We're on our way," Agent Young was now all business. And now, his business was to protect the Acting President of the United States and get her back to Washington and to the White House so that she could take the Oath of Office. He activated his radio. "All personnel...We are returning to the gate. President Harper has been killed. Acting President Bunnell must be taken to the White House. All agents use extreme caution and keep alert. No one, I mean NO ONE is to get near Acting President Bunnell until we are safely in the White House."

Patricia Bunnell heard the commotion but before she could say anything Agent Young was already near her and the look on his face meant trouble. "What is it, Agent Young?" Patricia asked.

"The President has been killed. We are returning to the gate and you are going to be taken to the White House where one of the Justices of the Supreme Court will meet you and administer the Oath of Office. Right now, Madam, you are the Acting President of the United States."

Secret Service agents converged on the jumbo jet as it came back to and entered the hangar. This would add additional security to which the agents and the Command Pilot agreed. Agent Young held the Acting President back while the cabin door opened. The movable stairs were brought to the doorway and all agents were on full alert with weapons drawn. When Gordon Young was satisfied that all was secure he lead Patricia Bunnell down the steps and right into the limousine. Several police and Secret Service vehicles sped out of the hangar and raced across town to the White House.

Patricia Bunnell was stunned and speechless. "What the hell is happening to me—to the world?" She thought. "It's all so unreal. I never thought I would become President...at least not like this."

Acting President Bunnell sat motionless but tense while the motorcade sped towards the White House. Agent Young was in constant chatter on his radio with all other agents directing this duty. Patricia's mind was swirling with a thousand thoughts at once. "Was this some kind of terrorist plot? First the Prime Minister, now the President—it had to be some conspiracy, some plot against the West. What will I do? I'm now responsible for over three hundred million Americans? I guess it is true that a Vice President is only a heartbeat away from being in the most powerful office in the world. And now, I am in that office." Patricia drifted in an out of her thoughts but one kept popping up that she couldn't get rid of— Flynn.

Quietly and unnoticed, a small tear welled up in her ocean blue eyes while she thought of the one man who could make some sense out of this and who she could rely on to assure her that everything would be all right. And, in that same train of thought, Patricia Bunnell came to the realization that he was now gone forever. She knew Flynn hated all politicians and now she was the politicians politician—President! There would never be anything between them again. "What will I do without you, Flynn?" Patricia whispered as the limo entered the safety of the White House.

The Chief Justice of the Supreme Court was waiting and within a few moments she was President Patricia Bunnell.

HOUSTON, TEXAS

From the moment that elevator # 3, opened into the Lobby and the bodies of President I. W. Harper, and four Secret Servicemen: Daniels, Edwards, Adams and Donovan were found poisoned by a deadly gas, confusion, commotion and chaos erupted in Houston with shockwaves rippling over the world.

The news media flashed bulletins to all parts of

the globe and a traumatic shockwave hit all who heard the terrible news. Network anchor men and women rushed to their studios to get on the air to relay the volumes of information that was streaming in from Houston to affiliates around the country and news services world-wide.

While emergency preparations were being made to fly the bodies back to Washington, the Federal Bureau of Investigation, the Secret Service, Homeland Security, the Houston Police Department, and even the Texas Rangers all joined in one of the most intensive homicide investigations in American history.

One man smiled when he heard the news. "The pieces of Operation Lifeblood are falling neatly into place," Tiger thought. "You got what you deserved Harper, you arrogant ass. Nobody gets in my way and lives!"

Upstairs in the Executive office of United Petroleum, CEO David Laird poured himself a tall glass of Crown Royal. He was visibly shaken by the news of Harper's death. "Marge," Laird addressed his secretary, "this shit is spooky as hell. Get me Kim Moon Jung on the phone, immediately. Christ, who would have believed he had the balls to kill the President?"

Laird chugged the whiskey down and poured himself another, adding a bottle of ice cold beer to go along with it while Marge made the call to Tiger's suite.

"Sir," Marge said into the intercom, "Mister Kim Moon Jung is on the line."

"Tiger," Laird said in nervous fright, "why Harper?"

"Don't play the fool, Laird," came the angered reply. "He was no longer of use to any of us in our plan.

He was becoming a source of annoyance to me and I could sense that it was time to stop his opposition. We need to have the weak woman in the White House. She can be controlled by our source there more easily than that ass, Harper." The Korean continued, "I trust you now understand that I will tolerate nothing that gets in my way!"

Laird was apprehensive. "Shall I notify the remaining others?"

"Yes," Tiger replied. Then with a sinister laugh he added, "No need to notify Foreign Minister Saunders, I have already taken steps to deal with him."

Laird couldn't control himself as he blurted, "Him, too?"

"Be careful, Laird," Tiger warned, "you are beginning to drink too much. And I have no need of a drunk in my plan."

Laird's glass of Crown Royal dropped from his hand and smashed on the floor.

THE ROAD TO SHAKER HEIGHTS, OHIO

Flynn was making good time in Jackie Armstrong's Corvette and was near the Ohio border when he needed to re-fuel the 'Vette. Flynn was just north of Pittsburgh, on I-79, when he pulled off the Interstate to gas up at the nearest station and convenience mart.

Flynn filled up the tank and noticed that the price of gasoline was at a record high. "What the fuck is going on with these prices for gasoline?" He mumbled while he went inside to pay and get a cup of coffee.

The young attendant was watching a small screen television when Flynn approached the counter with his coffee. Flynn stood there for a moment until he finally said, "Excuse me?" getting the young man's attention.

"Oh," the attendant said startled by the presence of Flynn at the counter. "I'm sorry, sir. Can you believe that news?"

Flynn was not looking for conversation but the young man's expression told him that something was troubling the young man. "What news is that?" Flynn asked.

"About the President. President Harper was killed in Houston this morning!"

"What?" Flynn said in concerned disbelief.

"Yeah, haven't you heard? The President was killed by poison gas in an elevator in Houston. Four body guards also died."

Flynn tensed with anger listening to the young man. Then he glanced over to the small TV that the attendant had been watching. The volume seemed to get louder while Flynn focused on the program. A network anchor was reporting to the nation on the tragic events of the murder of President Irwin W. Harper. Flynn took his change and raced for the 'Vette and tuned the radio to the first clear frequency broadcasting the news. Flynn gunned the engine and whipped back onto the Interstate while listening with keen interest to the reporters. Flynn couldn't quite believe what he was hearing. Indeed, the President and four Secret Servicemen were assassinated by an unspecified poison gas that was affixed to the top of the elevator car.

"Vice President Patricia Bunnell was apparently about to take off from Andrews Air Force base to attend the State funeral of British Prime Minister Nigel Sommerset when she was notified of President Harper's death. Now, Acting President, Miss Bunnell, will be sworn in at the White House within minutes by the Chief Justice of the Supreme Court, Calvin Brandt, who will administer the Oath of Office making Patricia Bunnell, President Bunnell.

"The body of President Harper is due back in the Nation's Capital sometime early this evening. The exact time of arrival is not being disclosed by the White House at this time. We will continue to bring you more details as they become available...."

Flynn suddenly thought of Patricia. "Now she's the President! Holy fuck! What must she be thinking right now. What kind of President are you going to be, Pat?" While he drove on he couldn't help but think that if he had quit his job at the Agency and stayed with her he could be...no, he could never live like that. He hated the political bullshit. The glad-handing, back-stabbing rotten life of a two faced liar was never in his make up.

For the next few hours that it took for Flynn to reach the Cleveland suburban city of Shaker Heights, Flynn listened to the news. Flynn immediately believed that the assassination of Prime Minister Sommerset and President Harper must be connected. "An international plot of some kind? For what purpose? How safe is Patricia? What is the motivational force behind these two murders?"

When he pulled into his driveway at 162 Parkland Drive, adjoining the Shaker Heights Country Club's fourth hole, Flynn said, "I've got to figure this out."

Jeremiah Flynn was home. He could think things out here in the privacy and safety of knowing that no one knew where he was. That simple thought alone gave Flynn comfort. He enjoyed his solitude. He was alone, again.

Flynn went to the spiral staircase and went up to the master suite. He flipped off his shoes and lay back on the king size bed. In a moment he was sound asleep.

It was a little past three in the morning when Flynn awoke. He showered, shaved and put on clean clothes. Flynn felt refreshed and relaxed.

"I should have come here for vacation instead of going to Alaska," Flynn mumbled. "At least here no one is trying to shoot my ass off." Flynn walked down the staircase through the living room and dining room to the kitchen. He hadn't eaten anything that he could remember. Unfortunately, the cupboard was pretty bare and the food in the freezer would take too long to cook. Flynn opened the refrigerator and took out a bottle of Dingler beer. "The breakfast of champions it's not," Flynn said twisting off the cap. He chugged it down in a few swallows. It tasted so good Flynn decided to have another. This Dingler he drank more slowly taking it with him when he went to the step down sun room off the kitchen. This room had a wall of glass doors looking out over his pool and expansive and secluded back yard. Flynn picked up a remote and turned on a flat screen, High Definition television.

Flynn sipped his Dingler while he watched the news channel repeating as many updated stories as they could on the assassination of President Harper and the four Secret Servicemen.

"....Correspondent Winston Chandler has Chief of Staff Admiral Moorehouse with him. Winston..."

"Thank you, Dan," the correspondent said, "I'm with Michael Moorehouse, President Harper's Chief of Staff. Admiral, what are the latest developments in this tragic story?"

"Not much more than you probably all ready know, Winston. The FBI, and Homeland Security are conducting the investigation along with assistance of the Houston police."

"Admiral," Winston Chandler asked, "are there any leads as to how, why or who might be responsible for this terrible crime?"

"None that I am free to discuss at this time. Other than we believe that the assassination of President Harper and that of Prime Minister Sommerset are somehow related and possibly the result of a rouge CIA agent who was recently given his burn notice by the Agency. This man, who was a lover of the alleged shooter of the British Prime Minister, Kristen Shults, may be leading a terrorist cell to disrupt the governments of the West."

"Can you tell us the name of the man you suspect, Admiral?"

"I'd rather not at this time. I will add that the National Security Agency, under the able leadership of William Pfohl, is tracking this man down and we expect to have him brought in for questioning very soon."

Flynn immediately knew that Moorehouse was implicating him in this plot."You no good motherfucker, Moorehouse!" Flynn screamed at the television. "You just made my shit-list!"

"Admiral, will you be continuing to serve in President Bunnell's administration?"

Admiral Moorehouse looked directly into the camera and said, "Let me assure and re-assure the American people that our government will continue to function under President Patricia Bunnell. The Constitution preserves that for all of us. And I, for one, will assist our new President, President Bunnell, in any capacity that she desires of me to make the transition to her administration as smooth as possible."

Flynn couldn't take anymore of Patricia's latest lover. He pushed the power off button on the remote and commented, "I'm sure you'll assist her, you fuck! You want to keep working under her, or is it the other way around, you sonofabitch!" Flynn threw the remote against the wall. Then he finished his Dingler. "All right, Sport," he said to himself, "let's get to work."

Flynn went into his office and unlocked the antique roll top desk and lifted the top. He opened a drawer and took out a yellow legal pad. His first notation was to call Jackie Armstrong and let her know that he still had her Corvette, and why it wasn't at Dulles as she expected. "I also need to find out what, if anything, she might have learned about my status being revoked. Why was I given a burn notice?"

Flynn jotted down three headings. The first, he wrote the name 'Kristen', the second column he headed with 'Patricia' and the third he labeled, 'United Petroleum'. Flynn stared at the paper for a long time. Then, directly under the 'Kristen' and 'Patricia' names, he wrote 'assassination'. Under the United Petroleum heading he noted the word, 'drugs' and 'Alaska'.

"The only connection I can see," Flynn thought studying the legal pad, "is that I am or were closely associated with both women. That I was the one who reported the drug activity in Alaska. And the fact that United Petroleum was stamped on the boxes."

The more Flynn recalled his Alaskan experience the more he began to realize that someone had monitored or intercepted his cell phone call to the Agency whereby he tipped them off to the drug smugglers. "And then that someone relayed my position back to those Koreans in Alaska with the fact that I had discovered their operation."

"Sonofabitch!" Flynn exclaimed. "someone at CIA...no, not necessarily," he re-thought. "It could be NSA, since they listen to phone traffic...there's a rat somewhere that I need to find. Either at Langley or at NSA headquarters. It's no wonder they issued my 'burn notice'. They want me dead but what's the big picture as to why?"

He wrote his name in the center of the legal pad and circled it over and over. Then he drew three lines— one from each column name to his own name. "What do they know or think that I know?" Flynn asked himself. "And what's the connection between the murders of Prime Minister Sommerset and President Harper, and drug trafficking through Alaska?"

Flynn pushed himself away from the roll top desk and began pacing about his office. Nothing came to him while he paced. Finally, "I have to call Jackie and see if she had discovered anything that might help me put the pieces of this puzzle together."

"But...can she be trusted?" Flynn stopped momentarily in thought.. "...Or can Mollie Farnham? Or even Deputy Director Dimmler?" Flynn came to the realization that, just like always, a good operative never truly trusts anyone. "I've got to be very careful. Especially since that dork Moorehouse has turned the hounds loose on me. But I've got to get some answers and to do that I gotta chance exposing myself. I don't like it, but I need to do it. So, I have to call Jackie."

Flynn looked at the clock over his desk. The illuminated numbers read: 5:07. Flynn sat back down at the desk and picked up his BlackBerry. He almost pushed the 'yes' to complete the call when he suddenly stopped. "There's someone listening, remember?"

Flynn decided to pick up a prepaid phone. "I'll use it once and throw it away." Flynn went to his wall safe and took out a 9mm Glock. He stuffed it behind his back in his pants. Then he went to a hall closet and put on a light, dark blue jacket before walking outside to Jackie's 'Vette. He drove over to the mall to the Wall-Mart.

The always open super store had a prepaid cell phone for thirty-two dollars. Flynn paid in cash and went back to the car to make his call to it's owner.

Flynn punched in the secret number that Jackie gave him. The call was answered on the second ring. "Jackie, my love," Flynn started but was interrupted by a sharp female voice on the other end.

"You bastard, Jerry," Jackie screeched, "what have you done with my car?"

"Sorry about that. But something came up rather unexpectedly at the airport."

"Where the hell are you?" Jackie asked before immediately answering her own question. "Never mind, don't tell me. I don't want to know." Then calming down she asked, "Are you all right?"

"Yes, my love, I'm still in one piece," Flynn responded.

"Good! Because when I see you I'm going to kill you myself! I had to take a goddamn cab all over Washington last night looking for my car."

"Jackie," Flynn replied sincerely, "I'm sorry about keeping your car. I needed it to get away." Then he got to the point of his call. "Were you able to find out anything about United Petroleum and why I am America's number one asshole as far as the Company is concerned?"

"It took me a while to find out some information on United Petroleum, but after my adventure last night, I know why you're the biggest ass in the Company."

Flynn shook his head, she wouldn't let it go. "I will make it up to you, I promise. Now, what did you find out?"

"I'm going to hold you to that promise, big boy. Okay, here's what I got. The list of Directors, Officers and major stockholders in United Petroleum reads like an international Who's Who. David Laird, President, and CEO, understandable...Kim Moon Jung, a Korean 'typhoon' who seeks unification for Korea and has some secret and undisclosed ties with Kim Moon-il of the North...."

"You mean TYCOON, don't you? Not Typhoon..." Flynn interrupted.

"Don't loose your sense of humor, you big lug," Jackie shot back. Then she continued, "Next, James Saunders, the British Foreign Minister. Sheik Mohammad al Anzarisad of Syria, Don Carlos Escobar of Venezuela, the world biggest drug pusher. And are you ready for the grand finale?"

"Come on Jackie, don't be a royal pain in the ass," Flynn said.

"The late President of the U. S. of A., Irwin W. Harper!"

"Jesus, Mary and Joseph!" Flynn exclaimed.

"No lover, they weren't on the list."

Flynn didn't follow her comment. "Who?"

"Jesus, Mary and Joseph...they weren't on the list."

"You are a twenty-four carat pain in the ass, Kid."

Flynn laughed.

"Yes, but do you still love me, Jerr?"

"You know it." Flynn couldn't help but like this woman. "Now, what about me?"

"You, Jeremiah L. Flynn, are a wanted man. Scuttlebutt has it that you are the Bureau's number one suspect in the murder of the President."

"What?" Flynn was astonished. "I was in Washington when he was murdered. You know that."

"Yes, I know that. But nobody else knows it—or will admit it. Seems you didn't check in with her highness as you were supposed to. There's some fucked up thinking going around the Agency that you went to Houston and killed the President so your girlfriend could get the top job!"

"Who's behind this load of bullshit?" Flynn asked in disbelief.

"None other than your friend and competitor for the hand of the new President, Admiral Michael A. Moorehouse."

"Sonofabitch. What does Dimmler think?"

"He's been conspicuously silent on the issue. It was he, or her highness, the slut herself, who slapped the lock on your file when you didn't report in as ordered. You went rouge-off the reservation-and a 'burn notice' is out on your ass, as cute as it is."

"This is unbelievable! I go on vacation for the first time in my career, some oriental assholes try to shoot me full of holes, and the next thing you know, I'm a flipped out psycho-killer of the President."

"That just about sums it all up, Jerry. Nicely done."

Flynn couldn't resist, "Does this mean that now

you won't marry me?"

Jackie Armstrong laughed hysterically. "What do you think? Is this an offer?"

"Legally it wouldn't hold up. You see you can't enter into a contract with a loony tunes."

"I thought so, you coward," Jackie laughed. Then she added in a more serious tone, "What are you going to do? This is getting too fucked up."

"I really don't know yet, what I'm going to do. But I don't want you getting in any deeper. All I can say for sure is that I will get to the bottom of this mess. And, when I do, somebody is going to be sorry and it won't be me."

"Okay. You let me know if I can do anything and I mean anything to help you," Jackie offered.

"You're a good friend. I've got your number and address. If something comes up I call you."

"What about my car?"

"Oh, yeah, your car," Flynn thought for a moment before he added, "Look, I'll call you early tomorrow morning and let you know where it is. Meantime, you take care of yourself, Jackie."

"Don't worry about me. You take care of yourself. I want all of you, you big hunk,"Jackie said disconnecting the call.

Flynn looked at the cell phone as if the phone conversation was as unreal as it seemed. "I'm the prime suspect in the assassination of the President? How absurd that anyone could or would believe such horse shit. I've spent my entire life defending the United States. Go figure."

Flynn continued, "Why does this asshole Moorehouse, want me out of the way so desperately? He's got the inside track on the Vice, er.. that would be-- Thee President, now. Who else would Patricia listen to now? Afterall they are lovers aren't they? And in her order of importance at this moment, I would be at the very top of the shit-list."

Flynn drove back to his house in silent meditation trying to sort out all that had happened. The only thing that mattered for Flynn at this moment was he would have to be extra careful. More careful than ever before. And he knew he had to help Kristen Shults.

When Flynn pulled into his driveway, he said, "Hold on, Kristen, I've got a plan. First, I need to get to Europe and out of the United States—unauthorized territory for a Special Operative anyway. And, when I do find you, we're going to kick some ass and take some names. If they think I am as bad as they do--they have no idea how bad I can be."

Flynn wasted little time in getting ready to leave for Europe as soon as possible. He activated his cell phone and checked the flight schedules. Flynn needed an edge from an old friend, so he made a reservation for a flight to New York's Kennedy Airport. From there he could pick any number of international flights. He went to the roll top desk and studied the legal pad and his notes before shredding the pages in his compact shredder next to the desk. He took a moment to look around the room. "I wonder when, if ever, I'll be back." He walked through the kitchen and activated his security system. Flynn took a deep breath and went out the side door to the driveway and Jackie Armstrong's classic red Corvette. Within a minute Flynn was off and heading to Cleveland's Hopkins International Airport.

Flynn drove the 'Vette into the long term parking

area and walked to the terminal to check in. The next flight to JFK was within the hour and, since he didn't have any luggage, it was easy to pass through security. He went to the gate and waited. Flynn used his cell phone to make an important call.

Flynn's call was answered on the second ring by a man with a heavy Italian accent.

"Ahllo."

"Vito Manderino, please. This is Flynn, Jeremiah Flynn calling."

There was a short pause before the man responded. "He'sah notta 'ere rightah now. You gimme a number and he callah you back."

Flynn understood the procedure. Vito Manderino was very careful about phone calls. In fact, he was a very careful man. Don Vito was also a very powerful man in the Mafia, as head of his own 'family'. Flynn gave the man his cell number and disconnected without saying another word. In exactly two minutes his ring tone advised Flynn he had the call.

The caller ID told Flynn who it was. "Don Vito. Thank you for returning my call."

"Mista Flynn," Don Vito replied, "what is it that I can do for you, my old friend?"

"Don Vito," Flynn began, "I need safe passage to Europe. I have to take care of some business."

"I understand, my friend. I have heard that you are not welcome by your Company anymore. I think that they do not know you like I do, eh?"

"Your sources are as accurate and up to the minute as ever, Don Vito. It's a very big misunderstanding on their part, of course."

"Yes, I know. But that it the way it is with them. If

they were smart, like you, they would be looking in their own back yard first or with that weasel at the 'phone company'."

Flynn knew what Don Vito meant by the term 'phone company', but wasn't certain to whom he was referring. "Can you be more specific, Don Vito?"

"Not on the phone, and not now. But I think I can help you. I never forget a friend who once did a great favor for me. Now tell me, Flynn, why do you want to go to Europe? The problem is not there."

"I believe it is all part of the same bad business that I must see to, Don Vito," Flynn explained. "And a very special friend of mine is in real trouble and needs my help."

"You see, Flynn," Don Vito said proudly, "this is why I like you. You worry about others more than yourself. Like a true friend."

"Thank you for your trust, Don Vito," Flynn answered humbly.

"You have earned it with me and my family, my friend." Don Vito added, "I owe you. Now tell me what it is you need."

"I'll need clean papers, some cash, an equalizer, and someone to check out my apartment in Amsterdam. I am sure that it is being watched."

"Can you get to New York today?"

"Yes, Don Vito. I have a flight to JFK from Cleveland, USAir flight number 2243, that should be there in about two hours."

"Good. I will have one of my people meet you. He will have everything you need to get to Europe. However, as far as Amsterdam is concerned, I will have to call another friend of the family. I will have a name and a number for you when you get here. And where and who to meet once you get to Amsterdam."

"I am very grateful for your help, Don Vito," Flynn said sincerely.

"Good luck to you, my friend," Don Vito concluded as he hung up.

Flynn decided to text Jackie on her private number to let her know that her Corvette was in the long term lot in Cleveland.

"It's in Cleveland!" Jackie screamed as she read his text. "I'm not going to Cleveland. You sonofabitch, Flynn." She thought for a moment and resigned herself that she would need to rent a car--another Corvette--and send him the bill.

Flynn's flight to New York's JFK was called and Flynn boarded without incident. The plane landed in New York only ten minutes later than scheduled. When Flynn deplaned and passed through the gateway to the main terminal he noticed a rather stocky man in a dark suit carrying an attache case at the end of the departure gate. Although Flynn did not recognize the man, he knew that he was sent from Don Vito.

"Mister Flynn?" the man asked.

Before he answered Flynn scanned the area, more out of habit than worry, for any undercover agent or police officer who might be watching for him. Flynn walked close to the man as if he didn't know who he was or who had sent him and answered softly, "Please follow me into the rest room."

Flynn walked directly into the nearby men's room and waited by the sinks. Don Vito's messenger followed at a safe and reasonable distance understanding the need for caution.

Don Vito's man came into the rest room and approached the sink next to Flynn. He put down the attache case on top of the sink between them. The man looked into the mirror, pretending to adjust his tie.

"Mister Flynn, Don Vito sends his regards," he whispered in a gravelly voice. "I believe everything you requested is in the brief case." Then the man reached into his inside coat pocket and pulled out an envelope setting it on the attache case. Flynn immediately picked it up and put it into his pocket.

The man from Don Vito continued. "There is a name in that envelope. He is a cousin to Don Vito. He can be reached in Amsterdam at the address and cell phone number which are also in there. You have a prepaid reservation on Air Alitalia leaving here at noon for Rome. The ticket is in the attache case along with a few hundred dollars, or so, some Euros and some British Pounds. You will have no problems getting on or off the plane. Once you have boarded, go directly to the first class washroom. There, taped under the sink will be a loaded piece. A custom's official in Rome has been alerted and will see you safely through. How you make it to Amsterdam is up to you. Do you have any questions?'

"No," Flynn responded. "Please thank Don Vito for me."

The man nodded to Flynn then turned without saying another word and left. Flynn took the attache case into the first available stall, locked the door and sat down. He placed the case on his lap and opened it. The entire bottom of the case was lined with stacks of 100 dollar bills, Euros and British Pounds!

Flynn gasped in disbelief. "There must be over a hundred thousand dollars here."

Everything else that Flynn had requested was also in the briefcase. He removed the passport papers, and a stack of the bills along with the airline ticket to Rome. Flynn closed the attache case, opened the stall then walked to the Air Alitalia boarding area.

Flynn passed through security and checked in at the gate. Flynn surveyed the other passengers and quickly assured himself that Don Vito's man was absolutely correct. There was no one who would bother him. Within a short time the flight to Rome was called and Flynn boarded. He was directed to his first class seat. Flynn thanked the flight attendant in perfect Italian, and excusing himself stopped in the first lavatory. He went in and locked the door. The pistol was exactly where Don Vito's man said it would be. Flynn examined the weapon and noticed it was a 'safe piece', no identification number, 85FS Cheetah, .380 caliber Beretta, fully loaded. He placed it in the attache case, closed it and returned to his seat. Flynn placed the attache case in the overhead compartment directly over his seat. He sat down and fastened his seat belt. The jetliner left JFK on schedule and Flynn was on his way to Rome, Italy.

It would be after midnight by the time the jumbo jet landed at Leonardo da Vinci (Fiumicino) Airport, Rome's busiest. "I will stay the night here in the Eternal City at the Hotel *Ara Pacis*, and enjoy the elegant 18th Century palazzo, right in the center of Rome itself." The hotel was more international in flavor—characterized by the typical ashlar-work on its facade, embellished by harmonious arcades on the ground floor, refined double lacet windows on the upper floors and lovely cornice topping off the attic, in a balanced combination of open and closed spaces. Flynn remembered that he often walked the short ten minutes to Via Condotti on some occasions, or made the fifteen minute walk to the Spanish Steps.

Flynn's superior room with visible wooden beams had a delightful little terrace where he stood and looked out at the night lights of the beautiful dome in the distance. His thoughts drifted back to the nasty business that he knew lay ahead. "Tomorrow morning," Flynn thought, "I'll rent a car from Auto Europa and drive to Amsterdam. It should take about fifteen hours, if I'm lucky. Oh, shit, that reminds me. Did I tell Jackie Armstrong where he 'Vette' is? Yes, but she won't go to Cleveland. No, on second thought, I'll send her twenty or thirty grand and buy it from her." Flynn wished that his trip was for pleasure and he could take time to enjoy it. But he was on a mission and his focus would have to stay on that mission. It was nearly two o'clock by the time that Flynn found sleep.

The next morning Flynn bought a few essentials and some clothing before he rented the Aston Martin V12, Vantage he would drive to Amsterdam. Once in Amsterdam he would make contact with Don Vito's cousin and see what information he had discovered. First, Flynn drove over to the International Bank of Rome and wire transferred thirty thousand dollars to Nick Cokely at the Munson Law Office, Boothbay Harbor, Maine. "I'll call Nicky later and have him contact Jackie Armstrong so he can send her the money for her Corvette."

WASHINGTON, D. C.

The body of slain President Irwin W. Harper was buried in Arlington National Cemetery with full honors. The nation had suffered another tragic, senseless killing of their elected leader. Amidst the countless stories surrounding his murder and the nation's sorrow, a growing undercurrent of distrust of the government's investigation of the heinous crime was seeping into news reports and into the minds of most Americans.

There was also a serious concern that the new woman President, Patricia Bunnell, would be fit to handle the job as President of the most powerful country on earth and the leader of the Free World. Many Congressional leaders saw this as an opportunity for them to exercise greater control of the Federal government. Top Cabinet advisors to the late President Harper began jockeying for position to place themselves in the Rheisilieuian role as the true power behind the throne of Patricia Bunnell. Political Washington resembled a feeding frenzy of sharks each attempting to rip out more of the flesh of the new President. None did this better than Admiral Michael Moorehouse.

Foreign governments as well were keeping a close eye on the events taking place in America. Many were also skeptical that a young woman President might not have the ability to make the tough decisions regarding America's overseas interests—allies or enemies alike. One country, Iran, was the first to test the new President.

President Jahmir with the blessing of the Ayatollah and the urging of Kim Moon Jung of North Korea test fired its first nuclear bomb. Although it was an underground low-level explosion, the news shocked the entire world, especially Israel. When intelligence reports poured into CIA headquarters and the National Security Agency, Deputy Director of Operations at the CIA, George Dimmler, ordered a call to the White House.

"Mollie," Dimmler barked into the intercom, "call the White House and get the President on the line."

Within a minute Dimmler's phone rang and he picked it up expecting to hear the President's voice.

"Hello, George, what's going on?" The voice was not the President's but that of Admiral Moorehouse.

Dimmler was annoyed. "Michael, I need to speak to the President about...."

Admiral Moorehouse interrupted him. "What's the problem, George, maybe I can help you."

"Goddamn it, Admiral, I need to speak to the President. What the fuck is going on over there?"

"Calm down, George," Moorehouse said trying to placate the Intelligence Special Operations Director, "The President's very busy..."

It was Dimmler's turn to interrupt. He bellowed, "Very busy! Jesus Christ Almighty! The fucking world is about to explode. Don't tell me she's too fucking busy. Goddamnit, who's running this fucking government?"

"We've got things under control here, George. Director Pfohl and I have been advising President Bunnell on this situation. We believe we can handle it at this end."

The Admiral's statement was not lost on the Deputy Director of Operations. His growing sense of urgency and frustration caused Dimmler's voice to quiver. "Michael, this situation is very, very serious. The President needs to make a decision on what policy we are going to take. The United States has obligations to our allies. This madman, thanks to his buddy in North Korea, has exploded a nuclear weapon! There are facts that she needs to know as our President and Commander in Chief or we could find ourselves with our tit in a wringer."

"I will brief the President, George. We'll get back to you if we think the situation warrants it." The Chief of Staff disconnected the conversation.

Dimmler looked at the phone in anguish. "We're in deep, deep shit," he said out loud. "We're not going to wait for any invitations. This shit has to stop!" Then George Dimmler pushed his intercom button again ringing Acting Assistant Deputy Director Mollie Farnham.

"Mollie, can you get me the latest intel report on the Middle East situation and have a call placed to Secretary of State Makoweic on the secured line?"

"Yes, sir, right away." Mollie answered. Then she added, "There's a message on your screen you need to see."

"Thank you." Dimmler swiveled in his chair and faced his computer monitor screen. He punched in his personal access code and five level passwords to bring up his confidential message file. The screen displayed the following message:

"TOP SECRET: HIGHEST PRIORITY—EYES ONLY.

PASSENGER ON KLM FLIGHT 53, D.O.A. AMSTERDAM. POSITIVE ID AS DAVID GREENE, BRITISH MI-6, CARRYING PAPERS OF JEREMIAH FLYNN, YOUR OFFICE. PRESENT WHEREABOUTS OF FLYNN UNKNOWN. BELIEVE LANGLEY OR NSA COMPROMISED. FBI INVESTIGATION OF HARPER MURDER BEING STONEWALLED BY

WHITE HOUSE. NO ONE IS BUYING THE FLYNN STORY. SANCTION CONTRACT NOW ON HIM. ONE MILLION DOLLARS. AT THIS PRICE EVEN HE CANNOT HIDE FOR LONG! CASEAR"

Dimmler studied the message for several minutes before he hit the escape key erasing all trace from the computer's memory. Just then his secured line rang.

"George, this is Mak," the Secretary of State began. "What's happening?"

"Mak, thanks for getting back to me so soon," Dimmler said. "The Israeli's are preparing for an air attack against Iran. Our sources indicate that the Iranian's test fired a small nuclear weapon and the Middle East is about to explode."

"Sonofabitch!"

Dimmler continued, "The worst part, Jim, is I can't get a call into the President. The fucking Admiral screens all her calls. I firmly believe we have to make a move before all hell breaks loose. What have you heard in the diplomatic circles?"

"As you might guess, not only the Israeli's are antsy but many of our so-called Arab allies are worried. Many are demanding a urgent meeting of the U.N.'s Security Council for later this morning. But like you, I haven't been able to get a personal call into President Bunnell. So our policy at State is still up in the air while the entire world waits for our response. All I can do for now is to reassure our allies that we will do whatever is necessary to protect and enforce our foreign alliance commitments."

"I can't believe this shit," Dimmler was annoyed. "Jim, we've got to get in to see the President, immediately!"

"I agree, George," Makoweic concurred. "Look, let's just crash the gate at the White House in one hour. Call and tell them it's a matter of National Security and that we ARE coming over!"

"I like the way you think, Mister Secretary," Dimmler agreed. "I think that the Joint Chiefs should also be there, too. As well as Bill Pfohl at NSA."

"I agree with you, George. However, it's my understanding that Pfohl has just about taken up residency there along with Moorehouse."

"Is that so?" Dimmler replied. "Well, I guess we won't need to call him then. I'll meet you at the White House in one hour. Maybe we can find out who is running this country of ours after all."

Dimmler disconnected the call wondering why Pfohl and Moorehouse were so tight. "Why is Patricia listening to them? What's it all mean?"

"Mister Dimmler," the intercom voice came in interrupting Dimmler's thought, "Acting Assistant Director of Operations Mollie Farnham's reports are here, sir."

"Fine. Please bring them in, Miss Ayers. But first, please call the Joint Chiefs and ask them to meet me and Secretary of State Makoweic for an emergency meeting at the White House with President Bunnell in one hour. Then notify my driver that I will be leaving right away. Finally, call White House security and let them know that we will be there in exactly one hour. Hold all calls for the next few minutes while I go over that report. Understood?"

"I got it, Sir."

Deputy Director of Clandestine Operations George Dimmler's thoughts momentarily drifted back to the context of the Top Secret message he had read moments ago. He jotted down a few notes on a small pad in a code that only he could decipher. Then he said to himself, "A million dollars on his head could make many 'friends' turn. That is, if he has any friends left anywhere."

"Here are those reports, Mister Dimmler," Miss Ayers said placing the binder on Dimmler's desk, noticing that he was in thought.

"Thank you, Miss Ayers," Dimmler responded in a soft tone.

After his secretary left his office, Dimmler opened his desk drawer and took out a secured cell phone. He punched in a series of numbers. The call was answered on the first ring by a female voice.

"Jaquin dry cleaning. May I help you?"

Dimmler began his encoded message. "Yes, I hope so. You see, I had a three piece suit cleaned there recently but I can't find the vest. Do you mind looking for it?"

"I'm sorry, sir. Of course we will assist you if we can. What is the number on that ticket?" The woman asked.

"JLF, dash RA 12553395. Did you get that?"

"Yes, I have it, sir. You understand, sir, that this may take a while. Often, however, items like this may never be found again. And if we do find it it may not ever be worn again."

"That's the chance I must take," Dimmler replied. "But I am particularly fond of this vest and I would like to have it back again. The suit won't be the same without it. Please do your best and let me know."

"We will, sir. Good Bye."

"Good bye." Dimmler put the cell phone away in his desk drawer and locked it. He picked up the report and went down to meet his driver. The Deputy Director was off to meet with President Bunnell come hell or high water.

THE WHITE HOUSE

Newly sworn in President Patricia Bunnell was working in the Oval Office when the call came in from her male secretary, Scot. "Madam President, I have been informed by the Secret Service that the Secretary of State, Deputy Director Dimmler of the CIA, and the Joint Chiefs are here to see you for a scheduled meeting. They say it is urgent."

"What?" President Bunnell asked incredulously. "Does Admiral Moorehouse know of this meeting? Is it in my appointment book?"

"No, Madam President, it is not in your appointment book." Scot added, "I haven't been able to reach the Chief of Staff. Apparently, he and NSA Director Pfohl are out of the office and they don't answer their cell phones. Now, what do I do about these men who wish to see you?"

"If they say it is urgent then show them in. I guess I'll see what they want. And, Scot, keep trying to reach Admiral Moorehouse."

"Yes, Ma'am."

The door to the Oval Office opened and the full entourage marched in. It was Secretary of State James Makoweic who spoke first. "Madam President, we need to talk to you."

"Well Mister Secretary, don't get your underwear in a bunch. Gentlemen please come in sit down and tell me what's this all about?" The President walked around her desk and shook hands with each of the men.

President Bunnell's style was more relaxed and informal than her predecessor and it was uncomfortable for many of the men present who were used to a more formal, business-like approach. Some of the group took this as a sign that the woman President was not in control of the job.

The President paused for a brief moment while each man took a seat. She remained standing directly in front of the assembled group. Her beauty was disarming even to the most calloused of the Joint Chiefs. Patricia immediately took control of the meeting before any of them knew it.

"Well, gentlemen," the President began, "what can I help you with? What's this all about?"

George Dimmler, who knew the President longer than the others, spoke up. "Madam President, there are two issues we need to discuss."

"Okay, George," she replied confidently, "let's take them one at a time."

"Very well," Deputy Director Dimmler stated. "The first is an issue of National Security interest. The Iranians have detonated an underground low level nuclear device which is a game changer in the Middle East. The Israeli's are preparing for a pre-emptive strike. Our so-called Arab allies are understandably nervous about a nuclear war in their backyard and our troops are about as stretched as thin as can be with our continued presence in Afghanistan, Pakistan and Iraq."

Secretary of State Makoweic now entered into the foray. "We have a political and military responsibility to our allies in the area. The Arabs and the Israelis are both on edge and in an uproar. We are sitting on a nuclear time-bomb! There is an emergency meeting of the United Nations Security Council scheduled for this morning to debate this issue." Secretary of State Makoweic looked around counting on his support before he concluded. "What we need from you, Madam President, is a statement of our policy in this matter."

"Quite frankly," Dimmler chimed in more forcefully this time, "Madam President, you have been isolated by Admiral Moorehouse and more recently, I understand, by NSA Director Pfohl. We have not been able to get a call into you since you have assumed the Office."

The President never flinched. She was a cold politician of the first order. She quietly sat on the edge of the front of her desk. Her shapely legs crossed at the knees. She glanced down at the gold ankle bracelet she wore—a present from Flynn--before she spoke. A momentary thought of him crossed her mind which she quickly dismissed.

"I assume," President Bunnell began, "that this is the second issue. The fact that Michael...Admiral Moorehouse, my Chief of Staff, is seen by you gentlemen as the 'palace guard' and you, my closest advisors, are unable to have free access to this Office. Is that correct?"

There was silence in the Oval Office while the President looked at each and every one of the men before her. Deputy Director Dimmler was the first to answer.

"Well, Madam President, to cut through the, the, er...."

"It's called bullshit, George!" Patricia Bunnell exclaimed finishing his thought. "Yes, gentlemen, it is bullshit. Let me assure each and every one of you that this Administration will run this government in a different fashion than the former one. As you may not know, and I apologize for not getting to all of you sooner, I have planned a full Cabinet meeting to discuss with you America's direction under this Administration and our focus and plan for not only this immediate crisis, but for a full outline of our foreign and domestic policies. I have been working on this agenda for the past week. Michael, Admiral Moorehouse, has been under my direct order to screen all calls to this office. Believe me gentlemen, he briefs me on each and every call. Right now, I don't think I could function without his assistance."

"Oh shit," Dimmler mumbled to himself. President Bunnell heard his gaffe, but decided to ignore it for the moment.

"Secretary Makoweic," President Bunnell asked, "how long will it take you and your staff to prepare a full blown public 'dog and pony show' about how dangerous President Jahmir's decision was to test an underground nuclear device while putting the world on the brink of World War Three? You know, the kind of technical display with satellite photos, etc., etc. to let the world know that the United States is committed to our allies?"

The Secretary of State thought for a moment and then declared, "Yes, Madam President, I believe I do understand what you mean. I think that we can put something together by the six o'clock news...if I can get the assistance of the CIA and the Air Force's recon photos and any intel that we could use."

The Joint Air Force Chief General Thomas Weatherup, stood up. "I will gladly assist Mister Secretary with everything we have." Then turning to Dimmler he added, "George, can you play ball with us on this?"

Dimmler felt like he was caught in a trap of his own design with no immediate way out. "Yes, of course. We will be happy to assist in any way we can."

Patricia Bunnell was again successful in casting her spell. She had a flair for the dramatic but not to the point of being incredulous. Dimmler watched while his colleagues became entranced under her spell. He admitted to himself that, "Yes, she does have a certain charisma. My only worry is does she have enough substance to go with all that form to lead our nation if a catastrophic war broke out in the Middle East?"

President Bunnell gave each man an opportunity to speak and add his input on the issue of the Iranian crisis. The meeting lasted for about an hour. By the time it was over President Patricia Bunnell had them all feeling good about themselves and her ability to lead the nation. While showing them to the door, she grabbed Deputy Director Dimmler's arm and quietly pulled him aside.

"George, may I speak with you for a moment?"

"Of course, Madam President."

President Bunnell closed the door to the Oval Office and spun around to face Dimmler. Fire shot out of her ocean blue eyes and her faced flushed with anger. "I won't have you making flippant comments about Admiral Moorehouse in front of the others. I wouldn't let anyone do it to you. If you don't like the fact that I rely on him a great deal, keep it to yourself!"

Dimmler was stunned. He thought that she hadn't heard his aside but now knew that she had. "Madam President," Dimmler addressed her in his best professorial voice, "I apologize for the way I said it, but I will not apologize for the fact that I did say it."

"Listen to me, George," Patricia spat back, "I am

President, now...."

Dimmler interrupted her. "I have heard those words before, Madam, from your predecessor. He took great pleasure in telling everyone that he was President and we were shit!"

"Goddamnit, George, your rudeness does not become you. Listen carefully to what I am saying and don't interrupt me again." The temperature in the Oval Office seemed to rise twenty degrees from the friction between the President and the Deputy Director of Operations. President Bunnell continued on the offensive. "I am not now, nor will I ever be, anything like that fucking, arrogant sonofabitch, who is hopefully burning in hell where he belongs. What I am saying is, I am the President now and need to rely on those whom I can trust, like Michael...."

Dimmler couldn't wait and interrupted her a second time. "How can you trust that over ambitious, backstabbing wimp? It seemed not so long ago that you had your eyes on and your hooks into Jeremiah Flynn. You have probably single handily, more than anyone, fucked Flynn up so badly he doesn't know right from wrong...."

Patricia Bunnell slapped Dimmler across the face. "I warned you, George!"

"You don't want to know or hear the truth do you?" Dimmler shot back at the President dabbing his lip which showed a trace of blood from her blow.

"The objective truth, yes!"

"Don't play these games with me, Patricia," Dimmler lectured. "The objective truth, the subjective truth. Truth is truth. One can't put limitations on the truth and call it the truth."

"Well, the truth is that you don't know what the fuck you're talking about," the President retorted.

"In that case, Madam President," Dimmler announced, "I resign!"

"The fuck you will, George!" Patricia Bunnell shouted. "I won't let you resign. I might fire your ass but you won't quit on me. And you won't quit on Flynn! Not when we need you the most. Who's playing games now, George?"

George Dimmler stood silent for a long moment. Slowly a slight smile appeared on his face. She had called his bluff. "Touche," Dimmler replied at long last. "How can I help you?"

President Bunnell smiled. "First, you can listen to everything I say."

"Agreed. No more interruptions. Forgive me."

"Forgiven. Now, as I tried to say, I need people with whom I can trust like yourself. And to a large extent, Michael. Don't think I don't know what kind of a person he is. I know him better than even his wife. But, we have been through a lot together and I know when he is trying to bullshit me and when he's not.

"I never expected to be President. But I am. I can handle the job. And woe to those who think otherwise. You are my eyes and ears, George. I need to know all the facts. Not sugar coated. Facts. And I need your advice and experience and expertise on just what the facts are and what they mean. I will make the foreign policy decisions based on your input and Secretary of State Makoweic's. I truly believe he is a very decent man. Very bright and very capable.

"I'd like to know who is putting out all the garbage on Flynn killing President Harper. I have a hunch, but I want to be sure. See if you can find out anything for me. And, speaking of Flynn, George, where is he? I need to talk to him. I need to know that he's all right and that he knows I believe in him and want to help him any way that I can."

The Deputy Director thought he saw a tear momentarily appear in her eyes although it disappeared as quickly as it appeared. "Pat, I don't know where he is. He is the best operative I have ever known. He has places to hide and people he knows all over the world who will hide him. People and places that even we don't know about. I would guess that some how--some time he will surface and probably with Kristen Shults. She's the woman accused of killing Prime Minister Sommerset, as you know. I only pray that when he does surface he doesn't get his ass blown off. There is a million dollar price tag on his head!"

"A million dollars? Who is responsible for that contract?"

"I am the head of the largest and most clandestine operation in the entire world but I don't have that answer. I only know that the price has been set and it's out on the 'street'."

"That's an unbelievable amount of money for a bounty on one man. And the bigger question, is WHY? What has Flynn done or what can he do or know that someone is willing to pay a million dollars to silence him?" The President became somber while she paused in thought. Then she looked at Dimmler and asked, "Can he make it, George?"

"Honestly?"

"Honestly, George."

"No!"

P'YONGYANG, NORTH KOREA

The city lights illuminated the face of the Tiger while staring out into the North Korean darkness from his office window in the Capital city. "The plan is so simple," he thought. "Cocaine for cash to control the oil market. By starting a war in the Middle East the major powers will have to focus all their attention there--thus the cocaine supplies will flow freely." Kim Moon Jung cracked a sinister smile while continuing his train of thought. "With the woman as President of the United States being controlled and manipulated by my insiders, the U.S. will never act decisively enough. The oil production will be in my control and the supply lines will be secure forever. Then, one by one, those greedy and mindless men of the 'Elite' will be eliminated as their value to Operation Lifeblood wanes."

The Tiger's thoughts turned to Flynn. "Only once there was a mistake. But that is being corrected. That bumbling American spy Flynn will be destroyed. Fortunately, we intercepted his message to Washington. He is now being hunted down like the dog that he is. No man can stay hidden with a million dollars on his head. Yes," Tiger nodded, "Flynn will be killed and with his death the security of our supply lines will be safely secured. Then all the world will be at my feet. Soon Kim Moon Jung, me, the Tiger, will rule before the Rise of the Crescent Moon."

AMSTERDAM

Flynn wheeled his rented Aston Martin V12 Vantage into a dark alley used for restaurant deliveries during normal business hours. He drove down the alley to the end which came out onto a one way street only two blocks from his Amsterdam apartment. He was careful to keep the Aston Martin in the shadows and out of sight from the street. Flynn would be gone before first light if all went well. He set the parking brake and shut off the engine. Flynn looked all around before he got out of the automobile making certain that there was no one in the area who might recognize him as he was too well known. Flynn left the vehicle and closed the door as quietly as possible. Staying close to the buildings and in the shadows for concealment, Flynn carefully made his way to the street.

The traffic on the street was light and Flynn darted behind a passing car to cross the street. He walked quickly to the doorway of an apartment house which he knew backed onto a courtyard shared by another apartment building and which fronted directly across the street where his apartment was located. Flynn glanced over the names on the mailboxes. He rang the bell for one of the upper floor apartments. A tired male voice answered in the speaker.

"Who is there?"

"Mister Smithsen," Flynn answered in perfect Dutch. "It's is me, Hans, in 202. I have locked myself out. So stupid of me. Could you please be so kind and buzz me in?"

"Why does everyone call me?" Mister Smithsen grumbled while pushing the buzzer unlocking the main door.

"*Danke*," Flynn said as he entered.

Flynn walked to the back of the building to a door that opened to the courtyard. He took a took a roll of tape from his jacket pocket and put a piece across the latch so the door would not lock behind him. He quietly made his way across the courtyard to the rear of the other apartment house. Flynn jumped up and pulled down the fire escape ladder then climbed up to the roof. Crossing the roof, Flynn crouched down in the front of the building's stone and brick balustrade.

From this vantage point Flynn could see his own apartment, up and down the street and the rooftops of the adjacent buildings. Flynn noticed two black SUV's below on the street while he studied the area. One was empty and the other was occupied by two men. "The Company men at work," Flynn mused. "Now where do you suppose the rest of them are?" His search was quickly ended by voices on the roof next to him.

"How long are they going to keep us up here on this fucking roof? You know that he's never going to show up here."

"We'll stay as long as they tell us for Chrissake. Quit you're bitching, you know it's part of the job." His partner then added something which Flynn hadn't known. "Besides, a million dollars is a lot of spending money when we bag him."

"Yeah, you're right about that. Say, what would you do with your cut?"

"Me? I'd buy a boat. A real fast boat. Ya know, one of those cigarette boats so I could pick up broads. Then I'd fuck myself stupid."

"You already are fucking stupid," Flynn thought.

The two men laughed at the idea then became silent again while they focused their attention back down to the street.

Flynn decided that he knew what he needed to know so he retraced his steps back across the roof and down the fire escape to the courtyard. Then he walked to the back door and opened it removing the tape across the lock. He went to the front door and crossed the street to his car.

"Four men," Flynn told himself. "Two up and two down." While turning the ignition key, Flynn wondered who might have put up a million dollars for his head. "Somebody really wants me dead." He drove out of the city to a small rural village further down the coast. He found an Inn still open and checked in for the night. In the morning, Flynn would place a call to Don Vito Manderino's cousin.

BELFAST, NORTHERN IRELAND

Kristen Shults was delivered to the Sisters of Charity at the convent at Noch Sheegan on the outskirts of Northern Ireland's capital of Belfast. Kristen's first few days in the cloistered convent were very disruptive for Mother Superior. It took several days and severe corporal punishment for the pretty young woman to accept the fact that she was now in a convent. A convent where no one was allowed to speak. Kristen was severely punished every time she blurted out any words. Kristen felt completely hopeless. She was totally isolated from the other nuns and forced into long hours of manual labor and prayer. Scrubbing for hours on her hands and knees until her skin bled, Kristen was in constant pain. Mother

Superior watched this new novice very closely and inflicted swift and harsh discipline on her daily attempting to break Kristen's will.

After a number of weeks, Kristen appeared broken in spirit. She seemed resigned to the fact that she was a prisoner. Her only hope, which faded as the days passed, rested with one man who might never find her. She found herself in constant prayer in spite of her predicament.

At first it was a prayer for freedom. But slowly, Kristen's prayers became more directed to repentance for sins she must have committed against the Lord. Her will was quickly being broken. The isolation and constant discipline were eroding her spirit and her very identity. She began to believe in and accept the tenants of the Order. Kristen Shults was evolving into Sister Maureen!

WASHINGTON, D. C.

President Patricia Bunnell was intently working late in the Oval Office and hadn't noticed Chief of Staff Admiral Moorehouse standing in front of the desk until he cleared his throat.

"Michael!" Patricia exclaimed momentarily alarmed. "I didn't see you there. What can I do for you?"

"What went on with this morning's meeting with Dimmler, Makoweic and the Joint Chiefs?"

President Bunnell put down her pen and looked up at Admiral Moorehouse. "We had a rather frank discussion of the troublesome events in Iran and the Middle East. They expressed their views and I gave them some direction on what our position will be *vis a vie* our political commitments."

"I thought that you agreed that I and Director

Pfohl would be included in any policy meetings."

"Well, Michael, neither you nor William Pfohl were around and these men just showed up..."

"You shouldn't have seen them. I make your appointments..."

"Hold it," President Bunnell raised her voice. "Apparently, you have been making too much of what your function is around here. Perhaps it's your sense that I need protection or that I'm incapable of making my own decisions without you or Pfohl's input. Let me make it perfectly clear, Admiral, that I am perfectly capable to handle this job. And, from here on, when I get a call from Deputy Director Dimmler, or Secretary of State Makoweic, or the Joint Chiefs, I want those calls put through to me directly. Is that clear?"

Moorehouse thought it better to retreat than to go forward. "Yes, Madam. Perfectly clear."

"Good," Patricia felt empowered by her stance. "Is there anything else on your mind, Michael?"

"Patricia," Moorehouse began slowly and softly, "I have some rather disturbing news about an old friend of yours." Moorehouse paused until she asked.

"News? What news? About whom?"

"You're not going to like this...but I feel that I have to tell you."

Annoyed by his childish behavior, President Bunnell shouted, "Come to the point, Michael!"

"Very well. It seems that your old friend Flynn is a double agent!"

Incredulously, the President exclaimed, "What are you talking about?"

"From my sources of information, Jeremiah L. Flynn has turned. He has, in the parlance of that sordid community, left the reservation and has a 'burn notice' placed on him."

"Explain yourself, Admiral," a livid Patricia Bunnell fired back.

"Apparently, he is responsible for the 'heart attack' that killed Daniel Kent at the Dubliner some weeks back. That, in fact, he was never in Alaska. It was just another of his treacherous cover stories and he remains the number one suspect in the death of President Harper."

Patricia Bunnell was shocked and angry at these statements. "Where did you get this bullshit from, Michael? Flynn is too loyal to do anything like you're suggesting. He has no reason..."

Moorehouse interrupted because he couldn't wait to see her reaction to what he was about to say. "He has all the reason in the world. You see, Kent had a complete 'DOGS' file on you and your love affair with Flynn all last year in Washington."

"That's so much shit," Patricia answered. "And so what? We were and are both single. There's no shame or scandal in what we did."

"You shouldn't be so naïve, Patricia. He was paid to assassinate Harper so you could become President and be controlled!"

"Controlled? Controlled by whom?"

"Flynn's Mafia buddies. Specifically Don Vito Manderino. You see, Flynn and the Mob are tight. It was, according to my information, the Mafia that helped Flynn leave the country. But now, because of the Shults woman, he has become a liability with them and their operations throughout Europe. So they have put a million dollar contract on him to cover their underworld asses."

President Patricia Bunnell was shocked by

Moorehouse's revelation which if true, or became public, would or could seriously jeopardize her ability to govern. She needed time to think this through. Angry and upset, she stood from behind the desk and shouted, "Get out! Leave immediately, Michael. Go home to your wife!"

Admiral Moorehouse turned to leave the Oval Office while a smile crossed his lips out of the sight of the President. He had planted the seed and now he could wait to see if it grew.

Within a few minutes, Scot rang the President. "Madam President, Director Pfohl from the NSA is on the line for you."

Patricia, still angry and attempting to sort out all the things her Chief of Staff had just told her, picked up the phone. "Yes, Director Pfohl, what can I do for you?"

"It's not what you can do for me, Madam President, " Pfohl began, "it's what I might be able to do for you."

Patricia wasn't ready for any more of these cute little word games. "Get to the point, Director Pfohl, please."

"Sorry, Madam President. Of course. We have intercepted phone traffic regarding the rogue agent, Flynn...."

"Christ, now what?" Patricia was exasperated.

"Clearly Flynn, it appears, has been turned by his lover Kristen Shults, a suspected IRA terrorist who murdered Prime Minister Sommerset. We have intercepted traffic that also ties Flynn to the murder of President Harper in Houston about the same time as the Shults woman's murder of Sommerset. Apparently, there is a connection with an organized crime family of one..."

"Don Vito Manderino," President Bunnell

finished his sentence.

Surprised by her remark, Pfohl said, "Why yes, Madam President. How did you know?"

"Chief of Staff Moorehouse was just here and told me basically the same thing. William," Patricia's head was spinning, "are you certain about this?"

"Yes, Madam President, I am very certain."

"All right," Patricia wanted to end this temporary nightmare. "Can you bring me over the recordings concerning what you have told me. You know so I can hear it for myself?"

"I'd be glad to, Madam President. When would you like them?"

"First thing tomorrow here in the Oval Office. Say about nine?"

"I'll be there. Good night, Madam President."

Patricia Bunnell didn't want to believe either Moorehouse or Pfohl. However, both of them said basically the same thing. And in the morning, Pfohl was going to bring the recordings that NSA intercepted. She turned in her chair and stared out the window of the Oval Office.

Her thoughts were confused. "Maybe Dimmler was right. Maybe I did selfishly lead Flynn along too much. So much so that he never knew how I really felt about him and how important he is to the success of this government and my administration. I would have wanted him to share this Office with me. But I knew deep down in my heart and soul that he could--would-- never do that. Even though he has always been there for me when I always needed him the most. But now, from what I have been told, he has 'snapped', turned on me and his country. Am I ever going to believe that? No. Flynn is Flynn.

Loyal, committed, and true. He has his faults, yes, but he would never betray himself and what he believed in or his country. So, I guess that if I truly believe in him as I do, he will somehow find and rescue the Shults woman. I can't image how Flynn will be able to show or prove that she is neither insane nor guilty of the murder of Prime Minister Nigel Sommerset. Go for it Flynn! Go off to wherever and save that love that I couldn't give you. Maybe you don't know that I still believe in you. And yes, I still love you. Even though I did lie to you back then. I admit that I committed the mortal sin of sins to you by lying to you about me and Michael when it was so expedient and easy for me to do. I am sorry Flynn. I will always love you. But I think I must finally let you go.

"So, I guess, Deputy Director Dimmler, you maybe right that it was me, who has 'fucked' him over. It is all my fault if anyone thinks Flynn doesn't understand right from wrong anymore. I can't, and I won't ever, believe it could be possible. Not Flynn! I just hope when this is over he will forgive me."

President Bunnell continued to stare out the window of the Oval Office for a very long moment. Finally, she turned back to her desk and made a call to Deputy Director Dimmler at CIA Headquarters in Langley, Virginia.

"George," The President began when Dimmler answered, "have you any news on Flynn or is he still off the reservation--as you spooks say?"

"I'm sorry Madam President, but I haven't heard anything from him or about him. There is one report that he left the country. However, an MI-6 agent, a David Greene, was found dead on a plane that landed in Amsterdam. He was carrying Flynn's papers. I don't know what to make of it, as yet."

"Oh my God, George, did Flynn kill the British agent?"

"I don't know. But the Brits think he did and they are pissed and after him now, too."

"Chief of Staff Admiral Moorehouse told me that and it was confirmed by NSA Director Pfohl, that Flynn has been working with the Mafia. A Don Vito Manderino, I believe they said, helped Flynn leave the country and travel over to Europe. Is that anything? Is there anything to that, George?"

"Look, Pat," Dimmler said in a fatherly tone, "I don't want to tell you that is a fact--but the Company has had the cooperation of some of the major crime syndicates for certain operations in the past..."

'I know that, George," The President interjected. "So, it is possible that they helped him?"

"Yes, it is possible."

"Okay. Assuming that is true, I have been told that they, the Mafia, has issued the million dollar contract on him...."

It was Dimmler's turn to interrupt. "That's simply not possible, Madam President. They don't operate like that. If they wanted Flynn dead they wouldn't have assisted him in getting to Europe."

"But Michael, I mean the Chief of Staff, said that they were now embarrassed because of of something Flynn did or didn't do. I don't know, George..."

"Don't believe anything like that," Dimmler assured her.

"One last thing. Admiral Moorehouse said that he had information that Flynn is a double agent. That he was paid by the Mafia to kill President Harper so that I could become President and be controlled by the mob. And that the Shults woman killed the Prime Minister in some sort of international conspiracy that the two of them concocted. It's making me crazy, George."

There was a long silence on Deputy Director Dimmler's end.

"George? George are you there?"

"Yes, Madam President, I'm here," Dimmler's tone was somber.

"Does your silence mean that there is some truth to this bullshit?"

"No, no, Madam President," Dimmler replied, unconvincingly. "I can't believe these rumors. But I have heard that there is some link between Flynn and Don Vito Manderino. Although there is nothing to really substantiate his working for or with them. Actually, it goes against Flynn's nature."

"Well, George, you're the Deputy Director of Intelligence. Where are these stories coming from? Who is behind this line of bullshit?"

"Pat, I don't know. I can only guess." Dimmler pause for a second, "There just isn't anything concrete to trace it to any one person or group."

President Bunnell understood the subtle innuendo about Michael and she bristled at his suggestion. "George, don't start on Michael."

"I'm not suggesting anything..."

"Yes, you are. And I don't like it."

"Like it or not Patricia, the Admiral is a bullshit artist. He's not one to be..."

President Bunnell wouldn't tolerate this insubordination and Dimmler's attack on her Chief of Staff. "Don't finish that statement, George. I have warned you for the last time. I believe that Michael has my best interests at heart. I know he is very jealous of the relationship I had with Flynn, but that's over! Michael is someone I trust and I can talk to."

"Very well, Madam President," Dimmler wanted out of this conversation as quickly as possible. She wasn't going to listen to anything as it related to her latest lover, Admiral Moorehouse. "I'll see what I can find out about the Manderino--Flynn connection and get back to you."

"Thank you," Patricia coldly concluded as she hung up.

Dimmler, as soon as he hung up from the President, made an intra-agency call to Mollie Farnham, Acting Assistant Deputy Director. "Mollie, there's something I'd like you to run down for me."

"Yes, of course sir, what is it?"

"Please check our files on Don Vito Manderino. More specifically, see if you can find anything that would connect Manderino and Flynn."

"Do you mean our Flynn, sir?"

"Goddammit, Mollie, who the fuck else do you think I mean by 'Flynn'?"

Mollie Farnham knew exactly what she was doing. She just wanted to put the Deputy Director of clandestine operations on record because every conversation at the Agency was recorded. Mollie smiled to herself before she answered. "Of course, Deputy Director, I'll see what I can find out."

LONDON, ENGLAND

Foreign Secretary James Saunders left his Ministry Office later that same evening and began his drive home. Earlier, his usual driver, William, had told him that he was not feeling well, and would be unable to drive him home. James Saunders was just on the outskirts of London when he attempted to navigate a rather sharp curve in the road. However, when he hit the brakes and attempted to turn the wheel, the Foreign Secretary discovered that the steering wheel spun freely in his hands. He had no control of his car and the vehicle hurtled itself over an embankment while the Secretary screamed in terror. The car crashed and suddenly burst in an explosion. The Foreign Secretary was burned to death beyond recognition.

The morning *London Times* was full of the news of the tragic accident which, within recent days, had claimed the second life of a high ranking government official.

AMSTERDAM, HOLLAND

Flynn was up before dawn as usual. He ate a small breakfast of coffee and toast, passing up on the bountiful platters of eggs, ham and potatoes. After he paid his breakfast check, Flynn opened his cell phone and push in the numbers he had memorized for Don Vito's cousin, Joseppi Penella.

Penella answered his cell phone. "International Warehouse, may I help you?"

"My name is Flynn. I'm calling for Joseppi Penella with a message from Don Vito Manderino.

Mister Flynn," Penella replied. "I have been expecting your call. How are things with my cousin, Don Vito?"

"He is well. He sends his regards to you and your family."

"Thank you, Mister Flynn. How may I help you?"

Flynn had assumed that Don Vito had already contacted Penella and understood that they were reluctant to go into much detail on the phone when talking about the family business. Flynn answered, "Don Vito has something he would like to give you. Would it be possible for us to meet somewhere today?"

Joseppi Penella thought for a moment before he said, "Of course. I know just the place. Are you familiar with the docks?"

Flynn replied, "Yes, I know the docks quite well."

"Good, good. Why not meet me here at my office near pier 24. You can't miss our building. International Warehouse, it is the largest building on the docks. Say about ten this morning?"

"I'll be looking forward to seeing you."

"When you reach the gate just tell the guard who you are and he will show you in—no problem."

"Thank you, sir."

"It's Joseppi, to all friends of my family."

Flynn smiled, "Thank you, Joseppi."

The drive across town to the docks would take about an hour Flynn calculated, depending on traffic. This would give him plenty of time to drive by Kristen's apartment and see how closely it was being watched as he knew it would be.

Flynn drove down *Brinker Strasse*, the street on which Kristen Shults' apartment was located. He drove slowly past the building and while looking, he noticed an 'Apartment to Let' sign in the window of the first floor. Flynn's curiosity was peaked. He parked on the street half a block away. He put on a pair of glasses, a hat and took a cane from the back seat. He started down the block walking with a slight limp supporting himself with the cane. "The best disguise" he thought, "is the least disguise."

Flynn took his time to approach the steps to the building. As he did so, he observed a man in a dark gray suit sitting on a bench ostensibly reading a newspaper. Flynn was certain that this man was an MI-6 agent. Flynn paused pretending to be short of breath before he attempted to climb the steps. He could feel the British agent's eyes watching him. Instinctively, Flynn prepared for the unexpected while he rang the bell for the superintendent's flat.

A small voice in Dutch came through a speaker by the door. "This is the superintendent, may I help you?"

Flynn replied in perfect Dutch, "Yes. I am inquiring about the apartment. Is it still available?"

"Yes, of course," came the voice. "I'll be right there to let you in."

While Flynn waited, he read the names on the postal boxes. He noticed that Kristen's name was still listed on her mail box. The inside door opened and an elderly man greeted Flynn.

"Hello, " Flynn said to the old man with a smile. "How are you today?"

"Come in," the man was all business. "It's four hundred Guilders a month. Is that a problem?"

"No, it is not a problem," Flynn answered, "but I would like to look it over first. Do you mind? The only possible problem would be if there are too many stairs or there is too much noise."

"Baah!" The old man exclaimed waving his hand. "It's on the third floor. And yes, we have an elevator. No need to walk up stairs."

"That's good," Flynn limped inside.

The superintendent showed Flynn to the elevator which was located in the center of the building. The old man opened the gate and Flynn joined him inside the cage. "There are four apartments on each floor," the superintendent explained while they rode up to the third floor. "One on each side of building and one in front and one in back."

The car stopped at the third floor. "I wonder if he is going to show me Kristen's apartment?" Flynn knew the building well having been a frequent visitor of the beautiful red-head on many occasions. Flynn was certain that he never before had seen this superintendent.

"Have you been the superintendent for a long time?"

"Yes, many years. But this is the first open rental I have had in many years. Most people stay for life. The one that is now open belonged to a widow who passed away last week."

The old man fumbled for the right key until he finally was able to unlock the door. "Go in, look around. It's a fine flat. You'll see."

Flynn was familiar with the layout but pretended to look around as if he weren't. It was small but clean and airy with many windows. Flynn couldn't believe this stoke of good fortune. "What a perfect place to keep an eye on Kristen's place and see who was watching it."

Flynn turned to the old man and asked, "Do the

furnishing come with the place?"

"Yes. Everything you see stays. Do you like it?"

"It's nice enough, I suppose. But what of the neighbors? Are they quiet. You see I need quiet. The slightest noise disturbs me. I must have quiet."

"There are no children here. All adults. It is a very quiet place. I do not tolerate noise in my building. There is an old couple over there," he continued pointing to the apartment across the hall. A professor at the University lives over there, and a young woman lives right next to this one."

"A young woman?" Flynn demanded, "Is she a working girl? You know, with many men guests?"

"No. No, nothing like that. She is an executive. Goes on business a lot." Then he turned to Flynn and inquired, "What business are you in?"

"I am a writer. That is why I need absolute quiet. I need to think in peace."

"It is very quiet here, I assure you. All good people live here."

"Very well, I will take it," Flynn declared. "But I insist it must be quiet."

"Baah!" The superintendent scoffed. "I told you it is very quiet. You will like it here. It is close to the library and the University. It will be perfect for you."

Flynn and the old man took the creaky old elevator back down to the superintendent's flat where Flynn signed a lease under the name of Frederick Von Honnold. He gave the old man forty-eight hundred Guilders for a full year's rent in advance. The old man was surprised but he gladly took the money, pleased that he had a new tenant.

Flynn took the key and as he began to leave

stopped before the old man could close the door. "It had better be quiet!"

"Baah!" The door slammed and Flynn cracked a smile.

Flynn walked slowly down the front steps to the street. He paused while looking up and down the street. The MI-6 agent was still sitting across the street on the bench watching Flynn. Flynn walked over to the man and sat down pretending to be out of breath.

Flynn glanced over to the man and in perfect Dutch said, "It's a lovely day, is it not?"

The British MI-6 agent looked at Flynn quickly then turned the page of the paper and grunted, "Yes, lovely day." His accent was decidedly British, and Flynn's suspicion was confirmed.

"You tourist?" Flynn continued, "or here on business?"

"A little of both."

"It is good to do both. Amsterdam is such a lovely city.

The Agent added, "There's good and bad in every city."

"Yes, I suppose that is correct," Flynn replied rubbing his leg as if it were in pain and he was trying to loosen it up. "The dampness does not help with this old leg."

The British agent looked at Flynn's leg without responding. The two men sat on the bench in silence for more than a minute. Finally, Flynn started to get up. "I must keep moving. If I don't the leg stiffens up too much. Enjoy your stay, young man." Flynn limped off down the street to his car. The MI-6 agent only watched Flynn for a few steps then looked away, bored with his assignment, never the wiser that the man with the bad leg was the wanted man Flynn.

Flynn got into the Aston Martin and drove off to meet with Joseppi Penella at his office down by the docks. The drive across town took about twenty minutes because Flynn made several left and right turns checking his mirrors each time to make certain that he wasn't being followed. He arrived at pier 24, International Warehouse's building exactly on time. The guards at the gate stopped him when he drove up. Flynn announced himself and the guards directed him where to park.

Flynn walked to the door of the warehouse where he was met by additional armed guards who showed him up to the stairway to Joseppi Penella's office. At the door, two additional guards armed with automatic weapons, patted Flynn down and removed his 10mm Glock before they let him enter to see their boss. They handed the weapon to Penella.

Joseppi Penella, upon seeing Flynn, stood up from his desk chair and extended his hand in welcome. Penella greeted Flynn as if he were an old and trusted friend. "Mister Flynn, it is a pleasure to meet you."

"Mister Penella," Flynn returned the warm gesture, "it is my pleasure to meet with you. Your cousin, Don Vito, sends his warmest regards."

"Thank you, Mister Flynn. Don Vito considers you a very close friend. He has asked me to help you in any way that I can. And, of course, I will gladly honor that request." He returned Flynn's pistol as a gesture of complete trust.

"I appreciate that very much," Flynn replied humbly. "There is one thing you can do for me right away, Mister Penella."

"Name it, Mister Flynn."

"You can drop the Mister. It's just Flynn."

Penella laughed. "Good, good. And you can call me Joseppi."

Joseppi Penella, in a show of bonding, took a bottle of Grappa from his desk and two glasses. He poured each of them with about two ounces then handed one to Flynn. "A toast! To my cousin, Don Vito, and to my new friend, Flynn."

Flynn looked at Penella raised his glass and added, "And to my new friend, Joseppi."

"Salute!"

"Salute!"

The two men down the shots of *Grappa* in one swallow. Joseppi put down his glass and embraced Flynn. Penella liked Flynn from the start. He now welcomed him into his 'family'.

Then Joseppi took a small mail sack from his desk and handed it to Flynn. "This is all the mail up to today that has been sent to your address here in Amsterdam since you left. I have a very good friend at the postal exchange. Now, Flynn, tell me how I can be of service to you."

Flynn looked at the man closely before he spoke. "First and foremost, Joseppi, I do not want to bring any kind of trouble to you or to your family. You see, there are people who want me dead. I would like to know who they are and why."

Penella was impressed by Flynn's sincerity. "You will not bring any trouble to me, Flynn. Do not worry about that. I will make some inquiries." Penella paused before adding, "What else is there, my friend?"

"I must have safe passage to London. I have to

pick up the trail of a woman, a close friend of mine, who is in a lot of trouble. She has been accused of murdering British Prime Minister Nigel Sommerset. Joseppi, I need to find her before they do."

"You are referring to Kristen Shults, are you not?"

"Yes, that is correct." Flynn continued not recognizing the familiarity. "Also, I would like to find out if there is any connection to United Petroleum and drug trafficking. And, if so, are they connected to the assassinations of Prime Minister Sommerset and President Harper?"

Penella interjected, "And the British Foreign Minister, James Saunders."

Flynn was shocked. "James Saunders was murdered?"

"Yes, my friend, last night. It has been called an 'accident' but I understand that his auto was tampered with..."

"Good Lord!" Flynn exclaimed. "He is, was, the uncle of Kristen Shults."

A somber faced Joseppi Penella then said. "I know....Let me ask around today. We shall meet again this evening for a late supper, say around nine o'clock at the *Cafe dur Amstel Haus*? Do you know where it is?"

"Yes," Flynn recalled the place, "I am familiar with it. I will see you there, my friend. Thank you for offering to help me."

"Flynn, that is what friends and family do for each other." Penella shook Flynn's hand before he left the office.

Flynn picked up the mailbag and left Don Vito's cousin's office. He returned to his car and his mind was racing faster than the Aston Martin while he drove back to the center of the city. The puzzle was becoming more complex. Flynn drove along one of the canals to a secluded spot and parked the car. He opened the mailbag and began sorting through the mail when he noticed a letter postmarked from the English port city of Liverpool. The envelope was written in Kristen's handwriting.

Flynn, tense with anticipation and curiosity, examined the entire envelope before carefully sliding a key under the flap to unseal the envelope. He took the one page letter out and read:

"Flynn, I am frightened and need your help. I have been wrongly accused of killing the Prime Minister. I was kidnapped and raped by three horrible men whom I believe did the killing. It is a long, terrible nightmare that I can explain if, and when I see you.

"I have managed to escape from those three men. Somehow I came to the village of Dobbinshire. Now, I am being helped by an Irish priest and a man named Timothy Hartnett. They also believe I killed the P.M. I think they are IRA. They said they are taking me out of England to safety in Ireland. I don't know if you will ever get this letter or if you do, that you will find me...alive. I am frightened to death. You were the first person I thought who might find me and help me clear my name and believe me without question.

"Please let my Uncle James know that I am not a murderer. Please tell him I love him. Kristen.

"P.S. I love you, too."

Flynn re-read the letter several times memorizing each word. His emotions ranged from deep compassion for this young woman whom, in his own way, loved and absolute rage at what had happened and what might be happening to her. He realized that this was the first clue in picking up her trail. Now he realized what he had to do. "Oh it's going to be payback time for sure," Flynn mumbled. "By God, or without Him, I am going to set things right. I am going to find you people and you are going to tell me where Kristen is, why you did this to her, and then I will send you to hell."

WASHINGTON, D. C.

Jackie Armstrong finished running the computer report she was directed to by Acting Assistant Deputy Director Mollie Farnham. She gathered the report carrying it to the elevator to personally bring it to Mollie. After the mandatory stop on the floor below the Executive level, where Jackie's identification was checked by security, she was permitted to the upper floor. While Jackie walked down the corridor, she couldn't help but think, "If I played politics and kissed ass the way Mollie did, I just might have been the Acting Assistant Deputy Director of Operations and Mollie would be bringing reports to me." Jackie continued her thoughts as she entered the outer door of Mollie's new office. "What does she want with this information on a possible link between Flynn and Don Vito Manderino? It's not unusual for field ops to to have all kinds of resources. Some are legitimate and sometimes some are not. After all, isn't what info they get that's important?"

"Jackie Armstrong to see her Highness," she quipped to the secretary.

"Yes, Miss Armstrong, the Assistant Deputy Director is expecting you." Mollie's young secretary buzzed Jackie into Mollie's office.

"That's ACTING Assistant Deputy Director,"

corrected Jackie while opening the inner door and not wanting to see the dirty look she knew she was getting.

"Here ya go, Mollie," Jackie offered causally. The report on the Flynn—Manderino connection you asked for."

Mollie Farnham had caught the tail end of Jackie's remarks to her secretary and bristled. "That's Miss Farnham, Miss Armstrong," Mollie demanded.

"Well, excuse me all to hell," Jackie snapped back. "Aren't we suddenly important."

"Listen to me, Miss Armstrong. You'd better adjust your attitude around here. This isn't a social club we're running but an important arm of the Federal Government."

It's more like the Mickey Mouse Club if you ask me," Jackie fired back at the pretentious woman. "Tell me, why in hell do you want to know about Flynn and this Manderino fellow? You know as well as I do that Flynn's the best man we've got in this Agency...."

Mollie interrupted, "You don't make policy here. You just run the computer operation. I don't want you to ever question why I want anything. I'm the Assistant Deputy Director and you answer to me!"

"Oh...Oh...Is it O-fficial? You're not still the Acting Deputy Director anymore?"

"You are being insubordinate! Keep it up and you'll be on Report!"

"Fuck you and your 'Report'. I knew you when you nothing more than a data entry supervisor."

"That's it! You are on Report for insubordination!"

"Kiss my Royal American Ass, Bitch!"

Mollie was red faced and livid. "GET OUT!" she shouted.

Jackie slammed the inner door. She saw the secretary smirk when she walked by her desk. "You two Lesbos deserve each other," Jackie fired at the young woman. Then she slammed the outer door and walked slowly to the elevator for the ride down to her operation.

It took Mollie Farnham less time for Jackie Armstrong to slam the outer door before she had dialed Dimmler's private phone. "George," Mollie began totally exasperated by the encounter with Jackie, "something has to be done about that Armstrong, Bitch!"

"Whoa, hold on there, Mollie," Dimmler was taken off guard but sensing a personality problem between two very competent women. "What has she done...this time?"

"I want....I demand that she be put on Report for insubordination. She can't talk to me me like that and get away with it."

"Mollie, calm down," Dimmler tried to reason with her. "What happened?"

"She's an insubordinate, jealous sonofabitch. She's trying to tell me what policy is and isn't. I'm fed up with her, George. She should be suspended or fired today!"

"Did you give Jackie something to do?"

"Yes, and she gave me and my secretary a ration of shit and made some disparaging sexual remarks... Just because she's in love with Flynn!"

"Wait a second, Mollie," Dimmler replied, sensing the the crux of the problem. "Who's in love with whom?"

"I know that she and Flynn are tight," Mollie ranted on, "and she thinks she has him all to herself..."

"Look," Dimmler continued, "We all know that Jeremiah Flynn is an inveterate bachelor. He plays all of you women like a violin. He's a schmaltz-er, and schmoozer. He couldn't care less about Jackie Armstrong. And, she is trying to upset you. Successfully, I might add. She's been like that for years. She also knows you have a soft spot for Flynn, as we all do. It's a competitive thing between you two and Flynn teases both of you for his own amusement."

"Bullshit. I don't have 'a thing' for Flynn or any man for that matter."

"Okay, okay. Let's get back to business. Do you have the report?"

"Yes, I have it. I, as I now first look it over, I don't see that there is any connection between this Manderino fellow and Flynn. There's nothing in his reports that...mentions...Manderino by name...Looking at the cross references....it appears that they have....many of the same acquaintances...none that I can...hold on a second.......Jesus Christ! I can't believe this!"

Dimmler was interested. "What is it, Mollie?"

"George I need to run another search report to verify this information. And if it pans out our 'Contra' connection may have been seriously compromised. It would be just like Flynn, too, that sonofabitch!"

Although Dimmler was accustomed to hearing disturbing news, if the 'Contra' connection was jeopardized, his ass could be in boiling water on Capitol Hill if that news ever got out."

"Drop everything else," Dimmler ordered. "Make certain...In fact, handle this personally. When you've assembled all the facts get back to me at once. Do not let anyone know what you find, except me. Is that clear."

"Yes, sir, it is very clear. I'm on it."

THE WHITE HOUSE

Secretary of Defense Phillip Raab was attempting to brief President Bunnell on the status of the United States' troop and naval deployment in the Middle East. Also at the briefing were Secretary of State James Makoweic, Chief of Staff Admiral Michael A. Moorehouse, and William Pfohl of the National Security Agency.

"Mister Secretary," President Bunnell began asking the Secretary of Defense, "what's our current military presence in the Middle East?"

"Madam President," Secretary Raab answered, "because of the Iraq, Afghanistan and Pakistan deployments, we are very short-handed as far as ground troops. As far as our naval resources, the Sixth Fleet is finishing training exercises in the Mediterranean. The Seventh is scheduled to begin similar exercises in the Indian Ocean this week, but we are on a holding pattern, pending your decision to deploy or remain."

Admiral Moorehouse interjected, "Well, it seems to me that we shouldn't be too hasty in canceling any of these exercises. I can't see that the Seventh Fleet needs to be deployed at this time. And, as far as the Sixth goes, there's nothing to be gained by having them steam into the Red Sea. They need to re-fit and hold their positions."

"But, Admiral, with all due respect," Raab argued, "if we don't start deployment now it could take weeks for us to get our fleets over there in case of a fire fight erupts."

NSA Director Pfohl spoke out, "That's pure speculation, I believe, on your part, Mister Secretary. I agree with the Chief of Staff on this one. As the Admiral has implied, if we come storming into the area Iran is going to see that as a belligerent attempt--a provocation, if you will, by the U.S."

Secretary Makoweic appeared agitated. "A provocation! For Chrissake, Mister Director, it's President Jahmir who's doing the provoking! He's the one who has been enriching uranium...making a nuclear weapon and is attempting to, in his own words, 'wipe Israel off the face of the earth!' If that's not provocation, then I don't know what is."

"Gentlemen," President Bunnell attempted to calm things down, "let's not let our emotions blind our reasoning. First of all, I believe we have to seriously consider our allies. Especially the Israelis. If we don't indicate that we are behind them they might just go it alone. And we would have an awful mess over there. I agree with Admiral Moorehouse and Director Pfohl right now, however. I don't wish to give the Iranians and the rest of the Arab world the wrong impression. I'm also concerned that we have spread our troops too thin. Frankly, I believe the American people are sick of these wars and would just as soon have all of our troops at home."

Chief of Staff Moorehouse glanced at NSA Director Pfohl and smiled slightly which went unnoticed by the rest of the group. Then Moorehouse said, "The President is right about this. The American people are tired of war. Remember the demonstrations and protests over Viet Nam?"

Secretary of Defense Raab shifted in his chair obviously upset at the way this briefing was going. "Damn it, Admiral, this is not Viet Nam. It it's not the same scenario as Viet Nam. A large and vital facet of the

American economy and the Western economy of our allies hinges on Middle Eastern oil! If we get cut off from that supply we have no other recourse than to take pre-emptive action to secure that oil."

"I have to agree with the Secretary of Defense," Makoweic exclaimed taking Raab's side. "We have to show the Iranians, the North Koreans and any other country that we intend to take a firm stand on this issue. No matter what!"

President Bunnell assumed control of the debate. "Gentlemen, we are not going to put the American people into another war if we can avoid it. I still agree with Admiral Moorehouse and Director Pfohl." Then turning to the Defense Secretary she continued, "Phillip, I want you to direct that the armed forces be put on stand-by alert. Have them continue with their training exercises." Then, addressing the Secretary of State, the President directed, "Jim, fly over to Tel Aviv and encourage the Israelis to exercise patience. Also, find out what Moscow's intentions are with regard to abiding by the U.N. sanctions. You'll also need to feel out the Chinese, as you know, they are North Korea's only protector and ally in the Far East."

"Is this your final decision on this matter, Madam President?" Raab asked.

"Yes, it is!" Admiral Moorehouse answered for the President.

Secretary of State Makoweic shook his head but remained silent for a moment before he announced, "Very well. I'll leave today. I just hope there is enough time."

Moorehouse, feeling powerful added, "Don't be so pessimistic, Mister Secretary. We know what we're doing."

The two Secretaries, Makoweic and Raab, stood and shook hands with the President then left the Oval Office.

Outside the Oval Office Makoweic took the Defense Secretary aside and calmly said, "Looks like we know who's calling all the shots, don't we?"

"That fucker!" Raab spit out. "He doesn't know his ass from first base. And that weasel, Pfohl, I thought he might know better. Well, as long as those two have her ear and Moorehouse her ass we're in a world of shit."

"I hear you, Phil."

After the briefing was over, Chief of Staff Moorehouse went back to his office. A short time later his private line rang.

"Yes?"

"I think you should know that there is a connection surfacing on the Contra Affair."

Moorehouse became concerned. "What connection? What do you mean?"

"I mean," the voice continued, "a link between you, Manderino and Flynn. We believe that he knows all about you and Don Vito's son, Santino."

The Admiral began to sweat visibly upset. "How does he know? How do you know that he knows?"

"Because Flynn was there right after your accident. Remember, you and Santino were trapped in the car when it caught fire? Well, did you know who pulled both of you out of that car and saved your lives?"

"No, I never knew, I was unconscious. I woke up in the hospital. I assumed it was the police or the EMT's...."

"It wasn't. It was Flynn! He saved both of your lives. He took both of you to the hospital before the police arrived. Flynn recognized Santino, of course. And, since you were with him, he must have believed you two were friends. He's not stupid. He obviously put two and two together rather quickly and covered the incident up. Don Vito knows that Flynn saved his son and now is indebted to Flynn. They work that way you know..."

"How did you find out about this? I was on leave and nobody knew anything that we were doing."

"Wrong, Admiral! It's in Flynn's confidential report-file. There was never a need for it to come to light except when certain individuals started running cross reference searches...By the way, what disc's does Flynn have?"

"The disc's! I thought they were destroyed in the fire!"

"Apparently, not. Flynn must have retrieved them and now has them somewhere."

"Who knows about this?" Moorehouse asked visibly alarmed.

"Fortunately, right now, only me. Perhaps one other, but I think I can take care of that."

"You'd better!" Michael Moorehouse threatened.

"Whoa there, Michael. Don't use that tone with me. Do you think I want this mess to get around? It could blow up in our face."

"I'm sorry," Moorehouse apologized. "It's just that...er, I didn't mean anything by it. I'm just looking out for the country's and the President's interest."

"Bullshit. You're looking out for your own ass. I just wanted to alert you to the situation. I'll try to handle things at my end. But as long as Flynn's alive and those discs are around he can destroy you and this whole Contra operation."

"But why hasn't he done anything about this if he really knows?"

"You don't really know him do you, Admiral?"

"Maybe not. But I do know that we've got to get that sonofabitch."

It's just a matter of time, Michael. It's just a matter of time." The call was disconnected.

Admiral Moorehouse was dripping wet with perspiration and he was as pale as a sheet. He sat down heavily in his chair and stared at the walls of his office. His whole body was numb while he thought, "Flynn saved my life and never said anything...Why not? And those discs. They have everything on them. The whole Contra operation. If it ever gets out, Watergate will look like a nursery rhyme compared to this." Moorehouse continued his thoughts, "No wonder Don Vito has helped Flynn. Santino is his only son, his life. And that bastard Flynn gave it back to Don Vito with no questions asked and no one ever was to know. The Code of Silence...but Flynn's not Mafia, not even Italian. But now Flynn is 'family' to Don Vito Manderino...Holy Shit!"

AMSTERDAM

Flynn put Kristen's letter in his attache case before he drove back to his newly rented apartment. He took his cane, put on his glasses and cap and limped up to the doorway. Again, Flynn pretended to be out of breath and fumbling for his key while looking around the street. The British Agent he saw earlier was gone although another had taken his place on the same bench. "They've still got the same old newspaper. Shit, can't they afford a new edition?" This thought brought a slight smile to his lips while he entered the building.

Flynn spent the rest of the day in his apartment trying to fit the known puzzle pieces in place and preparing for his journey to England and beyond in an effort to find Kristen Shults.

Flynn left his apartment at eight o'clock. "I need to call Jackie Armstrong," he mumbled while riding the elevator cage down to the main floor. "I hope she has uncovered some new information before I meet with Joseppi Penella." He drove through Amsterdam making a series of left and right turns, often back tracking, making certain that he was not being followed. Finally confident that he was not being followed, he took out his cell phone and made the call to Jackie's private number.

The phone rang four times and just as Flynn was about to disconnect she answered. "Hello...Dial-A-Date, may I help you?"

"I'd like to talk to Alice Long, please."

"Well, well, if it isn't Tommy Boyce....Or is this Bobby Hart?"

"You pick, Babe," Flynn quipped back.

"I'd like to kick your ass, Flynn!" Jackie joked.

"You'd need a very long leg, Darlin'. Did Nick get a hold of you?"

"You've got a lot of balls offering me twenty grand for my 'Vette, Flynn!"

Flynn laughed remembering he sent thirty thousand to Nick by wire transfer. "Well, it's used! The last guy to drive it put a shit load of miles on it."

"You're a bastard, do you know that?"

"Jackie, accept is a a down payment. If, and when, I get back and get your precious car back to you, you can keep the money and the car."

233

"I'd trade it all in for a gold wedding band," Jackie offered.

"I bet you would," Flynn added. "Now, what's happening?"

In a serious vein now, Jackie started her ranting on Mollie Farnham. "She's on a real Flynn search. Something about Don Vito Manderino and you. She's looking for some sort of connection. Do you have any ideas?"

"Yeah, I have a couple. Look, can you side-track her somehow? I don't think I want her to know too much right now."

I believe I can," Jackie smiled. "It might be fun. Unless she's already got the newest program. I'll see what I can do."

"Look, I told you before, don't get yourself in any hot water or trouble over me," Flynn advised.

"That's a laugh. I've already got in trouble over you. Today, when I brought the report she wanted on you....the first one, which only shows a hint of a link between you and Manderino. I told her to kiss my ass."

"Jesus, Jackie! Don't get fired! I need you."

"Fired by that bitch? Never. Fuck her anyway."

"Hey, have you found out anything new on United Petroleum?" Flynn asked, changing the subject away from Mollie.

"Nothing other than what I already told you. Actually it's been a little hectic around here. With the Middle East situation boiling, Foreign Minister Saunders getting terminated; and then SHE wanting me to run your name through eighty-eight gazillion files. You probably never knew how popular you are."

"No, I never thought I was except with you, 'Kid'."

"Don't pull that Bogart shit on me," Jackie laughed.

"Are you sure about Saunders being 'sanctioned'?" Flynn asked soberly.

"Affirmative, Jerr. Steering wheel box was tampered with..." A thought came to her. "Hey, just like your old girlfriend's husband's wreck on the Belt-way a few years ago."

"My who?" Flynn was confused momentarily.

"Your OTHER girlfriend, Madam President, that's who."

"You're being a real 'sport'. Do you know that?"

"No, seriously, Jerry, I'm not. I think I'll call a friend of mine and see what I can find out about that accident. Maybe there's a connection. His name was Spencer, wasn't it?"

"Yes." Flynn felt a cold chill run up his back while he pondered the possibility that this might be more than coincidence. He paused a few seconds before he finally concluded, "Okay. I've got to go. I've got a lead and I'm going to check it out. Try and find out what you can without getting caught. And, Jackie, see what you can do about sending Mollie on a red herring hunt as far as Don Vito is concerned. I'd like not to play that card right now."

"Roger, Dodger. Anything else?" Jackie asked.

"Nope, that's enough for now. You stay out of trouble."

"No sweat, Big Boy. You do the same." The call was disconnected.

The *Cafe dur Amstel Haus* was a quiet restaurant off the tourist trail and generally patronized by locals or well traveled business people who avoided tourist traps.

The food was excellent and the privacy was an unwritten trademark. What went on there stayed there.

Flynn arrived shortly before nine o'clock. He noted that Joseppi Penella had not as yet arrived. He took a seat at the bar and ordered a Heineken. Penella arrived before Flynn had finished his beer.

"Hello, my friend," Penella greeted Flynn careful not to mention his name. "I hope I have not kept you waiting."

"Not at all. I was a few minutes early..."

The maitre d' showed Penella and Flynn to a secluded table near the back of the restaurant. "May I get you something from the bar?" He asked handing each man a menu.

Joseppi deferred to Flynn who picked up his nearly empty Heineken bottle and said, "I have another one of these."

"And I'll have my usual, Otto."

"Very well. A Heineken and a vodka martini, extra dry, stirred, not shaken," Otto the maitre d' replied. Then he turned and left the men alone.

"It appears, my friend," Penella began, "that you are a very unpopular man."

"What have you found out?"

"There is a very sizable price on your head. A million American dollars."

"Any indication as to who put the contract out on me?"

"My family has made, shall I say, some subtle and some not so subtle inquiries concerning that. It might make more sense to you than me. Apparently, there is a syndicate of some powerful people who want you out of the way."

Flynn listened carefully to each word that Joseppi said. "Well, I know there is some of my own people who would like to pin the murder of President Harper on me...."

Penella interrupted Flynn. "The British also are looking for you. You eliminated one of their agents. An MI-6 man named David Greene."

"I knew David Greene. I talked to him at Dulles in Washington. But I didn't kill him. He was dead when I found him just before I was to get on a KLM plane to come over here."

"Whether or not you are responsible for Greene's death is of no interest to me. It is your business. And if you tell me that you did not kill him, well then, I believe you," Penella assured Flynn.

Flynn was about to speak but stopped when Otto brought their drinks to the table.

"Are you ready to order, gentlemen?"

"Otto, I'll have the sauerbraten over noodles." Then turning to Flynn asked, "What will you have, my friend?" Again, careful not to mention Flynn's name.

"The grilled swordfish will be fine." Flynn replied without making eye contact.

"A bottle of your very best wine too, Otto," Penella added.

"Excellent," the maitre d' smiled again leaving the two men alone.

"What can you tell me about this syndicate, Joseppi?" Flynn asked as soon as Otto left their table.

"We have been able to learn that United Petroleum has a very large contract to supply oil to North Korea in contravention of your country's economic sanctions against them. A man called 'Tiger' is behind a scheme to corner the supply and production of the world's oil. United Petroleum has contracts with its Middle Eastern partners including Iran, and South American partners in Venezuela. And, they are making very aggressive moves to establish a monopoly of the oil market for 'Tiger's' purpose."

"Who is this man you call, 'Tiger'?" Flynn asked.

"From what I have been told, he is a very powerful and ruthless North Korean, Kim Moon Jung. He is the real power behind Premier Kim Moon-il. He has been building an empire in trafficking drugs both in Asia and South America. He deals directly with Don Carlos Escobar, the Drug Lord of Venezuela.

"Jesus!" Flynn exclaimed.

"Does this mean something to you, my friend?"

Flynn explained, "Joseppi, the major stockholders in United Petroleum include Escobar, and a Korean—the man you called Kim Moon Jung, along with the late President Harper, Foreign Minister Sanders, Sheik Mohammed al Anzarisad, and David R. Laird, the company CEO!"

"Drugs, oil and much money!" Penella was seeing the connection.

"What I don't understand, is why was Harper and Saunders killed?" Flynn was puzzled.

"Perhaps they had a 'family' disagreement?"

Flynn thought for a moment. "Maybe yes and maybe no. But there is something or someone missing from the total picture. We're talking about major world governments involvement with high scale crime and corruption."

"This is not new, Flynn" Penella whispered. "You can't be that naïve."

"No, Joseppi, I'm not naïve. But this situation in the Middle East with Iran saber rattling, North Korea saber rattling...no, it's part of a plan." It suddenly became clear to Flynn. "Oh my God!"

"What is it?" Penella asked excitedly.

"If I'm right about this," Flynn tensed, "then I don't have much time to stop it."

Penella looked at Flynn trying to understand what he was talking about. "Is there anything I can do to help you?" Joseppi offered.

Flynn reiterated, "It's a plan! This whole thing is an orchestrated plot! The world crisis. The sudden spike in oil prices. Assassinations of Harper, Sommerset, Saunders...It's about control of oil, with the money from drugs. Don't you see? An international conspiracy!"

Penella did not fully comprehend what Flynn was trying to say. "He is either crazy or has stumbled on something that might be useful to the 'family'," Joseppi thought to himself. Penella quickly decided that Flynn was not crazy out of respect to Don Vito, his cousin.

The two men were served their meals and ate without further discussion. Flynn was silent because he needed to be. Penella was silent because a man's business is a private matter and he didn't want to appear pushy.

Near the end of the meal Flynn finally broke the silence. "Joseppi, I need to get to England, tonight!"

"Tonight?" Penella was surprised by the suddenness.

"Yes. I must move quickly. Time is of the essence. I apologize for springing this on you. Can you get me safe passage?"

"If it is this important to you, my friend, I will escort you there myself." Penella made a gesture to a man at another table who came over at once.

"Nunzio, go with Mister Flynn while he gets his things." Joseppi instructed quietly. "Then bring him by the airstrip. You remember where I keep my Baron."

"Yes, of course," Nunzio dutifully replied.

Penella looked at Flynn and affectionately explained, "This is my brother, Nunzio. He is a very capable associate. He will take care of you. When you collect what you need at your apartment he will bring you to my private airstrip and we will fly to England within the hour. Is this enough time?"

Flynn looked over the young man who appeared to be very strong. "Yes, an hour should be plenty of time. But I don't think you need to send your brother along with me. Just tell me where...."

"Nonsense, my friend. You have your ways and I have mine. I made a solemn promise to Don Vito that I would guarantee your safety while you were here in Amsterdam. And, I am determined to keep that solemn oath."

Flynn understood that nothing more he could say would deter Penella. He got up and shook hands with Nunzio saying, "Okay, Nunzio, let's get moving."

The young man did not answer but smiled at Flynn and shook his hand. Nunzio turned to his brother and gave him a slight nod of his head. The two left in Flynn's car for his apartment.

The ride was unusually quiet. Nunzio did not offer anything by way of conversation and Flynn thought it best not to try and pry anything from him. The trip took about twenty-five minutes. Flynn made his usual and careful evasive maneuvers to be certain that there was no one following. When they reached the block, Flynn stopped several doors away. He turned off the cars lights and engine and sat for a few minutes looking up and down the street. He noticed that the MI-6 agents were missing from their usual spot on the bench across from the apartment house.

"All right, Nunzio," Flynn said at last, "I'm going in. There shouldn't be any problem but keep your eyes open for anyone who might be watching too closely."

"I should go with you," Nunzio offered while Flynn put on his disguise which was in the back seat next to his attache case.

"No, it won't be necessary. Everything should be fine. I'll be out in about five minutes. You wait for me here."

Flynn got out of the car and limped his way down the dimly lighted street to the apartment house. He calculated that he was being watched, although unconcerned, having played this game several times before. He fumbled for his keys pretending to be short of breath before entering. Everything appeared normal. Flynn took the elevator to the third floor and walked to his door.

When Flynn began to unlock his apartment door a man came out of Kristen's apartment. Flynn immediately recognized him as the MI-6 British agent he talked to earlier on the bench across the street. Flynn instinctively went on alert.

"Good evening," Flynn said in perfect Dutch.

"Goot evening," the British agent replied in a poor accent.

Flynn opened his apartment door and started to enter when the British agent took a few steps toward him and this time spoke in English. "You almost fooled me again, Mister Flynn. But not this time."

Flynn turned to meet the man quickly and caught him off guard hitting the British agent in the solar plexus with the butt of his cane. The agent doubled over and was pushed backwards out of breath, gasping for air. Flynn grabbed the man's hair by the back of the head with his left hand while driving his right palm upwards into the man's nose. The nose bone broke and drove into the agent's brain killing him in an instant.

Flynn looked around the floor to see if there was any backup. No one appeared. Flynn dragged the man's body inside his apartment and closed the door. He gathered a small duffel bag with some clothes and personal items. He rechecked his weapon and slid it behind his back into his pants.

Flynn turned out all the lights before opening the door a crack to check the hallway looking and listening for anything or anyone. The floor was quiet, just as the superintendent had promised. Flynn picked up the dead agent's body and dragged him to the elevator in the middle of the floor, propping him up against the iron gate. Flynn pushed the lift's button for the fifth floor and rode up. Then he dragged the man's body over to a wall and sat him down against another apartment door. Flynn walked back to the elevator then rode it down to the main floor.

He was surprised to meet Nunzio at the entrance. Beside Nunzio were two bodies dressed in British tweed suits. Flynn looked at Nunzio and quipped, "My God, people are dying to get into this neighborhood, aren't they?"

"It's gone to shit," Nunzio answered with a straight-expressionless-face.

Flynn smiled at Nunzio and declared, "Let's get

out of here, my good man, before the entire Royal Army shows up."

The two walked back to Flynn's car and sped off into the darkness to Joseppi Penella's private airstrip.

Upon arrival at the airstrip, Flynn noticed that Joseppi's Baron was already warming up and going through a pre-flight checklist and ready for take-off. Flynn looked over at Nunzio and extended his hand. "Thank you, Nunzio, I owe you one."

"You're quite welcome, sir," Nunzio said shaking Flynn's hand. "But it's two!" Nunzio laughed for the first time and added, "Have a safe journey! I will see you soon."

"Right you are," Flynn rejoined. "And you take care, yourself."

Joseppi Penella was in the left seat when Flynn climbed in and buckled his seat belt. Then he tossed his bag and attache case behind him. Penella looked over at Flynn and asked, "Any trouble, my friend?"

"Nothing we couldn't handle. Thanks for sending Nunzio. He was very helpful."

Joseppi smiled and replied, "I thought he might be."

The plane, a twin engine Baron, taxied to the end of the runway and turned without stopping, full throttle, down the grass runway and up into the midnight sky. Flynn was on his way to the hunt. He looked out the window into the darkness while his thoughts drifted to better times with Kristen. He couldn't stop thinking and hoping if she were all right. Somehow, he knew that she was still alive. Anger and hatred filled Flynn throughout when he thought what Kristen probably had endured at the hands of her kidnappers. He knew that payback time was approaching for those who hurt her. He couldn't wait. "Hold on Kris," Flynn thought, "I'm on my way.... I'm on my way."

LANGLEY, VIRGINIA

Deputy Director of clandestine operations George Dimmler was at his desk when the intercom announced, "Mister Dimmler, Miss Farnham is here to see you."

"Send her in."

Mollie Farnham came crashing through the Deputy Director's door, her face was flushed and her forehead all furrowed in anger. "George," Mollie's voice was nearly a shrill, "I can't get into the the cross reference search program today! I've tried everything I know. But that little BITCH has done something to block me out!"

"Calm down, Mollie, what are you talking about?"

"Calm down! How can I calm down? You asked me to personally check out the cross reference search program on Jeremiah Flynn and Vito Manderino because I uncovered, or thought I might have uncovered, some connection which has National Security implications over and above..."

Dimmler cut off her tirade. "Yes, I know. So what exactly is the problem?"

"The problem is that fucking bitch, Jackie Armstrong! She's sidetracked the program somehow. All I can do is go around in circles. I cannot access the file without it sending me back to the beginning."

"Why would Jackie do such a thing," Dimmler asked in disbelief. "if, in fact, she did it?"

"If she did it?" Mollie's voice hit high 'C'. "Of course she did it! She's trying to protect Flynn. She's been chasing him for years."

Dimmler turned in his chair and thought for a moment. Then he spun himself back around facing Mollie and announced, "Mollie, sit down. I'll call her in right now and we will hash this out once and for all." He picked up his phone and speed dialed Jackie's number.

"Jackie Armstrong. May I help you?"

"Jackie, this is George Dimmler. Could you please come up to my office right away?"

"Yes, sir. I'll be right up."

Dimmler looked over at Mollie putting down the phone. "Now, Mollie, get your temper in check. I don't want this to be confrontational. Let me try and work this out. You two have got to work together."

"I can't work with that bitch! She's out to get me."

"That's enough name calling," Dimmler said sternly. "You've got to work together! I don't give a damn if you two don't like each other. That's not important here. What is important is we all have a job to do and we have to work together to get that job done. Do I make myself clear?"

"I understand. She's the one who doesn't understand."

The intercom announced, "Miss Armstrong is here, Mister Dimmler."

"Please send her in."

Jackie Armstrong opened the door making a 'Loretta Young-type entrance', twirling herself around while closing the door and smiling broadly.

"Good morning, Mister Dimmler," Jackie announced cheerfully. "Good morning, Acting Assistant Deputy Director Farnham." The obvious dig was not lost on Mollie who turned red with anger.

"Good morning, " Dimmler returned the greeting. Mollie remained silent.

"You wanted to see me, sir?" Sugar wouldn't melt in Jackie's mouth.

"Yes," Dimmler began. "Miss Farnham has a problem getting into a confidential report file...the eh..cross reference search program. Apparently, she keeps getting returned to the beginning of the program when she tries to search and reaches a certain point of reference. Can you explain why this is happening?"

"Well, sir," Jackie offered, "I'm not exactly certain what file Miss Farnham is trying to access, but our new programs should allow her to continue it if she uses the right accelerator code when she reaches a critical cross over point of reference."

"You've lost me," Dimmler said. "Can you put it in simpler terms that I might understand?"

Mollie decided that she couldn't remain silent any longer. "She's put a block on the file. That's what she's telling you. She doesn't want anyone else to do the search."

Jackie in her own defense replied, "That's not the case at all, Miss Farnham. The new programs automatically circle for security reasons unless you access the accelerator codes to bypass the initial search mode."

"Since when?" Mollie screamed.

Calmly and seizing control Jackie responded, "Actually for quite some time now. It was all explained in the memo some months ago."

"I never got any memo!" Mollie finally blurted out what had been pent up. "You're just trying to protect Flynn!"

Jackie looked at her then at the Deputy Director.

"Sir, all of our confidential field operatives files are so programmed. We're trying to insure the safety of all our field operatives. Isn't that what you want, Mister Dimmler?"

Dimmler shifted in his chair uncomfortably and answered, "Of course it is. But Flynn's status has been suspended. He's left the reservation, Jackie."

"Suspended?" Jackie pretended not to know. "Really? Why?"

"Yes, he's been suspended!" Mollie sneered. "And don't pretend you didn't know it."

"I have no knowledge of Flynn being suspended. When did this all happen?"

"Bullshit!" Mollie fired back.

Dimmler gave Mollie a look of disdain. "That's enough, Mollie!" Addressing Jackie he continued. "Jackie, I ordered the suspension on Flynn's status based on certain circumstances of late. We don't know where he is or with whom he is working or on what. He's been around here long enough to know the procedures. He hasn't checked in for some time. As far as we know he may have turned."

Jackie could not sit quietly while Flynn was being called a traitor. "How can you say such things, Deputy Director? You've known Flynn longer than anyone. You know he's the most loyal and best special ops guy in this whole Agency. Shouldn't we have a little faith and trust in our own man? Flynn is Flynn."

"Well, we can't let one man dictate Company policy. He's gone rogue!" Mollie exploded.

"Company policy?" Jackie fought back. "What's more important--a man's life or Company policy? What if Flynn's in trouble? Shouldn't we be helping him?"

Mollie turned to Dimmler. "See? I told you she was protecting him."

Dimmler thought a moment before he said, "We can't help him if we don't know where he is."

Mollie was going for the kill, spitting out fire. "Why don't you ask her where he is. I'll bet anything that she knows!"

That remark hit a raw nerve with Jackie Armstrong. "Listen, I've taken enough of your insults and innuendos. As far as I understood about Company policy, Flynn always checked in with you, Mollie. He has no reason to ever check in with me."

"Hold it ladies," Dimmler had heard enough of this cat-fight. "This type of bickering is unnecessary and unbecoming to both of you who are supposed to be professionals. I want it stopped. NOW!"

There was a sudden silence in the room. Dimmler then addressed them both. "Jackie I want you to work with Mollie and train her or show her how to use the proper accelerator codes. And, Mollie, I want you to start acting like the Assistant Deputy Director!"

"That's ACTING Assistant Deputy Director" Jackie interjected.

Dimmler blew his top. "Goddamn it! I don't want another word out of either of you! Or I'll make some changes around here and get rid of both of you!"

"Sorry, Director Dimmler." Jackie retreated.

"Now, both you get out of here and work this out. If I find out you can't I'll..."

"We'll work it out, sir," Mollie conceded.

"No problem from me either, sir," Jackie added.

"Good! Now let's get back to work. There are enough problems going on in the world right now. I don't need them in this office."

The two women left together. After the door closed, Dimmler spun around in his chair to face his computer screen. He pounded on the keyboard in frustration and said to himself, "Flynn you son of a gun! Even when you're not here you make my life difficult. Where are you my boy? Where in God's world are you?"

The computer screen flashed, "ACCESS DENIED!"

THE OUTSKIRTS OF LONDON

The Baron made good time crossing the English Channel with Joseppi Penella skimming less than two hundred feet over the waves below evading radar detection.

Penella brought the aircraft in over rural England, avoiding as much visual detection as possible. Finally heading his IFR to a remote farm some fifty miles from the London city limits. He skillfully slipped the Baron down on a grass strip. Flynn thought, "Joseppi's an excellent pilot who probably has made this journey more than once before on 'family' business."

When Penella taxied to a nearby barn he leaned over to Flynn. "Here you are, my friend. Safely delivered to England, as promised. I must leave now before anyone reports an unidentified aircraft flying too low. You are about fifty to fifty-five miles southwest of London, north of Southampton. There is a pickup truck in that barn which belongs to a cousin of mine. The keys are in it and it is full of petrol. He will not miss it. Use it for as long as necessary. When you are through with it, just leave it. You will find a map of the English roads in the glove box. If there is anything else I can do for you, you know how to reach me."

"Thank you, Joseppi." Flynn replied sincerely. "You have done more than I expected."

The two men shook hands, now more than friends. Penella smiled at Flynn, then said somberly as a warning, "Flynn, you be careful. There are a lot of men and women too, who would sell your head for a million American dollars. You are all alone on your journey, my friend. Good luck and good hunting!"

Flynn latched the plane's door and stepped back. Penella had already pushed the throttle forward to the 'max' and was down the grass runway and up into the darkness before Flynn made it to the barn. The roar of the twin engines going over caused Flynn to look up and see Joseppi Penella tip his wings in a farewell salute.

He was alone again. On the hunt for Kristen Shults and the men who kidnapped and framed her. A cool calm came over Flynn. He knew what he had to do.

The truck was exactly where Joseppi said it would be. Keys in the ignition and full of gasoline. Flynn started it up and drove down the bumpy farm road to a highway. He took his smart phone and plotted a route to Dobbinshire from his location. The drive to the rural village of Dobbinshire would take several hours. Once there, Flynn would visit a quiet Catholic church and have a chat with an Irish priest. Flynn calculated that he should arrive just before dawn. He was on the scent of Kristen's trail.

Flynn reached the village an hour before dawn broke over Dobbinshire. The quaint village was still quiet when Flynn drove in. He slowed the truck passing the Catholic church. Flynn noticed a light was on in the rectory. Flynn intuitively knew the priest was up and preparing for six o'clock mass. He pulled the truck over to the side a few doors from the rectory in order to do a little reconnaissance before he made any moves.

Flynn walked back into the darkness toward the rectory and made a sharp turn down a walk between the church and the parish house staying in the shadows. He made his way to the back of the rectory and looked into the lighted room which he immediately identified as the kitchen. There the old priest was drinking a cup of tea at the table while he was reading his Daily Office. Flynn watched for several minutes to make certain that there was no one else in the house. He was confident that the priest was alone in the rectory. A check of his Rolex indicated that it was five forty-seven. Flynn backtracked his way to the street. He would have to wait until Mass was over before he had a talk with this old priest concerning Kristen's whereabouts.

A couple of older ladies were approaching the church from behind him while an elderly man was arriving from the opposite direction. Flynn fell in behind the two ladies and entered the church. Flynn chose a back pew off to the left. The two women walked to the front pew, the elderly man sat near the middle on the right side of the aisle.

At exactly six o'clock the church bells rang in the loft as the priest left the sacristy for the altar. The old priest was wearing red vestments. There was no altar boy. Flynn thought back to his youth when he was a knight of the altar serving Mass. "Red vestments," Flynn thought, "another mass for a martyr."

Flynn remained until just before communion when he left the vestibule and out to the street. The sun was coming up but the village was still relatively quiet and free of traffic.

Within a few more minutes Mass had ended and the two elderly ladies and the old gent left the church and returned from the direction from which they had come. Flynn waited until the street was clear before he walked up the steps of the rectory and rang the bell. The door opened and the old priest looked at Flynn and asked, "Good morning, may I help ye?"

"Good morning, Father, I think that you might."

"Ah, a Yank," the old priest said. "Come in, lad."

Flynn was shown into the parlor. "Sit down, lad," the priest offered. "Now, tell me, how it is that I might help?"

"Well, Father, I am looking for a woman who told me that you had helped her."

The old priest's face flashed a look of puzzlement, which Flynn did not overlook. "I help, with God's Will, a number of people. Both men and women."

Flynn remained calm but insistent. "I believe you know who it is that I am talking about, Father. Her name is Kristen Shults and she wrote me a letter from here telling me that you and another man offered to help her."

"Did she now?"

"Yes, she did! And now I need to know where she is."

"I'm sorry, my son, but I don't know who it tis you're referring to." The old priest was becoming very uneasy.

"Please listen to me, Father," Flynn tried to remain cordial, "it is very important that I find her. She wrote me that you and a man called Timothy Hartnett were helping her to leave England."

The priest stood up. He was alarmed and was becoming agitated by Flynn's remarks. "I'm afraid I can't help ye. I have no knowledge of whom you're referring to or to whom you're talking about. After all, I am merely a simple parish priest in this small village."

"Cut the Blarney, Father," Flynn said directly. "It will be a lot easier if you tell me now. I will find her and either you, or this fellow Hartnett, will tell me. I won't leave Dobbinshire until I know where she is. I know that you know and quite frankly, Father, I don't care much how I find out. But I will find out."

"Are you daring to threaten a man of God?" the old priest visibly upset replied.

Flynn calmly stood and looked directly into the old priest's eyes. "No, Father, I don't threaten anymore. People tell me what I need to know...sooner or later."

"I want you to leave, sir, this minute. We have nothing further to discuss."

"Very well, Father. Have it your way for now. But I will be back. And when I do come back, I may not be as friendly as I am right now." Flynn left the rectory. He had hoped he put enough fear and panic in the old priest to flush him and Hartnett out into the open. Flynn slowly and deliberately walked up the main street to a public house where they were serving breakfast.

Flynn took a booth by the window where he could still get a view of the Rectory. He ordered some bangers, eggs and tea. While Flynn observed the rectory during his meal, there was no noticeable activity. It was just as he finished and paid his tab that Flynn saw a man enter the priest's home. Flynn hoped this was the man named Hartnett that Kristen mentioned in her letter. Flynn left the Pub and walked down the street towards the

Church and waited by the pickup truck.

A short time later the man who Flynn saw entering the Rectory came out and started walking in his direction. The man came up to where Flynn was waiting by the truck and stopped to address him.

"Ye shouldn't be threatening the old priest, Yank."

Flynn looked at the man and asked, "Are you Timothy Hartnett?"

"It's none of you fucking business. Now why don't you leave us alone before you get hurt."

"I will leave you all alone as soon as you or that old priest tell me where you took Kristen Shults."

"Never heard of her," Hartnett sneered back at Flynn.

"Well," Flynn remaining calm said, "that's not true. She says differently."

"You calling me a liar, now?"

"I guess I am," Flynn replied.

Hartnett took a swing at Flynn who anticipated the blow and, with a lightning move of his own, sidestepped the swing and drove his right fist into the side of Hartnett's face knocking him down. Hartnett got to his knees when Flynn smashed him again in the face breaking the man's nose. He went down unconscious and bleeding badly from the nose.

The old priest had been watching from his window hoping that Hartnett would have been the one to administer the pain and damage to Flynn. When he saw his man go down the priest bolted from the Rectory and came to Hartnett's aid.

"Look at what ye've done," the priest screamed at Flynn. "His nose is broken! There's no need for all this violence, now."

Flynn looked at the priest and said, "There's going to be more of the same, Father, if you don't tell me where I can find Kristen Shults."

The priest was kneeling down as Hartnett was coming to. "Who are ye? What do you want with the woman anyway?"

"I'm her friend," Flynn answered. "She wrote me that she was in trouble and she wanted my help."

"Saint's preserve us, man," the priest exclaimed. "all we did was help her. She's wanted for murder of the British Prime Minister."

Flynn helped the priest lift Hartnett up. Flynn took a handkerchief from his pocket and handed it to Hartnett to help stop the bleeding from his nose. Flynn then grabbed Hartnett's nose in his hand and snapped the cartilage back into place.

"Arrgggh!" Hartnett screamed in pain again.

"What are ye, some kind of a butcher?" the old priest shouted thinking Flynn was hurting the young man.

"He'll be all right in a little while," Flynn said. "Now gents, do you tell me or do I re-adjust his nose again?"

The old priest held up his hand motioning to Flynn to stop. "Come, help me get Timo into the Rectory so I can look after him."

Flynn put his arm around Hartnett and steadied him as the three men walked back to the priest's home. They went inside and back to the kitchen.

"Sit him down there," the priest motioned to a kitchen chair, "while I get a cold, wet cloth for his face."

"Look, Father," Flynn began, "You're wasting my time. I need to know..."

"Hold your whist now," the priest admonished

Flynn. "In due time." He took a small towel and soaked it in cold water and gave it to Hartnett to cover his nose. Then he went to the cupboard and brought down three cups and poured them all tea.

Flynn pulled his weapon out from the back of his pants and layed it on the table. "Father, I'm in a bit of a hurry."

"There's no need for that," the old priest replied looking at Flynn's pistol. "Have a spot of tea."

Flynn was becoming more impatient. "Look, Father, I don't care if you and Hartnett here are IRA, or whatever. That's your business. My business is getting to Kristen Shults and proving her innocence. And I know," Flynn took out Kristen's letter from his pocket and tossed it across the table at the priest, "she was here. And, I also know, that you and Timo here took her by way of Liverpool, to Ireland. Now, as I said, I'm on a tight schedule. Time is of the essence. So tell me now, or else...."

"Hold it, now. Hold it...there'll be no need for any more rough stuff," the old priest now realized that Flynn was serious. "You're right. We helped her. Timo took her to Liverpool so we could get her to Ireland, but she ran."

Flynn grabbed Hartnett's hand and with the butt of his gun smashed it down on his little finger breaking the bones.

"Aharrragh!" Hartnett screamed in pain.

The priest was shocked by Flynn's move. But before he could say anything else Flynn demanded, "Don't lie to me again, Father. It's a sin, remember? I'll break every one of his fingers and then his arms and legs if necessary, priest! Now, no more bullshit."

"Tell him, Father, or I will," Hartnett winced in

pain.

The old priest finally saw that Flynn meant what he said and he didn't want Hartnett to suffer anymore pain. "Very well, then. She's a novice in the convent of the Sisters of Charity at Noch Sheegan, near Belfast. She now goes by the name of Sister Maureen."

Flynn looked at the old man and then at Hartnett who was nodding in agreement with the priest's words. "This could have gone a lot easier, Father, if you told me earlier this morning. I didn't want to do it this way, but the sin is yours, Father, not mine. Now, if you're lying to me, I'll be back and both of you had better be in the state of grace because you will be seeing Jesus."

The old priest hung his head and looked at Hartnett who was in obvious pain. "I'm sorry, Timo," was all he could say.

Flynn left five, one hundred pound notes on the priest's table. "For his pain and suffering." In an instant Flynn was out the door and heading toward Liverpool.

Flynn's GPS guided him up the M-3, north to Oxford; then he took the M-40 around Birmingham to the M-6. Traveling on the M-6 to the M-62, west to downtown Liverpool. Across the Queensway Service Road and Bridge to Shore Road, then to the Egerton Wharf on to the Pump Road to Wallasey Dock. Once there, Flynn bought a ticket on the Belfast-Birkenhead Ferry from the Norfork Line for 172 Pounds Sterling which included his vehicle and a round trip--for two. The journey was going to take about eight hours. Flynn noted the departure time of 6:30PM, and figured he would be in Belfast around 2AM. "It's a slow boat," Flynn thought, "but it's a safer way to travel. I just hope Kristen is all right."

WASHINGTON, D. C.

"We have not intercepted any phone traffic from Flynn for a while, now," the voice on the line said. "Maybe the 'contract' has been accepted."

"If that's the case, why don't we have any confirmation. Certainly someone would want the million dollars, wouldn't they?"

"I suppose you're right. But how do you explain his silence?"

"I can't." There was a momentary pause. "Let me check something else."

"What is it?"

"GPS signals."

"I don't understand."

"GPS signals are tracking devices. We have them on our Agency cars so we know where they are. If Flynn is using his GPS, we might be able to track him. It's a long shot but we have the fastest computers and the up-links are already being monitored, so it might be worth it to look."

"Let me know if you find anything." The call was terminated.

BELFAST, NORTHERN IRELAND

Flynn saw the lights of Belfast while the Ferry approached the Victoria Channel. When the Ferry neared the Dock, Flynn prepared to exit. He looked at his watch and noted that it was past two thirty. A number of cars went before him and when it was his turn he drove up the Corry Road to Corry Link to Dock Street, making his way past the cars and lorries waiting to load back to Liverpool. On Dock Street, Flynn made a left on to Short Street and stopped at the *American Bar*. Fortunately, it was still open. Flynn parked and went inside.

"What'll ya have?" the bar tender asked.

"Double Jamison on the rocks," Flynn replied.

When the bar tender came back Flynn asked, "What's your name, young man? I hate to call, 'Hey You'"

The young man smiled, "It's Adam. Adam Fulgrahm, sir."

"Thank you, Adam," Flynn smiled. "Say can you tell me where the convent of the Sisters of Charity might be?"

"No, sir, I'm sorry. I'm kind of new here and don't know too many places. I could ask our night manager. She's a native."

"Thank you, Adam. What's her name?"

"Ashley Eldridge. She's right over there. You can't miss her. She's got some bodacious ta ta's."

Flynn looked over in the general direction of where Adam was indicating. He immediately saw what Adam was referring to when Ashley turned toward the bar. She was young, very attractive and Flynn smirked, "She does have some 'bodacious 'ta ta's', Adam. You're right. Never mind, I'll ask her myself."

Flynn walked over to the young woman. "Are you Ashley?"

The woman smiled and cheerfully replied, "Yes, and who might you be?"

"Flynn."

"Well, Flynn, do you have any other name?"

Flynn was slightly embarrassed and smiled, "Jeremiah Flynn."

"So what can I do for you, Flynn, Jeremiah Flynn?" Ashley bantered obviously taken with Flynn.

"Can you tell me how to get to the convent of the Sisters of Charity at Noch Sheegan?"

Ashley laughed, "What are you planning to do at a convent, Mister Flynn, Jeremiah Flynn, get into a bad habit?"

Flynn smiled at her joke. "That was almost as cute as you, Ashley,"

Ashley looked up into Flynn's deep blue eyes and said, "Thank you. You're pretty cute yourself."

Flynn took her by the arm and guided her to a table where they both sat down. "Can I buy you a drink, Ashley?"

"Sure." Then she looked over at Adam and waved. "Two of what this gentleman is drinking, Adam."

Adam waved back and fixed the two drinks of Irish whiskey and brought them to the table.

It was going on three o'clock. Flynn was tired and as much as he enjoyed the company of this lovely young woman he felt an urgency to go. He lifted his glass, "Here's lookin' at you, kid," Flynn imitated Bogart and downed the double shot.

Ashley downed her shot as well. "You can't get into the convent tonight, ya know."

"I guess you're right." Flynn agreed. "Is there a hotel around here?"

"Yeah, there's a few. But why not stay at my place?"

"It's a bit sudden isn't it?" Flynn smiled. "I mean, we hardly know one another."

"What's to know? As soon as I saw you I knew that I wanted you," Ashley confessed. "Come on." She took Flynn by the hand and led him out the back door to her car. There, Ashley pulled Flynn to her and kissed him deeply. Flynn held her close and swallowed her tongue as she did his, in rapid succession. She finally broke off the embrace and opened her car door. Flynn went around to the pickup and got in. He followed Ashley while she drove off down Dock Street passed the Arena Health and Fitness Club and pulled into the next driveway at an apartment complex. "We're here," she announced bounding out of her car and up to the apartment door. Flynn parked the pickup next to her car and followed.

Within a few seconds Ashley had the door open and was racing to the bedroom peeling her clothes off as she went. By the time Flynn reached the bedroom Ashley was completely undressed and waiting for him. They embraced and she fell back onto the bed. Within minutes Ashley was writhing in pleasure while Flynn made love to her over and over again. It was nearly five o'clock before they fell to sleep in each others arms.

Late the next morning, Flynn awoke. Ashley was still sleeping soundly. He dressed and quietly slipped outside to the pickup. Flynn backtracked to the Arena Health and Fitness Club, where he was able to shower and shave, after paying a modest guest fee.

When he left the Club, Flynn continued on to North Queen until he reached Antrim Road. There, he drove up Antrim until he reached Fort William Park where he took a left onto Somerton Road past the Dominican College, across from Saint Patrick's College. The convent of the Sisters of Charity was within a high walled enclosure and was tucked down a short, nameless road surrounded by tall bushes and trees. The landscaping made the convent look protected and isolated from the outside world. Flynn parked near the entrance and hoped that Kristen was inside and well.

Flynn walked up to the entrance where a sign read:

"The Noch Sheegan Convent of the Sisters of Charity is a cloistered Convent, where we do not speak, nor do we allow visitors. If you are making a delivery, proceed around to the back and unload at the portico. May God Bless You."

Flynn had not anticipated this roadblock to freeing Kristen. He thought, "I know that they have priests come in to say Mass and hear their confessions. And they need to eat, so some food has to be delivered." He drove around to the back to see what this 'portico' was like.

The rear of the convent building had a covered loading dock where any delivery packages could be left out of the elements. There was a bell next to a garage-type door that was locked from within. The deliveryman would ring the bell before he left to signal to the nuns inside that a delivery had been made. Flynn also noticed that a security camera was installed which would show whether the area had been cleared so that no nun would come into contact with anyone from the outside world. "This is going to be interesting," Flynn thought while studying the area.

"The walls are about fifteen feet high," he estimated to himself while he got back into the pickup. He would have to wait until dark. Flynn left the area and drove around looking for a hardware store. Driving up Woodstock Road, Flynn discovered Dawson Wright hardware at 355 Woodstock Road. He pulled the pickup in front of the store and went in.

Flynn was greeted by an elderly man, "Good day

to you, sir," the man said smiling. "May I help ye find something?"

"I'm looking for a twenty foot ladder," Flynn began, "and some rope."

"Right this way, sir," the gentleman answered, "right this way."

Flynn followed the man to the back of the store where there were a number of ladders in different sizes. Some were the studier wooden ones and the others were lighter aluminum ladders. "This is quite a store," Flynn was making small conversation.

"It 'tis. We've been in this same location now for fifty years," the elderly gent replied, proudly. "Would ye be lookin' for wooden or aluminum?"

Flynn looked over the selection before he answered. "Aluminum. I need something light, but it's got to be twenty foot."

"Then this one will do ye," the old gent said with a wink pointing one out to Flynn. It's light enough for one man to handle without any trouble, and it's study enough to hold your weight."

Flynn smiled at the man, "I'll take it. Now, sir, where's your rope?"

A stern look came over the elderly man, "Ye wouldn't be doin' yourself any harm, now would ye?"

Flynn laughed. "No, sir. I just need to bind a few things. Nothing to do with the ladder."

"I'm glad to hear that, lad. The rope is over there by the wall. You pick out what you need and I'll get the ladder to your vehicle. Where are ye parked, now?"

"The pickup in front."

Flynn found some nylon rope and measured out about twenty five feet of it and brought it to the counter.

While walking to the counter, he saw the elderly man easily carry the aluminum ladder to his pickup and lift it into the bed. The old man lashed the ladder to the pickup with some twine so that it wouldn't slide about while Flynn drove. Flynn thought, "This is one tough old rooster."

The elderly gent came back inside and walked behind the counter. "How much rope have ye got there?"

"Twenty five feet."

"Will this be cash or charge card, lad?"

Flynn answered quickly, "Cash."

The elderly man punched up the total and announced, "A hundred seventeen and six."

Flynn peeled off three fifty pound notes and handed them to the old gent. "Have you been working here long?"

The old man gave Flynn his change and smiled, "Since the day I opened."

Flynn nodded and smiled now realizing that this man was the owner and founder Dawson Wright. "Thank you, Mister Wright."

"Thank you for stopping by," Dawson Wright replied. "Come again, now."

Flynn walked out to the pickup and tossed the rope in the back. He returned toward Antrim Road and back to the nameless road where the Convent of the Sisters of Charity was holding a novice called 'Sister Maureen' against her will. Flynn untied the ladder and hid it and the rope in the shrubbery near the convent walls. Flynn looked at his watch. "I've still got nearly five hours til it gets dark. Just time enough for eighteen holes of golf." Using his cell phone's GPS and App, he located a nearby golf course.

Flynn drove up Antrim to Downview Avenue. He took a right and found the Fort William Golf Club. Flynn parked the pickup and went into the pro shop. "Can I get a round in today?"

The young man in the pro shop smiled, "I have a tee time open if you can be ready in five minutes."

Flynn replied, "Well, I can if you got a set of clubs I could rent."

"Not a problem, sir. We can accommodate you."

"Good. How much are your green fees?" Flynn asked.

"Twenty five pounds. The clubs are another ten, sir."

Flynn gave the young man the correct amount and within a minute he had a small bag of clubs and was ready to play. The rest of the afternoon and early evening, Flynn played golf and had dinner in the club's pub. Darkness came and Flynn went back to the business of rescuing Kristen Shults.

Flynn drove back to the Convent access road and parked in a spot near the area he had secreted the ladder and the rope. Flynn extended the ladder and leaned it against the wall. He climbed up the ladder and at the top of the wall looked below into the courtyard and surveyed the grounds. He could make out the chapel across the other side from where he was. To his right was what he believed to be the residence area and next to it was probably the library or some study area. To Flynn's left was the loading dock and the dining hall. All of the buildings were connected by walkways that met in the center of the courtyard where a statue of the Virgin Mary was located.

"If I'm right about this," Flynn thought, "getting

into the nunnery is not going to be the problem. Getting to Kristen's 'cell' is going to be the problem without anyone screaming for help. How do I find her directly?"

Flynn stayed still on his wall-perch for a long while watching and listening for any sound or activity. It was quiet and there was no noise coming from the grounds. Flynn checked his watch again. It was nearly midnight and time for action.

Flynn had propped the ladder against the pickup then tied the rope to a rung near the top and lowered himself down to the courtyard below. He kept himself low and in the shadows of the buildings, the bushes and trees. Deftly, Flynn made his way to what he believed to be the nun's sleeping quarters. He tried the main door and, not surprisingly, found it unlocked. He went inside keeping himself against the walls. The dimly lit hall was quiet. Flynn could make out a series of doors on both sides of the hall only eight to ten feet apart. The first door Flynn came to had a small sign indicating that it was the room of 'Mother Superior'. The next few doors did not indicate which nuns were in which of the rooms.

"Well, I can't peek in each one and call out to Kristen," Flynn thought. "Only one person knows where she is and that is the 'head penguin'." Flynn silently stepped back to the first room where the sign indicated 'Mother Superior'. He turned the door knob and the door opened. Flynn stepped inside but found to his surprise that it was an office and not the sleeping room of Mother Superior. Flynn turned on a lamp on the desk and looked around. Inside the top drawer of the desk was a 'residence chart' which indicated the names of the nuns assigned to each room. Flynn saw that a 'Sister Maureen' was assigned the second to last room on the floor. Flynn turned off the lamp and went back out to the hall and stealthfully walked to the second to last door.

Flynn opened the door and stepped inside. The cubicle was called a 'cell' in religious parlance for a reason. It was about the same size of prison cell. Just big enough for a cot, a small, open closet, and a small dresser with two drawers. Flynn could hear a woman breathing on the cot. There was no light switch. Only a bulb that hung in the center of the 'cell', obviously controlled by the Mother Superior. Flynn took a step toward the sleeping woman and covered her mouth to prevent her from calling out.

"Kristen?" Flynn whispered in her ear. "It's me, Flynn."

There was a gasp as Kristen tensed from fear at first and then from surprise. She grabbed his hand and sat up. Flynn felt tears on his hand when he uncovered her mouth.

"Is it really you or is this a terrible dream?" Kristen whispered.

"Susshhh," Flynn whispered. "It's not a dream. Let's get out of here."

Kristen wrapped her arms around him and hugged him. She sobbed quietly for a few seconds and then threw off the blanket and sprang to her feet. She rubbed his face and hair and made certain to herself that this was indeed real. He had come for her at last!

Kristen did not have any clothing except the nun's habit and a few under things. She slipped on the habit dress and took her shoes in her hand and pushed Flynn toward the door. He opened it and checked to make certain that the hallway was clear. The two made their way back out to the front of the residence hall leaving the building. Kristen slipped on her shoes while Flynn silently directed Kristen to the rope he had waiting.

"Climb on my shoulders and grab the rope and pull yourself to the top of the wall," Flynn whispered. Kristen did as he told her and was able to pull herself up to the top of the wall. She saw the ladder and climbed down and waited for the man she had prayed would come for her.

Flynn easily scaled the wall and pulled the rope up over the wall then descended the ladder. He no sooner hit the earth when Kristen jumped into his arms and kissed him.

"Come on," Flynn said, "we've got a long way to go and we're not out of this yet."

"Oh, Flynn!" Kristen cried with joy. "I hoped and prayed you'd get my letter and come for me. It's been a living hell. How did you find me?"

"I had a little 'talk' with an old priest and a young man named Hartnett. They told me where you were."

"Oh, my God. Do you know what happened to me?"

"Yes, I do. And now we need to get them and clear your name."

"I'd like to kill them all. Oh, I will see them dead for what they have done to me."

Flynn looked over at her and could see that there was a lot of anger and hate trapped up in this once beautiful and innocent person. She was still as pretty as he remembered on the outside, but inside her now was a different woman. She wanted revenge. Kristen would not settle for anything less.

Flynn pulled the ladder down from the wall and placed it behind the bushes out of sight. Then he and

Kristen got into the pickup and drove out of the area and toward the Ferry Terminal for the boat ride back to Liverpool.

"We're going to need to get you some different clothes," Flynn said when they reached the Belfast city limits.

"But where can we get anything at this hour?" Kristen asked.

Flynn thought for a moment about Ashley. She was about the same size as Kristen except Ashley's breasts were a lot larger than Kristen's. "A shirt and slacks or a skirt and a blouse?" Flynn thought to himself. Then he turned into Ashley's apartment drive and lot.

"Wait here," Flynn instructed Kristen. "I'll be back in a few minutes."

Flynn walked up to Ashley's apartment door and rang the bell. "She's probably still at the bar," he thought waiting to see if she answered. He rang the bell again. Flynn listened but could not hear any movement inside. He took out a credit card and slipped it through the door jamb and popped the lock. He hurried to Ashley's bedroom closet. He turned on a light and found a pair of jeans and a blouse. Flynn took them and went over to the dresser and grabbed a pair of panties and a pair of socks. He was on his way out of the apartment but stopped in the kitchen. He found a note pad on the counter and scribbled a note telling Ashley what he had taken. He also left two One Hundred pound notes as compensation. "Afterall," Flynn mumbled, "I'm not a thief, but just a gangster of love."

Back in the pickup he tossed the clothing to Kristen. "See if these fit."

Kristen looked at him in total disbelief. "Whose

clothes are these?"

"A friend of mine," Flynn said curtly. "Try them on."

Kristen immediately pulled off the habit and put on the panties and slacks."I guess you didn't think to get a bra."

Flynn smiled glancing over at her bare chest. "Trust me, it wouldn't have fit."

Kristen put on the blouse and immediately realized that it was too big. "Oh, I see. Another one of your conquests, I bet. And you always told me that more than a handful was a waste."

"I'm glad you haven't lost your sense of humor, Kris."

"You know, Flynn," Kristen began seriously, "I am in love with you. I often looked up at the Big Dipper and thought of you. Do you remember what you once told me?"

"Look Kris," Flynn replied, "We've got a long way to go so let's just focus on what we have to do..."

"Hey," Kristen interrupted him, "I'm not asking you to be in love with me. I'm merely telling you how I feel about you. There's no strings attached. If it bothers you for me to tell you that I love you...."

Flynn interjected before she could finish her sentence. "It doesn't bother me. It's just not the time to be talking about how we feel about each other, that's all."

Kristen slid over next to Flynn and gently took his arm and rested her head against his shoulder. "Thanks for coming to get me. And I mean it when I say I love you."

Flynn decided not to keep talking about her emotions so he kept quite while he drove through Belfast proper down the Antrim Road, passed the Clinton Street

Graveyard onto Clinton Street, around the traffic rotary to Westlink, A12. From there Flynn turned onto Dock Street, passed the *American Bar*. He noted Ashley's car still in the lot, smiled to himself and whispered, "Thank you." Flynn then proceeded down Dock Street to Corry Link and arrived at the dock of the Ferry Terminal. Flynn parked and, trying not to disturb a sleeping Kristen, went in to check on the next ferry to Liverpool, England.

When Flynn returned to the pickup he was surprised that Kristen was wide awake and noticeably anxious. "Where did you go?" Kristen asked.

"Take it easy, Kris. I just went to see what time the next Ferry was leaving. Are you all right?"

"I got scared not knowing where you were or where we were. I guess I must have fallen asleep. Please don't ever leave me again."

"I'm sorry," Flynn apologized sincerely. "I just didn't want to wake you."

"I understand," Kristen added, "but I'm afraid. I don't want you to leave me again, no matter what. I want to be with you all the time."

Flynn realized that Kristen must have been emotionally traumatized these past weeks so he held her close and offered, "I won't leave you. Right now we need each other. We need to find those bastards who did this to you. So, let's stay focused on getting back to England and settling the score and clearing ourselves, okay?"

"Okay. I'm sorry, too. I'm just so glad to be with you and free of that wicked place. And, Flynn," Kristen looked at him while her expression changed to contempt, "I will kill them. God strike me dead if I don't mean it. I will see them dead."

Flynn held her close for a very long time until he

could feel the tension from her hatred leave her body. Then releasing her said, "The Ferry leaves within the hour. Let's get this truck on board shall we?"

Flynn pulled onto the boat and parked. He paused gathering his thoughts trying to find the right words. Finally, he turned to her and soberly said, "I have to tell you some bad news."

His tone alarmed her, "What kind of bad news?"

"I don't know how else to tell you, so I guess I'll give it to you straight..."

"Stop!" Kristen shouted. "Don't tell me you're in love with someone else."

"No, it's not that. Please let me finish"

"Then it can't be bad news. That's the only bad news I couldn't take right now."

Flynn grabbed her by the arms and gritted his teeth while he stared directly into her emerald green eyes. "It's about your Uncle James."

"Uncle James?"

"Yes, he's dead!"

"What? How? Oh, my God, NO!" She began to sob uncontrollably.

Flynn held her tightly while she continued to cry. Within a few minutes Kristen regained some self control with tears streaming down her cheeks. She looked up at him still sobbing, "How did it happen?"

"It was an automobile crash." Flynn chose his words carefully.

"Is William dead, too?" Kristen asked referring to her Uncle's chauffeur.

"No, your uncle was driving alone."

"Why?" Kristen was puzzled. "He never drove alone. William always took him."

"I don't know why." Flynn went on, "It may not have been an accident."

Kristen sat silently for a moment before she asked, "Who would murder my Uncle James?"

"I don't know that he was murdered, Kris. But if he was then William was either lucky as hell or had something to do with it."

"William!" Kristen exclaimed. "Oh, my God, Flynn. I just remembered something else."

"What is it?"

"The day after I arrived at my Uncle's estate, the very next morning, in fact. Uncle James said he had to go on a government trip to the United States. Something to do with a meeting on the oil problem..."

"Houston," Flynn interjected. "There was a meeting in Houston with the late President Harper, and some others. I'm sorry. Go on."

"What? Did you say the late President Harper?"

"Yes, he was killed in Houston. And some think I did it. Even though I was not in Houston."

"I don't follow you," Kristen was confused.

"I'll explain later. Go on with what you were saying."

"Oh....well, the next morning I was taken by those horrible men. And William must have let them in. There is no other way they or anyone could get into that estate without someone letting them in." Kristen's mood changed suddenly. "That bastard! He let them do this to me! And he killed Uncle James, too! I'll kill him for this."

"Whoa, hold on Kristen," Flynn tried to calm her down as her rage flared up again. "Hold on. Stay calm. We'll get anyone and everyone who framed and..."

"Raped me! You can say it. They raped me, Flynn,

over and over! That's why I will kill them myself and William along with them!"

"If, as you say, William is in on this whole plot then we need to get William to tell us where the others are so we can..."

Kristen spit out venom. "So we can kill those bastards! William, Falso, Arthur and that slimy weasel, Willie!"

Flynn could see that Kristen's pain had turned into anger and hatred for these men. He didn't blame her for how she felt but he realized that he needed to keep an eye on her while she was in this state of mind. Finally he said calmly, "Well then, my dear, our first stop is to find our 'friend', William and make him tell us."

Kristen stared straight ahead into the darkness surrounding the cars and trucks now loaded on to the Ferry. She whispered a vow that Flynn overheard. "And when we do, I am going to kill him."

THE WHITE HOUSE

President Patricia Bunnell was being briefed on the Middle East situation by Secretary of State Makoweic and Deputy Director of Operations George Dimmler. Also present in this briefing were Chief of Staff Admiral Moorehouse and NSA Director William Pfohl. The Secretary of State had just returned from Tel Aviv and was explaining the Israeli position.

"The Prime Minister is adamant that if the Iranians continue to develop and enrich uranium, that they will not allow it," Makoweic told a somber room. "In fact, they are making preparations for a first strike on the Iranian plants."

President Bunnell asked, "Do you have a timeline or an estimate on how long before they attack?"

"Perhaps Deputy Director Dimmler could better answer that question, Madam President," Makoweic deferred to the CIA.

President Bunnell turned to the Director of Clandestine Operations, "Well, George, what have you got?"

Dimmler began, "Our latest intelligence reports inside Iran indicate that the Iranians have assembled a number of mobile missile launchers positioned around Tehran and their western border. Also there are unconfirmed reports that they have underground enrichment plants near Qom and somewhere in the Zargos Mountains near Esfahan."

Dimmler handed out a written report to everyone. "As you can see from the satellite photos, we have identified those missile locations."

The President studied the report for a brief moment before she asked, "What's the range and accuracy of these missiles?"

Dimmler took off his glasses and rubbed his nose with his thumb and forefinger. "The Russians sold them the launchers a few years ago. They have told us repeatedly that they did not include the computer programming for the guidance system. However, we believe that there range is easily within the fifteen hundred mile range. Maybe even farther."

NSA Director Pfohl spoke up, "They can definitely hit Israel. However, we think that this is just another Iranian bluff to get attention and to put pressure on China and Russia to soften up the United Nations' sanctions on them."

Admiral Moorehouse also concurred. "I agree with Director Pfohl. There isn't the imminent threat that the Israelis want us to believe. We should tell them directly that if they launch a pre-emptive strike against Iran that the U.S. will not back them."

President Bunnell for a moment ignored Moorehouse's breech of authority. She looked gravely concerned. After a moment of serious thought she addressed the Secretary of State. "Jim, I have to ask you to go back to the Middle East. You must convince the Israelis to restrain from launching any offensive strike. Also, meet with the Saudis and the Iraqis and request permission for our military to set up a base of operations in their respective countries. However, be sure to stress it is strictly for defensive purposes and assure them that we do not intend to launch any attack on Iran. I do not want to provoke President Jahmir or the Ayatollah. Yet," the President leaned forward, "I also believe it's time we showed them and the rest of the world that we will not sit back while they take over control of the oil supplies of the world or attack any of our Middle Eastern allies."

The President continued, "I will direct that our Ambassador to the U.N. introduce additional resolutions condemning the Iranian threat of nuclear war. I anticipate that if we garner enough support and draw the world's attention to this problem that we can stare down that madman."

"Gentlemen," Patricia Bunnell asked, "what do you think of a naval blockade?"

Chief of Staff Admiral Moorehouse stood up shocked at her question. "You can't do that, Patricia. It's an act of war."

Everyone was momentarily taken aback by

Moorehouse's sudden emotional response. National Security Agency Director William Pfohl saw an opportunity to add his support to the Chief of Staff. "I totally agree with the Admiral, Madam President. Any blockade will force the Iranians into a position that they will have to attack our ships."

Secretary of State James Makoweic interjected. "I disagree with you Director Pfohl, to a point. What if we stressed that it was an economic and not a military maneuver?"

"Nonsense! Nobody would buy that," Admiral Moorehouse shot back. "You people are blowing this all out of proportion..."

"Who the hell do you think you are to talk to me like that," fumed the redheaded President, obviously angered by Moorehouse's comments. "Don't forget, Michael, that I am the President and I'll make the final decision here. Don't you ever speak to me like I was your wife or some secretary in your office." She slammed her hand on the table and shouted, "Get Out! Now!"

The Chief of Staff was stunned by her rebuke. Deputy Director of Operations Dimmler couldn't help but crack a slight smile which was not missed by Secretary Makoweic who raised his eyebrows as he tried to cover his own amusement.

Admiral Moorehouse was visibly shaken as he tried to defend himself. "I...I..er..I"

"Just get your sorry ass out of here!" President Bunnell demanded.

The Chief of Staff gathered his papers while looking around the room for support before leaving, but no one was willing to make eye contact with the besmirched Admiral Michael Moorehouse.

There was a dead silence in the room for a few minutes after the exit of the Chief of Staff. Finally, the President broke the silence. "The Chief of Staff does not speak for me. Let me make that perfectly clear. I am the President and will make the tough decisions as necessary. Now, gentlemen, is there anything further?"

"I will head back to the Middle East immediately," Makoweic concluded getting up to leave. "I will do whatever I can to calm the Israelis and at the same time discuss your intentions of increasing our military presence in Saudi Arabia and Iraq."

"Good. Keep me posted, Jim. And buy us some time, please," the President responded. Then she turned to Dimmler and Pfohl. "You two have to be my eyes and ears during this crisis. I need both of you to keep me continuously updated on any intelligence you gather. We can't afford to make any blunders."

Dimmler looked at the President and marveled to himself how truly beautiful she was. His thought was interrupted by her words. "George, have you heard anything of Flynn?"

Before Dimmler could answer NSA Director Pfohl dropped his briefing papers and stooped down to pick them up, curious as to the answer. Dimmler calmly replied, "No, Madam President, not a word. He's off the reservation and is under suspension."

"Okay, George. Let me know if you hear anything, will you?"

"Of course."

The three men left the room as President Bunnell stood looking out the window. "Where are you, Flynn? I need you to give me a boost," Patricia Bunnell thought. "I should have made you Chief of Staff instead of that arrogant buffoon. But you wouldn't have taken it, I know. You hate Washington, politics, and me. Your cheerleader girlfriend, what's her name, Kathleen Murphy is it? No, it's Misses O'Toole. That's right. She got herself married because you were in some god forsaken black operation somewhere. Well, Flynn, I'm not married anymore and I miss you and need you." A tear welled up in the President's ocean blue eyes.

LONDON

Flynn parked the pickup on a side street two blocks from the residence of the late James Saunders. Flynn and Kristen sat in the shadows of a street lamp for a minute while Flynn looked around, then up and down the street. He took out his cell phone and found the number he needed to call. Looking over at Kristen, he said, "Kris, I've got to make a call before we do anything. Sit here. I'll be right outside the truck. Don't worry, I won't leave you."

"Okay," Kristen replied, "but don't be too long. I want to get that bastard tonight."

"Don't worry. I need to get some information before we visit William." Flynn pulled the door handle and got out. The wind was cold and damp and he pulled his jacket up over his neck while he pushed the send signal on his cell phone.

Jackie Armstrong answered on the second ring. "It's your dime."

"Flynn chuckled, "It's at least a quarter, maybe more."

"Hey you big hunk, where in hell have you been?"

"It's a long story. I'll tell you about it sometime.

What's the word?"

"The word is you have the little tramp with you."

Flynn attempted to rebuke her, "Now, now, Jackie. I don't travel with tramps. Besides, you're in Washington."

"Thanks for that, jerk! Are you and the Shults woman okay?"

"Yes, but how did you know I was with Kristen?"

"Jeezus, Jerry," Jackie Armstrong answered, "just because everyone in the world thinks the Company is filled with a bunch of coconuts we're not all stupid. British MI-6, Interpol, shit even the IRA knows you two are together. Seems that some nun in Belfast blew the whistle on you kidnapping one of her nuns and the two of you are on the loose."

Flynn thought for a moment. "And where do 'they' think I am? Where are they looking?"

"All right, I take it back...some of it back. They're not all too bright, but they're bright enough to know that you left Ireland....A convent, eh? The little bitch probably needed it..."

"Jackie, jealousy doesn't become you. You know that I could only love you."

"If that' so, then will you marry me?"

Flynn laughed, "Sure I will. Just as soon as I get back."

"I won't hold my hand on my ass waiting. The odds are pretty high that you won't even get out of London alive."

"So they think I'm in London, eh?" Flynn trusted the woman but he knew better than to volunteer any information especially if, as now, his and Kristen's lives depended upon it.

"Well, somebody seems to know a great deal about you, Flynn. Have you been leaving a trail behind you?"

"I didn't think so." Flynn was concerned. "What else?"

"Madam President would like you to call her, I'm sure. So would that bitch, Mollie. She thinks you'll call her. Have you?"

"You're the only one I've called, my love," Flynn teased. "Maybe you're telling them."

"Fuck you, Flynn!" Jackie was instantly angry. "If you think that then don't call me again."

"Now, Jackie, who's lost her sense of humor?"

"I don't find that humorous, Jerry. You're too important to me...Besides, I haven't had an offer in a long time."

Flynn smiled. "Then you'd better pray that they don't blow my ass away, kid. Anything else to report?"

"Just this," Jackie became very serious. "Bunnell's husband Spence, was murdered! The steering mechanism, you know, was tampered with. It was hushed up by someone very important, but no one is saying who. And one other thing, Thee Admiral is on the President's shit list right now."

"Why?" Flynn asked curiously.

"Don't know for certain. She blew up at him at a White House briefing today. She's starting to call her own shots. She's even thinking of setting up a naval blockade of Iran. Looks like there's going to be an explosion over there any day now. Makoweic is flying back to try and calm the Israelis down and set up some military bases in Iraq and Saudi Arabia. But that probably doesn't interest you, does it?"

"It would if it's a pissin' contest over oil and nukes, which it is. And, especially, since United Petroleum has a great deal of interest in those oil fields. You remember the cocaine coming through Alaska in United Petroleum's crates and barrels...me getting shot at on my vacation?" Flynn continued his train of thought into his cell phone. "If these assassination plots are tied in then I guess I'm right in the fucking middle of this shit, aren't I?"

"Christ, Jerry, you're right! God, you're as smart as you are handsome. I'm a lucky woman."

"That's why they pay me the big bucks, beautiful. Or I should say, that's why they USED to pay me the big bucks."

"You're right as rain, you big hunk. What else do you want me to do?"

"I'd like to know a couple of things. First, see if you can get a handle on who is following me or seems to know where I am. Second, keep your ear open to the situation at the White House, you know between the Admiral and Pat, er...the President."

"You're wasting your time and energy on the wrong woman, asshole. She's not right for you. You need a quiet, loving woman who will take care of your every need..."

"Third," Flynn continued, ignoring her remark, "get me a line on a William Smythe. He was the driver for the late Foreign Minister, James Saunders. Do you think you can get that info by this time tomorrow?"

"I will try. Anything else on your list?"

"Oh, yes. Just one more thing...."

"What is it?"

"You know I'll always love you...."

"Fuck you, Jeremiah Flynn," Jackie laughed as the call was disconnected.

Flynn walked back to the driver side door and opened it. Kristen was sitting motionless in the seat. Her face was expressionless. She stared straight ahead into the darkness almost as if she were in a trance. Flynn studied her for a moment and a thousand thoughts ran through his mind. He empathized with her pain and trauma. There was so much to be done in so little time. He thought briefly how this nightmare might end. He wasn't concerned for himself. He was trained to disregard his personal feelings in these tense situations. Yet, here was this once innocent, beautiful woman with so much to live for sitting in a pickup only blocks away from where this horrible twisted turn of events left her a fugitive.

When Flynn started the engine, Kristen never moved and continued her stare. Finally she spoke. "Can we kill him, now?"

Flynn reached over and took her hand. "No, not just yet. We have a lot of information we need from him first."

The pair drove off down the street slowly passing the house of the deceased Foreign Minister. A light was on in the back where William Smythe lived...at least for another twenty four hours.

Flynn drove on for a few more miles until he found the Royal York Hotel. There was nothing 'royal' about this old, run-down hotel. Flynn knew that they didn't ask a lot of questions and the rates were cheap. Flynn and Kristen checked in while paying in advance. Flynn signed the register Mister and Misses Jones. The clerk barely looked up at them minding his own business.

Flynn and Kristen went up to their room. She

remained distant and somber. Flynn had noticed the mood change come over her since they first left Belfast. He thought that he had better keep an eye on her. "How many times I've seen that same look on boys in combat," Flynn thought. "The horrors of war to some caused that same look. Most come out of it, although they never forget, and are able to function normally in a little time. I just hope that Kristen will snap out of it, too."

While Kristen slept, Flynn lay awake next to her sorting out his thoughts. "I hope that Jackie can find out who it is that seems to know where we are and where we're going. I'm almost positive that no one was following us. I kept checking constantly in the pickup's mirrors." Then his thoughts turned to William Smythe. "Why would he betray the Foreign Minister. Why did he allow Kristen to to be taken, raped repeatedly and set up as a murderer by three low life assholes?"

As he drifted toward sleep, Flynn also thought of Kathleen. He knew she married Michael O'Toole because Michael was always around and he wasn't. He also knew that Kathleen never really loved the man, but just needed someone to be with her. But now, she too, like the President herself, had gone from his life. "It's better this way," he lied to himself falling asleep.

LANGLEY, VIRGINIA

Deputy Director of Operations George Dimmler had just returned to his office from the meeting at the White House. His message light was blinking on his phone. Dimmler sat down in his leather chair and picked up the receiver then punched in the number that the recording gave him.

"Mollie Farnham," Mollie answered.

"Mollie, this is George. You left a message for me?"

"Yes, sir, I did. I have uncovered some additional information on the Shults woman as you requested."

Dimmler thought for a moment--finally remembering his directive. "Oh, yes. What have you got?"

"Well, sir, it seems that Interpol and British Intel are on the same wavelength. They have received some reliable information that Flynn and the Shults woman left Ireland yesterday and took a ferry to Liverpool. There Flynn must have had a car waiting because they are now reportedly in London."

"Two questions," Dimmler replied in amazement. "First, how in God's name did they find this out? And second, if they know where Flynn and the Shults woman are, why haven't they arrested them?"

"That presents a puzzlement, sir," Mollie speculated. "As near as I can determine they have been able to track Flynn through his GPS system in his cell phone. As far as the second question, the only directive that we have heard is to 'follow and report'. Apparently, MI6 wants to see what they do next. We believe that they are working on the theory that Flynn and Shults are part of an international conspiracy of terrorists; and they want to apprehend all the parties...."

"That's so much bullshit!" Dimmler declared. "Flynn isn't involved in any international terrorist conspiracy."

"We know that, sir. But we have removed Flynn from 'active operations status', and I would bet that they have learned that Flynn is a suspect in the assassination of

President Harper from the FBI.

"Jeezus H. Christ!" Dimmler was frustrated and angry. "You mean that our own Bureau is working with them?"

"And, apparently, NSA, too. How else would they have Flynn's GPS signal?"

Dimmler thought for a moment before he added, "Things aren't looking too good for our boy, are they? Can't we get a message to him?"

"We have tried, sir," Mollie said. "But he hasn't answered our ad in the *London Times,* per standard operations procedure. If he would only call in."

Dimmler was well aware of the procedure when a message was needed to get an agent to contact the Home Office. "But in this instance, Mollie," Dimmler recalled, "we asked him to contact the President directly, didn't we?"

"That's correct, sir. Per her order."

"Mollie, one more thing."

"Yes, sir?"

"Who do we have in London?"

"I'd have to get that information from Jackie Armstrong, sir. Her unit has all the operations data in their computers coded and classified."

"Okay. Never mind, I'll call her directly myself. Thanks for the update, Mollie." Dimmler disconnected the call and rang up Jackie Armstrong's number.

Jackie Armstrong was at her desk working when the phone rang. "Computer Operations, Armstrong." She was all business.

"Jackie, this is George Dimmler."

"Good afternoon, *Heir* Director. How might I serve you?"

"Can you get me the names of our people in London, right away?"

"Why of course, *mien* Director. It will be on your terminal in less than a minute. Anything else?"

"Maybe," Dimmler paused before he asked. "Jackie, I know that you have a special interest or spot in your heart for Jeremiah Flynn...."

Jackie interrupted, "Sir, I care for each and every one of our Special Operations and field agents."

"I appreciate that, Jackie," Dimmler conceded, "but Flynn's in real trouble. Can you get a message to him to warn him that MI6 is closing in on him?"

Sir, if I could I would. But he has been suspended, per your order, and his location is no longer in our field status files."

The obvious dig at the Deputy Director was not lost on Dimmler who took it very hard. Jackie knew that it was Dimmler who ordered Flynn's suspension and she took this opportunity to let him know it.

"Yes, yes, I know. I guess I was just hoping that maybe he contacted you, I'm sorry..."

"I'm sorry too, sir. He hasn't. You know, Deputy Director, that he was...IS our very best." Jackie knew how to work a nerve.

Dimmler didn't know what else to say, so he merely concluded, "Okay, I'll get back to you after I review those names of our London office."

Jackie Armstrong raised her middle finger to the phone but politely said, "They'll be on your screen in just a moment. Good Bye, Deputy Director Dimmler!"

Jackie hung up her phone while her fingers raced over the keyboard bringing up the information on the agents in London. Meanwhile her thoughts also raced as fast as her fingers. "I'll have to let Flynn know that MI6 is on his tail and closing in. And, I got a brief bio on William Smythe that he wanted. I just hope he calls as planned..."

While Jackie sent the information on to Dimmler's computer screen she had another thought. "Maybe there is one who could help Flynn, after all. Goddamnit, why didn't I think of it sooner?"

THE WHITE HOUSE

President Patricia Bunnell was meeting with Congressional leaders briefing them on the crisis in the Middle East and seeking their support for funding a military buildup in Iraq and Saudi Arabia when one of her personal Secret Service women, Mary Branson, entered the room with a sealed message.

The President took the sealed message and opened it and began to read. Her face became pale while she read on. Quickly the President regained her composure and announced, "Ladies and Gentlemen, I have to cancel the rest of this briefing. Something has come up that requires my immediate attention. Thank you all for coming."

The legislative leaders attempted to push the President on the urgency of the message. However, Patricia Bunnell refused to elaborate and left the conference room without further discussion. Once inside the Oval Office, the President re-read the message: *"Personal...Confidential...President Patricia Bunnell... Eyes Only...Jeremiah Flynn is in London and in serious jeopardy. Needs to see you at once. He has unlocked the key to the Middle East Crisis. Many involved include high U.S. and other government officials and corporate executives known collectively as the 'ELITE'. Your very life may also be in danger. Do not trust ANYONE. Flynn will explain all. He is in hiding in London and sitting on an international powder keg. Serious consequences for the World. Your cover story for the urgency to travel to London should include need to discuss Allied position regarding economic and political sanctions to defuse Middle East situation without military intervention. Further details on where to meet Flynn will be sent to you while en route on Air Force One. Code name Rubicon. Your compliance code number reply is 1600-736679582642, should be sent via computer to the code number below by 1730 hours this date. Caesar."*

President Bunnell had never heard of 'Caesar', nor did she have any idea from whom the message had come. However, she guessed that it must have come from inside the Central Intelligence Agency so she called Deputy Director Dimmler.

"Scot, get me George Dimmler at CIA. And put this call through the scrambled line."

"Yes, Madam President, right away."

While the President waited for her call to go through to George Dimmler, she pondered over the message. "Someone knows of my interest in Flynn," she thought. "Of course, the coded message for him to call me directly which the CIA posted in the European papers. That proves it's from Langley." She smiled at her cleverness continuing her thoughts. "What is this *'Elite'* business?" She stopped as she re-read the words: 'Do not trust ANYONE'. "What about Dimmler? Surely he can be trusted, can't he? After all he is a close friend of Flynn's...Wait...he did suspend Flynn's field operative status, though..." She was interrupted by the phone ringing next to her.

"Hello, George," President Bunnell said.

"Madam President, how might I help you?"

"George," she paused for a second, her mind racing. "I've heard some news on Flynn"

"He called? Thank God!" Dimmler was excited and relieved. "What did he say?"

"He didn't say anything, George. I didn't talk to him...."

Dimmler was now confused. "I thought you said you heard from him?"

"No, George. I said I heard some news about him." Patricia Bunnell was being guarded with her words, choosing them carefully, but she didn't really know why.

"I'm sorry, Madam President, I don't understand."

"I received a message...didn't you send me a message, George?"

"No, Madam President I did not. Why would you think it came from here?"

"I just assumed it did, George, because it was about Flynn. And, I thought only you and..." The President never finished, but quickly changed the subject. "...and, well, I just concluded that you had heard something and sent the message over, that's all."

"What does the message say?" Dimmler was curious.

"It wasn't very specific," the President lied. "It merely said that Flynn was still at large..."

"I see," Dimmler paused, thinking. "Was the message signed?"

"Yes, but it was a code name. That's one reason I believed you sent it over here. But now that I think of it, it must be from Director Pfohl at NSA."

"It might be, Madam President," Dimmler was serious. "But it disturbs me that anyone but my office should be giving you any information about one of my operatives."

"Yes, I can understand that, George. Look, I'll let you know as soon as I find out who sent it."

"Thank you, Madam President, I'd appreciate that very much."

Patricia Bunnell hung up her phone and now was more confused than before. She was interrupted by Chief of Staff Admiral Moorehouse who burst into the Oval Office unannounced. The President was terse. "What is it, Michael?"

"I just wanted to check to see if there were any changes in your schedule for the next few days, Pat."

"No. I haven't made any changes. Why do you ask?"

"Well, the way you abruptly left the meeting with the Congressional leaders had them murmuring that something urgent had just come up...that's about all."

"It's nothing for you to be concerned about. Do you know where the message came from?"

"I assume through the regular channels. Agent Branson brought it in from operations downstairs," Moorehouse replied. "You seemed upset."

The President turned and then ordered, "Michael, get me the operator who took the message. I would like to talk to him or her personally."

"What is it darling? What's the trouble?"

"Don't give me that 'darling' shit, Michael. Just get me the operator up here, NOW!" Patricia Bunnell was angry.

Moorehouse left the Oval Office and called down to the operations room in the sub-basement of the White House. After a moment with the supervisor, the Admiral was able to locate the operator who received the encoded message for the President.

"This is Specialist Jennifer Callahan," the female voice answered.

"Specialist Callahan, this is Chief of Staff, Admiral Moorehouse."

"Yes, Admiral?" Callahan nervously replied.

"I understand that you recently received an encoded message for the President."

"Well...yes, sir, eh..I did."

"The President would like to see you in her office right away. Bring your log book. "

"Yes, sir. Right away." Callahan replied.

"And Callahan," Moorehouse commanded, "stop by my office first. And keep this confidential. Do I make myself clear?"

"Perfectly, sir."

It took less than three minutes for Specialist Callahan to reach the office of the Chief of Staff. She was directed to go right in. The young woman was visibly nervous. She hadn't done anything wrong, but she had never been summoned before to see the President, either. Admiral Michael Moorehouse looked her over when she entered his office. He thought that she was rather attractive, young, but attractive in a business sort of way. Nothing flashy.

"Callahan," the Admiral's voice was intimidating. "You received a message for the President a short time ago?"

"Yes, Admiral. That's correct." Callahan's knees

were shaking.

"What was the content of that message?"

"I...I'm sorry, sir, the message was 'Eyes Only' and that means that only the President herself can see it. I'm not at liberty to disclose..."

Moorehouse raged. "I'm the Chief of Staff. I screen everything that goes to the President. I have to know everything that goes on around here. Is that clear?"

"Begging the Admiral's pardon," Specialist Callahan began reciting the training manual in her response. "Rule 22.3, paragraph five, indicates that 'Eyes Only' means absolutely that. No one but the President is to read the message when it comes from our unit. I have no authority to change..."

"Goddamn it Callahan," Moorehouse bellowed, "I am the authority around here. Do you hear me? I am to see everything that goes to the President. Now what was the message and who was it from?"

The young woman was frightened but she would not waiver from the rules even as tears formed in her eyes. "In all due respect to the Admiral, I am not allowed to disclose the information contained in an 'Eyes Only' message pursuant to Rule 22.3, paragraph five...."

"If you want to keep your job, Callahan, you'd better tell me, right now!"

It was just at that moment that the intercom rang and the President asked, "Michael, where is that operator?"

The Chief of Staff's voice immediately turned into sugary syrup when he answered. "She's right here in my office, Madam President...."

"Well, send her in here. What's she doing in your office, anyway. I need to see her. Now, if you please!"

"Yes, Ma'am." Moorehouse turned back to the shaking young woman, his personality changing as he spoke. "You have done well, Callahan. Sorry for the test, but National Security interests must come first, you understand."

Although Specialist Callahan didn't believe a word of this, she nevertheless pretended to go along just to get out of his office. Never in her years while working in the White House had she ever been the subject of such harassment and verbal abuse. She was still shaking when she entered the Oval Office, tears in her eyes.

President Patricia Bunnell had her back to the door when Callahan entered the Oval office so she didn't see the young woman crying. The President started to speak turning around to face Callahan. "I understand.....Good Lord, what's wrong?" The President was shocked to see the woman crying and visibly upset.

"Nothing, Madam President," Jennifer Callahan sobbed, struggling to find her composure. "It's nothing at all...."

"What happened?" The President demanded without expecting an answer, somehow sensing that Michael Moorehouse had interrogated this poor, young woman. Patricia went over to Callahan and put her arm around the young Specialist's shoulders trying to calm her down. Unfortunately, it had the opposite effect at first. Callahan cried uncontrollably.

"There, there, it's all right," President Bunnell assured the young woman. "There's nothing to fear." Patricia was full of anger at her Chief of Staff. She resolved to have it out with him in a few minutes. But first, the President needed the information that this woman might have. President Bunnell directed Callahan to a chair and then poured her a glass of water from her sterling silver water pitcher.

"Here, drink some water," the President said calmly. Specialist Callahan took the glass and drank some of the ice water. In a few moments she appeared to calm down. "Are you okay, now?"

"Yes, Ma'am. Thank you. I'm much better now. Forgive me."

"What's your name, young lady?" The President asked, not rushing her.

"Specialist, er... uh... Jen, er.. Jennifer Callahan, Madam President."

"Well, do you mind if I call you Jen?"

"No ma'am. Most people do."

"Good." The President was very comforting. "Now, Jen, I understand that it was you who took the 'Eyes Only' message for me. Is that right?"

"Yes, Madam President, I did. And I followed all of the procedures...."

"Yes, I'm sure you did."

"...to the letter of the Rules!" Callahan finished her statement.

"Of course, my dear. That's not why I asked you here. I need to ask a favor of you."

Jennifer Callahan couldn't believe her ears. The President was not the least bit upset with her. In fact, had she heard right? The President wanted a favor from her? "I'll do anything I can for you, Madam President."

"Okay," Patricia began now sitting on a chair next to Specialist Callahan. "Is it possible to tell where that message emanated from? Who sent it?"

Specialist Callahan thought for a moment before she answered. "Not necessarily, Madam President. I can tell you that it was a satellite feed...not wire. But, that's not unusual for 'Eyes Only' transcriptions. You see, they can't be intercepted as easily, especially since it was encrypted or scrambled...."

"Well then, how do we know that the message is legitimate?"

"Because they have the proper access codes...you know, from the daily random access PUB." Callahan tried to explain. "If the sender has the proper daily access codes then the computer can and will allow the message to enter..."

President Bunnell, although unfamiliar with the technology, was beginning to understand how it worked. "I see. I think." Patricia smiled. "So who has the daily access codes?"

"More people and departments than I could tell you. Defense Department, CIA, FBI, NSA, The Joint Chiefs, and more, I guess."

"So there is no way that you could trace the message?"

"Only if they included a return code. But then it wouldn't necessarily tell you who sent it, just where it came from."

The President looked over the message and remembered that there was a return code number. She handed the message to Specialist Callahan and asked, "What about the return code number here? Doesn't that indicate it came from CIA at Langley?"

Jennifer Callahan feeling more relaxed now, re-read the message which the President referred to, looking at the return code. She paused for a moment attempting to phrase her words so that there wouldn't be any misunderstanding.

"Not necessarily, Madam President. The reference to call back merely indicates which return channel the message is to follow. CIA, even NSA, has thousands of internal access lines and satellite feeds to their computers which are used merely to channel information to other departments' computers. Then the computers, by accessing the codes given, will automatically scramble or encrypt the message and disperse the data into an incoming network or channel. Only the operator or agency which has programmed the proper acceptance codes will receive the message and unscramble or de-code it. It could be anywhere in the United States or at one of our overseas locations."

President Bunnell was impressed with the young woman's demeanor and knowledge. However, Patricia was frustrated by the information that she had just heard. "Let me ask you one more question, Jen," the President began thoughtfully. "Is it possible to add a message to this return code? I mean, is it possible to say anything other than a 'yes' or a 'no'?"

"I believe it would be possible. You see, once the line is open, unless the computer has been programmed to shut off automatically at a structured response, then I'd say 'yes', one could insert a reply message."

"Well," Patricia Bunnell said encouraged by Jennifer's remarks, "let's give it a try." The President walked over to her desk and wrote down a reply message of her own.

Specialist Callahan sat quietly uncertain why the President would want to trace a message that was sent to her. "After all, doesn't she know who sent it? If not, why not?" Callahan thought. "And only the highest officials have access to the daily codes in the PUB. Who would send an anonymous message to the President? And if she didn't know who sent it, why in the world would she want to answer it?"

At last the President had finished writing. "I'm going to give you a message to reply to the one which I received. I want you to personally send this reply. No ONE is to know anything about this. This is a matter of the highest national security and top priority." President Bunnell handed the handwritten message to Specialist Callahan. "Can you read my writing?"

Callahan read over the message out loud:

"Eyes Only....Caesar...I need confirmation on the information regarding Flynn. I cannot just jet off to London without knowing more. It is imperative that I talk to you immediately. Call me at this number: 202-872-286-6355. If what you say is correct, I need more substantiation. The number is my private cell number and only I will answer it. There are many unanswered questions that must be resolved. You must understand my position as President and as a woman who, although cares about Flynn, must place the welfare of this country before him or myself. If you are unable to call within the next twenty-four hours, then I will presume the message is not justified. Signed, President Bunnell."

The President listen to the young woman as she recited the message. When Specialist Callahan finished her reading, the President confided, "I can't tell you how important it is to send this at once."

"Yes, Madam President, I understand."

"Remember," Patricia Bunnell cautioned, "no one else is to know."

Callahan's sudden uneasiness did not escape the President. "Ma'am," Callahan stammered, "does this

298

mean that Chief of Staff, Moorehouse isn't to know?"

President Bunnell slammed her hand down on the desk causing Callahan to jump and stiffen in fear. "Goddamn him!" Patricia exclaimed. Seeing that this outburst had frightened the young woman, the President immediately apologized. "I'm sorry, Jen. I didn't mean to frighten you. I just realized why you were crying when you came in here. He was interrogating you, wasn't he?"

"I...I...well, I..." Callahan stammered, still shaken.

Patricia walked over and put her arm around the young woman to console her. "It's all right. You don't have to be afraid of Admiral Moorehouse. I'll make certain that he won't bother you again. And if he does, I want you to tell me right away."

"He said he needed to know everything that went on but I wouldn't tell him anything, honest. I said it was against the Rules....then he said it was just a test..."

"I'll give him a test," the President decided. "Look, get going on that message. When you've sent it, shred the note. Tell absolutely no one. If anyone questions you, you tell them that you have a direct order from the President herself. You shouldn't have any further problems, okay? Now, get going and send that message."

"Yes, Madam President! Right away." Specialist Callahan replied. And, while leaving the Oval office, Specialist Callahan turned back to the President and blushed, "Thank you, Ma'am. I think you are a very nice person. And a good President. I'm very proud to work for you."

Patricia smiled at her sincerity. "Thank you, Jen. I'm proud to have you work here."

LONDON

Flynn awoke before Kristen. He watched her sleep for some time thinking about her ordeal and how her personality had changed since she found out her uncle James was killed and that his driver, William Smythe, was probably responsible. Flynn tried to suppress his personal feelings for the woman and only concentrate on controlling his professional instincts. He realized he couldn't let his emotions overcome him or both his and Kristen's lives would be in serious jeopardy. If there was ever a time that he needed to draw upon all of his experience, it was now.

Flynn sat back in the overstuffed chair which was still surprisingly comfortable despite being worn from the many years it had been in the room. He started sorting out the events in his mind that had happened over the past weeks from the very beginning in Alaska. While Flynn closed his eyes, he chronologically ran through the sequence of events, piece by piece. Then he went over it all again melding the various incidents into place. The pieces of this puzzle finally fit. Flynn sat up straight, his eyes wide open. "Yes! Oh, God," he thought, "it was really that simple." A rush of adrenaline was pumping as the sudden clarity overcame him. Flynn's focus and senses were now fully alerted.

Flynn leaped from the chair and began pacing around the room. His excitement brought on by the realization of the forces affecting his and Kristen's lives filled him with energy. He mentally reviewed the scenario again. "Yes, it had to be. What a diabolical scheme," Flynn mumbled to himself. "Turn the world upside down, manipulate governments, threaten nuclear war, all aimed at distracting the world's leaders, while gaining control of the world's oil supply." Flynn shook his head in disgust continuing his thoughts. "Then by using the cartel's drug money you buy, bribe and own high ranking government officials, purchase weapons and gain power. And in the end, you secure a stranglehold on the world's most powerful economies with one international cartel ruled by those who control the oil."

A small piece of the puzzle was still missing. Flynn shook Kristen awake. "Kristen, Kristen, wake up."

Kristen Shults awoke in a frighten start. "What's wrong?"

"Nothing," Flynn blurted excitedly, "Everything!"

"What?"

"I mean there's no emergency at the moment," Flynn explained. "But I think I know what is behind what's been happening...."

"To us?" Kristen asked as she rubbed her eyes.

"Well, yes, to a large extent. And to the entire world."

"I don't follow you, Flynn," Kristen was confused. "Slow down and tell me what you're talking about."

Flynn ran through his previous line of thought spelling out his reasoning to her as he elaborated. Finally he asked, "Kris, who has the most to gain by securing control of the world's oil reserves and supply?"

"Well," Kristen paused while she thought for a moment, "most of the Western economies are largely dependent upon foreign imports of oil from the Middle East and South America--Venezuela, particularly. However, there is one country that is totally dependent on imported oil and has the most to gain or to lose, depending on one's point of view, and that would be

North Korea."

Flynn listened carefully to her explanation before he said, "Jeezus, I think you're exactly right!" He reflected on a recent conversation he had with Jackie Armstrong about a group known as the 'Elite', one of whose principal directors in United Petroleum included North Korea's Kim Moon Jung, the Tiger! Flynn looked intently at Kristen and asked, "What do you know of a North Korean named Kim Moon Jung?"

Kristen's look was one of amazement while she answered, "He is known as 'The Tiger'. He is a very wealthy and powerful man who some believe controls Kim Moon-il, the reputed leader of the country. Kim Moon Jung," she continued, "is an absolutely ruthless individual with questionable mental stability."

"What do you mean," Flynn asked, "by 'questionable mental stability'?"

"He, like many powerful demagogues, has no conscience. He will do anything to get what he wants. However, unlike his Western counterparts, he has a very strong allegiance to North Korea and Korean unification under his terms. He has been quoted many times in various trade journals that he is a strict nationalist. That the good of North Korea transcends all other things. If it is in the best interest of North Korea he will see to it that North Korea will have it. His whole life's purpose is to serve North Korea and bring about a unified Korea under his terms and his control."

"Kristen," Flynn began, "I know who are the major shareholders and Directors of United Petroleum. And, I think there's a connection between the assassination of Prime Minister Sommerset, President Harper and your uncle James. Not to mention the reason we just happen to be on the world's shit list."

Kristen was baffled. "Flynn, I don't follow you at all."

"Well, look at it this way. The major stockholders also happened to be the Directors of U.P. They are: Kim Moon Jung, David R. Laird, President of United Petroleum, Don Carlos Escobar, a drug lord from Venezuela, Sheik Mohammad al Anzarisad of Syria, the late President of the United States, Irwin W. Harper, and....your deceased Uncle, James Saunders."

"Uncle James!" Kristen screamed in disbelief. "You...how do you know that?"

"Trust me, I do know it." Flynn replied. "And the next conclusion bothers me more than all the others." Flynn paused choosing his words very carefully while he continued. "Kris, you're not going to like what I'm about to say. But your Uncle James was behind your being kidnapped and set up as the assassin of the Prime Minister."

Kristen leaped up at him screaming in a fit of rage, "You're wrong! Uncle James could never have done that to me. He was like my own father....You're wrong, Flynn!" She tried to scratch at his eyes but Flynn deflected her wild assault grabbing her and holding her close to him. Kristen continued to pummel his back with her fists while sobbing hysterically. Flynn held her fast until she exhausted herself and went limp in his arms.

Flynn gently lay her back down on the bed. Kristen pulled the covers over her head sobbing into the pillow. She lay motionless for nearly an hour. As Flynn watched over her he strengthened his resolve to settle an overdue score.

It was nearly mid-morning when Flynn decided

that they needed to get moving. He knew he couldn't leave her alone so he roused her out of bed. "Kris, we've got to get going. There's much to be done today. Come on now, get up."

A little to his surprise, Kristen threw back the covers and got up out of bed. She sat up staring at the wall in silence for a long moment before gathering herself. Then she walked into the bathroom and showered. After her shower Kristen dressed quickly and in silence. Glaring at Flynn she finally asked, "Who are you?"

Flynn didn't understand what she meant. "What? You know who I am."

"Bullshit, Flynn! I want to know who you really are. You're not the man I thought you were all those years in Amsterdam. Now, please cut the shit and tell me who or what the bloody hell you are and who do you work for?"

Flynn didn't hesitate. There was no need to continue the charade any longer. He looked her straight in her emerald green eyes and calmly replied. "I work, or I used to work for the Central Intelligence Agency. I was a field operative, mostly special operations."

"You mean a spy, don't you!"

"Yes, we're sometimes called that...."

Kristen looked at him coldly. "Have you been using me all this time? Has our relationship been nothing more than an espionage episode in your work?"

Immediately Flynn came forth. "No! You were never part of my work! Our relationship was and still is, as far as I'm concerned, totally separate."

"Well, it isn't totally separate now, is it?"

Flynn paused for a moment. "It's our Karma. We

are in search for our mutual destiny. The forces of that destiny have thrown us together like two victims of an unfriendly god. I usually don't believe in such things, but it isn't a coincidence that we are in the middle of this. And how we find our way to destiny is going to be all part of that life experience."

"I don't know which one of you I'm supposed to believe. The intellectual oil analyst or the spy. I suppose," Kristen concluded, "that this is all some sort of a cover up."

"It's called 'cover'," Flynn corrected her softly. "And, Kris, I'm not two separate men. I am one and the same man you met."

"I don't know that I can accept that. I don't know what to believe anymore. Everything is so mixed up. I'm not sure I even know myself anymore."

"Yes, it is mixed up," Flynn concurred. "However, unless we can work together and you can trust me, it's gonna stay mixed up. You have to believe that you are still the same beautiful, lovely person you always were in spite of all the horrible things that have happened to you lately."

Kristen looked back at Flynn trying to decide if she could. Then she declared, "I guess I don't have much choice, do I?"

"Not if you want to stay alive."

"That's just it. I'm not certain that I do."

Flynn couldn't let her statement go unchallenged. "Well, I sure as hell want to live. If for no other reason than to get those people who have put me and you through this shit. What happened to that fighting spirit? You can't tell me you don't want to even the score. Besides," Flynn continued, "this is bigger than both of us.

These assholes are trying to take over and control the economies of the world for their own personal gain. And right now, as far as I know, we are the only two people in this damn world that know what they are trying to do. If we can't stop them, then I don't know who can."

Kristen still unconvinced shook her red hair. "That's just it. You said it yourself. It is bigger than either of us. We can't do anything to stop them....Christ, we don't even know who all THEY are. And, sure as hell, we can't take on whole governments. You don't even know who in America that you can trust to help us. They didn't waste any time turning their backs on you, did they? So don't try an feed me that bullshit that we can make a difference."

"Well, then," Flynn reasoned, "why don't you just walk out of here and turn yourself over to the police. Give up. I don't give a shit what you do if you feel that way. But I will tell you that I won't give up. It's not my nature to just roll over and quit. I never have and I never will. I'm going to do everything I can to stop these bastards or die trying. Which may be a distinct probability, by the way. At least, Kris," Flynn exclaimed forcefully, "I'm not afraid to try!"

Kristen looked at Flynn and slowly started to smile. Her eyes sparkled for the first time while she said, "You'll never make it as a psychologist, Flynn. Tom Sawyer was much better at it than you are. Maybe you might save those speeches for a pep rally. On second thought, you wouldn't have even fooled the children."

Flynn laughed, "It was that bad, huh?"

"Yes, it was that bad. However, you win. What the hell have we got to lose? At least I'd like the satisfaction of letting them know that they didn't get away completely unscathed. What do we do?"

"First, we need to make a few changes in our appearance. Nothing too radical, because the best disguise is the least disguise. Then, we need to go see an old friend of mine who can help us get new identities so we can get out of England and back to the States. Before that, however, we have some unfinished business with William Smythe and three of his friends. We'll twist his nuts until he gives us those three fucksticks who put you through hell. Once we even up with them, I believe the real key is in Washington. And, I have a hunch who that might just be."

Flynn and Kristen drove the pickup across town where they found a novelty shop. Flynn bought a pair of round glasses, a cap and a mustache kit. He chose a dark brown wig for Kristen and a jacket and cap. Then the pair drove over to a small print shop near the Thames River. Flynn parked the pickup a block away from the shop and the two walked back. Flynn remained on constant lookout, still concerned about what Jackie Armstrong had told him concerning someone seemed to know where they were at all times.

Flynn had used the services of Max Steiner many times in the past. Max was the best in the business. He could make passports and official papers as good as the real thing for any country in the world. The only concern Flynn had was that the CIA, and MI6, also knew of Max's talents and service and might be staking out the shop. Flynn had to chance it.

When Flynn and Kristen entered the shop, a little spring bell above the door announced their arrival. Flynn recognized the old man when Max approached from the back of the shop.

"How may I help you?" Max Steiner asked.

Flynn knew the routine. "I have a small printing job for you, sir."

"Well, Gov', that what we're in business for. What do you need done?"

Flynn realized that Max hadn't recognized him. "Max, it's me, Flynn."

The old man's eyes lit up. "Ah, Mister Flynn. I'm sorry I didn't recognize you. Very clever. Now, I see." The old man shook Flynn's hand before he turned somber. "You know, Flynn, you are very un-popular with certain people, you know. I assume this is Kristen Shults?"

"It is, Max. Does any of this present a problem for you?"

"It is none of my affair," Steiner replied waving his hand. "However, it is going to cost you more than usual. There is a great deal of risk. You understand."

"Yeah," Flynn smiled knowingly. "You're going to stick me up! Okay you old thief, how much?"

Steiner never hesitated. "Ten Thousand pounds!"

Flynn thought for a moment. "How soon can you have the papers and passports ready?"

"It's going to take a few days...."

Flynn's smile disappeared while he leaned over and got right in the old man's face. "For ten thousand pounds, Max, I want them tonight!"

The old man took a handkerchief from his pocket and wiped his bald head and then his face stalling for time to think. "You are asking the impossible, my friend. There is no way that it can be done so quickly."

"Look, Max, I know that's a bunch of bullshit. You can do it and we both know it. I need these papers and passports by tonight!"

308

There was a very long pause while the old man thought it over. "Okay, since it is you, Flynn, all right. Meet me here tonight at nine o'clock. Come around to the back of the shop and knock on the door. Right now, I will take your photographs and get your signatures."

Kristen and Flynn followed the old man to the back of his shop. They were properly photographed with their new disguised look. Flynn chose the name of his old friend. He and Kristen signed as Nicholas and Nora Cokely for their signature samples.

WASHINGTON, D. C.

Specialist Jennifer Callahan had completed sending the confidential, encrypted message from President Patricia Bunnell over the dedicated and scrambled line. She shredded the written message as instructed by the President. Callahan felt a sense of pride in that she had been selected by the President herself to handle such a confidential matter.

Meanwhile, at the same time as the message was being transmitted, a decoding program was intercepting the contents of the President's message and printing it on each computer screen within the access receiving mode. However, what neither Jennifer Callahan nor President Bunnell did not know was other interested parties' screens also intercepted and displayed the information each for their own purposes.

LONDON

TWA flight 1043, touched down at Heathrow at 2:07PM, local time. Don Carlos Escobar had left Caracas,

Venezuela nearly a day before catching a connecting flight from Rome, Italy. Don Carlos passed through customs without incident. He was met at the terminal by Falso, Arthur, and Willie, who were directed to meet him and take Don Carlos to an address on Bayswater Road across from Hyde Park. The journey from the airport through London center was made in near silence. The only conversation centered around whether or not the three had obtained the weapons which Escobar had requested.

Don Carlos was not pleased that the Tiger had ordered him to personally eliminate Flynn and any threat that he posed to the Operation Lifeblood plan. "Anyone of my top men could make this trip to eliminate this man Flynn," Escobar thought while they drove into London. "Even these three men, brainless thugs that they are, could have done the job. But no, Tiger would not hear of it. 'You must see to it personally,' was his order."

After the car pulled into the parking space adjacent to the apartment, Falso's curiosity got the better of him. "Hey, Carlos, how we gonna pick up this bloke, Flynn?"

Don Carlos raised his eyebrow sneering his response. "Senior, Falso, it is *Don* Carlos. And if you must know, Flynn will be sent to us. We will be told where he will be. And then, I will terminate this bug of a man." Don Carlos turned to Willie, "Now you, bring my bag." Before settling in to the apartment, Don Carlos added, "We must wait for the call." Willie turned to Arthur and nodded at the bag. Arthur understood that he was to carry it up to the room.

WASHINGTON, D. C.

Three separate computer screens lit up with President Patricia Bunnell's de-coded reply message to the phantom 'Caesar'. Neither of the three knew that the others had received the same message. Jackie Armstrong at CIA, Langley, copied the message on her printer and slid it into her purse. She would pass the information on to Flynn who would be calling her within the hour. Acting Assistant Deputy Director Mollie Farnham also copied the message and placed it in a secret folder in her office safe. A third copy was made by NSA Director William Pfohl who immediately went to his private scrambled line and made a call to his inside source at the White House.

HOUSTON, TEXAS

United Petroleum's President, David R. Laird's private cell phone rang. Laird answered it on the second ring-tone, immediately recognizing the caller on the cell's caller ID.

"Laird!"

"Yes, Tiger," Laird answered nervously. He didn't like these calls from the Tiger. It always meant something was about to happen and Laird felt an impending doom when he called. "What can I do for you?"

Kim Moon Jung could sense the anxiety and fear in Laird's voice. This empowerment filled the Tiger with power and control over the man who ran the world's largest oil company. The North Korean loved the feeling it gave to him. "Has Escobar arrived in London?"

Laird looked at his watch, then glanced at his wall which had clocks indicating the time in all the major capitals of the world. "His flight was due to arrive at two o'clock London time. It's now eight fourteen here...."

Kim Moon Jung exploded in anger. "Can't you just answer my question, Laird? I don't want to know what time it is. I want to know if you have heard from our source. Has Escobar arrived?"

Laird nearly dropped his cell phone while sweat poured over his hands and face. He was shaking. Instinctively, he reached for his ever-present glass of bourbon. Stammering, he brought the glass quickly to his lips answering, "Yes, yes, Tiger! I have heard that he arrived and is waiting at the Bayswater apartment for the call from Washington. He is being assisted by the same three we used before."

"You know, Laird, I am amazed that you ever got to the position you have. It is no wonder to me that the western economies are so vulnerable. It must be a reflection of your bumbling incompetence." The Tiger enjoyed belittling the man.

Laird attempted to defend himself. "I know the oil business pretty fucking well, Tiger. All this cloak and dagger shit is out of my line..."

"I will decide how well you know the oil business after I have accomplished my objective in Operation Lifeblood." The Tiger paused for an instant to let that last humiliation sink in before he commanded, "Now, get back to our 'source' in Washington. I want to know as soon as Escobar has eliminated Flynn. We are ready to begin 'Sandstorm'. Sheik al-Anzarisad and President Jahmir are waiting on my call to make their nuclear testing demonstrations both in Iran and Syria."

"Syria?" Laird was baffled. "When did Syria get the atomic bomb?"

"When I gave them one!" Tiger laughed. "You are as surprised as the rest of the world will be when both Syria and Iran test fire identical nuclear weapons simultaneously. This is 'Sandstorm' which will signal the beginning of Operation Lifeblood. Now, tell our source that there can be no failure. Flynn must be removed within the next forty-eight hours. Do I make myself clear?"

"But what if Flynn doesn't surface? What can we do?"

"He will if the 'source' does the job correctly. And, I will hold you personally responsible for making certain that it is done!"

"Jeezus, Tiger, I can't...."

"No more excuses, Laird! Your own life depends on it. See to it!"

"But...I..." Laird's hands were sweating as he fumbled his glass of bourbon causing the glass to shatter on the floor.

"I expect to hear from you soon, Laird." Kim Moon Jung disconnected the call. He smiled at his sense of power. Soon North Korea's source of unlimited oil will be secured. He would personally unite North and South Korea under his terms. It was his sacred duty. The new moon phase was nearly over and the rise of the crescent moon would soon be here.

WASHINGTON, D. C.

"I want an immediate tap put on a number." The command was direct.

"What number is it?"

"202-872-286-6355. And I want not only all calls

coming in and out recorded, but put on a computerized 'PIN' register, tone identifier, of all the numbers calling and being called. Do you understand my directive?"

"I understand. But is there proper authorization?"

"I am giving you a direct order. That should be authorization enough. This is a top priority of National Security from the White House. I don't want you to ever question my authority again. Just make it happen at once!"

"Sorry....of course...consider it done."

LANGLEY, VIRGINIA

Jackie Armstrong was sitting in her office reviewing the daily logs when her cell phone ring tone caught her immediate attention.

"Jackie Armstrong..." she answered.

"You're still my favorite girlfriend, Alice Long."

"It's about time you realized that, you big lug," Jackie replied smiling broadly.

"Look, lover, I have to get moving and I needed what info you had for me on William Smythe."

"You're going to drive me nuts," Jackie said while she quickly brought up the information on her computer. "I'll email it to you right now. What's your address?"

"I thought I made you nuts for me years ago," Flynn quipped. Then he quickly added, "flynnlawyer@hotmail dot com."

"Here it comes," Jackie replied forwarding the information to Flynn's email which he could retrieve on his smart phone. "I think he might just be your type, Jerry," Jackie teased. Then seriously added, "There was a message from your ex-girlfriend, the Prez, to 'Caesar'."

"What?"

"Apparently, the President received a message from this 'Caesar', who or whatever he or she is, and sent a reply message over the confidential code line asking for verification of this 'Caesar' message."

"What was the message?" Flynn asked curiously.

"I don't know what 'Caesar' communicated to her but the message asked 'Caesar' to call her at 202-872-286-6355, before she could just fly off to London. Hold on a second, I'll read it to you." Jackie took the message from her purse and read:

"Eyes Only...Caesar...I need confirmation on the information regarding Flynn....how sweet...I cannot just fly off to England without knowing more. It is imperative that I talk to you immediately. Call me at this number...202-872-286-6355. If what you say is correct, I need more substantiation....blah, blah, blah..You must understand my position as President, and as a slut, although who cares about Flynn, must place the welfare of the country before either he or myself...gag me with a spoon...If you are unable to call me within twenty-four hours, I will assume the message is not justified...President Bimbo."

"You ought to show more respect for your President," Flynn chided.

"Give me a break, Jerr, the woman is a bitch!"

"Now, now, Jackie. Don't let that green dragon overcome you," Flynn admonished jokingly before he concluded, "Hey, gotta go and pick up our new papers."

"New papers?" Jackie was surprised. "What kind of new papers?"

"Kristen and I went to an old friend of mine, Max Steiner. We need new passports and ID's to get out of

Dodge alive. Max owns the King Arthur Print Shop, which is basically a front."

"Can he be trusted?"

"Oh, yeah. For enough money Max could manufacture the Second Coming of Christ, and no one would question it."

"Are you sure?"

"Yeah," Flynn re-assured her. "He's okay."

"What time are you supposed to pick them up?"

"They'll be ready around nine tonight. Don't worry. I still love ya."

Jackie sounded concerned, "You be careful. You know I'm still a virgin, waiting for you..."

Flynn laughed out loud. "Right! And Santa Claus hates children!. I'll call you tomorrow night. Thanks, Jackie. Good bye."

"Hey, if I don't answer, just leave a voice mail. And never end with 'good bye', it's bad luck."

"Okay...good bye, Jackie." Flynn's call was disconnected. He brought up his email message from Jackie and looked it over.

The information was very specific: *"William Livingstone Smythe. Twenty-seven years in the Civil Service. Last position—chauffeur to late Foreign Minister, James Saunders...Never married...sill resides at Saunders estate...pending re-assignment from the Home Office....previously assigned to British Ambassador to U.S.A. for sixteen years... Smokes and drinks moderately....prefers the company of men over women....seems he left position with Ambassador to U.S. over a possible homosexual relationship/encounter with a North Korean....possibly being blackmailed by someone but MI6 has covered up any additional information with the usual smoke screen while being re-assigned to Saunders, claiming insufficient proof of any wrong-doing...The alleged influential North Korean-- named Kim Moon Jung!"*

"Holy shit!" Flynn exclaimed as he read the email. "It's starting to make perfect sense."

LONDON

"Don Carlos," the caller began, "I have just learned that Flynn and the Shults woman are going to be at the King Arthur Print Shop at nine tonight, your time. A Max Steiner is preparing new passports and identity papers. Perhaps you should cancel that order."

"*Si,*" Don Carlos Escobar replied, "I will be happy to do that. Do you have an address of the shop?"

"Ask any one of those 'three stooges' with you. They should be able to find it. And, by the way, when you cancel that order, cancel them too."

"That would give me great pleasure, *Amigo.*" Don Carlos disconnected the call. He turned to the three men and smiled slightly, "The fly is entering the trap. Do any of you know where the King Arthur Print Shop is located?"

Willie spoke up knowing right away the location. "Blimey, old Max Steiner's shop, eh? Sure, I know right where it is, mate. It's no more than twenty minutes from 'ere."

"Good," Don Carlos exclaimed slamming the clip into his 10mm Glock, semi-automatic. "Let's make sure to give this fucker Flynn a real surprise."

LANGLEY, VIRGINIA

Jackie Armstrong's private cell phone rang. She immediately recognized the calling number.

"Yes," Jackie said.

"As you know, Flynn is in London with the Shults woman."

"Yes, I talked with him recently," Jackie continued. "But I think he is walking into a trap."

"I believe you are correct. It has come to my attention that a notorious drug dealer and hit-man, a Don Carlos Escobar, has arrived here earlier today. I believe he is looking to cash in on the million dollar contract on Flynn's head. My information also indicates that he was met by three local small time hoods. Do you know where Flynn is now?"

Jackie paused for a brief moment, "No, but I do know that he and the woman are going to meet a Max Steiner at his print shop. Flynn and Kristen Shults are paying Steiner to make them new passports and ID papers."

"That only makes sense," the caller added. "When are they going to meet with Steiner?"

"All's Flynn told me was that the papers would be ready around nine o'clock tonight, London time."

There was a long pause before the caller concluded, "Thank you for the information." The call was terminated.

LONDON

Flynn and Kristen Shults arrived at the King Arthur Print Shop exactly at nine o'clock. He parked the

318

pickup truck a few doors past the main shop entrance so he could walk by and look through the shop window on his way back to the alley and to the rear entrance.

"Kris," Flynn advised preparing to get out of the truck, "you wait here. I should be only a few minutes. If for some reason I don't get back here in ten minutes, leave!"

"I'm not going to just sit here and wait all alone," Kristen protested, "I'm going with you."

"Look, humor me. Stay put. There's no need for you to come in....."

"No way. I said I'm not staying here all by myself. I'm going with you."

Flynn realized that this was one argument he wasn't going to win. "Okay, if you insist," Flynn conceded. "But stay right behind me in the shadows. And be quiet." He reached under the seat and pulled out a 9mm Glock and handed it to Kristen. "Take this just in case." Kristen looked at it for a moment and then slipped it into her jacket pocket.

The two of them left the truck and walked back towards the print shop. Flynn kept to the inside so he could look into the shop window. The inside of the shop was dark except for a sliver of light coming from the back room. The sign on the front entrance door read, 'Closed'. Flynn strained to see inside. Although he couldn't see anything out of the ordinary, the hairs on the back of his neck bristled instinctively telling him that something wasn't right. Flynn reached into his pocket and flipped the safety off his weapon.

They turned the corner and began a slow walk down the alley to the back of the shop. The alley was pitch dark and the London fog had rolled in making objects almost impossible to see. They were about to enter the building when Kristen's foot kicked a bottle across the alley. The smashing glass reverberated in the stone echo chamber. Flynn stopped cold pulling his Glock from his pocket prepared to fire at the sound. He identified the crashing sound almost immediately while his free arm slammed Kristen against the wall in a protection response.

The shock of the entire incident startled Kristen causing her to cry out, "Oouwah!"

Flynn was in her face snarling at her through gritted teeth. "I told you to be quiet! Why didn't you fucking ring a bell?"

Kristen held her hands over her mouth remaining motionless from fright. Finally she whispered, "Sorry, I didn't bring a bell..."

Flynn glared at her for a second or two before a wry smile crossed his lips. "You're a real comedienne, aren't you?"

"Sssshhhh!" Kristen whispered to him.

Flynn turned the final corner and saw the back door to the print shop was ajar. There was a halo of diffused light leaking from around the doorway. Everything was silent. Flynn's neck hair bristled again. He took in a deep breath while slowly pushing down on the latch with one hand while tightening his grip on his pistol with the other. The door opened easily and Flynn took a step inside. He nearly slipped on a pool of blood under his feet.

The back room of Max Steiner's print shop was a horrible sight. Steiner lay slumped over his desk in a puddle of blood. His throat had been slashed. Another body was behind him, shot through the chest. To the left of the desk a third body lay dead, shot through the head at close range. What was left of his skull and brain matter was splattered over the wall behind him. Flynn discovered the final body jammed into the ink-plate of the printing press also shot from close range. The last dead man stared agape at Flynn from against the far wall--his eyes and mouth wide open in terror in a ghostly death mask.

Flynn turned behind him to stop Kristen from coming into this scene of mass horror and death but he was a split second too late.

Kristen let out a frightened scream and then vomited.

Flynn grabbed her before she fell and spun her around out through the opened door into the darkness. He looked up and down the alley but could neither see nor hear anything.

Flynn led Kristen to the stoop. "Here, sit down. I'll be right back."

He re-entered the grisly room of the print shop with his Glock at the ready. He tried to piece the scene together. Three dead men unknown to him, and Max Steiner. Flynn ascertained that the murders had taken place moments before he and Kristen arrived. The killer or killers had fled. None of the dead men had fired his weapon which puzzled Flynn. "They were either ambushed or were surprised by someone who they knew and went with them," While Flynn looked around, something in the hand of the body by the door caught his attention. It was a business card. The word 'Caesar' was the only printing on the card. Flynn took the card and went outside to check on Kristen.

She looked up at him obviously still shaken and

asked, "What the hell happened in there?"

"It looks like someone knew we were coming. Max's throat was cut. The others were shot. Did you recognize any of them?"

"Yes. Three of them are the ones who kidnapped me. Falso, Arthur, and that little rat, Willie." Kristen paused before she concluded, "Those three deserved to die, but I never imagined how horrible it could be."

"Death isn't very pretty, sometimes. Especially when it's so violent and sudden."

"Why do you think someone knew we were coming?" Kristen asked.

Flynn pulled the business card out of his pocket and showed it to her. She walked over by the door where there was enough light to read, "Caesar?"

"This 'Caesar' has been following me since I left the States. He always seems to know where I am and where I'm going."

"How does he know all of that?" Kristen asked.

"I'm not sure. But it's like I have a ..." Flynn took out his cell phone. "Sonofabitch! This fucking cell phone is telling him. Either by the GPS or when I use it... someone is intercepting my calls!" Then taking Kristen by the arm ordered, "Come on we gotta get out of here, fast."

"What about our papers?"

"They're gone!"

"How are we going to get out of London?...England? Where are we going to go? What are we going to do now?"

Flynn hadn't released Kristen's arm while he directed her back up the alley and to their pickup truck. "I don't know just yet. But I'll think of something. We'll make it. Don't worry."

When Flynn and Kristen got to the truck there was a slip of paper stuck under the windshield wiper on the driver's side. He ripped the paper from the blade and read it.

"You are safe for now. We have taken Don Carlos Escobar with us. You and the woman return to your hotel. You will be contacted soon. Caesar."

Flynn slammed his fist on the hood of the truck making a loud sound. Kristen jumped in her seat. She watched Flynn. His facial expression confused and frightened her more. "What is it, Flynn? For God's sake what's happening?"

"Here!" Flynn snarled, angrily tossing the paper over to her and gunning the car. They sped away invisible--escaping into the darkness of the dense London fog.

THE WHITE HOUSE

President Patricia Bunnell's private cell phone rang. She picked it up and looked at it as the ring-tone signaled again. A momentary excitement overcame her when she answered the caller.

"Hello?" President Bunnell anticipated the message.

The voice of the caller was electronically disguised and sounded somewhat mechanical. "President Bunnell, I'm calling in response to your computer message request. I hope that your delay has not put Flynn in more jeopardy than he already is in."

"Thank you for calling." The President tried to remain calm and business-like. "What information can you tell me about Flynn?"

"I don't have any information other than what was already sent to you. Flynn and the Shults woman are in London and are in trouble. He is a target of a sinister group that wants the Middle East to explode for their own personal gain."

"How am I suppose to believe you?" Patricia Bunnell asked. "What can I do? Flynn's Agent status has been revoked and the Shults woman is wanted in connection with the murder of Prime Minister Sommerset." She paused and then declared, "I don't even know who you are."

"You don't need to know who I am. If you don't act soon there will be war in the Middle East and the economy of the United States and the rest of the Western world will be in chaos. Flynn can explain all of this to you."

"Where in London is he? And how could I ever find him, assuming that I were to go to London in the first place?"

"You will be contacted in flight on Air Force One. It is not safe at this moment to tell you any more---for both of you. You'll just have to trust me on that."

Patricia Bunnell was becoming frustrated and upset with the vagueness and secrecy of the caller's message. "Why should I trust you? I don't even know who you are or what is your motive in all of this. I can't just fly off to London because you, an anonymous caller, tells me to. Presidents simply don't do that."

There was a long silence before the mysterious caller spoke again. "What if I told you that these are the same people that murdered your husband, Spense?"

Patricia was caught by surprise by this remark and

exclaimed, "What? My husband was killed in an accident...."

"No, he was murdered," the caller calmly declared. "The steering mechanism was tampered with. The same thing that happened to Foreign Minister Saunders. He was murdered the very same way. It was supposed to look like an accident, but trust me it was murder. It was all part of a twisted plot to have you become President. That's why President Harper was assassinated, too. These people have infiltrated the government. They have people close to you in your administration that you trust and have been manipulating you for their own gain. Your own life may be in danger."

President Bunnell tried to sort out all of this shocking information which had come to her from this unidentified caller. "If what you say is true, how do I know that you are not one of these so-called people and are trying to 'manipulate' me, now?"

"I guess you don't." There was a slight tone of despair in the voice. "I just thought that Flynn meant something to you."

"How dare you presume anything about my feelings. I am the President of the United States. My personal feelings and emotions, whatever they are or might be, cannot override my duty and obligation to this country."

"Well, then, I guess there is nothing further for me to say, Madam President. If what you told me is true then Flynn's life means nothing to you. But, what if the information he has might avert a war and dies with him?"

"If Flynn has some knowledge of that he knows how to relay it through the proper channels."

"You know, President Bunnell, you really are a

Bitch! I don't know whatever he once saw in you." The caller terminated the call.

The President looked at the cell phone in disbelief. She sat back in her chair attempting to recall the exact conversation. When she did a small tear began to trickle down her cheek. Taking a tissue, Patricia wiped away the tears and went back to work.

ELSEWHERE IN WASHINGTON

"The call was made from a cell phone that was routed to several places around the globe. We are attempting to trace it down. The voices were electronically scrambled at both locations and a device was used by the caller to alter the voice. We are attempting to decipher and unscramble the call. It will take some time."

"Very well, when you have a clean tape bring it to me. See if you can match the voice to the voice print files you have. I need to know who made that call!"

LONDON

Flynn drove around London for nearly thirty minutes in total silence. He was frustrated and angry. Suddenly, without warning, Flynn pulled the pickup to the curb in front of a Pub. He jumped out and hurried around to Kristen's side pulling the door open. "C'mon," Flynn ordered, "I need a drink."

Kristen followed without hesitation still uncertain what was going to happen. She never saw this side of the man. He was moving too fast and his mood was sullen. She wasn't sure if he looked less confident or if she felt less confident in herself. She had to nearly run to keep up with his long strides.

Flynn entered the Pub and immediately went to the bar and ordered. "Two pints of Porter." He never asked Kristen if she wanted anything else. He brought them over to a side table while jamming himself into a seat. He took a long drink before he spoke to her.

"There's something rotten in Denmark. Something very, fucking rotten, and I don't like it."

Kristen looked at him not comprehending what he was saying while remaining silent waiting for him to explain.

"You know," Flynn began, "I think I am beginning to figure this whole thing out. Somebody is playing the puppeteer with us. Every time we get on to something they pull our strings and change our plans. I think we are unfortunately, caught in a power struggle between two separate factions."

"I don't think I follow you," Kristen broke her silence. "What do you mean?"

"Well, look at this way. I'm on vacation up in Alaska. I accidentally discover a massive drug smuggling operations with Asians and Latinos. When I call it in to CIA headquarters I get shot at. Not them. Then I find out that I'm on the Company's shit list. They burn me and I am framed for being a rogue agent and a possible, no, probable suspect in the assassination of President Harper in Houston. I never was in Houston, but that doesn't matter. Meanwhile, you are set up for the murder of Prime Minister Sommerset.

"Now, it doesn't take my people long to figure out that you and I are close friends so they anticipate that I'll do whatever I can to help you. Therefore, they know where to start looking for me. Sure enough, I find them all over Amsterdam checking out your apartment and mine. Some person or persons in President Bunnell's administration are on the take with these guys and are setting us up. They know that I have uncovered their plot to turn drugs into money to buy up oil futures and try to corner the oil market and start a 'little' war in the Middle East. This will lead to crippling the American economy as well as the rest of the Western economies that need the oil.

"Then they figure that they can kill two birds with one stone, so to speak, and they let me get to you. They figure that MI6, Interpol, the Yard, or the police will blow us away before we can tell the world what we know of their devious, fucking plan! And what has them pissed off? Is we have so far dodged them with the help of this 'Caesar', whoever the fuck that is."

Flynn stopped momentarily and downed the rest of the pint. Kristen glanced at him, sliding her pint over to him. Flynn, immediately embarrassed, realized that he hadn't asked Kristen what she might have wanted to drink. "I'm sorry," he apologized, "what would you like?"

"I don't need anything, really."

"Bullshit! What can I get you?"

Kristen quietly answered, "How about a gin and soda?"

Flynn got up and marched over to the bar and ordered her drink. In a minute he was back with the gin and soda. Kristen took a sip of the cocktail through a straw before she finally asked, "What is it that they want?"

"Well," Flynn began again, "one group, the one who calls itself 'The Elite', are international drug smugglers. They sell their shit for the money to buy people in influential positions and to buy these oil futures. They are attempting to corner the market on the supply of oil. This drives the price of oil skyward giving them more money while decimating the economies of the U.S. and the other developed countries. Then they have their hand-picked puppet in, say Iran, threaten a nuclear attack on Israel to distract everyone from their real goal. It doesn't take a genius to figure out that the U.S. and its allies cannot allow this. And, in order to protect their own self interests in keeping the oil supply flowing freely, launch an all out war. This, all the while, is being orchestrated by 'The Elite' for their own purposes as part of a global master plan."

"This is unbelievable," Kristen responded beginning to follow Flynn's reasoning.

"What's more unbelievable, Kris, is that your uncle and President Harper were members of this 'Elite'. So is Don Carlos Escobar."

"The man from the note?"

"Yes. He was with Larry, Curly and Moe at Max's place waiting to ambush us."

Kristen was puzzled. "Who?"

"The three stooges who kidnapped you."

"Oh, Arthur, Falso and that weasel, Willie."

"Yes," Flynn confirmed.

"Okay," Kristen leaned closer, "if what you say is correct about Uncle James and President Harper, why were they murdered?"

"You're not paying attention, Darlin'," Flynn replied. "Mister Kim Moon Jung, alias 'The Tiger', head of the 'Elite', simply didn't need them anymore. He probably had replacements all ready to take over for them or," Flynn frowned now in deeper thought, "he plans on getting rid of all of them eventually."

"Do you mean that the new Prime Minister and your President Bunnell are also part of this 'Elite'?"

"Either they are part of it or they're being controlled, unwittingly, by 'Tiger'."

Kristen shook her head and said, "This is crazy, Flynn. What is the motivation for whoever that wants us dead?" And, why is this 'Caesar', whoever that is, trying to help us? None of this makes any sense to me."

"You're right about one thing, this is certainly crazy all right. The 'Elite' wants us dead, no question about it. Me, because I stumbled upon their operation and know their plan. You, because of what you know about who framed you. With you out of the way, MI6 and Scotland Yard will simply say, 'case closed' she murdered the Prime Minister and look no further."

Flynn took another gulp of his Porter before continuing. "Another thing. If I could get to Patricia...President Bunnell. I think I could convince her that she is being used by someone close to her for their fucked-up purpose. As to 'Caesar', this is still a bit of a mystery to me. Obviously he or they have their own agenda which somehow conflicts with 'The Elite' and they are apparently helping us, if that's what's going on, because they think we can stop the 'Elite' if we stay alive. Truthfully, that part of this mess is still a mystery to me."

Kristen looked directly into Flynn's eyes when she spoke. "I have two questions I hope you can answer for me."

"Go ahead," Flynn replied, "But I'm not sure I know the answers."

"First," Kristen asked, "do you have any idea how

'Caesar' knows where we are or where we're going all the time?"

Flynn paused for a moment waiting to hear her finish. "And what's the second question?"

"One at a time, Flynn."

"Okay," Flynn began looking back into her emerald green eyes. "Simple answer, yes and no!"

"What do you mean, 'yes' and 'no'?"

"Well, either you're telling them, or I am."

"You've got me confused."

"Look, it's really pretty obvious. 'Caesar' knows where we are because you're telling them or I'm telling them. How? You see, every time I call my contact in the Agency, they get the information from my cell phone. Somehow this 'Caesar' is receiving my calls or my contact is forwarding the info on to them. Either way, I'm telling them."

Kristen reached over and put her hand on his while she thought for a moment before asking, "All right, if that's not true, then how am I telling them?"

"You could be making calls or leaving a drop message somewhere. Maybe," Flynn smiled at her, "you're an informer."

"You can't be serious. I haven't left your side since we fled from the convent."

"Don't lose your sense of humor, Kris. I don't think you're an informer. Actually, as I think about this some more, it has to be linked to my calls to the States. I'm just not sure yet, but I'll find out. Now, what's your second question?"

"I can't remember. It couldn't have been important." Kristen pulled her hand back and reached for her drink. While sipping on the gin and soda, she looked around the Pub. People were enjoying themselves. She thought, "I wish we were enjoying ourselves like they are. If only we weren't being hunted down like two common criminals. If I could only erase what has happened these past weeks we could be on a date. Oh, how did this ever happen?"

Flynn watched her for a few minutes. When he finished his drink he announced, "Let's get going. We've another appointment to keep."

Flynn's sudden announcement brought Kristen back to the present reality. "Where are we going?"

Flynn held out his hand to her and they both got up to go. When they went outside into the London fog he answered her. "We've got a date with Mister William Smythe, remember?"

They walked over to the pickup truck and drove off into the dark, foggy night. Within a few minutes they were outside the residence of Kristen's late uncle James Saunders, still occupied by Smythe. Flynn drove down the block and parked between the street lights. The dense fog made seeing difficult while Flynn and Kristen walked slowly back to the house.

"Where is the back entrance?" Flynn whispered.

"There's a sliding glass door on the other side of the garden. It leads to Uncle James' study. We can get there down the driveway," she answered quietly.

The pair hastened around the back side of the mansion where Flynn saw the garden and the door she had mentioned. Keeping to the shadows and following a hedge row, they carefully crossed the garden and came to the doors. Flynn tried the handle. It was locked.

"Is there another door or window back here?" Flynn quietly asked.

Kristen thought for a moment. "Back here," she answered starting for the garage. Flynn quickly followed.

The door, which had a number of small panes of glass above the knob, was also locked. Flynn took his Glock from his jacket and with the butt of the weapon smashed the glass.

The noise startled Kristen who exclaimed, "Jeezus, Flynn, why didn't you just fucking ring a bell?"

Flynn looked at her and smiled. He leaned close to her ear and whispered, "I didn't bring a bell." He reached his hand through the broken window and unlatched the lock. They both walked in. "Where are we?" he asked.

"We're in the garage. Go straight ahead and you'll reach the kitchen door."

Carefully they walked to the end of the garage and Kristen pointed to the door. "Over there."

This door was unlocked and Flynn slowly opened it, his Glock at the ready. Flynn paused as he entered the kitchen. Music was playing upstairs. Flynn led the way while Kristen stayed close behind. Flynn made his way along the hallway to the bottom of a staircase. The music was louder as they neared the steps. At the foot of the staircase Flynn stopped and took Kristen by the hand.

"You stay here," he ordered. "Keep your eyes and ears open. If you hear anything down here beat it out the back way we came in and make for the truck. I'll catch up to you. Do you have that pistol I gave you?"

Kristen reached into her jacket pocket and pulled out the 9mm. "Yes, right here."

"Don't use it if you don't have to. And for God's sake, don't shoot me!"

Kristen remained at the bottom of the stairs watching while Flynn tip toed up to the second floor. The music became much louder as Flynn approached the door from where it was coming. He could see light under the door. He reached for the knob while listening at the door for a moment. He could hear laughter and then two men's voices. Flynn flipped off the safety with his thumb preparing to throw open the door. He took a deep breath just before he turned the door knob and flung the door open. He propelled himself inside the room.

William Smythe and a younger man were totally surprised when Flynn burst in. They had been dancing naked but immediately stopped in shock when they saw Flynn and his weapon aimed at them.

"Don't fucking move!" Flynn shouted at the two naked men while smashing the CD player with his foot silencing the music.

The younger man threw himself onto the floor hysterically screaming and crying. Smythe froze as the younger man groveled. Smythe sneered at Flynn, "You bastard! Look what you've done to Jamie. What bloody right have you to barge in here?"

Flynn quickly glanced down at the younger naked man. Frightened, the younger man had urinated over himself and the floor. The sight of this disgusted Flynn who slapped Smythe across the face with his backhand sending Smythe reeling into the wall.

"You fucking brute," Smythe shouted wiping blood from the corner of his mouth. "What do you want?"

"I want some answers and I want them now!"

"Answers to what? I don't know what you're talking about."

"Who hired you to kidnap Kristen Shults?" Flynn demanded.

"Go fuck yourself, Yank!" Smythe scream back

defiantly.

Flynn pounced on the man and shoved his Glock hard into Smythe's nose breaking the cartilage with the force of his move. Flynn growled, "I'm going to fuck you up the ass with the barrel of this gun if you don't start giving me some answers!"

Smythe was now in pain and shaking in fright realizing that this man meant what he said. "Let's be reasonable," Smythe pleaded staring cross-eyed down the barrel of the Glock.

"I don't have time to be fucking reasonable, asshole," Flynn spit back. "Now I'm going to ask you just once more. Who hired you to kidnap Kristen?"

"The Foreign Minister told me to set it up. He said that she wouldn't be harmed. I only did what he asked me to do."

"Then you killed him," Flynn said.

"It was an accident," Smythe lied.

Flynn had had enough from this man. He shoved the barrel of his 10mm into Smythe's mouth, breaking off a partial denture. "I don't like lies. And I don't have time to play any games. Who ordered you to kill Saunders?"

William Smythe's eyes suddenly bulged catching sight of Kristen, now standing behind Flynn, with her pistol aimed at his head. Flynn hadn't heard her come up behind him.

Smythe started to gag on Flynn's barrel while he tried to mumble something before the back of his head blew apart from the gunshot. Flynn spun around in disbelief and looked at Kristen who was now turning her weapon on the younger man squirming on the floor. In an instant another shot rang out from her 9mm, splattering skull and brain matter all over.

Flynn lunged for the weapon, catching Kristen's hand as a third shot fired into the wall. "What the fuck are you doing?" Flynn screamed at her.

Kristen stood motionless with a fixed stare on her face. Flynn wrested the weapon from her hand and grabbed her. The smell of gunpowder and smoke filled the room.

At the same instant, the front door came bursting open and Flynn could hear heavy footsteps starting up the stairs. Grabbing Kristen by the still outstretched arm, Flynn pulled her with him down the back hallway while automatic weapons fire ripped around them. Flynn pulled Kristen close to him to shield her. Then turning his back to the window and pulling her close, he and Kristen crashed through the second story hall window. In an instant they were thrown into the garden hedge. The force of the fall caused Flynn and Kristen to tumble over and over before Flynn could get her and himself to their feet. Bullets rang out from the broken window above while Flynn and Kristen ran for cover in the darkness and the fog.

The pair went rushing out into the street in front of a passing car which came screeching stop just before them. Flynn ran to the driver's side and jerked open the car door shoving his Glock into the frightened driver's face. He pulled the man from the vehicle and shoved Kristen into the car. Then he got in behind the wheel. They sped off as more bullets rained around them and into the back of the speeding car.

Flynn drove around making a series of turns until he hit a four lane. He tromped down on the accelerator completing their escape. Several miles later he exited the highway and turned down the first street from the exit ramp. He pulled the car over and stopped. Kristen remained motionless. Flynn grabbed her arm and she turned toward him. He was just about to speak but Kristen calmly and quietly spoke first.

"I told you I was going to kill him, and I did. I'm not the least bit sorry for it. He deserved to die. They both deserved to die."

Flynn slammed his hands against the steering wheel in anger, "You sure as hell did kill 'em, all right. What the fuck for? He was just about to tell me who ordered him to kill your uncle and why you were kidnapped."

"Because he needed to die for all that he did to me and Uncle James."

Flynn took her head into his hands while he looked deeply into her emerald eyes. He recognized that she was in shock. He had seen the same expression on the faces of many young soldiers after combat in 'Operation Freedom'. Resolved that a major lead was eliminated, Flynn drove back to the Royal York in order for him to retrieve his briefcase. He knew he would need a lot of money to buy their way out of England. He could feel the net getting tighter around them and he hoped they could slip through before it closed completely.

Kristen waited in the car while Flynn dashed into the hotel. He was back by her side within a few minutes. Then turning to her began, "We're going to have to ditch this car and find a new place to stay tonight. Someplace that no one would ever think to look for us."

"You mean another sleazy room?" Kristen appeared to have come out of her shock.

"On the contrary," Flynn replied. "The most obscure place at a time like this is right where no one would ever expect us to go"

Kristen glanced over at him and asked, "And where might that be?"

"Why the bridal suite at the London Hilton, of course."

"You must be joking."

"No, it's perfect. But first I have to make a few calls." Flynn opened his cell phone. His first call was to the Hilton to make a reservation. The second was to a local taxi, and the third was going to be to Jackie Armstrong's private cell number. But as he went to look it up, a text message came through from her.

"Tommy, this is Alice. Copy carefully and respond in kind as in 5551212. Now here's just for you. R4, - L9, R4, R5, R5, - C2, C3, - R4, R6, - R5, R6, C6, L3 R6, C6, - L8, C8, C3, R7, - L7, L6, - C8, C7, L4, C3, C6, L8, - R4- R7, C3, C3, - C8, - R4,- C5, C6, R6, L9,- L9, C4, R6, - R2, L2, C3, R7, L2, C7, - R4, R7, -,L6, C3, C3, L8, -, L6, C3, - L2, L8, - C4, R6, C7, C6, L8, R6, C7, C7,C3, L8, -, L7, C8, C2, - L9, C3, L3, - L2, L8, - 2, L7, L6."

Flynn stared at her text message knowing that it was a code from the telephone number and its letter pad which told him the "C, R and L," indicated Center, Right and Left to identify the letter position on that pad and that the number itself was for the letter to spell the message. He deciphered it as: "I will be in London Tues PM. Urgent I see you I know who 'Caesar' is. Meet me at the Horn Dorset Pub Wed at 2PM".

Flynn texted his reply, "R6, C5,- C2, C8, L8,- L9, C4, L2, L8, - L8, C4, C3,- R3, C8, R2, C5?" ("OK But What The Fuck?")

Kristen could see that Flynn had a perplexed

expression on his face. "Anything wrong?"

Sarcastically, Flynn answered, "No, Kris, everything is just peachy."

Just as he finished his remark the taxi cab arrived and Flynn and Kristen were driven to the London Hilton.

The desk clerk gave Flynn and Kristen a skeptical look when they approached. May I help you, sir?"

"Reservation for Nicolas and Nora Cokely," Flynn confidently replied while beaming at Kristen and she beaming at him back, appropriately.

The desk clerk checked his computer and saw that indeed a reservation had been made for the bridal suite. He raised his eyebrow, again giving Flynn and Kristen the once over. "Yes, Mister Cokely, the bridal suite, of course. Any bags?"

"We eloped!" Kristen blurted surprising Flynn with her quick remark. "Does it show?"

The desk clerk cleared his throat and wryly smiled, "And how will you be paying for the room, sir? Credit card?"

"No," Flynn answered not taking his eyes from Kristen. "Cash. In advance for an entire week." He took out a wad of One Hundred dollar bills from his briefcase and slammed it down on the counter.

"Americans," the desk clerk thought. "How brash!"

Flynn filled out the reservation form and received the room key. He and Kristen walked arm-in-arm to the elevator and pushed the button for their floor. Within a few minutes they were settled in.

"Tomorrow morning we'd better buy some new clothes," Flynn said to Kristen who was on her way into the bathroom.

"Oh, that sounds lovely. I'm a bit tired of these 'rags'. But right now, I'm going to soak in the tub."

Flynn sat down and pondered over the message from Jackie. "Why was she coming to London? If she knew who 'Caesar' was she could have told him in the text message. Why 'urgent I see you'?" His thoughts drifted on. "I'm gonna have to figure out how we can get new passports....Maybe the one man I can ask who might know is Don Vito Manderino's cousin, Joseppi Penella. I'll have to call him tomorrow morning. He just might have the right connections. I just hope that I haven't run out of favors."

LANGLEY, VIRGINIA

Acting Assistant Deputy Director of Operations Mollie Farnham was reviewing the daily field reports when she came across the London report which immediately got her attention. "Scotland Yard reported that members of their SWAT team, assigned to stake out the residence of William Smythe, responded to gunshots at the residence. Smythe and his male lover, one Jamie Eggar, were found murdered. Agents fired on the two suspects--positively identified as Jeremiah Flynn and Kristen Shults who escaped by crashing through an upstairs window.

"Earlier that evening Scotland Yard discovered the bodies of three men with prior arrests, Arthur Grasse, Jonathan Falso, and William 'Willie' Bliss shot to death at the King Arthur Print Shop. Max Steiner, proprietor, also dead as a result of his throat being slashed. Flynn's fingerprints discovered at the scene. Both Flynn and the Shults women are now suspects in those murders as well."

Mollie took the reports down the hall to the Deputy Director's office. She was immediately buzzed in to Dimmler's office.

"Good morning, Mollie, what have you got?" Dimmler asked greeting his assistant.

"The London report, sir, is of particular interest," Mollie replied handing the report to Dimmler.

While Dimmler read the report a deep frown wrinkled his forehead. "What the hell is going on?"

Mollie offered, "It looks like our man has gone off the reservation and is on a rampage, sir."

"It doesn't make sense, goddamnit! This isn't like Flynn. Something just doesn't fit."

"What can we do, sir? The report clearly says that Flynn and Shults were identified."

Dimmler drummed his pencil while thinking for a moment. Finally asking, "Who do we have in the London office? Is Salient still the head man?"

"Jonathan Salient? Yes, sir. He's still there."

"Get a hold of him and tell him to see if he can get more on these two events from his contacts at the Yard. I'd like to get the ballistics report as soon as possible." Dimmler looked over the report again and then asked his assistant, "Does Armstrong know about this?"

"I'm not certain, sir. The time on the report is five twelve this morning which was after her scheduled time on her shift. Unless, for some reason, she happened to stay over time she wouldn't know."

Dimmler picked up his desk phone and called the computer operations room. "This is Deputy Director Dimmler. Can you tell me what time Jackie Armstrong signed out this morning?"

There was a momentary pause before he received the answer. "Five twenty-five, sir."

"Thank you," Dimmler said putting down the phone.

Mollie had been studying him during the call. When he returned eye contact with her Mollie asked, "She knows?"

"I'm afraid so." Dimmler answered calmly.

"Is there anything else you want me to do on this?" Mollie asked.

"Yes. Put a twenty four hour on Armstrong with a two hour call in."

"With pleasure," Mollie declared with a tone of satisfaction in her voice.

NORTH KOREA

Kim Moon Jung became furious while reading his text message. "Escobar has failed to close the London contract. All others terminated. Escobar is missing. Flynn still on the loose and becoming more of a threat. Should we send her to London? She might be able to close the deal. He trusts her."

Tiger slammed his hand on his desk in anger. Immediately he began to look up the number in his cell for his contact and made the connection.

"This is Tiger. Arrange it at once. I will fly to Washington this week. Meet me at my hotel suite at the Hilton three nights from today. Notify the other members. We will all meet at eleven P.M. your time three nights from now at the Heights Courtyard, as usual. I will make plans to take care of this troublesome Flynn matter personally."

WASHINGTON, D. C.

Jackie Armstrong removed the folded message from her purse and re-read it. The message troubled her. She didn't know what to do. She was uncertain if Flynn would ever call again. And, if he did, she wasn't sure what she could say to him. "Somehow," she thought, "our calls are being intercepted. Maybe Flynn hasn't figured that out and thinks I'm betraying him."

All morning Jackie paced about her living room. She looked at her cell phone hoping it would ring. "I need a shower to clear my head," she mumbled. While starting for the bathroom to undress, she looked out her window and noticed a car parked outside with two men sitting in it observing her house.

Jackie Armstrong had worked at the Agency long enough to recognize a surveillance team. She watched them for a minute being careful to not let them see her. She became apprehensive and found it difficult to swallow. Jackie quickly checked all her doors making certain the dead bolts were secure.

"Okay, okay," she began to ask herself. "What would a field operative do in a situation like this?" She tried to think. "I know. Pretend I don't know they're there and then lose 'em."

Jackie undressed and showered quickly. She dried her hair, put on a little make-up and dressed in jeans, a blouse and a sweater. She threw a change of underwear in a small handbag before she put on her running shoes. Jackie checked her wallet. "Credit cards, passport and a few hundred in cash. That's going to have to do."

Jackie turned on the television and a few lights

before she grabbed her leather jacket and the keys to her rented red Corvette. She walked quickly into the garage and pushed the automatic garage opener while buckling her seat belt. The engine came alive as soon as she turned the key. Then Jackie backed out into the street.

Slamming the 'Vette into gear, she sped past the two surveillance men watching them make a hasty U-Turn in her rear view mirror. "Catch me if you can," she smiled heading to the Belt-way.

Jackie headed north to Interstate 95. Her 'tail' was keeping a safe distance behind while she continually checked them in her rear-view. The morning rush hour traffic was heavy but flowing smoothly. Suddenly, Jackie pulled out into the outside lane and hit the gas. The well tuned 'Vette responded quicker than the Agency car. Just as they got out into the far left lane, Jackie swung right cutting off the surprised and angry morning commuters. She narrowly made the exit ramp--down shifting the 'Vette over loose stones. The Agency men were unable to make the same move soon enough and the heavy traffic stopped their attempt to follow.

"How do you like that, boys?" Jackie proudly said to herself. "Kiss my ass!" She had shaken her 'tail'.

Within a few hours Jackie drove into Manhattan and parked the rented Corvette in a garage on Eighth Avenue. She walked the few blocks to the Port Authority and bought a shuttle bus ticket to Newark International Airport.

Once inside the Newark Airport terminal, Jackie checked the British Airways departure schedule. Seeing that a flight to London's Heathrow was set to depart in a little over an hour, Jackie went to the counter and purchased a one-way ticket. She would be in London by supper time.

THE WHITE HOUSE

Chief of Staff Admiral Moorehouse was in on the morning briefing of the President. Secretary of State Makoweic, still in the Middle East, had just finished his telephone report that the Iraqis and the Saudis had agreed to let the U.S. buildup a military presence in their countries which pleased the Joint Chiefs. Plans were finalized on transporting men and material to Saudi Arabia and Iraq.

Moorehouse waited until the briefing was over and all of the others had left the Oval Office before he spoke to President Bunnell.

"Madam President," Moorehouse began, "I have received some information which you might find interesting...."

"What is it, Michael?" The President was still thinking about the Middle East situation that was heating up.

"It's the latest out of London this morning...." Moorehouse paused.

Jeezus, Michael, if you have something to say, then say it. Stop beating around the bush!"

Admiral Moorehouse handed a copy of the report sent to Langley detailing the gruesome murders and incidents involving Flynn and Kristen Shults the night before.

President Bunnell read the report over and then placed it on her desk. She glared over at the Chief of Staff and said, "Well, don't you have some cute little 'I told you so' comment to make?"

Moorehouse remained serious and a feigned puzzled look came over his face. "No, Patricia, I don't. I just thought you'd like the information. That's all. It's the first word we've had on him and his latest 'glorious' exploits."

"And what do you expect me to do about this?"

"I don't know that I expect you to do anything about it. I merely thought you'd like to know."

The President turned her back to him and said, "Thank you, Michael. That will be all for now."

The Chief of Staff left the Oval Office. Patricia picked up the copy of the report and studied it. A realization came over her while she reflected on the mysterious phone call and now this message. "This is a CIA internal report," her mind was racing. "How did it get into Michael's hands?"

President Bunnell made a decision. She picked up her intercom and rang her secretary. "Scott, make the necessary arrangements for Air Force One to fly to London this afternoon! I want to...no, I need to be in London tonight!"

"Yes, Madam President. But what of your schedule?"

"Cancel everything. This is a matter of National importance. Notify the Secret Service, and Press Corps. See if Deputy Director Dimmler and NSA Director Pfohl are available or their closest assistants. Have the Chief of Staff make arrangements with the Prime Minister and his staff. Alert the London Hilton to have the suites available, et cetera, et cetera. You know. We are leaving at noon!"

"Yes, Ma'am." Scott replied.

LONDON

The British Airways jet landed at Heathrow in time for Jackie Armstrong to make it to the London Hilton before the height of London's rush hour. She checked in and went directly to her room. She had made up her mind to stay in her room tonight and get a light supper brought up from room service. She checked her text messages and re-read Flynn's. He would meet her tomorrow as she planned at two P.M.

She chuckled again at his response, '...what the fuck?' "Tomorrow Flynn, you'll understand."

At the same time Jackie was having her supper, Air Force One touched down at Heathrow and the President and her entourage were ushered under the strictest security to London's Hilton.

Early the next day Flynn and Kristen had gone shopping. They both purchased several changes of clothing and new luggage. Flynn also purchased them some dark and clear eye glasses, hats and wigs. Although he suggested that Kristen dye her hair, she rejected that idea in lieu of a complete make-over at a nearby salon.

"This is going to take a few hours," Kristen advised him, "so do what you have to do. But meet me here in a couple of hours."

"All right," Flynn reluctantly agreed, "I'll be back. Don't leave without me. You keep the packages with you. I'm just going to take a few things." He put a few items in a small plastic bag and bid here good-bye.

Flynn walked a few blocks until he came to a Public House where he went in. He ordered a glass of Stout and found a quiet booth where he made his cell phone call to Joseppi Penella's business number in

Amsterdam.

A gruff voice answered. "Imports, Mister Penella's office."

"This is Jeremiah Flynn. Joseppi Penella please."

In a moment Joseppi picked up the phone. "Flynn it is good to hear from you, my friend. What can I do for you?"

"Hello, Joseppi. It is good to talk with you, too. How is your family, and Don Vito?"

"They are all well. Don Vito will be pleased to hear that you inquired of him. Thank you for asking."

Flynn wanted to get to the point but he understood that these men had a certain protocol and it was important to show respect. They appreciated only those who made the proper inquiries and showed them respect. "Joseppi," Flynn began, "I need to ask you for a favor. If it is possible?"

"Of course, Flynn. I will help you if I can. After all, Don Vito thinks of you as family. What do you need?"

"I need two exit Visas and passports to get out of England. Unfortunately, my original suppler was eliminated."

"I have heard that Mister Steiner met with an untimely death. A man named Don Carlos Escobar butchered him....from what I have been told. This man Escobar was sent there to fulfill the million dollar contract on you, my friend."

"Where is Escobar now?"

"Let me just say that he is no longer a threat to you or Kristen. However, you have other concerns. Your President is on her way to London to see you. But be careful, Flynn. All is not what it seems. Someone close to her is the 'Elite's' source...a 'mole' if you will, in her company."

Flynn couldn't believe what he heard. "No, Joseppi, I haven't heard of any news that the President was coming to London. Who's this 'mole' ?"

"We do not know. However, Don Vito and all of the family would be grateful if you could find out for us. This whole thing has been bad for the family business."

"I'll do what I can. I don't know how I am I going to get in to see the President. I'm not exactly welcome, as you know."

"Yes, my friend. But I trust you will find a way."

Flynn was confused about these new turn of events. He paused for a moment before he asked again. "What about the passports?"

"Yes, of course. There is a man named John Addams, with two d's. His number is listed under Addams International Diamond Imports in London. However, my friend, do not use him unless you must. Play the cards being dealt to you. If you do not like the game, then call him. I must emphasize that Don Vito would consider it a personal favor if you could uncover the identity of this 'mole'. He and his 'Elite' allies are enemies to both of us."

"I understand. One more thing, if I may?"

"What is it?"

"Do you know who 'Caesar' is?"

"He is your friend. I can say no more now. Good luck, Flynn." The call was disconnected.

Flynn closed his cell phone and checked the time. He had about a half an hour before his meeting with Jackie at the Horn Dorset. He was curious about what Joseppi had said about a 'mole'. "Could Jackie be that 'mole'? She knows I trust her and, after every time we talk, someone called 'Caesar' knows where we are. Why is she in London, anyway?" Flynn pondered these thoughts while he walked to the Horn Dorset to see if he could get some answers to these questions.

Flynn ducked down an alley and took a wig from the small bag he had with him. After he put it on he took a pair of wire rimmed glasses from the bag and put them on. "The best disguise is the smallest disguise," he thought while he turned and headed for his appointment.

Flynn arrived at the Horn Dorset, a well known Pub for locals who wanted to meet discreetly. The place was dimly lit with private booths. People who frequented this place minded their own business. Flynn found a seat in a booth near the back where he could view the door. He ordered a drink and waited.

At five minutes to two, Jackie Armstrong walked into the Public House. She glanced around and looked directly at Flynn, but didn't recognize him. She took a seat in a nearby booth. A waiter came over to her and she ordered a drink.

Flynn watched her for several minutes. He saw that Jackie was getting nervous and impatient. She kept looking at her watch and fidgeting in her seat. Finally, Jackie got up and went to the ladies room and Flynn moved his seat into her booth.

Jackie came back and was momentarily startled by this strange man in her booth until, imitating Humphrey Bogart as best he could said, "Of all the gin joints in all the towns in all the world, you had ta pick this one, eh."

Jackie immediately understood it was Flynn. "You sonofabitch, Rick, you really know how to treat a girl, don't you?"

"What brings you to 'Casablanca'? Got tired and

couldn't handle all the men in D.C.?"

"There's only one man I'd like to handle, you big lug. And that's you."

There little banter over, Flynn became serious. He leaned closer to Jackie and softly demanded, "What the fuck are you doing here?"

"This is what I'm doing here," she answered. She reached in her pocket and took out a copy of the report from the London branch which detailed the murders at the King Arthur Print Shop. She shoved it over to Flynn. "I thought you were in trouble and I could help."

"This isn't the first time I've ever been in a tight situation, you know. I don't get why you had to come here personally? With you here, I've got no contact back in the Sates. What gives?"

"Piss off you sonofabitch! If that's all you've got to say, then go to hell. I don't give two shits what happens to you and that little bitch you're fucking." Jackie got up to leave but Flynn grabbed her arm and guided her back into the booth.

"Hold it, Jackie, don't misunderstand me. It's not that I don't appreciate your concern, but now with you here, I got one more person to worry about. You've been a great help to me these past weeks, but you may have made this mess worse by coming over here."

"Hey, asshole, you don't ever have to worry about me. I can take care of myself. I don't need you or anyone. I've taken care of myself for a long time." She turned away trying to hid a tear welling in her eyes.

Flynn saw the tear. He reached over and took her hand. "Okay, you win. You're here. Let's think about this for a minute. No need to get worked up." He took a handkerchief from his pocket and handed it to her. "Here use this." She wiped her eyes. Then took a sip of her drink. Neither spoke for a long time.

"What do you want me to do?" Jackie finally broke the silence.

"I don't know right now. Where are you staying?"

"I'm at the Hilton," Jackie answered. She opened her purse and pulled out her room key. She slid it across the table and smiled, "It's room 1405. Take it, I have another. I was hoping that you, for once, might stay with me."

Flynn took the plastic card-key and put it in his jacket pocket. "That might cause a little problem."

Jackie realized what he implied. "Oh, yeah. Shults-ee. Two's company three's a crowd."

He didn't want to tell her that he was also staying at the Hilton, "Something like that."

Jackie leaned over and looked into Flynn's eyes. "Tell me, are you boffing her?"

"For one thing, gentlemen never discuss these things."

"Flynn, you're no gentleman."

"And secondly, I'm saving myself for you."

"You're a lying sack of shit. Wait," Jackie looked closer into his deep blue eyes, "Your eyes are turning brown."

"No, they're not. Look, Jackie," Flynn changed the subject. "I have to go and meet Kristen...."

"You are so boffing her. You're a slut just like the Prez. It's no wonder you got along with her, too."

Flynn didn't want to play this game anymore. "All right, that's enough. We've got more important things to worry about at the moment."

"Sorry," Jackie knew she went too far.

"It's okay. Maybe there is something you could find out for me."

"Sure. What is it?"

"Do you think you could bluff your way into the Agency's London branch?"

"I think so. Why?"

"I need as much info as you can get from the Company's files on Addams International Diamond Exports and a John Addams. That's spelled with two 'd's', in particular."

"Anything else?"

"See if you can find out who's here with President Bunnell. And why."

Jackie smiled, "That should be easy enough. Anything else?"

Flynn wondered how Jackie knew that the President was in London. He decided to let it pass for the time being. Instead he asked, "Can you get this information today?"

"I'm pretty sure that I can. Yeah."

"All right," Flynn concluded, "I'll be by your room tonight about eight. We'll go over everything then."

"Okay. Then I better get started." Jackie got up from her seat smiling at Flynn. She leaned down kissing him on the cheek. "See you tonight, Big Boy."

Flynn sat in the booth for a few minutes after Jackie left. "Joseppi said that someone close is the 'Mole'. It couldn't be Jackie. She's not close to the President. No, the 'Mole' is likely to be someone who's with her here in London. Someone who knows that she has come here to see me and find out what I know. And, probably has set up a trap to get me before I can get to her." Flynn finished his Stout. "I guess I'll just have to wait until tonight and see what Jackie has found out." He checked the time. He was going to be late to meet Kristen.

Jackie Armstrong had hailed a cab and instructed the driver to take her to an address further uptown to the London branch office of the CIA. The Company office was located in a high rise office building. It was a suite of offices which ostensibly indicated that they were occupied by 'Enterprise International, Ltd.', a phony commercial business. Jackie took the elevator to the twenty second floor. Jackie noticed a security camera was positioned outside a set of heavy wooden doors. Trying not to make direct eye contact, Jackie rang the buzzer to the right of the doors.

Within seconds the door lock released and Jackie entered a reception area. A receptionist sat behind a glass enclosure. There was a door directly behind her and another door to her right.

"May I help you?"

Jackie reached into her purse and took out her Agency Identification and held it against the glass. "My name is Jackie Armstrong and I'd like to see Jonathan Salient."

"Is Mister Salient expecting you?" The receptionist asked while still looking at Jackie's ID.

"No. This is an unscheduled visit. Part of a new policy from Headquarters. Mister Salient, I'm sure, got the memo from the Deputy Director, George Dimmler." Jackie bluffed perfectly. "Now, is he in? I have to inspect the computer operations and install a new program. And, I'm on a very tight schedule."

The receptionist never experienced a 'surprise visit' before. "I'll see if he's in." She picked up her phone and punched in a number. Jackie was unable to hear the conversation through the glass, although the receptionist glanced up at her several times while talking to someone. After hanging up her phone the receptionist addressed Jackie through the microphone.

"Someone will be with you momentarily."

Almost at once the door to the right opened. A small, slightly balding, thin man appeared. "Miss Armstrong? May I please see your identification?"

Jackie showed him her ID. "Mister Salient?"

"No, I'm Ernest Treadway. Mister Salient's Assistant. Mister Salient is out to lunch. How may I help you?"

"I'm hear to evaluate your computer systems and install a new--high level--encoded program...."

"No one notified us that anyone from the Agency Home Office would be coming here..."

Jackie continued her bluff. "According to the memo sent out by Director Dimmler, you and all other branches were notified that an unexpected visit could take place at any time. I guarantee that Mister Salient saw that memo."

"Is there a problem? I'm not aware of any problems with the data center."

"That's part of the reason I'm here today. To see if you do have any problems. And to install the new program. Now," Jackie began turning toward the door from which Treadway had come and more forcefully demanding, "if you'd be kind enough to show me the data center I can get my work done and out of your hair." She smiled looking at Treadway's receding hair line.

Treadway was flustered and taken off guard by Jackie's forward attitude. Unable to think quickly enough what to do next he stammered, "Yesss, of course. Umm, right this way."

Jackie Armstrong, immediately upon entering the data center, sat down behind a computer and began typing in her access codes. With a smile and a wave of her hand in a dismissing manner, Jackie discharged Treadway from the room. Once the codes were accepted, Jackie proceeded to 'talk' to Langley's Mainframe computer. She got the information that Flynn wanted on Addams International Imports and John Addams himself. She also accessed a top secret level six file emanating from the White House to the National Security Agency and the Department of State. "Holy shit. I need to get this to Flynn." Making sure that no one was looking, Jackie printed out the file's contents and stuffed then in her purse.

After she had finished, Jackie hurried to the door to leave. Treadway saw her and quickly jumped up from behind his desk. "Is there any problem?" He sheepishly asked.

"I'm afraid so," Jackie answered looking at her watch. "Does Salient always take more than an hour for lunch?"

"Oh, no." Treadway again was caught off guard. "He must have been unavoidably delayed."

"Well, I'll have to file a report. You understand." Jackie went to the doors to leave. Treadway followed her to the elevators.

"Is that really necessary?"

Jackie pushed the down button. "It's company policy. I have to file a report. And by the way, I'll be back tomorrow. I hope that Mister Salient will be available to see me." One of the elevator's car doors opened and she stepped inside. "Good Bye, Mister Treadway." Jackie said with a smug smile as the car's doors closed.

By the time Flynn got back to the Salon to meet Kristen he was nearly a half an hour late. Kristen was visibly nervous and annoyed when he finally arrived.

"Where the bloody hell have you been?"

"Whoa, there little woman. I'm sorry I'm a little late. I had some things I had to do."

Kristen remained livid, "A little late! You're nearly an hour late!"

Flynn took her by the arm and pulled her close to himself. Through clenched teeth Flynn fired back at her angry comment. "Let's get one thing perfectly clear. I'm trying to get us safely out of here the best way that I can. There are things that I have to do that I can better do alone! I don't get your attitude. I said I was sorry, now drop it!"

Kristen glared back at Flynn for a moment. She looked away then took a deep breath calming herself. "I was worried about you and I didn't know what to do without you. That's all. I just got frightened."

Flynn released his grip on her. Then more relaxed and stepping back, he smiled looking her 'new' image make-over. "My, my, but don't you look like a brand new woman. You are more lovely than ever, my dear. Shall we go?"

When Flynn led Kristen out of the salon she asked, "Are we going to take a taxi or walk?"

"Neither. We're going to take the bus." Flynn guided Kristen to a double-decker bus stop and both got on. When they got into their seat Flynn continued, "You're going to stay on the bus all the way to the hotel. I'm getting off at the next stop. Go straight to the room and wait for me. Do not let anyone into the room. And ignore all the security at the hotel. I'll join you later, I promise."

"Security? What kind of security?"

"President Bunnell has arrived here in London and is staying at the Hilton. The place will be crawling with Secret Service, British Intel, and assorted members of the Yard and I'm sure, local police. Just be confident. Walk directly with a purpose and avoid direct eye contact with everyone. Walk straight to the elevators and go up to our room. It won't be a problem."

"What if they recognize me? What do I do?"

"You'll have to trust me that they won't. They're looking for a couple. Not a beautiful, successfully-dressed and stylish woman like you, alone. You'll be fine. Don't talk to anyone and pretend you don't even notice them."

Kristen was about to protest but the bus stopped and Flynn bolted for the door. Kristen watched Flynn momentarily before he disappeared into the crowd. A sense of panic overcame her. The bus continued on its route finally stopping at the London Hilton.

Kristen got off the bus at the hotel and nervously marched into the lobby. She kept her eyes straight remembering what Flynn had told her, ignoring everyone while walking to the bank of elevators. She started to enter a car that just had opened when a man abruptly stopped her.

"Excuse me, Miss." The man said politely, "You'll have to take another lift. This one is reserved for the President's use...You understand."

Kristen held her breath. She was momentarily paralyzed. "He's a Secret Service Agent. What'll I do?" She backed up from the open car, "Yes, of course. Sorry."

Then another elevator car opened behind her and

she turned to get in. Kristen didn't notice that a woman slipped into the car just a second before the automatic doors closed. Unknown to Kristen, that woman was Jackie Armstrong. Jackie glancing over at Kristen thought, "Very lovely. And very expensively dressed." She started to turn away but quickly returned to look more intently this time, recognizing Kristen. Jackie waited until Kristen got off on her floor and followed her closely down the hallway.

Kristen inserted the key-card into the door to unlock it. The green light indicated the door was open. When Kristen started to go inside the room, Jackie suddenly burst into the door.

"Well, well. Kristen Shults, as I live and breathe." Jackie exclaimed.

"Who are you? What do you want? I'm not Kris...."

"Yes, you are," Jackie interrupted. "You're Kristen Shults. And you can relax, honey. You and I need to talk."

"What do you and I need to talk about?"

"Mutual friends."

ABOARD AIR FORCE ONE

Deputy Director of Operations Dimmler's cell phone rang while he was with the Presidential party heading to London on Air Force One. "Dimmler."

"Sir, this is Mollie."

"What's up?"

"I just received a call from Jonathan Salient in our London Office."

Puzzled and also curious Dimmler asked, "What did he want?"

"He said that Jackie Armstrong was in that office a little while ago. That she was doing a surprise inspection as you directed...."

"What?" Dimmler hadn't issued any such directive. "Okay, what did she do? Does he know?"

"Apparently, sir, Salient was out to lunch and she bluffed her way past Treadway and got access to the computer files. She claimed that she needed to install a new program. God only knows what damaged she might have done."

"Who's this Treadway?"

"He's the Executive Assistant under Salient, sir."

"All right. Then we know that she's now in London and probably close to Flynn."

"What do you want me to do at this end?" Mollie asked.

Dimmler paused momentarily before he ordered, "See if you can get a run down on her location."

"But, Director," Mollie interjected, "don't you think she might be using an alias?"

"Probably. But, if she used a credit card...."

"Of course," Mollie understood how she could trace the trail.

"When you locate her, let me know. No one else is to know about this and don't do anything else. If she doesn't know we are on to her she'll most likely lead us to Flynn."

"I'll get right on it, Director. I'll call you as soon as I find her location."

"Very well. I'll be expecting your call." Dimmler disconnected the call and Mollie went to work.

LONDON

After the Presidential party's arrival at the Hilton, the three executive floors were buzzing with activity. Last minute details were being finalized. The Secret Service was concerned that security was not what it should be because the President's sudden trip caught everyone off-guard.

President Patricia Bunnell had been receiving the latest briefings from her advisors on the Middle East situation. While leafing through the reports, President Bunnell asked, "Has anyone heard from the Secretary of State today?"

A deputy from the State Department answered her. "Madam President, Secretary Makoweic is in the air and returning to Washington at this hour. He is arranging a meeting with some foreign representatives..."

The President didn't let the deputy finish. "Okay, okay. Could you please call him and put him through to me. I'd like to get the latest from him on how the negotiations went and an idea on what course we might follow."

Although the President appeared calm and business-like, her thoughts drifted to Flynn. "How is he going to contact me. Am I suppose to reach him somehow? I know he's close but..."

Patricia Bunnell was returned to duty by the interruption of her private cell phone. The President saw the call was from Chief of Staff Moorehouse."Yes, what is it, Michael?"

"Pat, I just heard that Jackie Armstrong, a CIA computer supervisor, gave her people the slip back in Washington and she's now in London!"

"Slow down, Michael. I don't understand what you're driving at?"

"Jackie Armstrong works for the CIA. She is a close, and I mean real close friend, if you get me, to Flynn. She has been in constant contact with him since he disappeared. The Agency was apparently watching her but she managed to give them the slip in New York City and hopped a plane to London. Just this afternoon she conned her way into the London branch of the Agency and gave them some kind of story so they let her into the computer room..."

"I'm still not sure I get the total connection?"

"It's simple! If she's in London you can bet that Flynn is in London. They're probably working together. Speculation is that they are lovers!" Moorehouse had to throw in that last little zinger.

"I think you speculate too much, Michael." The President hadn't missed the deliberate jab. "Let me tell you something. Why do you think that I'm here in London?"

"I assume it's to discuss the allied position in the Middle East."

"Well, you would be wrong. I am here to meet with Flynn! I don't really care what the allies' position is at this moment. I think Flynn knows, or has some information on, how we can stop all this madness before it starts. And if I have to, I'll go on the BBC and beg him to come and talk to me."

"Have you lost your senses? The man is a wanted terrorist. He and that Shults woman are killers. Now he's got another dumb broad convinced..."

Angry at the implication President Bunnell fired back, "Who are you calling a 'dumb broad'?

"er...uh...Jackie Armstrong, who else?"

"I think you meant someone else, too, didn't you?"

"Who?"

"Why, me of course. Didn't you?"

"Jeezus, Patricia get a grip. Think of your Presidency. You need to focus. You're the goddamn President of the United States. Flynn's nothing more than a trained killer who is wanted by every nation on earth."

"I don't wish to discuss this any more. I will do whatever I can to avoid a war. And, if Flynn can help me, I intend to do everything in my power to talk with him."

"You can't trust him," Moorehouse pleaded.

"I think I can trust him enough. I've never known him to lie to me."

"Oh, yeah, I almost forgot about the two of you..."

"Cut the Bullshit, Michael. I sincerely like and trust the man."

"Have it your way." Moorehouse pouting added, "One more thing."

"What is it?"

"Just how are you going to talk with Flynn?"

"I think he'll find a way to get to me. I don't expect he'll have any problem doing that."

"You have lost it! What do you think the Secret Service is going to do? Let him just walk into your room?"

"He'll find a way. I'm certain of it."

"Yeah, well, if I were you, I'd be careful of that lunatic. Don't do anything foolish or stupid."

Patricia had had enough of this conversation and let the last comment by the Chief of Staff go unchallenged at this time. "Michael, I have to go. The Secretary of State is calling," she lied.

President Patricia Bunnell drifted back into her thoughts. "How will he contact me? Maybe I should never have come to London at all. Is Michael right? And who is this Jackie Armstrong? She might have been the one who sent me that message at the White House. Didn't Michael say that she was a computer supervisor at Langley? It might make sense, especially if she and Flynn are really that close. Maybe he's been using her as a conduit to me. And, if so, wouldn't he do it again? I hope that whatever Flynn is doing that he doesn't take too long."

The President was interrupted by a knock on her door. It was Mary Branson, one of the President's Secret Servicewomen. "Excuse me, Madam President, but your dinner is here."

"Thank you. Have it sent in."

The door re-opened and a waiter came in wheeling a serving cart. The Secret Servicewoman returned to her post outside the President's door.

"Good evening, Madam." The waiter said politely with a British accent while making the preparations to serve the President. Now, certain they were alone, the waiter added, "It's good to see you, Pat!"

Patricia knew immediately. "Flynn!" She hadn't recognized him because of his disguise. "Oh, my God! Is it really you?"

"At your service, Madam President." Flynn replied. "But before you have me taken into custody there's a few things I need to tell you. We don't have the time right now for me to explain it all. If I don't leave here in a minute your people will get very nervous and I don't need that. However, we need to talk. I'm staying here in room 1018...."

"You're here in this hotel?" Patricia couldn't believe it. "I just had a feeling you were close, but I never..."

"Look, when you can get alone later call my room and I'll explain everything that I know."

The door suddenly opened and the Secret Servicewoman appeared in the doorway. "Is everything all right, Madam President?"

President Bunnell turned toward her and smiling brightly replied, "Yes, Mary, everything is fine." Then Patricia turned to dismiss the 'waiter'. "That will be all for now."

Flynn made a slight bow. "Enjoy your meal, Madam President." Then he wheeled the empty cart out the door past the Secret Servicewoman, unchallenged to the service elevator. He pushed the 'Down' button. His mission was accomplished. He had made contact with the President. "Now, I hope we still have time to stop 'Operation Lifeblood' before the world explodes."

Flynn selected the button for the fourteenth floor. "Jackie should be back by now." When he reached the fourteenth floor, Flynn walked down the hall to room 1405. Taking out the key card that Jackie had given him at the Pub, he slid it into the lock. The green light appeared and Flynn opened the door to room 1405. The room was dark and Jackie wasn't in. He turned the light switch on and went to the room phone to call his room to check on Kristen. The telephone rang 'busy' several times that he re-dialed. Flynn became concerned. "Something isn't right about all of this."

Flynn turned off the light and went to the door to leave. It was just when he was about to open the door that he noticed shadows under the door in the hallway. Flynn looked through the security 'peep-hole' and saw two men standing outside Jackie's room. "From the looks of the dark suits they're probably 'Company'," Flynn thought.

Flynn waited until he heard one of the men slide in a pass key card then start to open the door. Quickly, Flynn yanked the door open while the Agency man, still holding the door handle, was pulled inside unexpectedly. Flynn smashed the tumbling agent in the temple--knocking him unconscious. The second agent instinctively tried to reach for his weapon but Flynn kicked out with alarming speed. The force caught the man squarely on the jaw sending him crashing into an unconscious heap against the far hall wall.

Flynn retrieved the agent from the hallway and dragged him into Jackie's room. He checked both their ID's. "NSA!" Flynn exclaimed. "What the hell is the National Security Agency doing here?"

While pondering this new development, he closed the door and left the room walking to the elevator to check on Kristen in their own room on the tenth floor. Then, while waiting for the elevator car, Flynn looked back towards Jackie's room. "She might have been followed or discovered. Something could have gone wrong at our London branch office or maybe she was just lucky not to be in the room when those two came calling. Obviously now, they know she's here and most likely know that I'm here, too. What I can't figure out is why would the NSA have any interest in Jackie or me, for that matter?"

The elevator opened and Flynn descended to the tenth floor and to their room in the Bridal Suite, room 1018. Flynn cautiously approached the room constantly checking the hallway--in his front and behind--looking for a possible trap. His weapon was at the ready as he drew nearer to the room. Upon reaching the room, Flynn paused to listen at the door. He couldn't hear anything. Instead of using his key card, Flynn knocked.

A female voice from within called out, "Who is it?"

"Complimentary champagne for the newly weds," Flynn answered holding his finger over the peep-hole.

The door opened. Flynn was surprised to see Jackie Armstrong standing before him with a pistol aimed at his head. "Jeezus fucking Christ, Flynn!" She paused lowering the weapon. "Where have you been?"

"Why Jackie," Flynn calmly answered, "I've been in your room entertaining two friends of yours. How did you get here--in my room?" Flynn looked past Jackie and saw Kristen sitting in a chair by the window. Her feet were up on the end of the bed. There was an open bottle of wine and three glasses on the table next to a full bottle of Jack Daniel's and an ice bucket. Jackie pulled him into the room. Then she checked up and down the hallway before closing the door.

Flynn glanced over to Kristen more intently this time, taking in her casual appearance. She was dressed in a pair of new jeans and a sweatshirt. Then he gave Jackie the 'once over'. She too, had changed clothing since he met her at the Horn Dorset. She was in tight fitting jeans and a tee shirt, no bra. Flynn noticed her nipples protruding through the cotton.

He smiled, "It looks as if you two have become quite the pair. Am I interrupting your party?"

"No, not at all," Jackie answered, "Kristen and I have been having a nice long chat. She even let me borrow some of her clothes. What do you think?"

Flynn returned his stare to her breasts. "I like the shirt."

"I'm glad you finally noticed," Jackie smiled. She walked over to the empty chair by the table and sat down. Then she asked, "What did you mean by 'entertaining two friends' in my room?"

"I went up to your room to see if you were back and if you had anything for me. I used the key card you gave me to go in. When I saw that you weren't there I got a little concerned and called up here but the line was busy. Any way, when I was about to leave I saw two 'dark suits' right outside your door. I surprised them...and, when I checked their ID's...it was me who got the surprise..."

"Company men?" Jackie asked interrupting.

"That's what I thought. But no...NSA."

"What? Why is NSA after me?"

"Good question. I don't know. But something isn't right."

Jackie looked at Flynn with a worried expression on her face. "So, they know I'm here. And that means they must think you're here. By the way, I found a top secret file today that might interest you. It claims that somebody named 'Tiger' is meeting with some very interesting people at the Washington Hilton in a couple of nights." She took the file paper from her purse and gave it to Flynn.

"Well, well, this is interesting."

"Who are those other people named?" Jackie asked.

"They are called the 'Elite', my dear. Did you see all the phone traffic in this message?"

"Not really. I did notice a couple of very familiar names though? What does it mean?"

Flynn never liked to reveal what he was thinking to anyone. "I'm not too sure right now." Then he picked up one of the empty glasses. He uncovered the ice bucket, took out a few cubes, dropped them into the glass, uncapped the Jack Daniels, then poured the sour mash whiskey to the top of the glass. Flynn stirred the drink with his finger for a moment while he turned and stared out the window. When he felt the drink was sufficiently cooled, he took a long sip.

Flynn remained gazing out the window while changing the subject. "So...what have you two been talking about?"

Kristen had just taken a sip of her wine and while setting down the glass answered, "You mostly. And what has happened and what might happen to all of us. Girl talk, you know."

"And a few 'mutual friends'," Jackie added smiling at Kristen.

Flynn's curiosity got the better of him. He turned to face the women. "What mutual friends do you two have?"

"Joseppi Penella," Kristen answered first.

"And his brother Nunzio." Jackie added.

Flynn was caught momentarily unable to speak at the revelations. He downed the rest of the whiskey in his glass. Then he asked, "How do you two know the cousins of Don Vito Manderino, the capo de capo of bosses?"

Kristen crossed her legs. "I dated Joseppi for a while a few years ago back in Amsterdam before you and I met. It was pretty common knowledge that he was 'connected'."

Flynn shook his head. "What's your story, Armstrong?"

"Well, when Nunzio and I were dating for a while a couple of years ago, I had forgotten that I had met Joseppi and Kristen once before. It was when Nunzio and I came to the Netherlands. Like I said, I had forgotten about it. And I since I couldn't remember Kris' last name, never put her name and face together until I saw her on the elevator today! Then one day, shortly after that one time meeting, Nunzio tells me he has a 'family emergency' and has to go back to Europe. I never heard from him again. And by the way, his 'family' nickname is...'Caesar!'"

"The world is really only about three blocks long," Flynn said philosophically. "What are the odds of this ever happening?" Flynn let out a small laugh. "Looks like I've been traveling with a couple of 'gun-molls'." He poured himself another drink.

"So, what do you make of all of this?" Jackie asked Flynn.

"The picture is becoming clearer to me," Flynn answered, "but there's still some unanswered questions. Who in the American government is in some way connected to the Manderino family and wants to stop 'Tiger' and the 'Elite'? And is using us to further those ends?"

Jackie thought for a moment and then exclaimed, "Well, it has to be someone high up with access to a lot of information and computer data bases." Then her face lit up as she burst out, "Holy Shit! It's either the Agency or NSA."

"Possibly," Flynn said. "Both the CIA and the National Security Agency have massive data bases and extremely sophisticated computer operations. NSA also monitors all phone conversations..."

Kristen sat up. "Would that explain how 'Caesar' knew where we were? From your cell phone calls, Flynn?"

"You're on the right track, Kris, I think." Flynn pausing in thought added, "That might explain some things. When I was in Alaska I stumbled upon the 'Elite's' drug smuggling operation into the country. I phoned it in to CIA headquarters and the 'Elite' has been trying to stop me ever since."

"Didn't you call in to Mollie?" Jackie asked.

"Yes, of course. I told her what I saw and the next thing I know my location is pinpointed and I'm a target."

"Then Mollie is the fucking rat!" Jackie screamed jumping to her feet.

Flynn held up his hand gesturing her to stop. "Not necessarily, Jackie. You're jumping to conclusions."

"She's a bitch and I'll bet she did it. It's pretty plain to me."

"Look, I know you don't like Mollie. But you can't let your personal feelings get in the way of rational and logical thought. You missed one important point."

"Yeah, what's that?"

"The phone calls. It could just as easily be someone at NSA listening to my phone conversation to her. And that person or persons could be the 'Mole', or are working with him or her, depending if the 'Mole' is a man or a woman...."

"Mole?" Kristen was puzzled.

"It's a term for someone inside spying for an enemy...like a double agent or a trusted friend who is really not your friend at all. ..."

"An undercover operative," Jackie added.

Flynn finished his Jack Daniels and poured

himself another. Then he turned looking back out the window into the darkness of London's fog. "So how do we flush out the sons'abitches?"

"Flynn, you're asking us?" Kristen questioned while pouring herself and Jackie another glass of wine.

"Maybe. Not exactly. But yes, possibly."

Jackie shook her head while listening to Flynn. "What the fuck are you talking about?"

"I was just trying to think out loud." Flynn then changed the subject. "You know I got in to see President Bunnell a little while ago...

This revelation caused both women to gasp, "You what?"

Flynn turned back to them and smiled. "Yes, I brought supper to her. Just before I came here."

"How the hell did you pull that one off?" Jackie was impressed.

"I went into the hotel kitchen and had an 'arrangement' with the waiter assigned to bring her dinner up to her suite."

"God, Flynn, is he still alive?" Kristen asked.

"Yes, but he won't remember anything. At least not for several hours..."

Jackie was curious, "So, what did you tell her? How much you still love her, or what?"

"No. Not much. I only had a minute. I just told her that I was staying here and for her to call me later when she was alone and could talk..."

"She knows what room you're in? Are you out of your mind? She'll have us all arrested."

"No, ladies, you're wrong. I think I know her well enough to know that she won't tell anyone......"

PRESIDNETIAL SUITE, LONDON

Chief of Staff Admiral Michael Moorehouse entered the room of President Bunnell just as she was finishing her meal. Moorehouse saw that the President appeared to be in a very buoyant mood, something that he hadn't seen in her in a long time. "What's up?"

President Patricia Bunnell smiled at him and replied, "What do you mean?"

"I mean, what's put you in such a happy mood? Did you get some good news that I'm not aware of?"

"You might say that, Michael. Yes...I...did."

"Well, are you going to tell me or not?"

"My mission here is accomplished. We're going home tomorrow morning."

"What? What mission are you talking about? We haven't discussed anything of importance with the Brits on the Middle east situation..."

"I don't need to discuss anything with the British or anyone else. I've seen Flynn!"

The Chief of Staff was alarmed and confused. "Flynn? Did you say you've seen that fucking madman?"

"Yes, and he's not and never has been a 'madman', Michael."

"Where? Where could you have possibly seen him. You can't be serious."

"He brought me my dinner. Right here under everyone's nose. Right here in this very room."

"Why didn't you call the Secret Service? The man is wanted."

"I told you that he has the information I need to stop this global madness before it goes any further. And, I also said that I would do anything that I could to talk with him."

"I don't believe this! Heads are going to roll around here! How could that man get in here without anyone knowing who he was?"

"He's just the best at what he does, Michael. And that really pisses you off, doesn't it?"

The irate Chief of Staff stomped out of the Presidential Suite livid. He started barking at everyone he saw. Patricia Bunnell couldn't help but laugh at his Rumpelstiltskin behavior. She walked over to the window and looked out over a sparkling lit London. For the first time in a long while she felt a little more at ease. She had a plan, too.

LONDON HILTON, BRIDAL SUITE

Flynn had never before experienced two beautiful women making love to him at the same time. There was nothing awkward about the entire situation. It just happened naturally. There was of course some discussion that, because Jackie's room was discovered, she couldn't return to it. Therefore, the most logical thing for her to do was stay in the bridal suite with Flynn and Kristen. There was plenty of room in the king-sized bed for all three. And, after another bottle of wine and a few more Jack Daniels, all inhibitions were dissolved. It wasn't planned, it merely happened. Flynn was pleasantly surprised that both women had no qualms about sharing him. Each selflessly seemed to understand the others wants, needs and desires.

Early in the morning, while the three of them lay exhausted in the bed, Flynn between them, the room to the door suddenly crashed open. Flynn sat up immediately only to find the room full of Secret Service agents with guns drawn aimed at them. Flynn recognized Agent Cathy Wilkins, one of the President's personal agents, from his 'association' with the President during his 'refresher course' in Washington.

Cathy spoke into her shoulder microphone. "We've got them all, Peter... Flynn, Shults and Miss Armstrong. Looks like Flynn was doing undercover work!" The pun was bad and Flynn didn't acknowledge it.

Flynn glanced over to both Kristen and Jackie. "I didn't know we were giving a party. Is it a birthday surprise?"

"Cut the wise cracks you perverted bastard. You're all under arrest. Now get out of that bed and get dressed. We have a plane to catch."

Flynn rolled over Jackie and was attempting to get up when Cathy's gun barrel smashed into the side of his head rendering him unconscious.

When he came to, Flynn was sitting fully dressed in the private quarters of President Patricia Bunnell aboard Air Force One flying back to Washington. His head was still throbbing from the blow while trying to focus on his surroundings. Standing before him was Secret Service Agent Cathy Wilkins.

"One false move, asshole, and I'll give you a matching lump on the other side of your head."

"I don't think that will be necessary, Agent Wilkins," Flynn weakly replied. What happened to Jackie and Kris?"

"Your concubine, Miss Armstrong, is up front with the President. We turned Shults over to Scotland Yard. You know," Cathy continued with a sneer, "you are disgusting."

"Don't knock it until you try it."

"You don't have anything I want to try," she snarled.

The private cabin door opened and President Bunnell came in. "That will be all, Cathy," the President said. "Go up front with the others."

"Yes, Ma'am. Are you sure you'll be all right alone with that scumbag?"

Patricia smiled, "Yes, I'll be fine. If I need you, I'll ring."

Flynn looked over at the President and sarcastically said, "It's good to see you again, Patricia."

"You don't let any grass grow under your feet do you?"

Flynn offered a weak smile but chose not to respond. Instead he asked, "What other surprises have you got up your sleeve?"

"Surprises? I'm not the one with the surprises. I thought there was something between us. I should have realized that you're no different than any other man--thinking with your dick first!"

Flynn rubbed his head then looked at the President. "There was something between us until I figured out whose side you're on. How long have you been working with 'Tiger' on Operation Lifeblood?"

A look of amazement came over her face. "What are you talking about? I'm not working with anyone called 'Tiger' or anyone else. And, I've never heard of Operation Lifeblood."

"Oh, cut the shit, Pat," Flynn was annoyed. "Then why do you have me as your prisoner?"

"Apparently, Cathy must have hit you too hard. I'm sorry about that. It wasn't the way I intended it. You're not a prisoner. My intent was to get you safely back to the U.S. What better way to get you out of England safely than under the diplomatic flag of the United States? I was, and still am, trying to help you so you can help me."

"Help you?" Flynn smirked, "Is having my head nearly smashed in the way you treat those who are trying to help you?"

"I said that it wasn't the way I wanted Cathy to get you here. She must have thought you were going to resist..."

"Resist? You can't be serious. How was I going to resist naked as a Jay bird, for Christ's sake?"

"Look, I'm sorry. I can't do anything about that now. The real question is will you help me stop the powder keg about to explode in the Middle East, or not?"

"It's my job, isn't it?" he replied coldly.

"Is that all it is to you, Flynn--a job?"

"That's all it can ever be between us anymore. My job. My duty to you, to the Agency. When, and if, I finish my 'JOB', I'm getting out. Getting out of this whole fucking mess. With the Company....and with you!"

Patricia Bunnell controlled her immediate desire to slap him across the face. She sneered instead, "Oh, yeah, I almost forgot. Your cheerleader girlfriend, Kathleen Murphy."

"Jealously doesn't become you, Madam President." Flynn retorted. "At least she never had my head bashed in for trying to help."

There was a long silence in the cabin. The President turned away momentarily, resigning to herself that she and Flynn would never be together. She walked over to her desk and sat down.

Still hurting inside she began, "All right. I get

it....Now, can we discuss what you know on a professional level? Will you do your sworn duty and tell me what you know about this 'Tiger' and Operation Lifeblood you spoke of?"

Flynn looked directly into her ocean blue eyes while he answered. "Yes. I'll tell you what I know and what I think I know." He straightened himself in the chair before he continued. "First, there is someone in your administration, someone close to you whom you trust, who is working against you and is helping 'Tiger' in Operation Lifeblood...."

The President interrupted. "Slow down. Who is this person you keep calling 'Tiger'?

'Tiger' is Kim Moon Jung. He's a North Korean psychotic. He's the power behind North Korean's desire to unify Korea by any means possible. He is also the head of a group of men who are called 'The Elite'. President Harper was one of this so-called 'Elite'. So was Foreign Minister James Saunders. Both of whom were murdered by 'Tiger' or one of his goons."

"Why?" President Bunnell asked.

"I'm not certain of the 'why'. Either they no longer served 'Tiger's' purpose or they were expendable for some other reason. It really isn't important. The fact is he had them assassinated."

"So, your 'girlfriend' Shults is working for him, then. She murdered the Prime Minister."

"No, Pat, she never did. It's a frame up just as they are trying to frame me for Harper's assassination."

"I never believed that..."

"Thanks, but someone close to you wants everyone to think that I did. And they are behind the frame up."

"Michael?" She whispered.

"You tell me. Who started that fucked up story that I was in Houston when in reality I was in Alaska?"

The President didn't answer that question. "Go on. What is this 'Operation Lifeblood' all about?"

"When I was in Alaska I came across a drug smuggling operation by Koreans and Latin Americans. I assume that Don Carlos Escobar, also a member of the 'Elite', and a drug lord from Venezuela, was behind the drug trade. Anyway, the shipments were in crates from United Petroleum courtesy of U.P.'s president, David Laird, another a member of the 'Elite'. The money from the drug trade provided 'Tiger' and his cronies with the ability to buy up oil futures with the intent to corner the oil market."

"I'm not sure I understand what you're getting at."

"It's easier when you know that Iranian president Jahmir, and Sheik Mohammed al-Anzarisad of Syria are also members of 'Tiger's' club. You see, Iran has a nuclear weapon, a gift from North Korea. Iran then rattles the world with a nuclear threat primarily aimed at Israel. Of course, you, as President of the United States, would have to come to Israel's defense. This threat, or alleged threat, distracts the major powers while the 'Elite' gain a majority control of the oil supply--all for the benefit of 'Tiger' and his warped sense of destiny--unification of Korea under his terms. This whole scenario would then undermine the economies of the West, causing a crippling effect on those countries so dependent on oil."

"But if what you say is true, what happens...I mean, why would someone in my administration want to do this?"

"Two reasons: money and power. They believe

they can do it. And, may believe they have been controlling or manipulating you to do what they want--all along."

President Bunnell was indignant. "Nobody is or has been controlling anything I do."

"Don't be so sure about that. Harper was assassinated which allowed you, a woman, to become President."

"My being a woman hasn't anything to do with anything. I'm not some weak-kneed little simple minded female."

"I know that. But in the minds of the 'Elite' you are. Except for Laird, and whoever else in your Administration, they are not Americans. They believe women are servants to men. Nothing more."

"How do you intend to find out who is the insider in my administration who, you claim, is working for this 'Tiger'?"

"I have an idea. Let me have a pen and a sheet of paper."

The President opened her desk and took out a legal pad and a pen and handed them to Flynn. While he wrote out a short note she thought over what Flynn had just told her. "Can it really be Michael? If not him, then who does Flynn suspect?"

Flynn finished his writing and turned the paper over to the President who read it. She looked over at Flynn incredulously but said nothing. Flynn continued, "I want you to give this message to these four people." He wrote down the four names on the legal pad and showed them to President Bunnell. "If you give this message confidentially to each of these people I think the last piece of this puzzle will fall into place. If I'm correct, then it's going to mean a major shakeup in your administration and the government's inner structure. Will you be able to do this?"

She re-read the message and then studied the four names Flynn had written down. "Don't worry about me. I can take the heat. However, I think you're way off base about any one of these people."

"Trust me, one of these people is the 'Mole'. I have a hunch who it might be and this should prove it, once and for all."

"It looks like you already believe it's the Chief of Staff, don't you?"

"Well, think about it. Who else has all the inside information? He's ambitious and above all, in my opinion, an asshole."

The President raised her eyebrow at his last statement. "I thought you were supposed to objective, Mister professional operative?"

"I'm giving him an option to prove me wrong. That's precisely why there are three other names on that list. After we land, give me a free hand for twenty-four hours. Once these people are given this message there is no other choice but for them to act."

"All right, Flynn. I'll see that you get the twenty-four hours. But if one of these people is the 'Mole', as you call it, your life is going to be in danger."

"It's part of the 'JOB', remember? Besides, these bastards have been after me since Alaska." Flynn looked out the plane's window for a moment. Then he turned back to her and apologetically offered "I wish it could have been different between us..."

"You've already made that decision, Jeremiah. We can't change the past." The President picked up the message and folded it. "Can you do me a personal favor? Actually two favors?"

"I'll try. What are they?"

"As you know, Spense and I weren't in a real marriage for a long time. Actually, I doubt that I ever really loved him or he me, for that matter. But it pisses me off that any of these people would murder him to advance their own interests thinking that they could manipulate me."

"Well, that's exactly what they are trying to do. So what's the favors?"

"I want you to get them all for me. And not just for me, but for our country. Even if it turns out to be Michael, get them all."

"Is this an Executive Order? To 'sanction' these..."

"BASTARDS!" The President finished his sentence. "Yes. Call it Executive Order number One. Terminate the *'Elite'!*"

Flynn watched her ocean blue eyes turn dark with anger. "I will do my best, Madam President. Now what's the other favor?"

"Stay alive. Please. I would be really ticked off if you weren't around to occasionally make me laugh."

"Don't worry, Patricia, someone has to keep you straight." Flynn smiled as he concluded, "after all, you are Thee President."

She smiled warmly at her former lover. "Okay, Flynn, how are we going to handle it from here?"

"You and your entourage leave the plane. Take Jackie with you when you all leave but leave me on board while they bring the plane to the hangar. Most importantly, however, deliver the message to each of these names, privately. This time tomorrow, we should have the 'Mole' in the trap."

Air Force One landed at Andrews Air Force base. The President, Chief of Staff, Director Dimmler, Director Pfohl, Jackie Armstrong, aides, and Secret Service all exited as Flynn requested. The Secret Service agents under orders from the President were informed that Flynn was to remain on the aircraft and not to interfere with him.

Flynn waited on board for about twenty minutes. He became apprehensive when the aircraft wasn't towed into its hangar. He glanced out a cabin window and watched while a good deal of activity caught his eye by the gateway. Four men in dark suits exited a limousine and walked toward the plane.

"This isn't good." Flynn mumbled. "I wasn't expecting a welcoming committee."

Flynn raced to the forward cabin door. He heard voices and footsteps coming up the steps of the ladder to the open front cabin door. Flynn couldn't get to the door quickly enough as the men stormed Air Force One. One of the men pulled his weapon from his jacket holster and started down towards the rear to where Flynn had retreated. Flynn looked over to his left and saw the emergency door. Without hesitating he forced open the emergency door and climbed down onto the jet's wing. With the men in hot pursuit, Flynn slid down the wing falling to the tarmac. He ran to the security fence and scaled it just as bullets whizzed around him and over his head.

He continued his dash in and out of the shadows and was nearly run over by an airman driving a jeep. Flynn spun around the jeep to the startled driver pulling him from the seat and tossing him to the ground. Flynn jumped into the jeep and sped off toward the guard gate. Without slowing, he crashed through the security gate barrier bar at the entrance to a public highway. He hit the highway at full speed, jumping the jeep over the median and reversing his direction towards Washington.

Once in the Capital, Flynn ditched the jeep down a dark street. He was now on foot. He was the lone hunter. "It's payback time."

Flynn walked several blocks until he came to a familiar neighborhood saloon. The clientèle was predominantly African-American. And, when Flynn entered the bar all eyes focused on him. Without hesitating, he went straight to the bar. "A bottle of 'Dingler'" Flynn ordered. Many of the customers began to close in on him--wondering what this white man was doing in their club.

Flynn gave the bartender a ten dollar bill for the beer. "Excuse me, sir," he asked, "could you do me a favor?"

The bartender, a tall muscular man, leaned over towards Flynn and replied, "What kind of favor would you want, man?"

"Would you kindly tell Charles E. Fromage that Don Vito Manderino's courier is here to see him?"

Amazed at the reference to Don Vito Manderino, the bartender signaled to the men behind Flynn. They backed off and went back to their own business. Then he pushed a button under the bar while gesturing to Flynn to go over to a door at the end of the bar. Flynn nodded a 'thank you' and walked to the door.

The door led up a stairway to another closed door at the top. Flynn climbed the stairs and upon reaching the closed door, knocked. A young black man opened the door holding a pistol in his hand. He started to 'pat' Flynn down when a gravely voice at a desk from behind said, "He's cool, Rakeem." Flynn walked toward the voice. "Well, well, if it ain't Mista Flynn. What the fuck brings you here to my establishment?"

"I was in the neighborhood," Flynn quipped, "and I thought I'd drop in to see an old friend."

The man laughed. "That's fuckin' rich, Flynn. You ain't 'zackly been a regular, now have you? It's been some time."

"Yes, it's been a while. I've been out of town. You know on 'business'."

"So I've heard. You ain't the most popular motherfucker in D.C. right now, you know."

"Or any place else for that matter. That's why I thought you were just the man who could help me."

"I might be able to help, if you tell me what you be wantin'."

"I need a gun, a car and," Flynn paused for effect, "plastique. Enough to blow up a small building."

Charles E. Fromage let out a deep laugh. "Motherfucker! Dat's rich! What the fuck do you think I am, Flynn, a fuckin' terrorist? Where do you think I can get plastique?"

Flynn put his hand on the desk and leaned forward. "We both know that you're the 'Big Cheese' around here, and a very resourceful man. I would consider it a personal favor. And so would Don Vito."

A broad grin crossed Fromage's face. "If, and I say if, I can get you what you want, what can I expect to get in return?"

The bargaining had begun and Flynn knew it. "What is it you're looking for?"

"Shit, man, I need a bigger piece of the action. I'm ready for expansion!"

"How much?"

Fromage went for more than he could expect. "I need another fifteen percent."

"Five," Flynn replied coldly.

"Go fuck yourself, Flynn. It's no deal."

"Have it your way, my friend. I will tell Don Vito you wouldn't listen to reason..."

"All right, I be a reasonable man," Fromage countered. "Ten."

"Am I speaking French?" Flynn continued. "I said five." He started for the door playing his bluff to the max.

"Motherfucker, Flynn! Hold on. Okay, five it is."

Flynn turned back to the desk and faced Fromage. "Good. Where can I pick the stuff up?"

Fromage opened his desk drawer and took out a 10mm Glock and slid it over to Flynn who checked to see that it was loaded. It was. Fromage then snapped his fingers and the young man by the door came over to the desk.

"Rakeem, take Mister Flynn to the east side apartment. You know the place. I will place a call to Ta'wan. He will give you a package. Give that package to Mister Flynn. And leave him the car. Someone will be over later to pick you up. You be gettin' all dat?"

"Yessir, I gots it."

Flynn looked over at Charles E. Fromage and said, "Don Vito will be pleased to hear how you co-operated. Thanks." He tucked the weapon into his pants and left with Rakeem.

Neither Rakeem nor Flynn spoke during the short ride to the east side apartment house. When Rakeem pulled the car over to the curb in front of the building, a small black man wearing wire rimmed eyeglasses appeared out of the shadows carrying a small box. However, when he approached the car and seeing Flynn, he turned to walk away.

Rakeem called out, "Yo, brother, it's cool. He's da man." The small man returned to the vehicle and handed the box to Flynn. Rakeem got out and Flynn slid over to the driver's side. "You be on your own now, man."

"That's just the way I like it," Flynn replied. He drove off into the darkness of Washington.

THE WHITE HOUSE

President Patricia Bunnell and the Chief of Staff, Admiral Moorehouse, were dining together in the private dining room. The President was sullen and unusually quiet. Her mood did not go unnoticed by Moorehouse.

"What's troubling you, Patricia? You seem distant?"

"It's nothing, Michael. I'm just tired," she lied.

"I'm not surprised. You had quite a whirlwind trip. I hope you're still not thinking of Flynn."

The President looked up from her plate and glared at Admiral Moorehouse. Her expression told him all he needed to know. She remained silent.

"Look, Pat," Moorehouse began, "he's no damn good. He's better off in custody where he can't hurt you or anyone anymore..."

She shot back in anger, "You don't know what you're talking about. Flynn's not in custody. For your information he's on his way to take care of 'Tiger' and the rest of the so-called 'Elite'.

Moorehouse was alarmed. "What are you saying? He's not under arrest? But he was met at the airport by..." He realized he had said too much.

"By whom, Michael? There wasn't anyone there to arrest him. He stayed on board to the hangar. Then he was going to track down 'Tiger' and his cronies who are scheduled to meet at the Hilton and clean up the mess they started. Does 'Operation Lifeblood' mean anything to you?"

"Are you crazy?" Moorehouse had overstepped his bounds and now was in a near panic. "How did he know 'Tiger' was holding a meeting at the Hilton? What happened to the NSA reception?"

"I never ordered any 'reception' by the National Security Agency." She realized that it was her own Chief of Staff who had ordered them to meet Flynn. "You sonofabitch! You ordered it, didn't you?"

"I was only thinking of your safety. Afterall, he's a goddamn killer."

"You bastard! By what authority...by what right did you dare order NSA to pick him up? You may have ruined everything, you jerk!"

"You don't understand. I only did it for you."

"You've gone too far now, Michael. I can't stand you being in my sight. You make me sick. Go home to your wife! Get the fuck out!"

The Chief of Staff stood momentarily as if he wanted to explain himself. Then, in a loss for words, he left in silence. Admiral Moorehouse now had other thoughts. He stopped in his office and made a call on his cell phone. He hoped that his reception party had Flynn in custody.

"Agent Simmons? This is Admiral Moorehouse.

Have you got Flynn?"

"Admiral," NSA Agent Simmons reported, "sorry, sir. No. We lost him."

Moorehouse was furious. "How the fuck could that happen?"

"He must have seen us coming, sir. When we stormed the aircraft he escaped out the emergency door and slid off the wing. We never expected that to happen..."

"Goddamnit, Simmons! I told you to expect anything from that sonofabitch. One simple job and you guys blew it!" Moorehouse disconnected the call.

The Chief of Staff opened his cell phone again. He needed to make another call.

"Flynn's on the loose. He knows of the meeting. Can you cancel it?"

"It's too late. Almost everyone is here. What can he possible do anyway? We have protection. He won't be able to even get to us. We'll take care of Flynn if he shows up, once and for all."

"I hope you're right." Moorehouse's call was disconnected. He left the White House and drove off.

Meanwhile, President Bunnell left the dinning room and walked into the Oval Office. She sat behind her desk and placed a call to William Pfohl Director of the National Security Agency.

Pfohl was in his limousine near Dupont Circle and the 'U' Street Corridor. He identified the call on his cell phone and knew it was coming from the President. "Madam President."

"Good evening, Director Pfohl. I have a question for you. Were you aware that the Chief of Staff had some of your people meet Air Force One this evening?"

"Yes, Ma'am. We discussed it on the way back to Washington. The Chief of Staff wanted to make certain that Flynn was taken into custody and I believed that you had ordered it, Madam President..."

"Well, William, I most certainly did not order it. So, where is Flynn being held?"

"Ma'am? I thought you already knew?"

Patricia Bunnell became concerned and feared what the Director might say. "Knew what?" She asked apprehensively.

"Why, Flynn escaped, Madam President. He exited Air Force One through the emergency door and slid down the wing..."

Relief came over the President. She smiled. "No, I didn't know that. Thank you, Director Pfohl. Have a good night."

"Good bye, Madam President." The call was disconnected just as the limousine pulled into the front of the Washington Hilton.

THE WASHINGTON HILTON

Flynn pulled the car that Charles E. Fromage had let him use into the hotel's parking garage. He drove down to the lower level and parked. Flynn walked up the stairs to the lobby. He went over to the house phone and called the front desk.

"Hello, I'm looking for Mister David Laird and his party. Could you tell me what conference room they're in? I'm a little late and I forgot the room number."

The clerk checked his computer screen for reservations."Ah, yes, sir. Mister Laird, a Diamond H-Honors member. He is holding a meeting over in the

Heights Courtyard at the Heights Executive Meeting Center."

"Thank you. But are you sure their not scheduled for the tenth floor Executive Level Meeting Center?"

"No, sir. Mister Laird specifically requested the Heights Courtyard. He likes the ambiance at the fire pit..."

"Yes, I guess that does ring a bell, now. Thank you for your assistance."

The clerk added, "You're quite welcome. But you're not late, sir. The meeting isn't scheduled until eleven tonight..."

"Of course. Thank you." Flynn hung up the house phone. After checking his watch, he had nearly an hour and a half before everyone of the 'Elite' would be assembled. He looked around and saw McClellan's Sports Bar off the lobby. "Hope it's not named after the Little General, Mac." Flynn thought of Civil War General George B. McClellan."Once I get setup, I'll have me a drink. But first, I gotta scope out the Heights Courtyard."

Flynn went down the corridor to the Morgan Room. Fortunately, the only people around were hotel staff setting up hors d'oeuvres and several bottle of liquor. "Excuse me," Flynn asked walking into the Morgan room, "Is this where Mister Laird's meeting is tonight?"

One of the wait staff glanced up at Flynn. "No, sir. This is just their break room. They'll be out there," he pointed out the glass doors, "by the fire pit."

Flynn walked through the Morgan room and out to the Heights Courtyard. He studied the layout and saw that chairs were being assembled around the fire pit. "Depending on how many armed guards they'll have, it looks pretty easy to get to." He walked back through the 'break room' and back to the lobby. He found a boutique and went in. He purchased a digital electric alarm clock, a box of cigars, and two pre-paid cell phones.

Flynn took his package to the men's room and walked into one of the stalls at the far end. Once inside the stall, Flynn assembled his bomb. "When I call this number it will detonate the plastique...Good-bye 'Tiger' and the entire 'Elite'," Flynn smiled. Flynn emptied the cigars temporarily into the boutique bag. Carefully, he placed his explosive components into the empty cigar box. Then he covered it with as many cigars as needed to hide the charge. Satisfied that everything was prepared, Flynn put the remaining cell phone in his pocket then left the men's room with the box and walked back to the Heights Courtyard.

By the time Flynn came back to the Morgan room the hotel staff had left. He quickly went outside to the fire pit area. Flynn placed the 'loaded' cigar box on a table near one of the chairs and left the way he came in. He returned to McClellan's Sports Bar and went in. He chose a table in the corner. A waiter came over and Flynn ordered. "I'll have America's beer."

The waiter hesitated for a moment before he understood. "Ah, yes, sir. A bottle of Dingler."

Flynn smiled and tipped the waiter a twenty immediately. "Have a few put on ice, would you? I like my Dingler cold. I think it's going to be a warm evening."

The waiter slipped the twenty in his pocket smiling at Flynn and cordially said, "Thank you, sir. I'll see to it immediately."

Flynn checked the time. "Just about ten. An hour to go." The waiter returned with his beer and left Flynn to himself. He looked over to the wide screen television.

The Nationals were playing the Phillies. He took a drink of the Dingler. "What could be more American than this-- baseball and America's beer?"

When the game ended, the news came on. Flynn perked up when he heard a story out of London. The reporter was standing in front of Scotland Yard.

"Scotland Yard has dropped all charges against Kristen Shults. She had been accused in the assassination of Prime Minister Sommerset. In recent developments, detectives discovered that the blood of a man, William 'Willie' Bliss, was found inside the stock of the rifle used to gun down the Prime Minister. Bliss was found murdered at the King Arthur Print Shop some days ago along with two other men and the owner of the shop, Max Steiner. We've been told that a DNA comparison of Bliss's blood was a perfect match from that blood found inside the rifle...."

"Thank God," Flynn said when the story concluded. He signaled the waiter who brought him another bottle of Dingler. He took a long drink before he checked his Rolex. It was five after eleven. "Almost time to go," he thought. "The fire pit's about to explode."

After he finished his last beer, Flynn paid his tab. Then, as he was leaving the bar, he saw Admiral Michael Moorehouse walking quickly into the lobby. Flynn stealthfully followed the Chief of Staff down the corridor toward the Morgan room. A pair of Oriental men dressed in black suits stood by the doorway. Suddenly, Flynn saw Moorehouse wave to the men in recognition then turn right into the men's rest room. Without hesitation, Flynn came in right behind.

Moorehouse turned back to the door as Flynn came in. "Flynn...." His words were cut off by Flynn's punch to the Admiral's mid-section. Moorehouse crumbled in a heap.

"You fucking traitor," Flynn snarled at the Chief of Staff. "This is going to be your last fuckin' night on this earth." He pulled out the 10mm Glock from behind his back that was tucked in his belt. Dragging Moorehouse to his feet, Flynn shoved the gun in Moorehouse's face.

The Chief of Staff was trembling with fear and nearly breathless, "Wait..."

Flynn sneered, "Don't beg, Admiral. It's un-professional."

Moorehouse shook his head groping for breath. "I'm not...I'm not begging. I came here to warn you..."

Flynn couldn't believe his ears. "What? You sonofabitch. You came here to warn me? I ought to blow your fucking brains out..."

"No. Yes." The Chief of Staff pleaded.

Flynn grabbed Moorehouse by the tie and pulled him close to his face. "Warn me of what?" Flynn aimed the weapon between Moorehouse's eyes. "Make it quick, Admiral, I've got a call to make to your 'Elite' friends."

Sweat ran down the Chief of Staff's face. He closed his eyes for a moment then opened them regaining his breath. "I'm working with Don Vito..."

Flynn was completely stunned by Moorehouse's statement. "What are you talking about?"

"Maybe you don't remember..."

"Remember what?"

"The accident. Santino. The night I had an accident. Santino Manderino and I were out drinking..."

Flynn now remembered the accident Moorehouse was referring to. The night he came across the burning car when he pulled both Moorehouse and Santino Manderino from the wreck just before it exploded. Don Vito's only son was saved. Flynn didn't know who Moorehouse was at the time, only that the man must be a friend of Santino's.

Flynn loosened his grip on Admiral Moorehouse and stepped back while still holding the Glock on the Admiral. "It was you?"

Michael Moorehouse took a deep breath nodding. "Yes, it was me. I never knew who pulled us out. I was unconscious. Don Vito told me later that it was you..."

"Then why have you been dogging my ass for all these years? Maybe I should have left you in the damn car."

"I'm glad you didn't." Moorehouse looked down shamefully as he continued. "I guess I have been jealous of you and Patricia. I wanted her to love me like she loved you. She always thought that you walked on water...I could never live up to her expectations after you and she....you know, I guess, no one could."

"Jeezus, you are really fucked up."

"You're probably right. In more ways than you can imagine...What did you do with the discs?"

Flynn was somewhat puzzled. "What disc's are you talking about?"

"The one's on the Contra Affair...Santino and I .."

"Holy fuck," Flynn exclaimed. "I turned them over to Langley."

Relieved that the CIA's special black operation would never be made public, Moorehouse sighed a grateful relief. "That's good to hear. Pfohl's been blackmailing me for years. I thought he had them."

Flynn remained silent for a moment trying to

absorb all of what the Chief of Staff had said. Finally, he looked at Moorehouse and said, "All right. What are you trying to warn me of?"

"They know you'd be here tonight. 'Tiger' has set a trap for you."

"A trap?" Flynn was puzzled. "What kind of trap?"

"I told one of the 'members' you'd be... that you'd be here tonight."

Flynn re-gripped the Admiral's tie and snarled, "So, just as I thought. You're the fucking 'Mole'."

"No, Flynn. It's not me. They think I'm in working with them. But I'm really trying to help Don Vito and the family...You know, for 'business' reasons. I owe it to him for almost killing his only boy..."

Flynn was still unsure whether or not to believe the Chief of Staff. "All right, then who's the inside man?"

"It's not one man, but two."

Flynn released his grip on the Admiral's shirt and tie and again stepped back trying to comprehend what Moorehouse had said. "Two?"

"Yes, Flynn, think about it. Who has the resources to intercept all phone calls?"

Flynn knew immediately, "The National Security Agency....Director Pfohl."

"Right."

"Wait a minute. How does that explain 'Caesar' also knowing where we were and helping us?"

"I told you, they think I'm in this shit with them. When Pfohl found out that you stumbled upon their operation, he told me how he could track you through your cell phone. I contacted Santino. The Manderino family put a GPS tracking system in the pickup you were given. 'Caesar' is Santino's cousin, Nunzio Penella and his brother Joseppi."

"Yeah, I figured that they were. But how does that explain why you started the bullshit that I murdered President Harper?"

"If I didn't do that you would never have been on the run. Who better to protect Patricia than you? Once they took out President Harper, who didn't want to go along with them anymore, their plan was to put Pat, thinking she was a young inexperienced President, in a position that they thought they could control. And, thinking they could use me...you know, being close to her and all, would help them."

"This is too much for me to believe, Admiral. Why would they kill the Prime Minister and blame Kristen?"

"It was no secret that you and the Shults woman were close. What better way to get you out in the open than to frame her? They, mostly 'Tiger', calculated you would be an easy target figuring that you would try to rescue her...."

Flynn lowered his weapon while he stepped further back analyzing what Moorehouse was saying. "If this shit is all true who is the other traitor besides Pfohl, if it really isn't you trying to save your own ass?"

Admiral Moorehouse wiped the sweat from his face with his shirt sleeve. "Who is the most powerful Cabinet member? Who also has designs on being President? And who presents the U.S.'s position in the world theater?"

It all fit in Flynn's mind. "Secretary of State Makoweic... I'll be a sonofabitch."

"Yes, for once I must agree with you." The Chief

of Staff smiled in relief.

While Flynn momentarily reflected on all that had happened, Michael Moorehouse added, "Look, I have to go into that meeting right away..."

"No, you can't. I planted a bomb in there. I'm going to blow the fuckers up."

"A bomb?" Moorehouse was shocked. "How? Where?"

"It's hooked up to explode when I call this number." Flynn took the cell phone out of his jacket pocket and showed it to the Chief of Staff who studied the number. "When that number is connected," Flynn explained, "the bomb will go off and blow the Heights Courtyard to hell."

"Holy shit, Flynn, how are you going to know when to call?"

"Don't worry about that, Admiral, I'll know."

No sooner than Flynn finished his statement, the mens' room door burst open and the two Korean guards who were waiting by the Morgan Room came crashing in with automatic weapons drawn. Flynn was unable to react fast enough to shoot.

"This is Flynn!" Moorehouse shouted, "He's here to kill 'Tiger' and all the 'Elite'!"

Flynn looked at the Chief of Staff in disgust. "You fucker."

Moorehouse stepped over and took Flynn's Glock. "Take him to the 'Tiger'."

The two Koreans ushered Flynn from the restroom and led him through the Morgan Room out to the Fire Pit and the assembled 'Elite'. Moorehouse followed. When Kim Moon Jung saw the guards with Moorehouse and Flynn, he stood up. Moorehouse made the introduction.

"Tiger, this is Flynn."

"So this is the man who has been trying to stop Operation Lifeblood all by himself." He walked over to Flynn and spit up in Flynn's face.

"And you're the little psycho who wants to conquer the world." Flynn said calmly. "I suppose that you and your gang of assholes here thinks you are going to succeed." Flynn reached into his pocket for the cell phone.

"Stop him. He's got a bomb!" Moorehouse commanded while slapping Flynn's hand away from his pocket. The Chief of Staff reached in and pulled out the cell phone.

"You know, Admiral," Flynn began contemptuously, "you almost had me believing you a while ago."

Secretary of State Makoweic alarmed by the prospect of a bomb stood up from behind the fire pit and walked over next to Moorehouse. "What's this about a bomb, Michael?"

Flynn glared at the Secretary of State, "You fucking traitor..." Moorehouse struck Flynn on the head with the barrel of the Glock knocking him down and unconscious. Flynn was dragged to a chair by a round metal cocktail table back from the group. One of the guards stood covering him with his weapon.

"You have done well, Admiral," Kim Moon Jung said patting the Chief of Staff on the back. "Now, gentleman, let us get on with our meeting."

James Makoweic was still uneasy. He asked again, "What's this about a bomb? Admiral, didn't you say Flynn had a bomb? Where is it?"

"I don't know," Moorehouse answered while

putting Flynn's cell phone in his pocket."He told me that but I think he just made that shit up. He's too much of a 'cowboy' to have anything like that. He thought he could just come in here and shoot everyone. He's a fucking loser." All of the members of the 'Elite' sat down and listened to 'Tiger' as he outlined the next phase of his Operation Lifeblood plan.

Flynn slowly regained consciousness. He didn't move and opened one eye just enough to see and survey his situation. After a few minutes, Michael Moorehouse spotted the cigar box which was over in front of National Security Advisor William Pfohl. "Mister Director," he addressed William Pfohl, "would you please pass me a cigar?"

The Director of NSA picked up the box and walked over to Moorehouse. There was an empty chair next to the Admiral and United Petroleum's CEO David Laird, so he sat down. The four Americans were all together while on the opposite side of the Fire Pit sat Sheik Mohammed al-Anzarisad, Iranian President Jahmir, and Kim Moon Jung, the 'Tiger'.

Chief of Staff Moorehouse opened the cigar box and looked in. He picked out a cigar and unwrapped it. Slowly, as the 'Tiger' continued talking, he reached his hand in his pocket. Flynn watched from the distance. "He's memorized the number I showed him! He's going to access the number!" Flynn instinctively moved. He flipped over the metal cocktail table before anyone could react. There was a loud explosion when the plastique was ignited. The guard who was next to Flynn was blown across a wall. A ball of fire and debris flew around the over turned table as Flynn crouched behind it for protection.

The next instant there was silence. Flynn arose from his protective table and saw the devastation. All that remained of the members of the 'Elite' were body parts. Flynn found what was left of the cellphone still attached to a hand. "That took guts, Admiral. You played your role well." Flynn walked through the shattered glass and left out the back service doors to the parking garage. Then he drove off to find a phone. An all night superstore was open. Flynn went in an picked out a new BlackBerry. Within a few minutes he made a call to Jackie Armstrong's number.

"Hello?" Jackie answered not recognizing the calling number.

"You're still my favorite girlfriend, Alice Long."

Immediately Jackie knew it was Flynn. "Where the hell are you? Did you hear about some explosion at the Hilton?"

"Yeah, I did hear it. I happened to be in the hotel bar..."

"Don't tell me.." She paused. "Holy fuck, it was you! Did you get them all?"

"I don't want to say. Look, tell Dimmler I'm out. I've had enough of this shit. And, ask him to tell the President that Executive Order Number One has been accomplished"

"What are you talking about?"

"I quit. I'm going home and then I'm going away."

Jackie sensed that there was more to what Flynn was saying and feeling than he wanted to talk about. "Okay. I guess you need to take a little time off. I understand..."

"Are you going to be all right?" Flynn asked changing the subject. "You know at the Agency and with

Dimmler and everyone?"

"Yeah, no sweat. I got a thirty day vacation but they said I can come back as long as I keep my nose clean...George was pretty good about it. But, there is one condition..."

"What's that?"

"That I will now have to report directly to that Bitch, Mollie."

Flynn laughed. "You'll be fine. She's not as bad as you think, kid. And now that I'm out and won't be around, you two will have no more jealous reason to fight over me.

"You know, Flynn, you're an arrogant prick."

"Wouldn't that be an arrogant, GIANT prick?"

Jackie smiled remembering the night of the London three-some. "Naw, more like little prick. I've seen bigger."

"Good-bye."

"I'll miss you, Jerry. Please come back to us."

"So long, Alice." Flynn disconnected the call.

Jackie Armstrong called Deputy Director George Dimmler immediately after she had talked to Flynn. A 'cleaning' crew was instantly detached to the scene and assumed complete control over local authorities.

The next morning's *Washington Post* ran a short story 'of a gas explosion at the Washington Hilton. Forensic experts were attempting to positively identify the remains of the bodies.'

That same morning President Patricia Bunnell was visited by CIA Deputy Director Dimmler. "Madam President, it appears that you are going to have to replace a few positions in your administration."

Patricia understood. She had given the message to

all four names on Flynn's list. The only man still alive was sitting in front of her at this very moment. "I can't believe all three of them, George. And what happened to Flynn? Is he...?

"No, he's alive. He reported that Executive Order Number One is accomplished. I assume you know what that is?"

"Yes, I do." Then President asked, "All right, George, how do we spin this mess?"

"A plane crash always works. They all happened to be in the same plane. You make a directive that no two high level people can ever ride together again in order to avoid such a tragic...you know, political bull.."

"Okay. I'll work on it." The President walked around the desk and sat on the edge. She crossed her legs and looked down at Dimmler still sitting in a chair. "Now, Mister Deputy Director, where is Flynn?"

"I honestly don't know. He told Jackie Armstrong that he quit. That he was out."

"How can he walk out on me....I mean...us, like that?"

Dimmler knew that she was upset for Flynn leaving without a word. "Give him some time, Madam President. I'm sure he'll be back. He loves the action too much."

"And his cheerleader girlfriend in Ohio. Maybe she's enough 'action' for him."

"Kathleen Murphy?"

"I believe your intelligence is the same as mine, George."

"I'll call him in a few weeks. He's a good soldier. He does this after every mission. He says he quits, then before you know it, he's bored to tears and he's back doing only what Flynn does best--righting wrongs." Dimmler paused for a moment then added, "There's another serious problem brewing down in Colombia. Flynn's been there before and I could use him there again, soon."

"Is there any place on this earth that there isn't a problem brewing?"

"Welcome to the Presidency, Madam President."

THE END

17931026R00215

Made in the USA
Charleston, SC
07 March 2013